# THE LAST GOODBYE

*Recent Titles by Margaret Pemberton from Severn House*

*The Hong Kong Saga*

A TIME TO REMEMBER

THE LAST GOODBYE

*The Saigon Saga*

UNFORGETTABLE DAYS

THE TURBULENT YEARS

A DARK ENCHANTMENT

FROM CHINA WITH LOVE

THE FOUR OF US

A MANY SPLENDOURED THING

A REBELLIOUS HEART

THE RECKLESS MISS GRAINGER

VIOLINS OF AUTUMN

A YEAR TO ETERNITY

# THE LAST GOODBYE

## Margaret Pemberton

This title first published in Great Britain 2007 by
SEVERN HOUSE PUBLISHERS LTD of
9–15 High Street, Sutton, Surrey SM1 1DF.
First published 1988 in Great Britain
under the title *A Multitude of Sins*.
This title first published in the USA 2008 by
SEVERN HOUSE PUBLISHERS INC of
595 Madison Avenue, New York, N.Y. 10022.

British Library Cataloguing in Publication Data

Pemberton, Margaret
  The last goodbye
  1. British - China - Hong Kong - Fiction 2. Women pianists
  - Fiction 3. World War, 1939-1945 - China - Hong Kong -
  Fiction 4. Love stories
  I. Title
  823.9'14[F]


  ISBN-13: 978-0-7278-6450-5    (cased)

*All Severn House titles are printed on acid-free paper.*


Printed and bound in Great Britain by
MPG Books Ltd., Bodmin, Cornwall.

# 1

The Blantyre Castle steamed languorously through the South China Sea towards Singapore, and Elizabeth tried to retrieve the peace of mind that Raefe Elliot had so disastrously destroyed.

She had hoped that the voyage would give her a chance to reaffirm her love for Adam, to show him physically how very much she loved him. Her hopes had been dashed when, on their first night at sea, Adam had complained of a severe head-cold. He had taken himself to bed alone with a hot brandy and lemon, and she had been ashamed of the relief she had felt. However sincere her intentions, she knew that it was not possible to re-create with Adam the passion she had experienced with Raefe.

Whatever explosive ingredient existed between herself and Raefe Elliot, it did not exist between herself and Adam, and never had done. They were friends, gentle lovers with a wealth of shared and treasured memories behind them; and as Adam began to feel better, and they strolled the decks hand in hand, she realized with thankfulness that her passion for Raefe had not altered her feelings for Adam in any way. They played deck quoits and tennis, they danced together in the evenings, and incredibly it was as if nothing had changed between them. With utter certainty she knew that nothing would. Not if she were strong. Adam had a right to her companionship and the quiet love she felt for him, and he would have both for as long as he wanted. That part of her life was the same and had no connection with the sexual madness that had erupted between herself and Raefe Elliot.

Memories of their fevered lovemaking on the beach rose up to torment her constantly, and she ruthlessly subdued them. It was over. Her true nature had been revealed to her, but for Adam's sake she would never succumb to that animal-like hunger again. She had turned her back on Raefe Elliot, both metaphorically and physically. She would not capitulate to him again, and the memory of how she had capitulated, her frenzied, lascivious eagerness, filled her with mortification. She slid her arm through Adam's, hugging it tight for reassurance. Raefe Elliot was a thousand miles away and, no matter how Adam urged her to return to Hong Kong, she would not do so. Not until she had rooted out and killed her carnal desire for Raefe, until she could meet him and be as indifferent to him as she was to Tom Nicholson or Ronnie Ledsham.

'Penny for them, darling,' Adam said, smiling across to her as they leaned on the deck-rails watching a school of flying fish.

A flush of colour touched her cheeks. 'I was wondering if Singapore will be much different from Hong Kong,' she lied, her eyes remaining resolutely on the fish.

'I imagine so. It's all South-East Asia, isn't it? There'll be the same polyglot mix, the same heat and the same sort of smells. Sweet spices, dried fish, frangipani. The smell of the tropics. It's never far away, even on board ship.'

'I'm looking forward to it,' she said with a fierceness that made him raise his eyebrows. 'Perhaps we can go up-country. To Johore and to Kuala Lumpur?'

'You really have got the travel bit between your teeth, haven't you?' he said, amused. 'What about Li Pi and the tuition you were looking forward to?'

The flying fish dived from view, but she kept her eyes firmly on the creaming waves. 'Li Pi will still be there when we return to Hong Kong,' she said with a lightness she was far from feeling. Li Pi had been the sacrifice she had had to make in order to free herself from Raefe. Even now, the cost of it filled her with so much pain she could scarcely breathe. 'Let's go down to the bar and have a drink,' she said, turning away quickly so that he would not see the anguish in her eyes.

The talk in the bar was all of war, and as Adam and the friends they had made on board discussed the news that Warsaw had surrendered to the Germans she struggled to recover her composure and her equilibrium. By the time the conversation had turned to America, and its determination not to be involved in the conflict rending Europe, she was once again cool and in control. She would not think of Li Pi. She would not think of Raefe. She would think of nothing but Adam, and his dear honest face. Nothing but of how he loved her and needed her. Of how fortunate she was to be his wife.

'It's a bit flat and drab after Hong Kong, isn't it?' Adam said, puffing on his pipe as the *Blantyre Castle* approached the sea-lanes outside Singapore's harbour.

'It's not as pretty,' Elizabeth agreed, standing beside him on the deck, the sea-breeze cool and refreshing against her face.

There were no magnificent mountains rising sheer from the sea. No soaring rocks, silver-grey, silver-tawny. Instead, in the dancing, almost liquid heat, Singapore lay spread out before them, an unromantic line of godowns and shining petrol-tanks on the left, and on the right a fringe of coconut palms and flurry of sampans and junk masts.

'The terrain is the only thing that *is* different,' Adam said with a grin an hour later, as he guided her down the gangplank and a blast of hot air hit them in the face. 'Just listen to that racket! It's even worse than Victoria!'

The dockside teemed with coolies, their clamouring cries and chants as they loaded and unloaded cargo rising deafeningly – nearly, but not quite, drowning the strident shouts of their Chinese overseers. Street-hawkers added to the din, plying their wares to disembarking passengers.

3

The boats around them were unloading spices from Bali and Java and the Celebes, and the fragrance rose into the air, mingling with the smell of the Singapore River and the swamp that stretched out on either side of it.

'God, but it's hot,' Adam said, wiping the back of his neck with his handkerchief as they stepped on to the dockside. 'I thought I'd got used to the heat in Hong Kong, but it's like a blanket here!'

Elizabeth laughed, looking exquisitely cool in a white linen dress that emphasized her slender curves, a broad-brimmed straw hat shielding her face from the sun. She felt headily free. Hong Kong was behind her, and she was determined, with all her might, mind and strength, that she would not return to it until she knew that her marriage was no longer in danger. Leaving Li Pi, leaving Raefe, had been the hardest thing she had ever done, but somehow she had found the strength and now, standing on the crowded dockside, she felt pride at having emerged victorious from her long hard private battle.

'Where to now?' she asked, taking his hand as their luggage was trundled ahead of them by a clutch of black-clad coolies.

'Raffles,' said Adam, beginning to think that the trip had not been such a bad idea after all. There *was* something exciting about a new city, and his instinct told him that Singapore was going to be an interesting and perhaps even more exotic city than Hong Kong had been.

She walked quickly at his side, her hand held firmly in his, ignoring the appreciative glances she drew from certain sections of the crowd – husbands waiting to greet their wives, businessmen waiting to meet colleagues.

'I'm looking forward to it,' she said, her eyes sparkling in a way they had not done for weeks, and then she looked away from Adam to the gate leading from the docks to the road, and her face whitened, her hand clutching convulsively on his arm.

'Welcome to Singapore,' Raefe said, stepping towards them, his rich deep-timbred voice ripping wide all her hard-won intentions and sending them scattering. 'Did you have a good voyage?'

He was speaking to Adam, but his eyes, dark and determined and full of heat, were on Elizabeth. She couldn't look away from him. She was held by his gaze, drowning in it, riveted by it.

'Yes,' Adam said with unaccustomed curtness. 'I didn't know you were in Singapore.' His eyes flicked past Raefe, looking for a taxi. 'Are you here for long?'

'I don't know,' Raefe replied easily, his eyes still on Elizabeth. 'It depends.'

His eyes were burning hers, scorching her with their heat. She tried to speak and couldn't. She had tried so hard, run so far, and all to no avail. She had merely run from the frying-pan into the fire. In Hong Kong there were friends who could, simply by their presence, offer her a measure of protection against her crippling desire for him. In Singapore there was no one. And he would pursue her until she capitulated, not just for a few stolen hours, but for ever; his eyes and the tight harsh lines around his mouth told her that. Her fingers dug deeply into the soft linen of Adam's tropical jacket. She felt as if she were going to faint.

'Where are you going? Raffles?' Raefe asked Adam, dragging his eyes reluctantly from her.

'Yes.' Adam's voice was chill. He didn't like Elliot. He didn't like his reputation or his negligent insolent attitude. And he didn't like his being in Singapore, or the coincidence of his being at the docks at the precise moment they had disembarked.

Raefe turned round and raised his hand, and immediately a yellow Ford taxi-cab purred to a halt at their side.

'Thank you,' Adam said stiffly as the coolies began to load their luggage into the boot.

'Singapore is my city, almost as much as Hong Kong,' Raefe said, his eyes once more on Elizabeth's pale strained face. 'I look forward to showing you around.'

Adam made a polite noncommittal reply. He had no

intention of spending time with Elliot, in Singapore or any-where else. He helped Elizabeth into the rear of the taxi and climbed in after her. Then he leaned forward to the Chinese driver. 'Raffles, please,' he said, and did not even look in Raefe Elliot's direction as the taxi pulled away from the kerb and into the main stream of traffic.

Raefe was uncaring. It was about time Adam Harland realized that he was losing his wife. And he *was* losing her. Had already lost her. A small tight smile touched his mouth. He knew how much she had wanted to hurtle into his arms, how desperately she had wanted to turn her head as the cab drew away, to look at him as he was looking at her, until she was no longer in sight.

'You tried hard, my love,' he said softly as the dockside crowds and rickshaws and taxi-cabs surged around him. 'But even you cannot escape the inevitable.' And then he turned to the chauffeur-driven Lagonda waiting a mere few feet away. 'Robinson Road,' he said as he settled himself into its luxurious interior, wondering how he would endure the hours until he saw her again.

Elizabeth leaned her head weakly against cracked hot leather. Dear God, what a fool she had been to think that she could escape him so easily! As the taxi hurtled away from the docks she could see a godown, the name 'Elliot' emblazoned in large scarlet letters across its front. Elliot. A name synony-mous with rubber and tin. A name as well known in Singapore as it was in Hong Kong. She remembered her first dinner-party at Tom Nicholson's and Julienne saying that it was when Raefe had returned from a business trip to Singapore that he had found Jacko Latimer in his wife's bed. She closed her eyes as the cab sped past neatly laid-out flowerbeds and the white elegant façades of government buildings. She should have known. She should have remem-bered. Ever since she had left Hong Kong she had been living in a fool's paradise. A man of Raefe's wealth didn't waste time in travelling to Singapore by ship. He flew down. And he had done so the minute he had been told where she was.

'Did you know Elliot was in Singapore?' Adam asked, his voice unusually brusque as the taxi veered into a tree-lined road.

'No.' She opened her eyes. She felt so drained, so shattered with the shock of seeing Raefe, of knowing that she could summon up no resistance to him, that if Adam had asked her then and there whether she was having an affair with him she would have admitted it.

He said irritably: 'I can't stand the man. There's something insufferably arrogant and insultingly self-assured about him. It wouldn't surprise me at all if he had murdered Jack or Jimmy Latimer, or whatever his name was, in cold blood.'

It was so unlike Adam to speak harshly of anyone that Elizabeth felt as if cold hands were on her heart. 'He didn't,' she said, hating herself for the position he had put her in. A woman defending her lover to her husband. 'The jury was all agreed that his action was unpremeditated and that he merely meant to give Jacko a thrashing.'

'It's a pretty vicious thrashing that leaves a man with a smashed skull,' Adam said tightly as they turned left into Beach Road and approached the traveller's palms that signalled Raffles.

She remained silent. She didn't want to discuss Raefe with him. Her feelings were in tumult as it was, and to hear Raefe's name being spoken so derogatively by someone she loved and whose opinion she had always respected was almost more than she could bear. She wondered if he knew. The tension emanating between herself and Raefe had been almost palpable, and she knew that another, more worldly man would have guessed the truth instantly. But Adam was not worldly, not when it came to sexual indiscretions, and he had never had any reason to suspect her of unfaithfulness.

The cab drew to a halt. Bellboys ran to assist with their luggage. An Indian doorman, tall and turbaned, saluted them into the marble-flagged reception area. Thanks to her childhood, she was a connoisseur where great hotels were concerned and she had looked forward to staying at the legendary Raffles. Now her pleasure was nonexistent, and she scarcely looked about her as a bellboy led them to their rooms.

'I suppose he's down here on business,' Adam said pugnaciously, refusing to let the subject drop. He tipped the bellboy and closed the door on him. 'The name Elliot was plastered all over the godowns near the docks. He must own half the damned city.'

'I don't think so,' she said, sitting down on one of the beds and easing off her shoes. God, the last thing she wanted was a discussion with Adam about Raefe's wealth. 'I feel suddenly ridiculously tired, Adam. Would you mind very much if I had a sleep? We can go for a look-around later on, after lunch.'

He looked across at her with a concerned frown. Her beautifully etched face was ivory pale, and there were dark shadows beneath her eyes that he had not seen there earlier.

'Of course I don't mind,' he said, immediately solicitous. 'Would you like me to ring for a cup of tea?'

'No, thank you,' she said, forcing a smile. 'I just need a sleep, Adam, that's all.'

He walked across to her. 'I shouldn't have gone on so about Raefe Elliot,' he said apologetically. 'It isn't as if the man is of the slightest interest to us.' He leaned over and kissed her on the forehead. 'Have a good rest, darling. I'll wake you in an hour or so.'

The door clicked quietly behind him. The fan, hanging trembling from the ceiling, turned lazily and sunlight fell in slatted shafts through the rattan blinds. She stared up at the glistening white ceiling. All she had to do was not to see him. With a little persuasion, she could surely coerce Adam into leaving immediately for Kuala Lumpur or Johore. Her good intentions didn't have to lay shattered in smithereens around her. She could still salvage a remnant of self-respect from the wreckage.

She thought of the way he had looked when their eyes

had met over the heads of the hurrying coolies and disembarking passengers, tall and broad-shouldered, his silk shirt open at the throat, his white flannels snug about his narrow hips, his glossy black hair sheened blue by the sun, and desire shot through her, convulsing her with a physical longing raging to be assuaged. Dear God, but she wanted his hands on her body, his mouth on her flesh. The mere thought of it made her hot and damp, made her quiver in hungry anticipation.

With a sob she rolled over on to her stomach, her fists clenched as she slammed them into the pillows. She would *not* give in to him! She would not sacrifice her life with Adam because of her animal-like craving to lay spread-eagled on her back beneath Raefe Elliot's hard thrusting body. She would not! She would not! She would not!

When Adam returned she had showered and was wearing an apricot cotton dress with a narrow waist and full skirt, and matching high-wedged peep-toe sandals.

'Feeling better, darling?' he asked, sliding his arms around her.

'Yes,' she lied, leaning against him, wishing with all her heart that her body would react to his in the same wild impassioned way that it reacted to Raefe's. 'Adam?' Her arms tightened around him as he looked down questioningly at her. 'Could we leave tomorrow for Kuala Lumpur? I've heard that the scenery up-country is superb and—'

'Good heavens, Beth! We've only just got here!' he said, laughing indulgently. 'Let's leave Kuala Lumpur till next week or the week after. It won't run away.'

Her heart began to beat in short thick strokes. She could never remember his refusing her anything, and this was so important! If they didn't leave Singapore, if she had to face Raefe again, then the whole structure of their lives would fall apart.

'Please, Adam,' she said, slipping her hands up and around his neck. 'Please, darling. It would mean so much to me.'

His smile faded. 'That's what you said about coming to

Singapore, Beth. I gave in to you, and we came, but I don't particularly want to find myself in transit again for at least two weeks. It simply isn't reasonable.' He squeezed her and then released his hold of her. 'Come on, darling. I got talking to a couple of planters and an up-country tin-miner in the Long Bar. I'd like to introduce you to them.'

'Please, Adam,' she said again, her voice taut. 'I know it seems ridiculous, but it *is* important to me!'

'But why?' he said. 'Why this urge to be constantly on the move? Is there something wrong? Something you're not telling me?'

She looked up into his dear, kind, puzzled face, and knew with despair that she couldn't tell him. It would hurt him too much, and the dreadful inadequacy at the heart of their marriage would lay exposed. He would know that his gentle reverent lovemaking had never aroused her. That, though she loved him dearly, she was not in love with him in the way that a woman ought to be with her husband. And nothing would ever be the same between them again.

'No,' she said wearily. 'No, there's nothing wrong, Adam.'

He took her once more into his arms, holding her close. 'I can't bear it if you're unhappy, Beth,' he said, his voice muffled against her hair. 'I love you so much, sweetheart. You mean everything in the world to me.'

'I know.' Her voice was choked. 'And I love you, too, Adam.' Her arms tightened around him. At that moment it seemed inconceivable that she could ever hurt him. All she had to do was remember how very dear he was to her. And refuse to see Raefe Elliot ever again.

They had a couple of drinks in the Long Bar, and Adam introduced her to the planters and the miner that he had met earlier. Later, as they ate lunch, the sound of music filtered through into the dining-room. 'That's the band,' Adam said with a grin. 'There is dancing here every afternoon. Rather decorous, I suspect, but still fun.'

When they had finished their coffee they strolled along the arcade that led to the dance-floor. 'How about a slow foxtrot before we launch ourselves on the town?' Adam asked her, putting his pipe away in his pocket. 'It's years since I did this sort of thing at two o'clock in the afternoon. It makes life feel quite *risqué*!'

For the rest of the day, as they explored Singapore by rickshaw and taxi-cab, she wondered when Raefe would next attempt to get in touch with her. And where.

The city was more open, more laid-out, than Hong Kong, the contrasts between the different parts of the city sharper and more obviously defined. The Chinese part of the city, the crowded and dark little shops, was familiar enough to them after Hong Kong, but only a few streets away the noise and bustle vanished and Chinese faces were replaced by Indian faces, black pyjamas by vivid silk saris, hectic frenzy by Asian languor.

They paid off their taxi-cab, strolling through a street-market, its stalls piled high with mounds of mangoes and papayas and pomelos and chillies, the ground daubed with the scarlet stains of betel nuts. Later, when they were tired, they took a rickshaw back towards Raffles, the narrow crowded streets replaced by broad avenues with trim grass verges and luxuriant and carefully tended flowerbeds.

'That's the Tanglin Club,' Adam said, pointing out a low white building amidst spacious grounds. 'If we're going to be here for any length of time, we must become members. Alastair says it has the best swimming-pool in the city.'

As they neared the government and business section, she saw the name 'Elliot' emblazoned high over an office block and her stomach muscles tightened. She didn't want to be in Singapore long enough for it to become necessary for them to join prestigious all-white sports clubs like the Tanglin. She wanted to leave Singapore, and Raefe Elliot, far behind her.

'It's a far more attractive city than it first looked, isn't it?' Adam mused as their rickshaw bowled down the broad tree-lined expanse of Battery Road. 'Every street leads to

11

either the sea or the river. There's water and ships everywhere.'

She agreed with him. Singapore *was* a beautiful city, with its parks and gardens, its straight streets bordered by exotic flame trees and trim grass verges, but she couldn't take the pleasure in it that Adam was taking. As they neared Raffles Place, she could think only of Raefe. Of whether he would be at Raffles when they returned. Of how he would take her adamant refusal to see him again. Of how she would summon the strength to remain steadfast against her crippling need of him.

Dusk was falling rapidly as their rickshaw-boy drew up with a flourish in front of the traveller's palms. 'You go ahead for a shower, Beth,' Adam said as they walked into the hotel. 'I'm going to slip into the bar for five minutes and have a cooling stengah. My throat is parched.'

She was only too happy to go straight up to their room. A brief glance into the barnlike lounge had shown no sign of Raefe, but he would be nearby somewhere, she was sure of it. Her hand trembled slightly on the banister as she walked quickly up the wide stairs. She was filled with such a mixture of dread and longing that she felt as though she were being torn inwardly apart. Once in the comparative safety of her room she closed the door and leaned against it, her eyes closed.

Would he have the temerity to join them for dinner? Was he even now sharing a drink with Adam? His determined pursuit sent waves of aching pleasure licking through her. He could have any woman he wanted for the asking. And he wanted her. She opened her eyes and moved across the room, switching on lamps, closing the blinds against the moths and the night-time sounds of crickets and bullfrogs. When she listened to people talking about him, even people who liked him, such as Julienne and Helena, she felt as if they were talking about a stranger. They weren't talking about the Raefe that *she* knew. The Raefe who was as oddly vulnerable and as inwardly lonely as she herself was. The Raefe with whom she identified so completely.

12

She unbuckled the narrow belt of her dress and stepped out of her shoes. There had been an almost instant fusion between them, not only physically but also mentally. She felt as if she had known him all her life. She laid her dress on the end of the bed and walked into the bathroom, turning on the shower, unfastening her bra and letting it fall to the cool tiled floor, removing her panties.

The water gushed hot and strong, and she stepped beneath it, turning her face upwards. She wanted to be with him more than she had ever wanted anything, ever, in her life. Even more than she wanted success as a pianist. She wanted his face to be the last thing she saw at night when she closed her eyes. She wanted him to be the first thing she saw when she woke. She wanted to eat with him, sleep with him, laugh with him, cry with him. She wanted to sit across the breakfast-table from him, she wanted to watch him shave, she wanted to share his dreams and hopes. She wanted to be part of his life. Tears mingled with the hot rush of water. If only they had met years ago. If only she hadn't married Adam. If only. . . . If only. . . .

'There's quite a good bunch down in the bar,' Adam called out to her as he entered the bedroom. 'Tin-miners out on the town. What they don't know about the Japs isn't worth knowing. You don't mind if I have another chat with them later, after dinner, do you, Beth?'

'No, of course not.' Beneath the roar of the shower her voice was unsteady. She wiped the futile tears away from her face, deeply ashamed. How could she ever wish that the last few years with Adam had never taken place? It wasn't possible. Adam had always been a part of her life. His strong compassionate nature had been her support and her sustenance ever since she had been a child, and she could not wish herself free of it now, simply because the deeply sexual side of her nature had, at last, been unleashed.

She stepped out of the shower and wrapped a towel around herself. 'Was there anyone else in the bar?' she asked, forcing her voice to sound uninterested. 'Anyone we know?'

'No,' he said, his brows pulling together slightly. 'It would be hardly likely, would it? The only person we know who's in Singapore is Elliot.'

She crossed to the dressing-table, sitting down before it and reaching for her make-up. He had told her all she wanted to know. Raefe wasn't in the bar. And he hadn't approached Adam suggesting that they all dine together. She felt a surge of relief that was immediately followed by fierce excruciating disappointment.

Adam gave her a long puzzled look, and then walked into the bathroom to shower. Had she been referring to Elliot? Was she expecting him to be in the Long Bar this evening? Had she perhaps known all along that he would be in Singapore? He unbuttoned his sweat-soaked shirt and tossed it to the floor. The Singapore heat was getting to him, and he was being ridiculous. Elliot being at the docks when they had disembarked had been nothing but coincidence. And there was nothing remotely odd about him being in Singapore. His business interests must demand that he visit the city often.

The water gushed hotly over his head, and as he reached for the soap he began to whistle. The idea of Beth indulging in an adulterous affair with Raefe Elliot was as ridiculous now as it had been when Alastair had first hinted at it. He grinned to himself, thinking how outraged she would be if she knew he had even considered such a thing a possibility.

'Put your silver dance-shoes on,' he called out to her as he soaped his chest and shoulders. 'We'll have another spin on the floor and a bottle of champagne to celebrate our first night here!'

All through dinner she tried to relax and failed miserably. While Adam talked about the differences between Singapore and Hong Kong, her eyes flicked nervously away from his animated face and around the crowded dining-room. There was no sign of Raefe. She felt her throat tighten, torn by conflicting emotions.

'One of the chaps I was drinking with earlier used to be a

stockbroker, travelling up to town from Brighton every day on the eight-fifteen. He threw it all in five years ago and came out here. He says he hasn't regretted a day of it.'

Elizabeth smiled and toyed with her *satay*, wondering if, concealed by one of the many giant potted ferns, Raefe was watching them as they ate and talked.

Later, in the Long Bar, she did her best to listen attentively as Adam and his new-found friends discussed the Japanese and their empire-building intentions.

'I'm sorry . . . I didn't quite hear,' she said apologetically as one of the planters waited, his eyes appreciative, for her to respond to the last remark he had made to her.

'I said that the war in Europe has been no bad thing for Malaya,' he repeated obligingly, wishing to God that her husband wasn't there and that he could let his eyes rove below the enticing neckline of her dress. 'America is panicking like mad and demanding more rubber than she has been doing for an age. We have over three million acres of it under cultivation, you know, and half the world's tin.' His Australian accent was full of pride, as if he were personally responsible for the country's natural richness.

She managed a smile. 'Then, it's no wonder the Japanese have an unhealthy interest in Malaya.'

The Australian laughed. She was intelligent as well as stunning to look at. 'Have another drink,' he said expansively, turning round and banging his fist on the bar to attract the barman's attention.

Elizabeth suppressed a shudder and touched Adam's arm lightly, saying; 'I really don't want any more to drink, darling. Or any more of this conversation. Do you mind if I slip away? It's been a long day, and I'm tired.'

'No, of course not,' he said, his eyes darkening with concern as they always did at the least indication that she was uncomfortable or unhappy. 'Do you want me to come with you?'

She shook her head, knowing that he was enjoying his conversation about Japanese intentions and Britain's ability to deal with them. 'No, of course not. I'm going to go for a short walk in the grounds and then have a long bath before I go to bed.' She gave his arm a loving squeeze, said goodnight to the disappointed Australian, and walked quickly through the lounge and along the arcade that skirted the ballroom and led to the gardens.

Raefe hadn't been in the dining-room, and he hadn't been in the bar. She had been wrong in her assumption that he would be. As she stepped out into the hot sultry darkness she knew that if only she could persuade Adam to change his mind and leave Singapore in the morning for Kuala Lumpur or Johore, then the confrontation she so dreaded would be avoided.

The narrow gravel path she had taken wound down between soaring traveller's palms and high banks of ghostly blossomed hibiscus and sweet-smelling juniper. Thousands of stars spangled the night sky, burning with breathtaking brightness, and she paused, looking up at them, recognizing the Pleiades and Orion and the familiar curve of the Hyades.

From somewhere behind her, in the scented darkness, there came a soft footfall and the sound of a match spurting into flame. She spun round, her heart leaping into her throat, knowing who it was even before he rounded the curve of the path. A second later the hibiscus blossoms trembled, milk-white petals fluttering to the ground.

'I thought you were never going to have the sense to come out here,' he said, and the match and the cigarette he had just lit both went fizzing down among the dry juniper needles as he covered the distance between them in an easy stride, taking her in his arms.

# 2

She tried to push herself free of him, tried to cry out in protest, but the touch of his hand on her flesh, the hard muscular strength of his body, the feel of his heart slamming close against hers were too much for her. With a groan she swayed against him, brought almost to insensibility by the pleasure of his touch.

'No . . .,' she whispered desperately as he raised her face to his. 'Oh, please, Raefe, no. . . .'

In the moonlight his lean high-cheekboned face was merciless. 'Yes,' he breathed harshly, lowering his head to hers, holding her with brutal strength.

Vainly she tried to wrest her mouth from his, but her need of him, her raging urgent desire confounded her and left her helpless. For one brief brave moment she struggled and then his hair was coarse beneath her fingers, his hands hard upon her body, and his mouth was dry as her tongue slipped past his lips.

Her capitulation was total, irrevocable. When his hands slid up beneath the soft silk of her dress, she made no protest, pressing herself closer to him with shameless hunger.

'I want you, Lizzie. . . . Want you . . .,' he uttered hoarsely, and though beyond his shoulder she could see the lights of the ballroom gleaming between the trees and the painted Chinese lanterns that decked the terrace she said only in a wanton raw voice that she no longer recognized; 'Yes! Here! Now! Oh, please! Quickly. Quickly!'

17

There were no preliminaries; he didn't even lower her to the ground. Like a stag on heat that cannot wait another moment for copulation, he slammed her against a tree and took her where she stood.

Afterwards, as they clung together in the hot moist darkness, reverberations of their shattering climax still shuddering through them, he said: 'You will, of course, tell Adam what has happened? And return to Hong Kong with me.'

She moved away from him slightly, and her hair, which had fallen free of its pins, shimmered in wild disarray about her shoulders. 'No,' she said quietly, her voice brooking no argument. 'I shall not tell Adam. It would break his heart. And I shall not return to Hong Kong with you.'

His brows flew together. 'This isn't a repeat of what you said to me at Shek O, is it?' he asked fiercely. 'You can't possibly imagine that you can walk away from me again! That I would even *allow* you to.'

She shook her head, and her hair gleamed in the moonlight, pale as ivory. 'No,' she said softly, her arms tightly around his waist, her head against his chest. 'I shall never walk away from you again, but if you want me, Raefe, it must be on my own terms.'

'And those are?' he demanded harshly, tilting her face to his, his eyes burning hers.

'That I remain with Adam.' He made a savage sound of protest, and she continued, her voice almost as fierce as his had been: 'I owe Adam my loyalty, Raefe. He has loved me and cared for me all my life, and I care for him. Very much.' His frown deepened, and she said more gently; 'Don't confuse my loyalty with my love, Raefe. I can only give one to Adam. You have both. Surely it is enough?'

He said, his voice still tight: 'It isn't what I want.'

'It's all I can give.'

All around them crickets rattled their legs in continuous whirring. From the terrace there came the sound of subdued laughter and the clink of glasses. There was a

18

long silence and then a small grin crooked the corners of his mouth. 'Then, it's what I shall take,' he said, and this time when he kissed her it was with the knowledge that she would never be lost to him again.

She was sitting at the chintz-flounced dressing-table in her nightdress and négligé, brushing her hair, when Adam returned to their room.

'I thought you'd have been in bed and asleep long ago,' he said cheerily, happily inebriated at having drunk far more stengahs than he was accustomed to.

He shrugged himself free of his white evening jacket, draping it over a convenient chair, undoing his bow tie and tossing it on his bed, unfastening the top button of his dress shirt as he walked across to her, giving her a kiss on her cheek.

'Mmmm, you smell nice, sweetheart,' he said appreciatively and, instead of walking away and continuing to undress, his voice thickened and his hands slid up her arms, cupping her shoulders. 'I miss you when you're not with me, Beth. I didn't see another woman all evening who was half as beautiful.'

She forced a smile, putting down her hairbrush with an unsteady hand; her passionate, physical, total love for Raefe had not diminished the deep affection she felt for Adam. But she couldn't make love with him tonight, not while the heat of Raefe's hands still lingered on her body. 'I'm glad,' she said, rising to her feet and walking over to the chair and his discarded jacket and picking it up. 'Did the ex-stockbroker from Brighton join you after I had left?'

'No.' His voice was deflated. He had never, ever, made love to her when he had thought she was tired or unwilling. Her action in moving away from him signalled that tonight she was perhaps both, and he felt acute disappointment. He sat down on the edge of the bed, slipping off his shoes. 'I have some news for you that you will like, though,' he said, pulling his shirt over his head, his spirits rising as he anticipated her pleasure. 'There's a train leaving for Kuala Lumpur at ten tomorrow morning, and we can be on it if you still want to be.' He turned his head so that he could see the delight on her face.

She was in the act of hanging his jacket in the wardrobe. He saw her hand falter, but she didn't turn her head in his direction, and when she spoke her voice sounded oddly high and brittle. 'That's very kind of you, Adam, but I've changed my mind. I'm quite happy not to do any further travelling.'

She began to pick imaginary specks of dust from the lapels of his jacket, and he said, puzzled: 'But I thought you were quite desperate to go. You said it was important to you.'

His kindness, and the knowledge of how she was repaying it, made her cheeks burn with shame and mortification. She kept her back firmly to him, beginning to examine a lightweight suit for nonexistent dust specks. 'Not any longer,' she said, trying to inject a note of lightness into her voice, as if her contrariness was an example of female perversity and should be laughed away.

Adam shook his head in mock despair. 'I can't keep up with you, sweetheart. You haven't set your heart on any other far-flung destination, have you?'

She emerged from the wardrobe at last. She had set her heart elsewhere. Not on a destination, but on Raefe. 'No,' she lied, giving him a quick squeeze and moving away towards her own bed before he could interpret her gesture as sexual willingness. 'And from now on we'll go where *you* want to go, Adam. I promise.'

He grinned. 'OK,' he said, settling himself into bed. 'That means that tomorrow we hire a car and drive across to the north of the island. I want to see for myself how easily Singapore can be defended against the Japs. And I want to see what defences have been built, and if there's anything Hong Kong can learn from them.'

She smiled at him, her affection for him so deep that she felt tears sting the backs of her eyes. 'You should have stayed in the Army and become a general. Good night, darling. God bless.'

He blew her a kiss across the narrow divide of their beds and turned off the bedside light, happy that he wasn't travelling to Kuala Lumpur the next morning, and happy that Beth was no longer consumed by the restlessness that had seriously begun to worry him.

She didn't see Raefe for three days. Unspoken, but understood between them, was their mutual desire that Adam should be treated with as much respect as was possible. There would be no apparently 'innocent' meetings when Adam was present.

She was no longer torn apart by inner turmoil. She had reached her Rubicon and crossed it, and there could be no going back. The knowledge brought with it a peace of mind that she had thought she would never regain. The next morning they hired a car and explored the island at their leisure. It was rich and verdant, the city sprawling out till it merged into an exotic jungle of casuarina trees, and flame trees and bushes with thick juicy leaves, infested by screeching monkeys and vividly coloured birds. They drove across to the north coast, looking out over the narrow strait that separated the island from the Malay Peninsula.

'The Japanese couldn't possibly attack Singapore in the same way that they could Hong Kong,' Elizabeth said, standing on the palm-fringed beach and shielding her eyes against the sun as she looked towards Johore. 'They would have to fight their way down the entire peninsula. It simply couldn't be done. The ground is too mountainous and the vegetation too thick, even for tanks.'

She was wearing a pair of white slacks and a cornflower-blue blouse, open at the throat. He looked across at her and grinned. 'You sound even more knowledgeable than Denholm Gresby.'

She laughed and then said, a small frown puckering her brow: 'I don't think Sir Denholm is knowledgeable at all. At least, not where Hong Kong is concerned.'

Adam raised his binoculars, sweeping them round in an attempt to locate strategically placed pillboxes. There was none to be seen. He was not unduly surprised. There was no urgent necessity for them. Singapore, unlike Hong Kong, was a fortress that was impregnable, and he had been wrong in thinking there would be anything to learn in the way of coastal defence.

'Well, where Singapore is concerned, there's not too much to worry about,' he said, lowering his binoculars. 'Though where the Japs are concerned anything could happen. They're just crazy enough to believe an attack could succeed.' He wiped a bead of perspiration from the back of his neck with his handkerchief. 'Where to now? What about the Sea View Hotel for a nice curry tiffin? The fellows in the bar highly recommended it.'

'Fine,' she said agreeably as they turned away from the sea and began to walk back towards their car. 'Where is it? Back in the city?'

'No, it's on the east-coast road. Apparently the Britishers here treat it as a kind of English village pub. You know, drinks before lunch on a Sunday and a good old sing-song into the bargain.'

She slipped her arm through his. 'You're making me feel homesick. I haven't thought of Four Seasons for ages. Do you think Sundays at home are still the same, or do you think the war will have altered everything?'

'For the moment, I suspect they will still be the same,' Adam said as he opened the door of their hired Mercedes tourer. 'The newspapers are calling it the phoney war. Nothing seems to be happening at the moment. Let's hope nothing does.'

It was on the Wednesday that Adam asked her if she would like to spend an afternoon, free of his company, shopping. She knew immediately that it was because he had plans of his own that he wanted to follow.

'Where is it that you want to go?' she asked teasingly.

22

'On a binge with your drinking chums of the other night?'

'Not exactly,' he said good-humouredly, filling the bowl of his pipe with tobacco. 'There's a card game on, and I wouldn't mind chancing my luck. That is, if you don't mind.'

'Of course I don't mind. Just make sure you don't lose your shirt, that's all. I imagine that those rubber-planters are pretty sharp card-players!'

She had telephoned Raefe at the number he had given her, and told him that she was free for the whole afternoon. 'But I'm supposed to be shopping. Could you pick me up at Robinsons? I'll call in there first and buy a dress.'

'You have ten minutes,' he threatened, his voice thickening with desire. 'If you're not at Robinsons' front entrance by ten past one, I shall come into the dress department and carry you bodily out of it!'

'I'll be there,' she said, her eyes shining, her cheeks flushed as she put the receiver back on its rest, grabbing hold of her handbag and running from the room.

Robinsons was a huge store in Raffles Place, only a stone's throw from the hotel. She hurried up to the dress department, taking the first dress she saw and waltzing it over to be wrapped and boxed without even trying it on.

'But, madam, surely it would be wisest to see if it fits . . .,' the shop assistant protested in dazed bewilderment.

'It will fit perfectly,' Elizabeth said, feeling as euphoric as if she were drunk. 'Please wrap it for me quickly; I'm in a terrible hurry!'

He was waiting for her as she emerged five minutes later. 'You only just made it,' he said, laughing down at her as she hurtled into his arms. 'I was on my way in to retrieve you.'

In the strong sunlight his black hair had a blue sheen and the lean sunbronzed planes of his face looked almost Arabic. Uncaring of the shoppers thronging around them, her arms slid up and around his neck, her lips parting eagerly as he lowered his head to hers.

A few shoppers gave them a bemused glance and made

a detour round them, but one particular shopper stood rooted to the spot, staring at them in stunned disbelief.

Miriam Gresby had been about to enter Robinsons to meet a woman friend for coffee in the new air-conditioned restaurant. Denholm was in Singapore on official business and was, that morning, meeting Sir Shenton Thomas, the island's governor. She far preferred shopping in Singapore to Hong Kong, and so she had accompanied him, and now she stood, hardly able to believe her eyes, as the cool, beautiful, exquisitely mannered Elizabeth Harland threw herself publicly into Raefe Elliot's open arms.

It was disgraceful behaviour for anyone, but *Elizabeth Harland*! She watched as the fervent embrace came to an end and he took her hand, leading her across the pavement and towards an open-topped Chrysler. Her mouth, which had at first dropped open in amazement, closed like a trap. There would be no more dinner invitations issued to the Harlands, and she would certainly see to it that none would be accepted from them.

As the Chrysler pulled away and into the main stream of traffic, she remembered the other occasion when she had thought she had seen Elizabeth Harland with Raefe Elliot. It had been outside the Peninsula Hotel, but the idea had been so ridiculous that she had assumed she had been mistaken. Her eyes narrowed as the Chrysler was lost to view. She knew now that she hadn't been. The flagrant affair was one of long-standing duration. She marched into Robinsons, her rocking-horse nostrils flaring, eager to share her outrage with the friend who was waiting for her.

He had never taken any of his Singaporean girlfriends to his house at Holland Park on the outskirts of the city, and Melissa had never visited it. It was a large sprawling white bungalow and it had been his childhood home. Perhaps, subconsciously, that was the reason he had never used it as a cheap love-nest. Whatever the reason, as he lay beside Elizabeth's creamy pale body on the large brass-headed bed, he was supremely glad that no woman had lain there before her.

They hadn't drawn the blinds, and there were no curtains, but outside the window there was a vine sifting the sunlight so that the walls of the bedroom were delicately patterned with the moving shadow of leaf and tendril.

'Slowly,' he said, his rich dark voice full of love as she turned towards him, pressing the length of her body against his, her breasts soft against his chest. 'This time, my love, there's no need to hurry.'

Teasingly his lips played with hers as his hands caressed, aroused, explored. She had a tiny mole beneath her left breast, a small scar on her hip, and her pubic hair was golden-blonde, crisply curled.

'You're so beautiful,' he breathed as he held himself in firm control, his hands running over the silky flesh marvelling, fascinated, enchanted.

'Aaah, Raefe . . .,' she sighed deeply beneath him, her fingers curled in the ram's fleece of his hair, filled once again with that fierce chaotic tumble of urges to unite with him, to be part of him, to complete herself by joining with him.

'I love you, Lizzie, I'll love you always,' he said passionately, his mouth open on hers.

She arched herself towards him, aching for him to take her. 'I love you,' she whispered against the heat of his flesh.

He looked down at her, his dark face brilliant with an expression of such fierce love that it was transfigured. 'Always?'

'For ever.'

They pressed themselves close to each other, savouring each moment of their leisured lovemaking, and then, at last, he entered her and she gasped and then purred with pleasure, her body melting boneless into his. He took her to the very brink of sexual convulsion, holding her there with infinite skill, teasing, tantalizing, until she begged and pleaded for release.

He refused to acquiesce, withdrawing until she thought she would die, and then plunging deeply into her, his eyes tightly closed, a look of agony contorting his features.

25

'Now,' he uttered harshly. 'Now!' And she cried out beneath him, brought to an orgasm so stabbing, so victorious that it filled her with joyous terror. Their bodies were slippery with sweat, the sheets tangled around them as they lay intertwined, the sunlight streaming golden across the floor.

Colonel Landor put down Raefe's latest report and said, with a note of weariness in his voice: 'It would seem that every photographer and barber in South-East Asia is a Jap spy!'

'Mr Mamatsu, the photographer who plies his trade behind Raffles Hotel certainly is,' Raefe said grimly. 'He makes a feature of giving cut rates on soldiers' souvenir photographs to send back to wives and sweethearts, that sort of thing. His shop is crammed with military personnel at all hours of the day and night.'

Colonel Landor rose from behind the desk and walked thoughtfully across to the window, staring out across a green-lawned square. It irked him that his best intelligence officer was an American and not British. He disliked Americans. All Americans. They were too cocky, too self-assured. And with Elliot he could never rid himself of the feeling that he was being held in contempt. 'As long as we know who these beggars are, and as long as we can intercept and decode their messages, I don't think too much damage is being done,' he said coldly.

Raefe's mouth tightened. He hadn't expected the Colonel's view to be any different. It had been a while since his last visit to Fort Canning, and the five Japanese seconded from the Japanese army for the supposed purpose of learning English were still happily ensconced in Hong Kong, as was the barber at the Hong Kong Hotel. 'I beg to disagree,' he said tightly.

Colonel Landor turned reluctantly away from the window. The sun was shining and the grass was green, and it was a perfect day for cricket.

'It isn't your position to agree or disagree, Major,'

he said, holding on to his patience with difficulty.

Raefe's eyes smouldered furiously. Landor was a Whitehall wallah. Following the official line laid down by men in pinstriped suits, thousands of miles away. Men who had no real understanding of the East or the Eastern mind.

'With respect, Colonel,' he persisted, 'we're being too complacent. I've travelled the length and breadth of Malaya, I know the country like the back of my hand. Whitehall's boast that it is unassailable is misplaced.'

Colonel Landor picked up his swagger-stick and slammed it against the four-foot-high map pinned to the wall. 'A backbone of granite mountains rising to seven thousand feet, zig-zagging the length of the country! Four-fifths of the land covered with dense tropical jungle, with rainforest. How can it be?'

'Despite what army intelligence would like us to believe, the Japanese army is highly trained, and it is highly trained in bush warfare. They'll land on the coast and they won't be deterred by jungles or by rainforest. They are accustomed to those conditions in a way none of our own troops are. They'll use enveloping tactics rather than a head-on assault, and they'll be at the Johore Straits before we've had time to blink!'

Colonel Landor's nostrils were pinched and white. 'I find that kind of talk defeatist, Mr Elliot. The Japs have to be so sure of our military superiority that they will never dare to attack! Our belief in ourselves and in our ability is crucial!' He strode back to his desk. 'Your report about Mr Mamatsu will be dealt with. Good day, Mr. Elliot!'

Elizabeth sat in a wicker long-chair on the glass-covered veranda of the hotel, a notepad on her knee. She was writing her regular monthly letter to Princess Luisa Isabel, but was not filling the pages up as rapidly as she usually did. She looked down at what she had written. 'Singapore island isn't mountainous or as magnificently beautiful as Hong Kong, but the city is far lovelier and Adam is enjoying himself hugely, making friends with rubber-planters and tin-miners, and brushing up on his poker-playing.'

The words were innocuous, accurate, and very misleading. She was conjuring up a picture of an idyllic vacation, and she was giving no hint at all of the cataclysmic turn that her life had taken. She put down her pen, staring out across the gardens. At the frangipani trees. At the hibiscus.

Voluptuous pleasure licked through her. Hibiscus, and Raefe rounding the path in the darkness, and their shameless fevered lovemaking. She picked up her pen again. 'There is so much I would like to talk to you about, Luisa. So much has happened that is hard to put down on paper. . . .' She paused, knowing that she could not be more explicit, that it would not be fair to Adam.

A small bird with jewelled coloured wings darted down from a nearby tree, and as she watched its flight she knew with sudden certainty that, if and when she told Luisa about Raefe, Luisa would not be surprised. That she would have been expecting such an event for a long time. 'The East has brought me to maturity,' she wrote, her pen beginning to flow more easily across the paper. 'I have been a little girl in a woman's body for too long. I am so no longer. . . .'

She saw Raefe only once more before he flew back to Hong Kong. Adam had fixed up a game of singles with the ex-stockbroker from Brighton, and she had left him on the tennis-courts and taken a yellow Ford taxi-cab to the padang on the waterfront, where Raefe was waiting for her.

'I haven't got long,' she warned as she slid into the Chrysler's front passenger-seat beside him. 'Only an hour or two.'

'Then, don't waste time talking,' he said practically, pulling her towards him and covering her mouth with his.

They had driven to Holland Park and made love and then they had gone down to the river, walking along its banks, their arms around each other's waist, painfully conscious of the sun sliding away to the west and the precious minutes ticking rapidly away.

'How long will it be before you return to Hong Kong?' he asked, hating the thought of leaving her, acquiescing only because he understood her feelings towards Adam and respected them.

'I don't know. A week, perhaps two weeks.'

'And you will be sailing back?'

'Yes.'

'So it could be over a month before I see you again.'

She was silent, knowing how much he wanted her to leave Singapore with him, knowing how impossible it was for her to do so. The river wound through the heart of the city, narrow and alive with sampans.

'What will you do when you return to Hong Kong?' she asked, her head resting against his shoulder as they walked.

He flashed her a sudden down-slanting smile. 'I shan't be seeing Alute, if that's what you're thinking.'

'I wasn't,' she said gently, utterly sure of him, as she knew he was of her.

His smile faded. 'I shall probably be spending most of the next few weeks with Melissa,' he said, a slight edge to his voice. 'She needs all the support I can give her at the moment.'

'Is it very bad for her?' she asked curiously. 'I don't know anything at all about heroin.'

'It's a killer,' he said briefly, 'a by-product of opium. In wine-drinking terms, if opium is regarded as a light hock, heroin is a mixture of brandy, methylated spirit and cyanide.'

A light breeze from the sea blew coolly against their faces, heralding a tropical shower.

His profile was grim. 'It's been hellish for her. She isn't a person who has ever had to fight for anything. Whatever she has wanted, some man has supplied. Her father always indulged her, her boyfriends indulged her, and, God help me, I indulged her. Instant gratification was what she always demanded and to hell with the consequences. If you'd asked me six months ago if she could have fought a nightmare like heroin addiction, I would have laughed in your face. But she is, and she's doing it with more guts than

29

I ever gave her credit for.' He stared out towards the sampans, so closely packed together that children were jumping across from one to another. 'I've come to respect her in a way I never did when I lived with her. She's. . . .' He sought for the word and then said with a crooked smile: 'She's gallant. And she'll win through, in the end.'

The next morning, just after dawn, he flew from the airfield, piloting his Northrop himself. She had slept restlessly, and as morning sunlight seeped through the shutters she slipped out of bed and dressed, being careful not to disturb Adam. She wanted to breakfast by herself. She wanted just a little time of privacy in which to come to terms with the knowledge that Raefe was once again thousands of miles away from her.

The dining-room was nearly deserted, except for a few planters up early to catch a flight north. She could never in her life remember missing anyone so badly. Not her father; not Adam. She ordered papaya with fresh limes, and the porridge that was a Raffles speciality, and toast with Cooper's Oxford Marmalade and coffee. Even as she ordered, she knew that the only thing she wanted was coffee. The rest was just something to toy with, an excuse to remain in the dining-room, to delay returning to Adam.

The fruit and the porridge were returned to the kitchens untouched, but she ate a slice of toast and sipped her coffee and became aware that she was not only feeling heartsick, she was feeling physically sick. She took another sip of coffee and put down her cup. It tasted foul.

A middle-aged American couple, looking as if they were tourists, sat down at a nearby table.

'. . . and so I thought we could take a rickshaw this morning and buy some silks,' the wife was saying.

Elizabeth took a deep breath and swallowed. It was no use. She had only eaten a slice of toast and drunk half a cup of coffee, but incredibly she was going to be sick. She rose abruptly to her feet, running from the room.

The Americans stared after her with raised eyebrows. 'I

30

wonder what's wrong with her?' the husband said. 'She looked white as a sheet. Where did you say we could buy the silks?'

Elizabeth kneeled on the cool tiled floor of the lavatory, retching over the pan. The toast and coffee came back easily. After that she continued to retch, bringing up dark green bile. At last it stopped, and she staggered to her feet, crossing to the sink and pouring herself a glass of water. Gingerly she sipped it, wondering what on earth could be wrong with her.

The middle-aged American woman came in, putting down her handbag, opening it and taking her make-up purse out.

'Heavens, what we suffer to become mothers,' she said, beginning to repair her make-up.

'I'm sorry, I don't understand . . .,' Elizabeth said, still leaning weakly against the sinks.

The woman laughed. 'Morning sickness,' she said understandingly. 'If men suffered from it, the birth rate would soon fall!' She pressed her lips together to set her lipstick, popped her lipstick back into her handbag, and said as she walked towards the door: 'Never mind, honey. It's worth it in the end. I have three and I wouldn't be without one of them!' The door swung to behind her, and Elizabeth was left gripping on to the sinks for support, ashen-faced and trembling.

# 3

She told herself that the American woman had jumped to a ridiculous conclusion. People were often taken suddenly ill in a climate like Singapore's. She had eaten something, or drunk something, that had disagreed with her.

The next morning it happened again. And the next.

'Oh God!' she whispered as she kneeled on the floor, heaving up the scrambled egg she had manfully forced down in an attempt to prove that there was nothing wrong with her. 'Oh God! What now? What on *earth* do I do now?'

She had crawled out of the bathroom and sat at her dressing-table, opening a drawer and lifting out a small diary. She had kept it meticulously for over three years. It was the diary her gynaecologist had advised her to begin to keep when she had first become anxious about her fertility. The dates of her monthly menstruation were carefully marked. As were the dates when she was most likely to conceive, and the dates she and Adam had made love. She turned the pages with a shaking hand, knowing what it was she would find.

Her last period had come to an end the day before she had gone to Shek O with Raefe. Guilt had ensured that she had not made love with Adam in the immediate ensuing days, and then they had left Hong Kong aboard the *Blantyre Castle* for Singapore.

She had been lovingly affectionate to him on the voyage, wanting to make up to him for her betrayal of him, wanting to re-establish the firm foundation of their marriage. But there had been no lovemaking. Adam had been

32

tired, suffering from a severe head-cold and a general feeling of malaise. They had held hands, they had danced together, they had stood at the deck-rail with their arms around each other's waist, but they had not made love.

She put the diary down. She had no need to check the days since their arrival in Singapore. Although Adam had approached her lovingly several times, she had always made a gentle excuse, wanting to give herself more time before she committed what she saw as the final act of treachery – entering his bed with the heat of Raefe's hands still on her flesh, his kisses still hot on her lips.

She stared at her reflection in the dressing-table mirror. She looked like a ghost, her eyes darkly ringed, her face deathly pale. It had been obvious that she was unwell, and she had told Adam that she thought she was coming down with the virus he had been suffering from on the voyage out. His concern had only made her feel more wretched.

'Oh, Adam,' she breathed despairingly. 'Oh, darling, *darling* Adam! I didn't want it to come to this! I didn't want to hurt you!'

Tears slid down her face. She had thought she could continue to give him all the deep affection she had always given him. That their life together would continue as it always had, unscathed by her passionate love for Raefe. Now she knew that it was not possible. There could be no balancing of the two separate halves into which her life had fallen. She could not have both her calm, steady, sheltered life with Adam and the turbulence and tumult of her love for Raefe. One of them must be lost to her. And she was bearing Raefe's child. She pressed her hands against her face, and the tears rolled mercilessly down between her fingers and on to her négligé.

'Damn, damn, damn!' she sobbed. She had longed for a child for years. She had counted dates. She had waited in a fever of hope and longing month after month. And at last what she had most longed for had been given her. She was expecting a baby. And the father was the man she loved. But it was not her husband. It was not the baby she had

33

dreamed about, the baby that would make Adam so happy. The baby that would be the crowning happiness of their life together. 'Oh God, Adam!' she whispered brokenly, lowering her head to her arms. 'I'm so sorry, darling. So desperately sorry!'

'So you've changed your mind completely about this jaunt to Kuala Lumpur?' Adam asked her as they ate lunch at the Sea View.

She had been toying listlessly with the sweet and sour prawns on her plate and now she put down her chopsticks and said carefully: 'If you would like to go, Adam, then I'm quite happy to go with you. But there's no need to visit Kuala Lumpur for my sake.'

He had been smiling, happy with the game of tennis he had played earlier before leaving Raffles, happy with life in general. Now he said, a frown puckering his brow: 'Are you sure you're all right, Beth? I mean, are you not wanting to travel north because you feel so unwell?'

She shook her head and pushed her plate away. 'No, there's no need to worry, Adam.'

She knew that she had to talk to him, but she couldn't bring herself to do so yet. She didn't know the words to use. She didn't know how it was possible to break such devastating news to someone she cared about so much, someone who loved her so deeply.

His frown deepened. 'I really think you should see a doctor, Beth. It's ridiculous saying that you'll be right in a day or two. You're hardly eating anything and you look ghastly.'

She forced a smile. 'That's not a very complimentary thing to say to a lady!'

He grinned. 'You know what I mean. It isn't safe to let things run their course in a climate like this.'

He was wearing an open-necked cotton shirt and a pair of shorts, but the sweat still gleamed on his forehead and glistened on his neck. He turned round, looking for a waiter and raising his hand to indicate that he wanted another stengah.

'If you don't want to travel further north, then perhaps it's

34

about time we returned to Hong Kong,' he suggested, turning back to her as a waiter indicated his stengah was on its way.

'Yes,' she said, avoiding his eyes and looking seawards to where a small group of Malay fishermen were collecting their catch from their fishing-traps. The sooner they returned to Hong Kong, the sooner she could tell Raefe about the baby. And the sooner Adam would have to be told.

A Chinese waiter, balancing a tray of gimlets and stengahs and Tiger beer, weaved his way dexterously between the crowded tables towards them. Adam signed for his drink and then said: 'Then, we'll sail for home on the first available ship.'

The fishermen were walking away across the beach with their catch. In the brilliant sunlight, the small green islands in the distance were as insubstantial as mist. She drew her eyes away from them, looking across at him, saying curiously: 'You really do think of Hong Kong as home now, don't you?'

He shrugged. 'Why not? It feels like home.'

'And Four Seasons?' she asked, wondering if she would ever return there. If it would ever be a home to her again.

'I've never thought of Four Seasons as home,' he said with his usual honesty. 'I always think of it as being exclusively yours. Which it is.'

'But you enjoyed living there?' she persisted, suddenly wondering if she had always assumed his contentment and his happiness. Wondering if, perhaps, there was far more to him than she had previously suspected.

'I would enjoy living anywhere with you,' he said, his voice thickening, reaching across the table and taking her hands. 'A palace or a shack, it would make no difference. As long as you were there, Beth. I would be happy.'

She couldn't have spoken, even if she had wanted to.

He squeezed her hands and said decisively: 'That's it, then. We'll call in at the shipping office on the way back to the hotel and book two berths. I wonder if much has changed while we've been away. I imagine Alastair is still trying to persuade Helena to marry him and that she is still refusing.'

As they rose to leave, she felt dizzy at the thought of how much had changed. Their whole lives. And he didn't know. Not yet. And she hadn't the courage to tell him.

They walked along the Sea View's pillared terrace and beneath an incongruous dome of Grecian splendour, towards their waiting Mercedes. Adam had discovered that driving in the Singapore heat was not much fun and after their first few days there he had hired a *syce*, a Malay chauffeur. The *syce*, who had been squatting down, sheltering in the shade of the car, jumped to his feet at their approach, opening the doors for them with an efficient flourish.

'Julienne's probably notched up at least three new lovers,' Adam said drily, wincing against the heat of the leather seat. 'God knows how that marriage survives. I don't.'

Again Elizabeth said nothing. There was nothing she could possibly say. They called in at the shipping office in Robinson Road and booked a double berth in a ship leaving the following Monday. She was both longing to leave and loath to leave, her feelings as agonized and contradictory as they had been when she had left Hong Kong.

'I'm tired, Adam,' she said truthfully, as they stepped out of the air-conditioned coolness of the office and into the blistering heat of the street. 'I don't know what you have planned for this afternoon, but I'd like to rest for an hour or two.'

He looked down into her wan face, distressed at the deep circles he saw beneath her eyes. 'You should have said so sooner,' he said, concerned, his hand beneath her arm as they walked towards the car. 'I'll tuck you up and then go for a swim at the club.' Their *syce* drew out into the main stream of traffic, refusing to be intimidated by aggressive rickshaw-drivers who regarded crowding a foreign car off the street as a duty. 'And if you're feeling no better by the time I return,' he continued sternly, 'then I'm calling for a doctor, no matter what you say.'

She had rested and drunk some milk of magnesia, and by the time he had returned she had been able to say, with an element of truth, that she felt much better and that there was no need for him to carry out his threat.

On the following Monday, they sailed out of the great harbour, and northwards towards Hong Kong. If Adam thought her unduly quiet, it was only because he believed her to be still suffering from the enervating virus he himself had suffered from for a while. He had enjoyed their trip to Singapore far more than he had anticipated, but he wasn't sorry to be leaving. He wanted to be in at the inception of the proposed Hong Kong Volunteer Force. He wanted to have a good old chin-wag with Leigh Stafford about the apparent invincibility of Singapore. He wanted to sit on his veranda, a sundowner in his hand, and look out across his garden and the lush tropical greenery of the Peak down to the glittering harbour and the distant cloud-capped hills of Kowloon.

'We're home,' he said with satisfaction, as their ship nosed its way up the Lei Yue Mun Channel between a scattering of small, stony, uninhabited islands.

Elizabeth stood beside him, her hands on the deck-rail, her knuckles white. She no longer knew where home was, or who it was with. It was late afternoon, and the Peak was half-hidden in cloud, scudding shadows of high cirrus smoking down the ravines and ridges, the scent of hibiscus and frangipani drifting fragrantly across the water.

She had not told Raefe that she was on her way back to him. Unless he had tried to contact her at Raffles, he would think her still in Singapore. He would not be waiting for her when they docked, and she did not want him to be. When they did meet, she wanted to be the one who was in control of the situation. Whatever decision was taken about the future, it would be *her* decision. Not Adam's. Not Raefe's. Hers.

There was the usual pile of mail. Business letters for Adam. Cards and invitations. Half a dozen envelopes bearing Princess Luisa Isabel's embossed coat of arms. Chan and the other houseboys carried the luggage upstairs, and while Mei Lin supervised the unpacking Adam retreated to a comfortable chair, a gin and tonic in his hand as he settled down to read the backlog of letters.

Elizabeth pushed her pile neatly to one side. There was no way she could cope with party invitations and frivolous gossip at the moment. She didn't even want to open Luisa's always cheery letters. Restlessly she went upstairs, saying to Mei Lin as she deftly sorted the unpacked clothes into piles for the laundry, piles to be pressed, piles to be put neatly away: 'Have there been any messages for me, Mei Lin?'

'All the messages are on the telephone-pad, Missy Harland,' Mei Lin said, her gold cheeks rosy with pleasure at having her mistress back in residence again.

'But have there been any other messages?' Elizabeth persisted. 'Any personal messages?' She had already flicked an eye over the names written with meticulous care by Mei Lin on the telephone-pad. Raefe's had not been there.

'I very careful,' Mei Lin said, a trifle defensively. 'I put every name down, Missy Harland. I leave none out.'

So he hadn't rung. But, then, he had had no reason to. She had told him that she would get in touch with him when she returned. From downstairs she could hear Adam calling her name and she hurried out to the head of the stairs.

'There's a letter here from Stafford,' he called up to her. 'Sounds as if I should see him straight away. I'll be back in an hour.'

A second later the door slammed behind him. She walked slowly down the wide open staircase, her heart beginning to hammer in her chest. She was on her own and she had to take advantage of the fact. She had to ring Raefe now, before Adam returned.

'I have sent a message to the wash-amah to tell her that you are back and that she is needed,' Mei Lin panted as she carried the laundry through into the kitchen. 'She will be here in an hour.'

'Thank you, Mei Lin.'

She stood looking at the telephone on the hall table for a long moment and then walked quickly into the drawing-room where she would have more privacy. She wouldn't tell him about the baby over the telephone. She would only tell him that she was back. And that she had missed him every single second she had been away from him.

His houseboy answered the telephone.

'Could I speak to Mr Elliot, please?'

'Velly solly,' his houseboy said in broad pidgin. 'Mr Elliot not in. Can I take message?'

Her disappointment was so intense that she physically slumped against the wall. 'Tell him Mrs Harland rang,' she said, feeling ridiculously as if she were going to cry. 'Tell him that I am home again. That I am in Hong Kong.'

'Yes, missy. Velly good, missy.'

She was filled with the sudden humiliating thought that he had probably taken hundreds of such messages in the past. From Mrs Mark Hurley, from Alute. From women whose names she didn't know and had no desire to know. The feeling of humiliation was fleeting. He had never before taken one from a woman with whom Raefe was in love, of that she was sure. She walked across to the large window that looked out over the Peak and the bay and, despite all her misery at the hurt she was about to inflict on Adam, happiness bubbled up inside her. Raefe would ring her back within minutes, within hours. They would be together soon. 'Oh, but I love you,' she breathed, hugging her arms around her waist as she looked down towards Victoria. 'Raefe Elliot, I love you!'

Raefe took the message from one of his Chinese informers. This time the titbit was not about Yamishita, the Japanese barber at the Hong Kong Hotel, or any of the other known

Japanese spies masquerading as photographers and waiters.

'Your friend, Mr Nicholson, is in great trouble,' the familiar sing-song voice said urgently. 'Mr Kaibong Sheng knows of his involvement with his daughter. The Tong are on the streets looking for him.'

Raefe blanched. The Tongs were the hired killers of the Chinese underworld, and if Sheng had discovered that his daughter had been deflowered, then there was nothing more certain than that he would have hired the Tongs to exact his revenge.

'Do you know where Tom Nicholson is now?' he demanded urgently. 'Do you know where Lamoon Sheng is?'

'No,' the sing-song voice expressed neither regret nor curiosity. 'I only know that Sheng was told an hour ago that the Englishman has soiled his daughter's honour. And that the Tongs have been given their orders.'

Raefe blasphemed, looking at his watch. It was four-twenty and it was Thursday. The day that Lamoon ostensibly attended nursing lessons at the hospital. By four-thirty, Tom would have taken her back to the hospital so that she could slip in through a side-door and emerge seconds later through the main door where the chauffeured Rolls would be waiting for her. Only today the chauffeur would not be the only person waiting outside the hospital. The Tongs would be there as well.

Raefe slammed open his desk drawer, taking out a revolver and a shoulder-holster, strapping it on as he strode from the room, grabbing his jacket from the hall coat-stand, running out of the house and towards his car. Tom would be unarmed and unprepared, and the Tongs were not likely to have had instructions merely to give him a beating. For the sin Tom had committed, Raefe doubted if old man Sheng would be satisfied with anything less than his death.

He vaulted into his Chrysler, gunning the engine into life, the tyres squealing as he shot out of the parking-bay and into the main stream of late-afternoon traffic. Thank God he had been at the apartment when he had received the message, and not at the Peak. If he had been, there would have been no chance at all of him reaching Tom in time. He swerved past a Buick, pressing the heel of his hand on the horn, making no concessions for rickshaws or cyclists or even pedestrians.

What car did Tom drive? Was it a Mercedes or an Opel? A Packard. It was a Packard. He sped across a busy inter-section, aware of a squealing of brakes in his wake. It was four twenty-nine. Tom was probably there now. He was never late in delivering Lamoon back to the hospital – doing nothing, as he thought, to arouse her father's suspicions. He screamed around a traffic island, sending rickshaw-boys scurrying for their lives. Tom had been a naïve fool even to imagine the affair could continue without someone, somewhere, seeing them and informing on them.

The hospital loomed up on his right-hand side, and he saw the unmistakable powder-blue of the Sheng Rolls-Royce parked outside the front entrance. He took the next corner on two wheels. The Tongs would be waiting for Tom at the side-entrance. They would wait until Lamoon had entered the hospital before they pounced. Their orders would be not to involve her in the violence. And if Lamoon had still not walked out of the front entrance. . . .

It was four-thirty. The side-street was crowded with office workers leaving as early as they could for home. There were black-clad Chinese on bicycles and half a dozen Chinese stall-holders and a pedlar selling jade, all a mere yard or two away from the side-entrance door. He was just about to breathe a sigh of relief, believing he had got there before Tom, when he saw the Packard parked at the other side of the street and Tom's tall broad-shouldered figure walking through the crowds towards the entrance, Lamoon's diminutive figure at his side.

He was still fifty yards away from them, and the street was jammed with traffic. He slewed the Chrysler to a halt, slamming his hand hard upon the horn as he did so. The crowd of office workers turned their heads, staring at him as if he had lost his senses, but Tom was too deep in conversation with Lamoon to take any notice of a maniac let loose on a car horn. Raefe jumped from the car, shouting his name, forcing his way at a run through the office workers and shoppers and tourists who crowded the pavement.

'Tom! Tom!' he yelled. The Chinese cyclists were no longer with their bicycles. They were all moving in behind Tom as he approached the side-entrance of the hospital. One of the stall-holders, too, was no longer intent on selling his wares to passing pedestrians.

Tom and Lamoon were at the side-entrance. A Chinese was standing over the open bonnet of Tom's Packard, busily disabling it to ensure there would be no escape in that direction.

'Tom!' Raefe yelled at the top of his lungs. This time Tom heard him. His head swung round, his eyes widening as he saw Raefe hurtling towards him. Lamoon was still in the doorway, a bewildered expression on her face. The crowds who a second earlier had thronged the street had now, sensing danger, hurriedly scattered, leaving the side-entrance of the hospital an open space apart from Tom, and the Chinese, and Raefe.

'It's the Tongs!' Raefe shouted to Tom as the jade-pedlar, judging that there was no longer time to wait for Lamoon to disappear before launching his attack, hurled his tray at Raefe and then dived towards Tom.

The tray caught Raefe full on the chest, and he fell to his knees, scrambling to his feet again, gasping for breath, seeing through a blood-red haze the gleam of a blade and then Tom's fist as it shot out, sending the jade-pedlar sprawling.

Desperately he tried to reach Tom, but there were hands around his throat, pulling him chokingly backwards, fingers gouging at his eyes. He kicked backwards, knocking his assailants off balance, snatching his gun from his holster.

Tom was on the ground, barely visible as he thrashed beneath a welter of kicks and punches, and then the stall-holder grabbed hold of the jade-pedlar's knife and as Tom was held, staked to the ground, he sprang forward, the knife lunging down towards Tom's heart.

The blow from the gun's butt knocked him senseless, just as the blade pierced Tom's flesh. Raefe was aware of Lamoon screaming, of a police siren wailing, of feet running. Tom gasped, dazedly imprisoned beneath the weight of his attacker, blood oozing from the shallow wound in his chest. Raefe tried to tell him to lie still, but when he spoke the words were fuzzily incoherent and to his surprise and indignation his legs buckled beneath him and he dropped forward on to the pavement. He pressed his hand to his side to ease his breathing, and when he withdrew it his fingers were dark and sticky with blood. Tom wasn't the only one who had been stabbed.

The whine of the police siren came nearer and nearer; Lamoon was running towards them, her eyes wide with terror, and then Raefe saw the Sheng chauffeur sprint around from the front of the building. He tried to warn her, to tell her to run towards the approaching police car, but his desperate warning was barely audible. He was going to faint. 'Christ!' he whispered disgustedly, slumping forward into a deepening pool of blood as the chauffeur seized Lamoon and dragged her, kicking and screaming, away.

When the telephone rang Elizabeth leaped towards it, her heart racing. Adam was down at the tennis-courts, inspecting the nets in the last flush of light before darkness fell.

'Yes,' she said eagerly, 'Elizabeth Harland speaking.'

It wasn't the rich dark voice she so longed to hear.

'It's Helena,' Helena said briefly. 'I knew you were back. I saw Adam with Leigh Stafford in the Long Bar at the Pen a couple of hours ago.'

'Oh, Helena, it's lovely to hear from you,' Elizabeth

began, trying to tear her thoughts away from Raefe. 'I was going to ring you, but—'

'There's been an accident.'

Elizabeth's hand tightened on the telephone receiver. She knew now what the strange curtness was in Helena's voice. It wasn't pique because she hadn't rung her the instant she had returned from Singapore. It was the sound of sobs being barely suppressed.

'Oh God,' she whispered, her stomach muscles tightening, thinking immediately of Jeremy and Jennifer. 'What is it, Helena? What has happened?'

'Someone told Kaibong Sheng of Tom's affair with Lamoon,' she paused, trying to steady her voice. 'He ordered the Tongs to kill him. . . .' She began to cry, and Elizabeth sat down very slowly, keeping the telephone receiver pressed tight to her ear.

'Yes, Helena?' she prompted, terrified of what Helena was about to tell her.

'They were waiting for him when he brought Lamoon back to the hospital. . . . They tried to stab him. . . .'

Elizabeth clung tightly to the word 'tried'. 'But they didn't?' she asked urgently. 'Tom isn't hurt? He's still alive?'

'Yes.' There was another pause while Helena blew her nose. 'I can't stop crying. It's the shock. The thought of that evil old man giving orders for Tom to be killed.'

'What happened?' Elizabeth asked again. 'Tom brought Lamoon back to the hospital, and the Tongs were waiting for him. What happened then?'

'Someone – I don't know who – rang Raefe and told him what was planned. He reached the hospital just in time to shout a warning to Tom and to help him. . . .'

Elizabeth felt the blood leave her face.

'There was a dreadful fight on the pavement. Tom's nose is broken and two of his ribs are cracked and he has a shallow knife-wound in his chest.' Her voice trembled. 'It would have been much worse. It was Raefe who saved his life. . . .'

44

Elizabeth said tightly: 'He's hurt, isn't he? Raefe's hurt?'

Helena began to cry again. 'He was stabbed . . . the knife punctured the pancreas. They operated on him an hour ago. . . .'

'Jesus God!' The room rocked sickeningly around her. 'I must go to him. What ward is he in? Where is he?'

'He's in a private room just off ward three, but you can't go to him, Elizabeth! There's Adam to think of! I'm going down there now. I'll see him. I'll tell you how he is!'

'No!' Elizabeth shook her head, her eyes frantic. 'I'm going there myself!' And she slammed the receiver back on its rest, running for the door.

'What on earth is the matter, Beth?' Adam asked in amusement as he entered the room and she hurtled into him. 'Where's the fire?'

He had put his hands steadyingly on her arms, and she wrenched herself free. 'I'm sorry, Adam,' she gasped, 'I have to go down to Victoria.'

She ran out into the hall, scooping her handbag from the hall table, seizing her jacket from the bamboo coat-stand.

'But why?' he asked perplexedly as he followed her. 'What on earth has happened?'

She was scrambling in her handbag for her car keys. 'Lamoon's father has discovered she is having an affair with Tom.' Her fingers curled round the keys. 'He sent the Tongs to kill him!'

'Dear Lord . . .,' Adam's face paled.

She ran to the door, opening it and looking back at him, her eyes anguished. 'He's all right, Adam. He has a broken nose and a couple of cracked ribs, but he's all right.'

'Then, I don't understand why there is all the urgency. . . .' He took a step towards her. 'We can visit him tomorrow, together.'

She shook her head. 'No!' she whispered, knowing that she could not stay to explain to him, that every minute was precious. 'Raefe's been hurt, too. He's been stabbed. They operated on him an hour ago!' And she wheeled on her heel, running out of the house and across the gravel towards the garage, slamming open her car door without even looking back towards him.

For a long moment he couldn't even move. He felt as if he had been kicked savagely in the chest. By the time he managed to stumble to the door, her car was already screeching down the drive towards the road.

'Beth!' he shouted vainly. 'Beth!' He ran down the shallow steps of the portico, but it was no use. With a scream of tyres she had slewed out on to Peak Road, and he could hear the engine tone change as she slammed through the gears and into fourth.

He leaned against one of the portico's flower-wreathed pillars, sick and disorientated. *What* had Beth said? Surely she couldn't have meant it? Surely he had misheard, as he had misheard Alastair in the golf-club bar. A flock of blue magpies, disturbed by the raucous noise of her departure, wheeled over his head before settling again in the flame trees. *Elliot?* She had gone racing down to Victoria like a woman demented, all because Raefe Elliot had again involved himself in an act of violence? It didn't make sense. It *couldn't* make sense.

He could no longer hear the sound of her car engine. The magpies had settled down again in the branches of the flame trees. And it did make sense. It made the most awful, most diabolical sense. Like an old man he pressed his hand against the pillar in order to launch himself into a tottering walk. He hadn't misheard Alastair. He had told Alastair they were leaving Hong Kong because Beth was having problems, and Alastair had immediately assumed that her problem was Raefe Elliot.

He walked slowly into the house, his shoulders hunched, his hands pushed deep into the pockets of his cardigan. Alastair was a man who hated gossip and never indulged in it, and yet he had known about Beth's passion for Elliot. And if Alastair knew, then Helena must know, and Julienne and Ronnie. He poured himself a large measure of whisky. Probably the whole island knew. His hand shook as he raised his glass to his lips. He had never known such pain. He couldn't even begin to imagine how he would live with it. A world without Beth. It was inconceivable. The glass fell to the floor, whisky seeping and staining the pale beige carpet as he lowered his head to his hands and wept.

Helena was in the hospital foyer waiting for her when she arrived.

'How is he?' Elizabeth asked, running across to her, her eyes fierce with anxiety.

'I haven't been allowed to see him. I don't think he's fully recovered consciousness yet. The sister says there's no need to worry, that he's going to be all right. The knife missed the lungs and, though it pierced the pancreas, she says that no lasting harm has been done.'

Her relief was so intense that she swayed slightly. 'I must see him, Helena.'

'They won't let you. It's strictly next-of-kin so soon after surgery.'

A new look flashed into Elizabeth's eyes. 'Does Melissa know yet? Has anyone told her?'

Helena pushed an untidy mass of dark hair away from her face. 'I don't know. Perhaps the hospital has. I never gave Melissa a thought.'

'She should be told!' Elizabeth said vehemently. 'I'm going up to the ward now. The sister will know if she's been told or not.'

'And if she hasn't?' Helena asked, her beautiful square-jawed face troubled.

'Then, I will tell her,' Elizabeth said, leaving Helena with slightly raised brows as she walked swiftly off in the direction of ward 3.

'No, Mrs Elliot hasn't been informed,' the ward sister said apologetically. 'I understood that Mr and Mrs Elliot were separated and that Mrs Elliot was living in the New Territories.'

'They are separated, but she isn't living in the New Territories,' Elizabeth said, her eyes going to the door of the private room opposite the sister's office. 'She's at the family home and she should be told what has happened.'

'Of course.' The ward sister hesitated. 'Perhaps, if you are a family friend, it might be less of a shock if you were to contact her?'

'Yes,' Elizabeth said, her eyes still on the door of the private room. 'I will telephone her when I leave. After I have seen Mr Elliot.'

'I'm afraid Mr Elliot only returned from surgery two hours ago. There will be visiting tomorrow evening,' the ward sister said pleasantly.

Elizabeth turned and looked at her. 'Please let me see him. I don't want to be here tomorrow when perhaps Mrs Elliot may be visiting.'

The ward sister drew in a deep understanding breath. It hadn't occurred to her that the lovely Mrs Harland was here in any other capacity but that of family friend.

'Please!' Elizabeth repeated, her eyes urgent.

The sister hesitated and then said compassionately: 'All right, but only for five minutes. And don't expect him to make much sense, because he won't. He'll still be fuzzy from the anaesthetic.'

With her legs almost buckling with relief, Elizabeth followed her out of the office and across the corridor to the private room.

'Five minutes only,' the sister said again as she opened the door.

Raefe made beautiful sense. 'Hello,' he said as she reached the bed, his voice heavily slurred as if he had been drinking. 'I love you, Lizzie.'

Tears stung her eyes. 'I love you, too,' she said softly, shocked at how pale he looked.

He gave her a crooked smile. 'Bloody Tongs,' he whispered expressively. 'They can't do anything right. It was me they damned near killed, not Tom.'

She took hold of his hand. 'It would take more than Tongs,' she said with a wobbly smile.

His hand tightened on hers. 'I'm glad you're back,' he

said weakly. 'Another week and I would have come for you, Adam or no Adam!'

She thought of Adam as she had left him. White-faced and shocked. Knowing at last of her passion for Raefe. 'Don't worry about Adam,' she said sombrely. 'I shall never leave you again, my love.'

The sister stood at the door. 'Your five minutes are up, Mrs Harland. Any further visiting will have to be at the appointed times.'

She squeezed his hand. 'Melissa doesn't know yet. I'll telephone her tonight.'

'Good,' he said wearily. 'She'll be grateful. Goodnight, sweet Lizzie.'

She withdrew her hand reluctantly from his. 'Goodnight, my love,' she said, blowing him a kiss, knowing that from now on her life would be shared with him. That there were no more decisions to make, no more choices to agonize over.

The door closed behind them. 'So you will telephone Mrs Elliot?' the ward sister asked, disguising the prurient curiosity she felt.

'Yes. Could I do it from your office, please?'

The sister nodded. It would be as well to know that the news was broken in the proper manner. 'Of course,' she said, leading the way across the corridor. 'You will need to ask the switchboard for an outside line.'

Helena was waiting for her when she walked back into the foyer. 'How is he?' she asked, rising to her feet. 'Did they let you see him?'

Elizabeth nodded. 'For five minutes. It was strange to see him so weak and so pale.'

'But he's going to be all right?' she asked anxiously, not able to imagine Raefe either weak or pale.

'Yes,' Elizabeth said as they stepped out into the darkened street. 'He'll probably be discharged by the end of the week.' Her voice was tired, drained of energy.

'Let's go for a drink somewhere,' Helena suggested, knowing exactly how she felt. 'The Pen, perhaps, or Grips?'

49

Elizabeth shook her head. 'No, Helena. I have to get back home. I need to talk to Adam.'

They had stopped near her Buick. Helena looked at her in alarm. In the garish light of the street-lamps Elizabeth looked almost ill. 'You're not going to tell him about Raefe, are you?'

'There's no need,' Elizabeth said wearily. 'He already knows.'

Helena's face was horrified. Elizabeth bent down and unlocked the Buick's door. She didn't want to talk to Helena about Adam. Not yet. Perhaps not ever. 'You didn't tell me what happened to Lamoon?' she said as she opened the door and slid behind the steering-wheel. 'Was she hurt as well?'

'No. At least, I don't think so.' Helena was still thinking of Adam. How on earth would he have taken such news? Of all the men she knew he least deserved such a blow.

'Where is she now?' Elizabeth asked curiously.

'Lamoon? I don't know.' She dragged her thoughts away from Adam. 'I don't think anyone knows. I don't think we will ever see or hear of Lamoon again.'

Elizabeth turned the key in the ignition. 'Poor Tom,' she said bleakly. 'Goodnight, Helena. I'll give you a ring tomorrow.'

Helena stood on the pavement, watching her as she drove away. 'Poor Tom,' she repeated, heartsick. 'And poor Adam. I wonder what he will do now?'

Elizabeth sped away from the hospital, driving through Victoria's neon-lit streets and squares and towards Garden Road and the slow climb towards the Peak. Magazine Gap Road was deserted, and as she climbed higher she could see the silky blackness of the bay and the distant twinkling lights of Kowloon. The feeble orange glow of the street-lights lit her on to Peak Road. She drove carefully, mindful of the precipice on the left, catching occasional glimpses of white stuccoed mansions hiding palely between the trees, thinking of her telephone call to Melissa.

Melissa had sounded disorientated when she had first

spoken to her; and then, when she understood what the message was, and what had happened to Raefe, she had been genuinely distressed.

'Can I see him now? Tonight?' she had asked uncertainly, wondering if the chauffeur was in his quarters and if he would drive her to Victoria.

'I think it is probably too late now,' Elizabeth had said awkwardly. 'There is visiting tomorrow.'

There was a long pause, and then Melissa said: 'You've already seen him, haven't you?'

'Yes,' Elizabeth had said unhappily. 'Yes, I've already seen him.'

There was another long pause, and then Melissa said: 'I'm sorry, but I don't know your name.'

'Elizabeth. Elizabeth Harland.'

There had been a slow intake of breath on the other end of the telephone, and then Melissa had said in a flat defeated voice: 'Thank you for telephoning me, Elizabeth. It's more than I would have done if our positions had been reversed.'

She had put the telephone receiver down, and the conversation had come to an end. What the listening ward sister had made of it Elizabeth neither knew nor cared.

The road wound between high banks of thick foliage and tall dense pines. It had been a disconcerting conversation, but one that had done nothing but increase her sympathy towards Melissa. There was a far more terrible conversation lying in wait for her. She eased the Buick off Peak Road and on to the narrow track that led towards the drive of her home. The lights were on as she had known they would be. She slid the Buick into the double garage, closing the door quietly behind her, hating herself to the bottom of her soul as she walked reluctantly towards the house, and Adam.

51

# 4

Julienne and Derry were in a small sailing-boat, drifting pleasantly in a dead calm off Cape d'Aguilar.

'I can't understand why the devil he wasn't arrested,' Derry said, a note of admiration in his voice as he sprawled at the helm, wearing nothing but a small gold crucifix and chain and a pair of white shorts that had seen better days. 'It's only months since he was cleared of Jacko's murder. How he can rampage the streets with a loaded revolver and get away with it is beyond me.'

Julienne leaned against the side of the boat, her hand trailing languorously in the jade-green water. 'But he knew the Tongs were lying in wait for Tom. And he didn't burn the gun. He only pistol-whipped the Chinese who was attacking Tom.'

'Fire,' Derry corrected in amusement. Julienne's rare lapses of idiom always entertained him. 'You *fire* a gun, sweet love. You don't burn it.'

Julienne shrugged a naked shoulder imperturbably. Her shorts were cerise, very brief, very French, and her halter top was a sizzling shade of apple-green. 'Fire, burn, what does it matter? All that matters is that he did not shoot the man. He simply prevented him from murdering Tom. And for that, *mon amour*, I am very grateful.'

Derry looked across at her speculatively. He wasn't sure, but he thought she had once been Tom's mistress. If she had been, he didn't want the affair to rekindle now that Tom's rash affair with Lamoon had been brought to an abrupt conclusion. If he didn't know himself better, he

52

would have said that he was headlong in love with Julienne. As it was, he merely considered himself delightfully infatuated. But, infatuation or not, he was seriously disturbed at the thought of losing her. Ronnie he could come to terms with. He had no choice. But the thought of Julienne romping in bed with anyone else made cold sweat break out on the back of his neck.

'Come over here,' he growled, feeling a rising in his crotch as Julienne withdrew her hand from the water, her nipples straining full and taut against the thin cotton of her top.

She smiled across at him lazily. 'A sailing-boat is not a very good idea for what you have in mind, *chéri*. You will get yourself very wet and very bruised!'

'I'll get myself very fucked and I won't care about the bruises,' he said, his electric-blue eyes dark with heat. 'Now, for God's sake, get yourself over here, Julienne!'

She giggled and rose to her feet, moving carefully as the sailing-boat rocked gently. 'I think, *chéri*,' she said mischievously, 'that you are going to have to be very, very careful!'

She slid down next to him, and as he slipped his arm around her shoulders she said. 'How long will Raefe be in the hospital? Does anyone know?'

'No.' A light breeze had sprung up, and Derry eyed the sails doubtfully, wondering if he should put a couple of reefs in them. He didn't want to capsize off Cape d'Aguilar with his shorts around his ankles. The breeze petered away, the sails flapping desultorily. He relaxed, saying: 'Melissa went to visit him the day after it happened. They seem to be on extraordinarily good terms at the moment. You would think, now that the divorce is going ahead, that they'd hardly be speaking to each other.'

'Divorce?' Julienne asked curiously. Her cheek had been resting against his shoulder. Now she turned her head and looked up at him. 'I didn't know that they were getting a divorce. I thought she had moved back in with him.'

Derry shook his head. The sun had bleached his hair, and the spray from the sea had tightened his curls, so that he reminded her of a statue she had once seen of a Greek god. 'She's back in the house they used to share, up on the Peak. But Raefe isn't living there. He's moved permanently into his apartment in Victoria. I can't imagine him staying there once he has remarried. It's only small.'

'Remarried?' She sat bolt upright, her eyes wide. '*Tiens*! He can't be going to marry again! It isn't possible!'

'It's very possible,' Derry said, a slight frown touching his brow. 'You haven't had any hopes in that direction yourself, have you, Julienne?'

She looked genuinely shocked. '*Non*! How can you think such a thing?' She kissed him, open-mouthed, pressing herself against him. Derry enjoyed the embrace, but did not allow himself to be distracted.

'Then, why does the news shock you so much?' he asked when he finally drew his mouth away from hers.

'Because I know who it is he is in love with. And never, in a million years, would I have believed it possible that she would leave her husband for him. It is amazing! Incredible!'

The breeze was beginning to lift again, filling out the sails. Derry ignored them. 'Who is she?' he asked, fascinated. 'I know it isn't Mark Hurley's wife, because she's been looking as miserable as sin lately. And I haven't seen him with his Chinese girlfriend for weeks.'

'I don't think I should tell you, *chéri*,' she said teasingly. 'It would not be very discreet of me.'

'To hell with discretion,' Derry said thickly, his hand sliding down inside the low neckline of her halter top. 'Now, who is it? Tell me or I'll throw you overboard!'

He had begun to caress her nipple, and familiar sweet urgings were centring in her vulva. 'I don't think you would do such a thing,' she said, her eyes beginning to darken with her desire. 'But just in case. . . .' She laughed throatily as he lowered his head to her breast. 'It is Elizabeth Harland, *chéri*. And never did I think she would be so reckless. So very un-English!'

'We English,' Derry said hoarsely as he slid her down beneath him and the boat rocked wildly, 'can be *very* reckless. . . .'

His hands were on the waistband of her shorts. She undid the button and zip, wriggling obligingly as he eased them down over her hips.

'Why is it your pussy hair is an even spicier red than the hair on your head?' he asked as the tight tousle of curls sprang erotically against the heel of his hand and his fingers slipped inside her.

'*C'est joli, non?*' she whispered, pushing herself up against him, her eyes closed, her lips parted. 'Oh, but that is good, *mon amour*. Very, very good.'

The breeze was blowing landwards, filling the sails. Derry felt the boat begin to scud, and an edge of water creamed over the side, splashing down on them. He ignored it. The tide was on the turn. The worst that could happen was that they capsized or were blown ashore, still fucking. He kicked his shorts from around his ankles, Julienne's silky-dark nipples were erect against his chest, her legs were wide, uncaring of the sea-water that now slopped around them. He took his prick in his hands. He wasn't going to stop now. Not even for old Father Neptune. He grinned as he thought of the sight they would make as they neared the shore. He hoped no one would be so daft as to think they were in difficulties and send out help. He didn't need any help. None at all. He was going in hard and strong and with all flags flying.

Late the next afternoon Helena visited Tom for the second time that day. She felt incredibly tired. Tom had not wanted to stay another night in hospital, and it had taken all her persistence to ensure that he did so. He wasn't badly hurt. His nose had been broken and would probably set a trifle crooked, but his good-looks had always been of the rugged kind and she did not think they would suffer. His broken ribs had been strapped. The wound on his chest had required only half a dozen stitches. His mental suffering far exceeded his physical suffering.

'I must see Lamoon!' he said to her fiercely when she entered his room. 'I must know that she is all right!'

'She wasn't hurt,' Helena repeated for the twentieth time. 'You told me yourself that the chauffeur merely dragged her away.'

Tom slammed his fist down on the tightly tucked-in sheets, his eyes blazing. 'She was fighting him for all she was worth! Anything could have happened to her! A man crazy enough to try to have me killed isn't exactly going to be lenient with a daughter who is completely in his power, is he? Christ!' He ran his hand through his hair. 'And I just laid there! I didn't lift a finger to help her!'

'You can only have been semi-conscious,' Helena said practically. 'When the police arrived seconds later, you were flat out and that horrid Chinese was lying senseless on top of you. How could you have helped her?'

He swung his legs from the bed, wincing with pain from his ribs as he did so. Helena put her hands restrainingly on his shoulders. 'Oh, no, you don't,' she said firmly. 'You're not leaving here till tomorrow morning at the earliest. Even if you did, it wouldn't do any good. You can hardly call in person at the Sheng mansion and ask for her, can you? Not unless you want more thugs to complete yesterday's unfinished task!'

'But I have to know what has happened to her,' he repeated despairingly. 'I'm responsible! I knew the risks she was running and I encouraged her!'

'Lamoon knew the risks as well,' Helena said quietly.

Tom groaned, not wanting to put into words what he most feared. That she was no longer even in Hong Kong. That he would never see her again.

'I'm going across to see Raefe,' she said, satisfied that he had accepted the futility of storming out of the hospital. 'He has Chinese friends who will be able to tell us what has happened.'

'How is he?' Tom's eyes darkened. 'I tried to go over and see him this morning, but that dragon of a ward sister said the doctor was with him and that I couldn't see him until tomorrow.'

'She probably had her instructions from the police,' Helena said drily. 'I imagine they want to keep the two of you apart until they have finished taking statements from you both.'

'They can take statements till they're blue in the face!' he said savagely. 'Any injuries we inflicted were in self-defence. If Raefe hadn't shouted out to me when he did, that bloody Chink would have knifed me with no one on the street being aware of it!'

'And if he hadn't hit the supposed stall-holder, where your first attacker failed, the second would have succeeded,' Helena said, her face going pale at the thought of how near he had come to losing his life. 'I hope the powers that be decide it wisest to take no action against Raefe. He's suffered enough as it is. I don't believe he was half so indifferent to the murder charge that was brought against him as he would have had us believe.'

'I don't believe he's half so indifferent about a lot of things as he would have us believe,' Tom said wryly. 'Underneath that devil-may-care swagger of his, there hides a damned nice bloke.'

'Yes,' Helena agreed wearily as she turned to leave. Raefe Elliot *was* a damned nice bloke. And he had saved Tom's life, which made it all the more difficult for her to blame him and to dislike him for the unhappiness he was causing Adam.

'So there's no news at all of Lamoon?' Raefe asked her, propped up against pillows, his hard-boned face oddly pale, his eyes burning blackly.

'No, you are the only person I know who has access to the Chinese grapevine. I wondered if you could find out what has happened to her?'

'Yes,' he said unenthusiastically. 'I can do that, Helena. But I can already give a pretty good guess. She won't still be in Hong Kong, that's for sure. She will have been sent to

57

relatives as far away as possible. And she will stay with them until a suitable marriage can be arranged for her.'

'Poor Tom.' Helena's deep blue eyes were bleak. 'He loves her so much.' She crossed the small room to the window and stood for a moment, looking out, seeing nothing.

'There was never even the vainest hope of them being able to marry,' Raefe said, his voice oddly flat. 'For families like the Shengs, mixed marriages are out. There are no exceptions.'

Helena continued to look out of the window. 'What a stupid world we live in,' she said bitterly. 'There is so much unhappiness that can't be avoided. You would think, by now, the human race would have stopped inflicting misery that *can* be avoided, simply because one person's skin is a different shade from another's. Surely all that matters was that they loved each other? Surely loving each other is the *only* thing that matters?'

'It may be, one day, but that day hasn't dawned yet, Helena.'

'Do you think it will ever come?' she asked, turning towards him once again. 'Not an ideal world with every-one loving one another, but a *decent* world. A multi-racial world, where people are judged by their worth, and not by their colour or social status?'

'If enough people want it, and work for it, and are pre-pared to die for it, then it will come,' Raefe said sombrely, 'but it won't come in a world dominated by Hitler or the Japanese.'

Helena managed a tired smile. 'Oh dear, what a subject to bring into a sickroom! I meant to try to cheer you up, not cast you into a pit of depression.'

'Then, cheer me up,' he said, his eyes watching hers closely. 'Where the hell is Lizzie? I haven't seen her since yesterday evening, and I was too groggy then from anaes-thetic to appreciate her visit properly. I expected her to be here this afternoon.'

'Perhaps she thought Melissa would be visiting,' Helena

said awkwardly. 'I know that she telephoned her from here late last night.'

Raefe's eyes narrowed slightly. 'Melissa has been and gone. A telephone call to the ward would have told Lizzie that. Where is she, Helena? What do you know that you're not telling me?'

Helena wished that she had remained standing at the window where she could avoid Raefe's all too perceptive eyes. 'I don't know,' she said uncomfortably. 'We parted outside the hospital at about nine last night. I had suggested we go for a drink together, but she. . . .' She faltered, cursing herself for a fool.

'But she what?' Raefe demanded, his nostrils pinched and white, his mouth tight.

'She said she was tired,' Helena finished lamely.

Raefe's near-black eyes held hers mercilessly. 'Don't lie to me, Helena,' he said tautly. 'Why wouldn't she go for a drink with you? What was it she said?'

'That she had to go home to talk to Adam,' Helena said at last, defeatedly. He had saved Tom's life. She couldn't lie to him, no matter how much she wanted to.

'Talk to him about what?' Raefe demanded, every muscle in his body tightening with tension.

'She said that Adam knew about her affair with you. I imagine that was what she needed to talk to him about. He loves her very much, and—'

'Christ!' He swung his legs from the bed, pulling free the drip that was inserted in his arm.

'Now see what you've done!' Helena cried out, horrified. 'Stay where you are! Don't move until I can get a nurse!'

'I don't need a damned nurse!' he snapped, but to his fury the sudden movement had made him sick and giddy, and as she rushed to the door to get assistance she was relieved to see that he was swaying unsteadily and was not hard on her heels.

It was the ward sister who came in answer to Helena's call for help. She took one look at Raefe, his face bone-white, and said crisply: 'Thank you, Mrs Nicholson.

59

Perhaps you would leave now. Mr Elliot is far weaker than he believes himself to be.'

'Telephone Lizzie,' Raefe said to Helena, knowing defeat when he met it, and accepting it with appalling grace. 'Tell her I want to see her. Tell her if she doesn't come to me, then I'm coming to her!'

'Not without my permission you're not,' the ward sister said tartly.

Helena grinned. She doubted if Raefe had ever been spoken to in such a way before. Then, sensing that a full-scale battle was about to commence, she made a hasty and diplomatic exit. At the public telephone booth in the hospital's foyer she dialled Elizabeth's number.

'Mr Harland, Missy Harland not home,' Chan said before she could even state who it was she wished to speak with. 'Please to telephone back another time.'

'Could I leave a message . . .?' Helena began, but Chan had already severed the connection. The line was dead.

Helena replaced the receiver on its rest, perturbed. It was unlike any of the Harlands' houseboys to be rude or curt. As she walked through the busy foyer and out into the street she was convinced that Chan had been so because he had been lying. Adam and Elizabeth *were* at home. But they weren't answering the telephone, not even to her. She unlocked the door of her open-topped Morgan and slid behind the wheel, wondering what on earth was happening in the Harland home, and whether she should drive up there.

Julienne walked with hip-swinging pertness down the hospital corridor towards Tom's private room. She was wearing a suit of sizzling lemon linen, the waist nipped in tightly, a peplum emphasizing the curve of her hips. She wore no blouse beneath the jacket, and the collar was open deeply, revealing honeyed skin and a small diamond on a chain nestling at the cleavage of her breasts.

'Mr Tom Nicholson, please,' she asked the ward sister, her red hair glinting, her eyes bright with health and love of life.

60

The ward sister put down the sheaf of notes she had been carrying. The private lives of her two most recent patients was growing increasingly interesting. She knew very well who Julienne was – and of her reputation. 'Certainly,' she said, her face revealing none of her thoughts. 'This way, please.'

Julienne's treacherously high-heeled shoes tip-tapped in the sister's wake, along the corridor towards Tom's room. 'How is Mr Elliot?' she asked the sister, her eyes flicking over the names on the doors of the few private rooms. 'Is he going to be all right?'

The ward sister turned her head, her eyes meeting Julienne's. 'Yes,' she said, wondering which man it was that Julienne was most interested in, and what her relationship with both of them was. 'But he needs rest.'

If there was any irony in the sister's voice, Julienne was blithely unaware of it. '*Vous avez été très gentille*,' she said as the sister opened the door of Tom's room. 'You have been very kind.' And then, on seeing Tom, his chest heavily bandaged, her smile faded. '*Oh, mon pauvre petit!*' she exclaimed, the heady fragrance of her French perfume filling the room as she hurried to his side.

Tom was genuinely glad to see her. They hadn't been lovers for over two years but, unlike most of the women he knew, Julienne had a capacity for friendship, as well as for love, and his affection for her ran deep.

'*Ça va?*' she asked urgently, taking his hand. 'Are you all right?'

'I'm fine, Julienne,' he said, not looking fine at all. 'A couple of cracked ribs and a broken nose. That's all.'

She ignored the stiff-looking chair by the side of his locker and perched on the bed. 'You do not look fine, *chéri*,' she said, her kittenish face unusually sombre. 'You look very, very unhappy.'

'I am.' Worry and anxiety had carved deep lines on his handsome face, and his long mobile mouth was tight with strain. 'You know about Lamoon?'

Julienne nodded. Helena had told her. She had not been

61

surprised. She had known that a man as virile as Tom must have been conducting a love-affair with someone, and the fact that he had never brought that someone with him to picnics and parties indicated that she was, perhaps, a Chinese.

'I am very sorry for you both,' she said sincerely, 'but you must have known it was hopeless, Tom. A girl like Lamoon . . . I don't even understand how you managed to meet undiscovered for so long.'

'Elizabeth and Adam Harland gave us hospitality and the use of their summerhouse,' he said bleakly.

'*Tiens!*' Julienne's pansy-dark eyes were shocked. 'I would never have believed it in a million years! I always thought the Harlands so prim and so very proper, and now I discover that Adam is really a romantic at heart, and as for Elizabeth. . . .' Words failed her.

Tom looked at her curiously, unused to such an occurrence. 'What about Elizabeth?' he asked, sensing that something was wrong.

'She's in love with Raefe,' Julienne said simply. 'Derry tells me that Raefe intends marrying her.'

Tom stared at her. 'I don't believe it,' he said at last.

Julienne's shoulders lifted in a tiny shrug. 'I do not blame you, *chéri*, but I think it is the truth. I think that very soon the nice steady Adam is going to be a very unhappy man.'

'Christ! Tom continued to stare at her in disbelief. 'Raefe and Elizabeth. It never occurred to me. . . .'

'It has been going on for quite a while,' Julienne said knowledgeably. 'Since before Jeremy's birthday party.'

'Christ!' Tom said again. He had been so immersed in his affair with Lamoon that he hadn't given a thought to his friends' private lives for months. 'Poor old Adam. . . .'

Julienne took his hand. 'And poor Tom,' she said gently. 'There will be no more Lamoon, *chéri*. You are going to be very lonely.'

His face tightened. 'I can't accept that yet, Julienne. I *have* to see her again! God damn it! I *will* see her again!'

Julienne shook her head slowly. 'No, *chéri*,' she said regretfully, 'I think not. I think your Lamoon is already very far from you.' She rose to her feet, looking down at him compassionately. 'Perhaps in a few days, if you *are* lonely, perhaps it might be a good idea to telephone me? Old lovers should be able to give comfort when it is needed. *C'est compris?*'

Despite his grief he grinned. He understood very well. 'You never know,' he said, his heart breaking inside him, 'I might just do that, Julienne.'

She smiled and blew him a kiss. '*Au revoir*,' she said, hoping very much that he would do so. 'God bless.'

Dusk had fallen and the lights were on in the corridor as she walked towards the sister's office. She hesitated a moment outside the door that bore Raefe's name. She wanted very much to go in and see him, if only for a few moments. A few yards away from her, in her glass-fronted office, the ward sister put down her pen and watched her with interest.

A small frown puckered Julienne's brow. Surely he would not mind if she went in and asked how he was? But she wasn't sure. Nothing about Raefe was predictable. It was one of the reasons she found him so devastatingly attractive. She knew very well the kind of reaction she could arouse in Ronnie or Derry, or even Tom. But Raefe Elliot was different. And she didn't want the humiliation of forcing her company on him if he preferred to be alone.

'Another time, *chéri*,' she whispered beneath her breath, smiling to herself as she continued to walk down the corridor towards the stairs. Elizabeth was a very lucky lady, and she didn't blame her in the least if she was about to burn all her boats behind her. If she were in Elizabeth's position, she would be very tempted to do the same thing herself. But tempted only. After all, she was married to Ronnie, not to Adam. And Ronnie was fun and made her laugh. She ran down the last few steps and into the foyer. She felt very sensuous and Ronnie was meeting Alastair at the Pen at seven o'clock. She would have to hurry if she wanted to detain him before he left the house.

Adam stared at Elizabeth as she entered the drawing-room. He looked hunched and gaunt and suddenly very old.

'You're in love with him, aren't you?' he asked without preamble.

'Yes.'

The word fell between them like a bomb. She saw him stagger slightly and then regain his balance. He was standing in front of the flower-filled fireplace, his pipe clutched tightly in his hand, the tobacco long since burned out.

'Oh, Adam, I'm so sorry,' she said heartbrokenly, moving towards him. 'So very, very sorry.'

He fended her off with his arm. 'No!' he said, his voice thick with grief. 'Don't come near me, Beth! Don't touch me! I can't bear it! Truly, I can't!'

The tears were pouring down her face. 'Sit down, Adam. Let me fetch you a drink. . . .'

'I don't want a bloody drink!' he shouted explosively. 'I want what I've always wanted! I want you, Beth!' He raised his arm against his eyes. 'I want you,' he said again, brokenly. 'God help me, Beth. I don't know how to begin to live without you. You're all I've ever wanted . . . ever since you were a little child.'

She moved towards him once more, taking his arm and leading him towards a chair. 'Sit down,' she said gently, and as he did so she crossed to the table that held decanters and glasses, and poured a large brandy. 'Drink this,' she said, pressing it into his hand. 'Oh, Adam, oh, my dear, if only you knew how hard I've tried not to let this happen!'

He drained the brandy in one swallow, putting the glass down unsteadily, saying with sudden bitterness; 'So you've *tried* to stay with me, have you? You've *tried* to love me and not him?' His face was ashen with anger and grief. 'I don't understand it, Beth! I thought we were so happy together!'

'We were . . . we are. . . .'

She was crouching at his feet and he leaned forward,

64

seizing her wrists with surprising strength. 'Then, *why?*' he howled. 'In the name of God, Beth! *Why?*'

He was hurting her, but she couldn't pull away. 'I don't know why . . .,' she cried truthfully. 'But when I'm with him I feel whole. Complete. I feel as if he is the other side of my personality. I want to be with him all the time.' She saw the agony on his face but she couldn't stop. 'I want to share his life. . . .'

He released his hold of her, springing to his feet with such suddenness that she fell on to her knees. 'You've taken leave of your senses! Men like Elliot don't marry the women they sleep with! You don't mean anything to him, Beth! He doesn't love you! *I* love you!'

She pulled herself up against the chair, tears dripping down on to her hands, her dress, hating what was happening to them, hating herself for allowing it to happen. 'No. . . . It isn't like that, Adam. He does love me. He wants me to share his life with him.'

He physically flinched, as if he had been struck. 'You can't mean that. . . . You can't intend *leaving* me for him? For a man who doesn't know the meaning of the word "faithful"? A man who is a *killer?*'

The room was suddenly very still. She felt as if she were on a stage set. As if nothing that was happening was real. She said, unutterably wearily, all passion spent, 'I have to leave you, Adam,' and then, as he stared at her, refusing to believe her, she said with brutal simplicity: 'I'm carrying his child.'

His groan was deep and terrible. He put his hands out, like a blind man, seeking for somewhere to sit. 'Oh, no . . .,' he said as he lowered himself into a wing-backed chair. 'Oh, no . . . no. . . . I don't believe it. I won't believe it!'

She walked across to the mantelpiece, leaning against it for support. 'I don't know what I'm going to do,' she said bleakly. It wasn't a cry for help; it was simply a statement of fact. 'Raefe doesn't know yet. Whatever I do, though, I can't stay here, Adam. I'm going to move into the Pen.'

He shook his head, struggling for words. When they came, he said desperately: 'No! There's no need, Beth! Stay here. Stay with me!'

'I can't,' she said, her heart breaking. She moved across to him, kneeling down in front of him, taking his hands in hers. 'There is no way I can expect you to understand, Adam. But I love you. I've always loved you.'

His eyes were tired in defeat, aged by pain. 'But not the way you love him?'

Her hands tightened on his. 'No,' she said, her voice cracking, 'not the way I love him.'

For a long time neither of them spoke; and then, at last, he said – a new note of desperation in his voice: 'There's no need for you to leave, Beth.'

She raised her face to his.

He was struggling inwardly, coming to terms with the most dreadful crisis he had ever faced. 'You say Raefe doesn't know about the baby? Don't tell him. Don't tell anyone.'

'I'm sorry, Adam, I don't understand. . . .'

His thumbs pressed so hard on to the backs of her hands that she winced with pain. '*We'll* have the baby, Beth! *I'll* be the father! We can live together as we've always lived! We've been happy, Beth. You said so yourself! We can be happy again! *Please*, my darling. Please stay! Please let me take care of you both!'

She began to cry, great racking sobs that could not be controlled. She had always known that he had loved her, but that he loved her so deeply that he would forgive her infidelity, accept another man's child as his own, tore her apart. He was offering her all he could possibly offer, and it wasn't enough. Nothing ever could be. Their life together had come to an end, buried beneath a carpet of hibiscus blossom.

'No,' she whispered brokenly, rising unsteadily to her feet, wondering if her life would be long enough for her ever to forgive herself. 'I think you are the kindest, most loving man in the world, Adam, but I can't do as you ask. I can't live with you any more. I'm going back down to the Pen tonight.'

He made no move towards her. He didn't even try to rise from his chair. His world had collapsed around him. She was going, and there was nothing he could do to make her stay.

'I love you,' he said tonelessly as she walked towards the door. 'God help me, but I still love you, Beth.'

She swayed, one hand on the knob of the door, and then walked blindly out of the room. She packed only one suitcase, carrying it down the stairs herself, not calling for Chan or for Mei Lin. She paused in the mosaic-tiled hallway. The drawing-room door remained closed. She didn't move towards it. There was nothing more she could say to him. The most horrible thing of all, the most horrible part of the whole dreadful scene that they had endured, was that, deeply as she cared for him, not once had she had any doubts about the decision she had made. She had none now as she walked tiredly towards the door, closing it quietly behind her, walking across the dark gravel towards the garage and her Buick.

'My God, I don't believe it!' Helena said, thunderstruck. It was nine in the morning. She had driven over from Kowloon, determined to see either Elizabeth or Adam, worried sick by the repeated refusal of Chan to put through any of her calls.

Adam smelt of stale brandy. His cardigan looked as though it had been slept in. 'It's true,' he said bleakly. 'She's at the Pen.'

'But she'll come back!' Helena cried in desperate reassurance. 'When she has had time to think, she will come back!'

Adam shook his head. 'No,' he said flatly. 'She won't come back, Helena.' He paused for a moment and then said: 'She's pregnant by him.'

'Holy God!' She stared at him, so shocked that she felt physically ill. 'Oh, Adam, my dear. I'm so sorry. . . .'

67

'It isn't pity I want,' he said tautly. 'I just want Beth back again.' His eyes met hers urgently. 'Talk to her for me, Helena. Try to make her see sense. I've told her I don't care about the baby. I don't care about anything as long as she comes back to me!'

'I'll talk to her,' Helena said, but her voice, even to her own ears, was defeated. Elizabeth's decision would not have been taken lightly, and if she were pregnant with Raefe Elliot's child, then Helena could not imagine her returning home. 'Come along,' she said to him. 'You look ghastly. Have a shower and change your clothes and we'll have breakfast together. I'll ask Chan to put on some eggs and to lay the table.'

'Thank you, Helena,' he said gratefully, knowing through his pain that her maternal bossiness was exactly what he needed.

He left the room slowly, his limp more pronounced than she had ever seen it before. 'Damn you, Raefe Elliot,' she whispered beneath her breath. 'Why the hell couldn't you have fallen in love with Julienne? Then no hearts would have been broken.'

# 5

She booked into the Peninsula, tired and drawn, asking for a single room and saying that she would want it indefinitely. She knew that Raefe, when he knew, would immediately want her to move in with him, but she had no intention of doing so. Not yet. She had not left Adam in order to live with another man. She had left him because she was carrying another man's child. Because she could no longer give him the love and loyalty that were his due.

She moved wearily around the room, putting her toilet things on a small glass shelf in the bathroom, laying her nightdress on the bed. There was a carafe of iced water on the dressing-table, and she poured herself a glass, drinking deeply. She didn't want room service. She didn't want a meal, a hot drink. She didn't want to do anything but sleep.

She undressed with slow tired movements. Her face was swollen from the tears she had shed, her head ached. She moved her clothes to the back of a chair, took a long cooling shower, and lay down on the bed.

She had left Adam. She had left the one person who had never, ever, intentionally hurt her. Her agonized mind sought oblivion in sleep. The day began mercifully to recede, grow confused, grow dim, the sound of traffic on nearby Salisbury Road began to blur and fade. . . . She had done the only thing she possibly could do. She had told Adam of her love for Raefe. She had told him about the baby. And she was going to have the baby. The merest touch of a smile softened her lips as she closed her eyes and slept.

The next morning she didn't drive first to the hospital. She drove instead down Nathan Road and towards Li Pi's Kowloon apartment. If she was embarking on a new chapter of her life, then her music was going to have first priority. It had taken a back seat for far too long.

She looked ill and pale as he opened the door to her, but her eyes were burning with an expression he was all too familiar with and he wasted no time in upbraiding her for her absence. Neither of them had time to spare.

He took her straight to the keyboard, but not in order that she could play for him as she had played previously. This time they were starting from the beginning. 'I would like you to play for me a C-major scale in double octaves,' he said to her without preamble. 'As *legato* as possible and in one continuous gesture.'

He stopped her after only the first note. 'You must sit differently. You must sit on the *thighs* so that the pelvic and knee joints are mobile. Now, once again.'

It was exactly what she needed. For three hours she did not think of Adam once. Or of Raefe. Or even of the baby.

At lunch-time, as they shared a light meal of fish and rice together and before she had returned to the keyboard, she told him how difficult she always found Bartók's second piano concerto. He smiled, his old Oriental face creasing into a hundred lines.

'There is no such thing as a difficult piece, Elizabeth. A piece is either impossible or it is easy. The process whereby it migrates from one category to the other is known as practising.'

She had laughed, knowing that he was right, loving the feel of once again working, of having achieved something of worth.

'You will be here tomorrow?' he asked, when at last he escorted her to the door.

'I shall be here every day,' she said, and her beautiful face was no longer etched with strain. She felt clear-headed, confident.

'Remember,' he said to her. 'Remember when you

practise that in performing the scale, the *tempo* must not be too slow, otherwise it will break down into a series of isolated impulses; nor must it be too fast, or *staccato* emerges.' He gave her his gnome-like grin. 'Till tomorrow. Joi Gin. Goodbye.'

It was late afternoon, and the streets were crowded as she drove back towards the ferry and Victoria. She felt almost light-headed. Her life was not lying in pieces all around her. It was beginning to take shape. She no longer felt as if she were being manipulated by emotions outside her control. She felt in command of what was happening, and the feeling brought with it a heady sense of freedom. When she walked into the hospital it was with the swing of new-found confidence.

'Is Mr Elliot feeling stronger?' she asked the ward sister as she passed her in the corridor.

The ward sister raised an eyebrow slightly. It was because Mrs Harland hadn't visited earlier in the day that Mr Elliot had been demanding he be discharged.

'If his temper is anything to go by, he is,' she said drily.

Elizabeth grinned. Raefe wouldn't make an easy patient. 'Can I see him now?' she asked.

'The sooner the better,' the ward sister said practically, 'but if he tells you he's discharging himself dissuade him. He won't be fit to go anywhere for at least another week.'

Elizabeth nodded. She was wearing a full-skirted dress of pale eau-de-nil silk, and the skirt rustled against her legs as she walked into his room.

His head spun towards the door. 'What the hell time do you call this?' he demanded, but his eyes told her his anger was only feigned. They blazed with pleasure at seeing her. 'It's nearly six, God damn it!'

'I had things to do,' she said mischievously, walking across to his bed and sitting demurely on the stiff little chair beside his locker.

'Come here, woman!' he growled. 'Where I can get my hands on you!'

She did as he demanded and, despite the saline drip and

71

his heavily bandaged chest, it was a long time before either of them spoke again. When she finally pulled herself gently away from him, she said hesitantly: 'I have something to tell you.'

'I know.' She was sitting on the bed, her hands imprisoned in his. 'Adam knows about us. Helena told me.'

There was unconcealed satisfaction in his voice. She withdrew her hands from his and rose from the bed, walking across to the window.

His brows flew together. 'What is it, Lizzie? He had to know some time. What's the matter?'

'I didn't want him to know so suddenly, so dreadfully.' She paused for a moment and then said: 'I've left him. I had no choice. I've taken a room at the Pen.'

His elation was tempered instantly by the realization that there was still something she hadn't told him. He waited, every muscle in his body tense with expectancy.

At last she turned to face him, the sunlight streaming through the window behind her, burnishing her hair to silver. 'I'm having a baby,' she said simply.

He didn't even ask her if it was his. He didn't need to. 'The devil you are!' he breathed exultantly. 'Come over here where I can kiss you!'

A smile curved her lips. 'Are you pleased?'

'Let me show you,' he said, reaching his hand out towards her, pulling her down against him. 'Why on earth did you move into the Pen? You should have gone straight to the apartment.'

'No.' She pulled away from him a little. 'I'm not moving into the apartment, Raefe. Not yet.'

He stared at her, as if she had taken leave of her senses. 'Why ever not? It's large enough.'

She shook her head. 'It has nothing to do with size. It's just that I don't want to walk out of Adam's life and immediately into another domestic arrangement. Does that make sense?'

'None at all,' he said, his brows once more flying satanically together. 'I want you with me every minute of the day. You want to be with me. We're having a child. You living at the Pen and me living alone in the apartment just doesn't make sense!'

She had known that he wouldn't understand. 'It makes sense to me,' she said quietly. 'It's what I need.'

'What you need is a good hiding,' he said grimly, 'but I'm in no condition to administer it.'

A smile touched the corners of her mouth. 'Then, you'll have to accept what I'm saying.'

There was a new-found assurance about her, and a determination, that he knew he could not argue with. Not yet. 'How will you manage?' he asked, thinking that he had found her Achilles heel. 'The Pen is ruinously expensive. I can't imagine Adam footing the bill, and I'm not going to.'

Her smile deepened. 'There's no need for either of you to foot any of my bills,' she said, enjoying her new-found independence. 'My father left me very adequately provided for.'

'Blast him,' Raefe said, his eyes gleaming once more. He didn't imagine that little fact had pleased Adam Harland. A financially independent lady was one who could call her own shots, and it was obvious that that was exactly what Lizzie intended doing. 'Who was your father?' he asked curiously. She had talked about him but she had never told him his name.

'Jerome Kingsley.'

He frowned, trying to remember. 'Kingsley ... Kingsley,' he said to himself, and then his face cleared. He'd got it. Jerome Kingsley, financial wizard of the thirties. No wonder the Peninsula's bills left her unperturbed. 'At least', he said wryly, drawing her gingerly back into his arms, 'you're not marrying me for my money.'

'I'm not marrying you at all,' she said, a shade of laughter in her voice.

He grinned complacently. 'Oh, yes, you are. Just as soon as Adam can be persuaded to divorce you. Do you think you could rearrange yourself a little? I have a knife-wound there that's giving me hell. What I need is a glimpse of your breasts to take my mind off it!'

'*Je ne comprends pas,*' Julienne said bewilderedly. 'I do not understand it. Raefe is now out of hospital and living in Victoria. And you are in a single room at the Pen. It doesn't make sense.'

'So I've been told,' Elizabeth said, amused.

'Doesn't Raefe *want* you to move in with him?' Julienne asked, wondering if she had been unnecessarily tactless.

They were at the Swimming Club, relaxing at the poolside with long iced drinks.

'Yes,' Elizabeth replied. 'Don't look so concerned, Julienne. I'm at the Pen because I want to be there.'

'*I* wouldn't want to be there. Especially in a single room!' Julienne said emphatically. She looked across to where Elizabeth lay on her sun-lounger, her swimming costume still wet from their swim. 'You know, Elizabeth,' she said thoughtfully, 'I do not think that staying at the Pen is very good for you. I think perhaps you are beginning to eat a little too much.'

Elizabeth grinned. Julienne did not yet know about the baby. 'Yes,' she said contentedly, eyeing her slightly thickening waistline, 'I think you could quite possibly be right, Julienne!'

The last few weeks had not been easy for her. Although adultery was rife in Hong Kong, the desertion of a husband or wife was not. Her action in moving out of her marital home had shocked and dismayed. Lady Gresby had crossed her firmly off her list, and so had a lot of other people. Leigh Stafford had been excruciatingly embarrassed when they had met accidentally at the Hong Kong Club. People she had regarded as friends now no longer spoke to her and openly avoided her. She had been uncaring. She was living her life as she wished to live it, and the friends who mattered to her had all stayed loyal.

\*      \*      \*

'Adam tells me that you've asked him for a divorce,' Alastair said to her when they met one day for lunch at the Parisian Grill. 'Is that wise, Elizabeth? So soon? It's a very final step.'

'So is having a baby that isn't his,' she said quietly.

Alastair blanched. 'I'm sorry . . . I didn't realize.' He toyed with his smoked duck and then said: 'Wouldn't it be easier if you moved in with Elliot? People wouldn't find the situation quite so puzzling.'

'I can't help it if people find my personal life puzzling, Alastair,' she said with unusual crispness. 'And it doesn't bother me. It isn't any of their affair.'

'No,' Alastair agreed, with little conviction. He was a man who liked things to be neat and tidy. He didn't like loose ends or messiness in personal situations, and he was growing increasingly miserable over his failure to persuade Helena to marry him.

'How are things with you and Helena?' she asked, sensing the direction of his thoughts.

He shrugged dismally. 'The same as they have always been. I love her. I'm damned sure that she loves me. But she won't marry me.'

'Perhaps it's still too soon for her. She's only been a widow for two years.'

'It isn't two years,' Alastair corrected. 'It's nearly three now. She used to talk to me about it, but she won't any more. I think she talks to Adam more than she talks to me.'

'Adam can be a very sympathetic listener.'

'Yes.' He looked across at her curiously. 'You still see him, don't you? I mean, not just casually and by accident. You see him by arrangement?'

She nodded. They had needed to meet and talk, and she had not wanted to keep returning to the home they had shared. He had suggested they lunch at the Pen, and they had continued to do so at least once a week.

'Is he happy about a divorce?'

'No.' A shadow crossed her eyes. She didn't like talking about Adam with anyone, but Alastair had been a good friend to her and he deserved to know something of what was going on. 'He won't instigate proceedings yet. He's still hoping that I will return to him.'

'And you won't?'

Her green-gold eyes met his unflinchingly. 'No, Alastair. I'm in love with Raefe. Even though, for my own reasons, I'm not living with him, my future is with him.'

He sighed. 'I wish to God Helena felt that her future was with me,' he said wearily. 'If the Japs continue being belligerent, I can see women and children being ordered to leave the Colony. And if Helena goes, then I may never see her again. She may just slip away from me, and I couldn't bear that, Elizabeth. Truly I couldn't.'

'Are things really getting worse with the Japanese?' Elizabeth asked, unable to give him any words of comfort where Helena was concerned.

'Oh, yes. They're playing a waiting game, but I don't think they will wait much longer. An expeditionary force landed at Bias Bay last month. That's only thirty-five miles north-east of Hong Kong. Canton has been captured. In practical terms our isolation is almost complete.'

'And, as if it isn't enough, the Germans are rampaging all over Europe, the Russians have invaded Finland . . .,' she said bleakly. She looked round the luxurious restaurant. It seemed very hard to believe that half the world was at war. Silver gleamed on white napery, a trio of musicians played discreetly. There were Sydney rocks oysters for hors-d'oeuvres, smoked salmon, strawberries, champagne and fifteen-year-old brandy.

'I know,' he said, reading her mind. 'It doesn't seem possible, does it? But it will come here as well, Elizabeth. It's just a matter of time.'

'Would it help this period of adjustment you're giving yourself if we took a trip to Australia?' Raefe asked her as they lay in bed in his Victoria flat.

'Australia?' She turned her head towards him, her hair brushing his shoulder. 'Why Australia? Do you have to go on business, or does Fort Canning want you to go?'

'Neither, sweet love,' he said, amused, his hand resting comfortably on the growing rise of her belly. They had no secrets from each other. She knew far more about his intelligence work than he should ever have told her. 'Roman is on tour there. The orchestra is giving concerts in Sydney, Melbourne, Adelaide and Perth. I thought we could meet up with him on the last leg in Perth.'

She sat up in bed, looking down at him, her eyes shining. 'Oh, that would be wonderful, Raefe. It seems forever since I heard a great orchestra!'

He leaned back against the pillows, loving her so much his heart hurt with it. 'He wants to hear you play.'

Her eyes widened in horror. 'You're joking! He's one of the greatest conductors in the world! What could I possibly play for him?'

'Bach, Schubert, Beethoven, anything that you like,' he said grinning. 'Don't tell me you're not capable of it. Not after all the work with Li Pi.'

She laughed down at him. Her horror had only been because he had taken her by surprise. She knew her capabilities very well and she was more than ready to play for a conductor of Roman Rakowski's stature. The prospect sent adrenalin singing along her veins. 'Roman Rakowski . . .,' she said again in awe. 'I can hardly believe it. . . .'

He pulled her down beside him. 'Don't say his name with quite such adoration or I might change my mind and keep you as far apart from him as possible!' His hands reached out for the full lusciousness of her breasts. 'They're getting bigger, Lizzie. How many months is it yet?'

'Ages and ages,' she said languorously, sliding her legs between his, luxuriating in the pleasure of his touch. 'Another six months at least.'

He lowered his head, his tongue circling her silk-dark nipple, his lips pulling gently. She gave a soft moan, pushing her pelvis against him, hot and damp with reawakened desire.

'Twice before breakfast can't be very good for my

health,' he murmured teasingly as her hands moved caressingly downwards. 'I'm thirty-two, sweet love. Not twenty-two.'

'You're wonderful,' she murmured, her lips on the bronzed flesh of his shoulders, her legs spreading wide, her breath exhaling on a low deep sigh of fulfilment as he entered her. 'Wonderful . . . wonderful . . . unbelievably wonderful. . . .'

They arrived in Perth on Christmas Eve. Neither of them had wanted to spend Christmas in Hong Kong. It was too emotive a time. Raefe was sure that Adam would ask her to spend the day with him and, if he did, knew that she would feel bound to do so. As it was, she had been able to tell him that she would be in Australia and she had been deepiy relieved by Helena inviting Adam to spend Christmas with her and Alastair and the children.

Melissa had gone, of her own choice, back to the farm in the New Territories. She didn't want to be surrounded by the curious eyes of family and friends. Every day was still a battle for her, and she wanted to fight her battle alone and in private.

'It seems funny to see Christmas trees and imitation snow and snowmen when the sun is blazing down,' Elizabeth said as they window-shopped in Perth, looking for a Christmas present for Roman. He tucked her hand more tightly in the crook of his arm. 'I keep forgetting that you've never spent a Christmas in the southern hemisphere before. We'll spend tomorrow on the beach. That will really disorientate you.'

They passed a news-stand, the headline on the month-old papers from England headlined with a defiant 'COME ON, HITLER! WE'RE READY FOR YOU!'

'I wonder what next year will bring?' she said, suddenly sombre.

He patted her hand. It was Christmas. He didn't want to think of Hitler, or the Japanese, or the darkness the world was plunging into. 'It will bring a baby,' he said, deliberately misunderstanding her. '*Our* baby!'

Her sombreness lifted as he had intended it should. She hugged his arm. 'The nurse at the clinic says that it should start to move within the next few weeks. I wonder what it will feel like?'

'Uncomfortable, I should imagine,' he said with a grin.

They were passing a shop window. Backed against a neutral screen of shot-grey silk, stood an exquisite bronze head.

Raefe turned and glimpsed it. He stopped. 'Our window-shopping is over,' he said, drawing her near to the glass. 'Look.'

She looked and saw the name, edged in gold: 'Wolfgang Amadeus Mozart.'

'Oh,' she said, letting her breath out slowly. 'It's beautiful, Raefe.'

'And perfect for Roman. Come on. Our shopping expedition is over.'

'It's wonderful!' Roman Rakowski said, his eyes shining as he lifted the bronze carefully from its tissue wrappings. They were in the empty auditorium of Perth's concert hall. Elizabeth and Raefe had sat, spellbound, as Roman had taken the great orchestra through its rehearsal for the evening's performance. Now the three of them were alone, with Elizabeth excruciatingly aware of the Steinway grand standing off-centre on the platform above them. His present to them had been a small painting of the boy David, his sling in his hand, his eyes fearless, as he faced Goliath and the Philistines.

'I thought it apt,' he said, his deep voice filling the empty hall. 'A small force facing a larger one. It reminded me of your situation in Hong Kong.'

'It's lovely,' Elizabeth said truthfully. The colours glowed with vibrancy and there was something so pure, so brave about the boy's stance that her throat tightened. She had nearly forgotten Rakowski's Jewishness. He was not at all what she had expected. He was a big bear of a man with a shock of dark-gold, unruly hair, and an engaging habit of running his fingers through it whenever he explained a point to the musicians. He was ridiculously young for a conductor of such stature, but she could see why he had achieved such eminence. There was a presence, a vigour, an authority about him. Enthusiasm emanated from him in waves.

'What do you think, my friend?' he had demanded, bounding down from the rostrum when the musicians had been dismissed, hugging Raefe as if he were a long-lost brother. 'The sound has changed, eh?' He had turned towards Elizabeth, his smile wide, his eyes welcoming. 'The sound of the orchestra now comes from the string-playing. Did you hear it? We are softer in the brass section, not so dominating as other orchestras, and in the strings we do not have this very *spiccato* off-the-string way of playing. I think, especially for classical music, it is wrong. This is better, don't you agree?'

He had put his arms around them both, leading them to the far right of the platform where he had a flask of coffee tucked away.

'It's not much to greet you with,' he had said, shrugging his huge shoulders apologetically, 'but the champagne will have to wait until after tonight's performance.'

There was a permanent undertone of suppressed laughter in his deep bass voice, and Elizabeth felt herself instantly drawn towards him, liking him unreservedly.

When they had drunk the coffee he had looked down at her, lines crinkling around his eyes as he said: 'The concert platform is yours, Elizabeth. Make yourself comfortable. Play whatever you want.'

A moment of pure undiluted terror coursed through her veins, and then, as he touched her arm encouragingly, she remembered who she was, and what she was, and she stepped up on to the concert platform with the confident knowledge that it was where she belonged.

The first flawless notes of Grieg's Piano Concerto filled the hall, and Raefe let out a sigh of relief. She hadn't been overcome by nerves. She was playing to the best of her ability. God damn it! She was playing like an angel!

Afterwards, as they sat in a tiny Polish restaurant that served the icy bortsch soup that Roman loved, Raefe asked him: 'Where do you go next?'

Roman broke a roll of rye bread in half. 'Palestine,' he said with deep satisfaction, 'as guest conductor.'

Raefe gave an impressed whistle. 'That must mean a lot to you,' he said, pouring more wine into Elizabeth's and Roman's half-empty glasses.

'It does.' Roman's voice was suddenly sombre, and all three of them fell silent, thinking of the musicians who formed Palestine's national orchestra. Musicians who had fled the horror of Hitler's Europe.

When Roman spoke again it was to say tersely: 'Did you know that the British are restricting the entry of refugees into Palestine?'

Raefe nodded, and Elizabeth said uncertainly: 'I'm sorry, I don't quite understand. . . .'

'There are hundreds of thousands of Jewish refugees seeking to enter Palestine,' Raefe said to her quietly, 'and as Palestine is a British-mandated area the British have control of the numbers being accepted.'

Elizabeth's face was pale. 'What happens to the refugees that Britain refuses entry to? Where do they go?'

'They are shipped back to whatever country they fled from,' Roman said, his grey eyes bright with fury. 'And the persecution they tried to flee continues. They will be herded into ghettoes, sent to concentration-camps.'

Raefe took Elizabeth's hand. 'It isn't only the British who are being deaf and blind,' he said gently, sensing her shame. 'The Americans are being just as bad.'

Roman ran his fingers through his hair. 'Why the hell can't they realize the gravity of the situation?' he asked despairingly. 'Why can't they forget about numbers and quotas? The bureaucracy of it all is beyond belief!'

'Bureaucracy always is,' Raefe said tightly, and his rage

and frustration weren't directed only at the faceless governments who were closing the doors against those needing sanctuary. It was directed at the bureaucrats of Fort Canning as well. At the high-ranking military personnel still obstinately adamant that there would be no war in the East.

That evening Elizabeth and Raefe sat in the concert hall in the seats that Roman had reserved for them. The atmosphere was electric. Many of the music-lovers in the audience had never been to a Rakowski concert before but they knew of his reputation and they were waiting in tense anticipation to see if it was justified.

There was a storm of applause as Roman strode out on to the concert platform and made his way towards the podium.

Elizabeth felt the familiar surge of almost unbearable excitement that she always experienced in the few moments before the baton was raised. Only this time it was different, even more heart-stopping. This time the superbly elegant figure in white tie and tails was not a stranger. It was Roman. Raefe's friend, and now her friend.

She withdrew her hand from Raefe's, clapping wildly as Roman took his place on the podium and turned to the audience, acknowledging their applause. His unruly dark-gold hair had been brushed into submission and gleamed sleekly. His exquisitely cut evening jacket emphasized his powerful physique. As he bowed and the applause intensified, Elizabeth felt a sense of shock run through her. It was obvious, even before he raised his baton, why he aroused such fevered enthusiasm in his audiences. There was a virility about him, a personal magnetism that was overwhelming.

Elizabeth slipped her hand once more into Raefe's, squeezing it tight. The concert hall fell silent. There was a long pregnant moment of waiting and then Roman raised his baton. Elizabeth could hear her heart beating. He was opening with Mahler's Fourth. It was one of her favourite symphonies, and one she had heard conducted magnificently by Wilhelm Furtwängler at the Albert Hall in London. That the performance she was about to hear could even begin to compare with Furtwängler's seemed an impossibility.

There was utter silence, and then Roman brought his baton down and almost from the first instant she knew that she had no need to worry. He was in complete and utter command of the orchestra, his rhythm flawless. The music flowed and surged, sank and rose again with glorious unforced urgency.

She sighed rapturously, succumbing to Mahler's sensuous richness and lush lyricism. Roman was a bold conductor, his use of *rubato* so adventurous he nearly took her breath away. At times he would pause for an instant of delicious expectation before launching into a heart-easing melody, at others he would press forward within a phrase towards its climax. Whatever he did he did with utter confidence, revealing a deep, almost mystical understanding of the score. 'Oh, wonderful! Wonderful!' she breathed when the last exquisite notes had died away and the auditorium erupted in applause.

The applause died down, to break out again when the young man who was to play the solo in Tchaikovsky's Violin Concerto in D walked on to the platform.

It was as good as the Mahler. Roman's conducting was big and bold and soaring. He possessed a charisma that not only excited the audience, but magnetized the orchestra as well. They played like angels for him. As the last, unbearably beautiful notes died away, Elizabeth could feel tears pricking the backs of her eyes and then she was on her feet with the rest of the audience, shouting out 'Bravo! Bravo!' and clapping until her hands hurt.

'I told you he was incredible!' Raefe shouted to her as Roman strode from the concert platform and the applause rose frenetically for his return.

'I know . . . but I'd never imagined he would be quite so *demonic!*'

Raefe laughed, and the applause reached fever pitch. Once again Roman strode across the concert platform to the base of the podium, sharing the applause generously with the orchestra, perspiration gleaming on his forehead, his dark-blond hair no longer smooth and sleek but gloriously unruly.

'Bravo! Bravo!' the shouts continued, the orchestra clapping as unstintingly as the audience.

As he took his fifth and final bow he looked laughingly down to where Elizabeth and Raefe were cheering, his eyes shining with elation and satisfaction.

'Do you always achieve such an effect when you conduct Mahler?' Raefe asked later as they sat at a candlelit table in the little Polish restaurant that had become their regular haunt.

Roman grinned. His thick shock of dark-gold hair was still damp with perspiration, his eyes as brilliant as live coals. 'What effect is that, my friend?' he asked, attacking mushroom-stuffed beefsteak rolls with relish.

'For the entire audience it was as if they had died and gone to heaven!'

Roman laughed. 'Was that how it felt? Then, that is good. That is how Mahler *should* make you feel.'

Elizabeth and Raefe sat opposite him, their plates empty. They had eaten before the concert and were not hungry, but Roman signalled for the waiter, asking for a fruit compote to follow the beefsteak. 'I'm not usually a big eater,' he said apologetically to Elizabeth, 'but after a performance it takes hours for my nervous energy to subside, and while it is doing so I eat like a horse!'

Elizabeth smiled across at him, and at that moment, as their eyes met, she knew that they were truly friends. That they would have been friends even without Raefe's influence. She knew exactly how he felt after such a performance, and he knew that she knew. She sipped at the Polish wine that Roman had insisted they drink, wondering if she could ever acquire a taste for it, and said: 'Is Mahler very difficult to interpret?'

The plate of mushrooms and beefsteak was cleared away and replaced with the compote. Roman ate a spoonful appreciatively and then said: 'No, for me he is one of the easiest of composers.'

Elizabeth rested her arms on the table, leaning forward slightly. She was wearing a sleeveless lemon silk dress. 'Why is that?' she asked with professional interest, her hair falling softly to her shoulders.

Raefe grinned. The rapport between Roman and Elizabeth delighted him. He loved watching Elizabeth's face, laughing and animated, as she and Roman enthusiastically discussed musical personalities and orchestras, and the vital question of whether there should be breaks after the fermatas in Beethoven's Fifth. That he was able to take very little part in these discussions bothered him not in the least. Music was the world in which Elizabeth belonged and one in which he was determined that she should take her place. The day would come when Roman, with his connections and his influence, would be a great help to her.

'Mahler was a conductor himself,' Roman was saying exuberantly, 'and it shows in his scores. He puts in so many marks and verbal instructions that it is impossible to go wrong. For instance, in the second symphony. . . .'

Raefe gave a mock groan. 'It's nearly three in the morning, Roman. Have some pity, please.'

Roman gave a deep chuckle. 'You are a Philistine, my friend,' he said indulgently. 'But, for your sake, no more Mahler for the moment. Instead, let us drink Brudershaft together.'

'Brudershaft?' Elizabeth asked, hoping fervently that it wasn't another Polish wine.

'It is a ceremony we have in Poland. A declaration of life-long brotherhood. You fill your glasses, so. . . .' He generously replenished their half-full wine-glasses. 'And then, still holding your glasses, you link your elbows around each other, so. . . .' He linked his elbow with Raefe so that their arms were intertwined. 'And then we drink from our own glass at the same time. It is a pledge. A promise that our friendship is for ever.'

Entranced, Elizabeth watched as, their eyes holding each other's fast, the two men drank. Despite the difference in their colouring, there was something uncannily similar about them, as if they really were brothers. They were both tall and broad-shouldered, and though Roman was heavier-built than Raefe he possessed Raefe's pantherlike grace, moving with the easy strength and agility of a rigorously trained athlete. They shared other qualities in common, too. With both of them there was a sense of power under restraint, an impression of controlled vigour and sexuality. A self-confidence so total it was almost insolent. She suppressed a smile, wondering how their prestigious American university had survived them.

'And now we will drink Brudershaft together,' Roman was saying to her.

Feeling slightly drunk, she lifted her glass, linking her elbow around his, and as she drank she felt overcome at her good fortune. She had Raefe, whom she loved with all her heart; she had all her friends in Hong Kong; and now she had Roman's friendship, too, and looking into his brilliant grey eyes she knew it was a friendship that would last throughout her life.

Four days later, when the time came for them to part, their regret was almost unbearable. Roman was returning with the orchestra to London, and then flying out immediately to Tel Aviv. They were returning to Hong Kong. None of them knew when they would meet again.

'The next time we share a concert platform, it will not just be at a rehearsal, it will be before an audience,' Roman said thickly to her, hugging her so tight that she thought her ribs were going to crack. He turned to Raefe, his eyes suspiciously bright. 'Uwazaj, na siebie,' he said huskily. 'Take care, my friend. Goodbye.'

*     *     *

It was early dawn when they arrived back in Hong Kong. Their aeroplane squealed to a halt on the tarmac of Kai Tak Airport, and through the windows she could see the sun rising golden over the Peak.

'We'll soon be home,' he said to her, a curious gleam in his eyes as they stepped down on to the tarmac. She was carrying the painting that Roman had given them, holding it close to her chest. It had stood on the dressing-table of their hotel room all the time they had been in Perth. Now she would have to part with it. It had been given to them both, but it belonged now in Raefe's flat, not in her impersonal hotel room.

'You had better take this now,' she said regretfully, handing it to him as they walked across to the parked Chrysler.

He opened the door for her, quirking an eyebrow, making no move to take it. 'Oh, I think not,' he said airily.

She stared at him. 'But surely you want it on the wall of your room?'

He closed the door on her, walking round to the other side of the car, opening the driver's door and sliding in behind the wheel. 'Of course,' he said unperturbedly. 'Most definitely.'

The engine snarled into life, and as they drew away from the airport she said suspiciously: 'You're playing games with me, aren't you? What is it that is so amusing you?'

He flashed her a down-slanting smile. '*You* amuse me, sweet Lizzie.' He pulled out into Argyle Street. 'You don't really think, after the week we have spent together, that I'm docilely going to return you to the Pen, do you?'

'The majority of my clothes are still there,' she said without much vehemence.

His smile deepened. 'No, they're not, dear love. They were removed the day we flew to Perth. They are now cosily nestling against my clothes in the extraordinarily large wardrobe that had to be bought to accommodate them. You are a very *greedy* girl, where clothes are concerned. I've never seen so much stuff. Armfuls and armfuls of it. . . .'

'Your bedroom at the apartment has fitted wardrobes; a

large wardrobe would look preposterous in it,' she inter-rupted. 'I don't believe a word you're saying!'

He turned left into Waterloo Road. 'You're quite right. A wardrobe *would* look preposterous in the apartment. How-ever, it does not do so in our new bedroom.'

She gurgled with laughter, still holding the painting against her chest. 'And where is that?' she asked. She had no intention of arguing with him. She had known ever since Christmas that the period of adjustment was at an end. She no more wanted to return to the Pen than he wanted her to.

'Sit still, keep quiet, and you'll soon find out,' he said, shooting down Nathan Road towards the vehicular ferry.

Once on Hong Kong Island, he drove eastwards through the still quiet streets of Victoria and the gaudier streets of Wanchai.

'Where on earth are we going?' she asked, her arm through his, her head resting on his shoulder.

'Patience,' he said in loving chastisement, taking the road out towards Sai Wan Ho.

He drove on, past Lei Yue Mun Bay and Chaiwan, and then, as the morning sun bathed Mount Collinson and Pottinger Peak in liquid light, he took a small turning up into the foothills. The track wound round, bumping and swaying over the ruts which marked the course of winter overspills of mountain rain. It churned its way up round a steep bend and ground to a halt, the dust of its wake hanging thickly in the air behind them.

'Oh,' she breathed rapturously. 'Oh, Raefe, it's beautiful.'

The house was small, secluded, nestling against a back-drop of fern and mountain pine. Away in front of it the hills rolled down to the bright blue glitter of the sea.

'I warn you now, it isn't furnished,' he said as they stepped out of the car and began to walk towards it. 'Apart from two or three essential items, that is.'

It was unlike any other house she had seen on the island. There were no pillars, no porticoes, it bore no resemblance at all to the luxury houses of the Peak. It was built of stone, with an outside staircase leading to the floors above, each step whitened at the edge, and on every step there were terracotta pots and tubs of flowers. Deep drowned purple pansies; scarlet geraniums; milk-white anemones with lamp-black centres; a tangle of honeysuckle tumbling riotously. The doors and shutters had been painted cornflower blue and had been thrown open welcomingly.

'We can have something much grander if you like,' he said, seized by sudden doubt as to its suitability, as they stepped over the threshold.

She shook her head vehemently. 'Oh, no, Raefe. This is what I want. This is perfect!'

The sun streamed in through the windows on white-washed walls and gleaming pine floors. She walked through the rooms, the scent of the flowers drifting in fragrantly through the open shutters. His two or three essential items of furniture were a large brass-headed bed, the bed-linen snowy white and lavishly trimmed with lace, an enormous wardrobe holding all her clothes, and a Steinway concert grand. 'I thought you would want to choose the rest of the furniture yourself,' he said, standing close behind her, his arms around her waist. 'I want your personality in every room, Lizzie.'

She turned in the circle of his arms, touching his face tenderly in absolute love. 'We can start furnishing it now,' she said softly. 'This very minute.' And she gently freed herself from his embrace and walked out to the car, returning with Roman's painting of the boy David.

They hung it in the sun-filled room that looked out over the sea. He held her close. 'And we can start living in it now,' he said huskily, lifting her up in his arms and carrying her towards the bedroom and the snowy-white bed.

# 6

The master bedroom of Tom Nicholson's house was in deep shade, the blinds drawn down against the fierce brightness of the afternoon sun. A slight smile touched Julienne's lips as she lay on her back, her hands moving caressingly over his shoulders and up into the dark thickness of his hair. Tom had never been a very imaginative lover. He, unlike Derry, would never have considered making love in a rocking sailing-boat off Cape d' Aguilar. But his very prosaicness made a change, and her appetite for change was inexhaustible.

'That is good, *n'est ce pas?*' she whispered, her hips moving with increasing speed as she sensed that he was coming to a conclusion.

She closed her eyes, the sexual images she conjured up amply compensating for Tom's deficiencies. His mouth ground deeply on hers, his hands tightened convulsively on her breasts, and as he groaned in the agony of climax she knew without offence that he wasn't making love to her at all. It was Lamoon who was filling his head, Lamoon he was mentally expending his passion on. She was merely giving him sexual relief, easing his pain. Her arms cradled him close, the knowledge giving her a satisfaction that was far deeper than the transient satisfaction of successful copulation.

When, at last, he rolled his weight away from her, lying exhaustedly on his back, she raised herself up on one elbow, looking down at him compassionately. 'Do you feel better now?' she asked, her fingers playing slowly across his chest.

He grinned. 'You sound like a nurse.'

She giggled. 'I *feel* like a nurse. A very *personal* nurse, *chéri*.'

His grin faded, and his eyes darkened with affection. 'You're worth your weight in gold,' he said huskily, pulling her down beside him, grateful for her sexual generosity and her blessedly uncomplicated nature.

She nestled against him, her vibrant red hair tousled, her breath soft against his flesh. 'I am having lunch with Elizabeth tomorrow,' she said as he reached out to the bedside table for cigarettes and lighter. 'Having a baby suits her. She looks more beautiful than ever.'

Tom blew a wreath of cigarette smoke into the air. 'I still can't believe that she has left Adam.' A smile tugged at the corner of his mouth. 'I had ideas myself once where Elizabeth was concerned.'

'*Quand*?' Julienne demanded, sitting upright, her eyes widening with interest. 'When? Tell me!'

'It was when I first met her, aboard the *Orient Princess*. I thought maybe an affair with her would help me to say goodbye to Lamoon.' He was silent for a minute or so. He never talked about Lamoon. The pain was too deep, too raw. She waited, and at last, when he had regained control of his voice, he said: 'I never approached her, of course. She seemed to be so happy with Adam, and I couldn't imagine her being unfaithful to him in a million years.'

Julienne gurgled with laughter, swinging her legs to the floor and reaching for her scattered clothes. 'That is where you made your first mistake, *chéri*. You should never assume. Especially where women are concerned!'

The next day, at the Floating Palace Restaurant in Causeway Bay, she said to Elizabeth: 'Lamoon might just as well have vanished off the face of the earth. No one knows where she is, or what has happened to her. Tom won't speak of it. If he did, I think he would simply go to pieces.'

Elizabeth put down her menu, unable to decide whether to have lobster or oysters or fresh crab. Raefe had done everything he could to discover Lamoon's whereabouts, but even he had failed. The Chinese grapevine was ominously silent. It was almost as if Lamoon had never existed.

'Raefe thinks she was bundled out of Hong Kong and married to a man of her father's choosing, while he and Tom were still in hospital,' she said, her voice vibrant with the rage she still felt. 'It's unbelievable that in this day and age a girl of twenty can still be treated as if she's nothing but a chattel!'

Julienne lifted her shoulders in mutual disbelief. 'I agree with you, *chéri*. It is medieval. Thank your lucky stars that you are a European.'

A waiter weaved his way between the crowded tables towards them. The restaurant had been decorated to resemble a Mississippi steamboat, and he looked curiously out of place with his oriental face and high-collared white-buttoned jacket.

'I'll have oysters, please,' Elizabeth said, her choice dictated by the knowledge that the lobster and crab were at present swimming below the restaurant in large cages.

'I will have the lobster,' Julienne said, suffering from no such qualms, 'and a bottle of Chablis, please.'

She looked round at the neighbouring tables, but there was no one she recognized. She felt unbelievably tired. Keeping Ronnie and Derry happy, as well as Tom, was proving to be quite a feat, even for her.

'You're looking unusually pensive,' Elizabeth said, resting her hand on her tummy as the baby gave a definite kick. 'Is anything worrying you?'

'No,' Julienne said with a little sigh. 'I was just thinking that maybe it is time I settled down a little. I shall be twenty-seven in June. Perhaps I should be thinking of having a baby, like you.'

'Have you told Ronnie about this burgeoning maternal instinct?' Elizabeth asked, amused.

Julienne's pansy-dark eyes finished their reconnoitre of the restaurant. She had seen no one of interest. 'I do not think Ronnie would mind,' she said, a note of surprise in her voice. 'I think he might even be quite pleased.'

The waiter was at their side again, piling the table with appetizers of spring rolls and spare ribs and dumplings. Elizabeth ignored them. She was six months pregnant now, and the baby was playing havoc with her appetite. Some days she was ravenously hungry; others she had to force herself to eat even the lightest of meals.

'Doesn't it give you a guilty conscience, Julienne?' she asked musingly as Julienne lifted a dumpling from its basket with her chop-sticks.

'*Comment?*' Julienne asked, startled, wondering if Elizabeth was referring to Derry or to Tom.

'All this food,' Elizabeth said, indicating the laden table. 'I don't know what things are like in France, but ever since the beginning of January bacon and butter and sugar have been rationed in Britain, and now the government has announced that every Friday will be a meatless day and that no beef or veal or mutton will be sold on Mondays or Tuesdays.'

'It is those pigs of U-boats in the Atlantic,' Julienne said graphically. 'Ronnie says that once the Navy has put paid to them, and supplies are able to reach Britain from America, without hindrance, then there will be no further restrictions on how much food people can buy.'

'I'm sure Ronnie is right,' Elizabeth said without much conviction. 'But it's March now. How much longer can it go on?'

It went on all through April. On the ninth, two German divisions invaded Denmark and Copenhagen was taken within twelve hours. On the same day German troops landed near Oslo and the fierce and bloody battle for Norway began.

'At least we're fully prepared against an enemy attack in Hong Kong,' said Adam at the beginning of May. They were seated at a corner table in the Peninsula's flower-filled restaurant. Their weekly meetings had continued, but the reconciliation that Adam had hoped for was as far away as ever. She was happy. She was in love with Raefe. And with

93

great reluctance, prompted by the existence of the child she was carrying, Adam had agreed to institute divorce proceedings against her on the grounds of her desertion and adultery.

He was trying hard not to think about that now. For the next hour he had her entirely to himself. It was what he had looked forward to and lived for all through the week. With dogged determination he refused to allow thoughts of their pending divorce to blight his fleeting happiness.

'The Hong Kong Volunteer Defence Corps will soon be a force to be reckoned with,' he said with pride. 'We're carrying out training now on a regular basis. Leigh Stafford has joined, and even Denholm Gresby is giving us his support.'

The formation of the Volunteer Defence Corps was his major interest. It ensured that when the time came men like himself would be able to fight in an officially recognized unit. 'We have all types of men offering their services,' he continued enthusiastically. 'Businessmen and bankers, Customs officers and clerks. My God, but we'll give the Japanese a run for their money when the time comes!'

She smiled. Despite his heavily greying hair and the deep lines that now ran from his nose to his mouth, there was something eternally boyish about him.

'A lot of people still think that the Volunteers are unnecessary and that there will be no call for them,' she said, toying with her sweet and sour pork and finally pushing the plate away from her.

She didn't feel very well. The baby was lying uncomfortably, and she had been awake through most of the previous night with a severe attack of heartburn.

'I hope you're not one of them,' Adam said, shocked.

She managed a smile. 'No, of course not. I've been aware that the Japanese threat is real for a long time now.'

'Then, who is it who thinks the Volunteers are unneccessary?' Adam persisted.

'Late-night drinkers at the Jockey Club,' she said vaguely, knowing that if she gave any names he would immediately single the offenders out the next time he met them, demanding that they explain themselves.

'Then, they're misinformed idiots,' he said contemptuously.

Elizabeth's smile deepened. The gentleman in the Jockey Club bar who had loudly stated that the Volunteers were flapping and there wasn't the remotest possibility of an attack by the Japanese had been a high-ranking executive of the Hong Kong and Shanghai Bank; she shifted uncomfortably on her chair, wishing that the baby would rearrange itself.

'Are you all right, Beth?' Adam asked quickly, immediately concerned for her.

'I'm fine,' she said reassuringly. 'It's just that I'm so big now that it's difficult to be comfortable.'

'How much longer have you to go?' To her bemusement he had never found any difficulty in talking about the baby. It was Raefe that he would never mention.

'Six weeks or thereabouts.'

An all-too-rare smile touched his mouth. 'I'm surprised that you can still sit at your piano.'

'It isn't easy!' she said with feeling. 'I must be the only pupil Li Pi has ever had who has to have her back rubbed at half-hourly intervals!'

They laughed, and for a few brief seconds it was almost possible for Adam to believe that she had never left him. That they were sitting as they used to at Four Seasons, or on the terrace of their home at the Peak, sharing a drink and chatting about each other's day. His laughter died. They weren't in their own home. They were in an impersonal hotel restaurant, and the baby they were referring to was not his. He said tersely: 'Are you happy, Beth? Truly happy?'

The old pain coursed through her. She was, but the agony of telling him so almost crippled her.

He had stretched his hand out towards her across the table, and she took it. 'Yes, I'm happy, Adam,' she said quietly, her throat tight. 'Please don't keep asking me. My answer hurts you so much, and I can't bear it.'

'Then, come home!' he said fiercely, his fingers tightening on hers. 'It isn't too late, Beth! The baby can have my name. We'll leave Hong Kong. We can go to America or to Canada. No one there will ever know. We can be a family again.'

She shook her head, futile tears stinging the backs of her eyes. 'No, Adam. I've made my decision, and it has been the right decision. For me.'

His shoulders slumped, and he looked suddenly ill and tired. 'Then, that's it,' he said defeatedly. 'I shan't ask you again, Beth. But the offer will always be there. Even after the baby has been born. Even after the divorce.'

She squeezed his hand, unable to speak. The musical trio in the far corner of the room began to play 'Night and Day', and she rose to her feet. 'I must go,' she said thickly. Raefe was leaving that afternoon for a flight to Singapore and a meeting with Colonel Landor, and she wanted to drive him to the airport. 'Goodbye, Adam. Take care of yourself.'

'Bye, Beth.' He rose heavily to his feet. 'Take care of yourself, sweetheart.'

She nodded, aware that Miriam Gresby was lunching with a friend half a dozen tables away, and that she was staring across at them with outraged curiosity. She walked quickly from the room, her back straight, her head high, graceful despite her advanced pregnancy.

Miriam Gresby had seen to it that no one in Hong Kong had been left uninformed of her desertion of her husband. The most surprising people no longer even spoke to her. And the most surprising people had continued to be unfailingly kind and courteous. Major-General Grassett's wife, for example. And Lady Northcote, wife of Sir Geoffrey Northcote, the Colony's Governor.

She slid herself with difficulty behind the wheel of the Chrysler. Raefe had tried to persuade her to allow a chauffeur to drive her, but she enjoyed the mechanics of driving and she wanted as few household staff as possible intruding on their privacy. Their only resident servants were Mei Lin, who had timidly asked Adam if she could follow Elizabeth to her new residence, and Raefe's long-term houseboy.

The vehicular ferry was nearly empty, and she stepped outside the car and leaned her arms on the rail as the short crossing between Kowloon and the island was traversed. She still didn't feel very well. Her stomach muscles were uncomfortably tight, and there was a pain low in her back that she couldn't ease.

They docked in Victoria and she drove the car off the ferry, wondering if perhaps Raefe was right, and it wouldn't perhaps be more sensible to have a chauffeur, at least for the next five or six weeks. The temperature was in the eighties, and the heat, unalloyed by any breeze, drove down from the sky as from a burning-glass. 'Next time I venture into pregnancy,' she said to herself as she turned the Chrysler's nose towards Mount Collinson, 'I'll make sure that the last few months fall in the winter!'

The sea was glorious as she skirted the coast, rippling out through jade-green to aquamarine to deepest indigo. She turned right, twisting up into the flank of the mountain, wishing that Raefe wasn't leaving for Singapore. He would only be away for three or four days, five at most, but she knew how intensely she would miss him. The Chrysler's tyres rolled over a bed of dried verbena and turned the last corner before the house.

She slowed the Chrysler to a halt, savouring the sight of it. Blue convolvulus looped down the side of one wall in long belled strands. Scarlet geraniums flamed against the blue paintwork. Carnations of every shade, from deep flame to mother-of-pearl, crowded the white-edged steps. She slid the car forward again, happiness striking through her like an arrow. This was where she belonged. This was where her heart lay.

He was in the bedroom, putting the last of his things into a small overnight case. 'I was beginning to think you were planning sabotage,' he said with a grin. 'Delaying coming back until it was too late for me to catch my flight.'

'It would have been a very sensible idea,' she said,

stepping into the circle of his arms and laying her head against his chest. 'I wish I had thought of it.'

His arms tightened around her. 'It won't be long,' he murmured tenderly against her hair. 'Just a few days.'

She nodded, and he hooked a finger under her chin, raising her face to his. 'I shall miss you,' he said, lowering his head to hers, kissing her lingeringly.

The drive back across the island to Kowloon and Kai Tak Airport was one she could have done without, but it never occurred to her to tell him that she was not feeling very well. She wanted to be with him right until the last possible moment. And that meant driving with him to the airport, and then driving herself home again.

It was six o'clock by the time she wearily took the coast road eastwards for the second time. She determined to go to bed early when she arrived home. She would ask Mei Lin to make her a cup of hot chocolate and she would have a long leisurely bath, and then she would go to bed and read. A trail of lilacs lay, unbruised, across the track. She steered the car round them, leaving them as perfect as before; and, as she did so, something damp and warm seeped on to her legs and her abdomen was seized by a cramping pain, as if it were in a vice.

She sucked in her breath sharply, her hands clenching the wheel. The Chrysler wavered slightly and then straightened. The pain eased and began to die. She let out a grateful sigh of relief, the alarm-bells in her brain awakened but not yet ringing. By the time she reached the house they were ringing so loudly that she was deafened by them.

The doctor who had been attending her at the antenatal clinic had told her exactly what to expect. And it wasn't what she was now experiencing. He had told her that the pains would start gradually and intermittently, that she would have plenty of time in which to arrange to be driven into Victoria to the maternity hospital.

She stumbled into the house, gasping for breath as another strong convulsive pain seized her. 'Mei Lin,' she called, an edge of panic in her voice. 'Mei Lin!'

98

'Yes, missy,' Mei Lin answered, stepping forward to meet her, a smile of welcome on her face. It vanished in an instant as Elizabeth leaned back against the wall for support, beads of perspiration on her forehead, her face chalk-white. 'Missy! What the matter? What happened?'

'The baby is coming,' Elizabeth gasped. 'Help me to bed, Mei Lin. Telephone the doctor! Telephone Mrs Nicholson!'

'Yes, missy! At once, missy!' Mei Lin panted as she helped Elizabeth into the bedroom.

She fell on to the bed. The pains were getting harder, and they were six weeks too early. They began to merge into one another so that there was no respite, no abatement in which she could gather together her strength and her stamina. Six weeks too early! The words beat like a tattoo in her brain. Something had gone terribly, dreadfully wrong. She should be in hospital. Raefe should be at her side. She should be welcoming decently spaced-out contractions, working with them, breathing with control, not thrashing in agony attended only by a terrified Mei Lin.

By the time the doctor came she was barely conscious. 'It's all right, Mrs Harland,' he said reassuringly, his voice reaching her from what seemed like a vast distance. 'An ambulance is on its way. Now, do exactly as I tell you.'

She clung to consciousness and to the sound of his voice. She was dimly aware of towels being spread on the bed, of her underclothing being removed.

'The baby is breech,' she could hear him say tautly. 'I'm going to have to try to turn it round. . . .'

He tried once, twice, three times. Someone was screaming long and low. Mei Lin placed a wet cloth against her brow, and she realized with horror that the person screaming was herself.

'Have . . . you . . . done . . . it . . . yet?' she croaked, her voice barely audible.

He shook his head, knowing it was too late to transfer her by ambulance to the hospital, knowing that unless he succeeded in turning the baby soon he would lose both child and mother.

'Now! Again!' he said fiercely. 'When the pain is at its height!'

Some dim far-removed part of her brain wanted to laugh. When the pain was at its height! It had never been anything else. It ripped through her, stunning her with its savagery. She sucked in her breath, groaning in agony as once again his hands reached deep inside her. This time he gave an exclamation of relief.

'That's done it! I'm sure of it! Now, summon up all your strength, Mrs Harland! Push!'

She could no longer do anything of her own volition. She could only cling desperately to the last shreds of her strength, praying for it to be over. Praying for the baby to be born. Praying for it to be all right.

'That's it! Wonderful! Once again!'

She was drenched in sweat, barely able to hear him, no longer able to see. She was being split apart, rent in two. She heard herself cry out, a long primeval ululation of victory as her exhausted body finally succeeded in expelling the child from her womb. She wanted to open her eyes, to see, to speak, but she was falling into a vortex of black rushing winds.

'My baby . . .,' she whispered. 'My baby. . . .' And as the winds closed over her head, submerging her, she was aware that something was wrong. Something was not as it should be. She tried to think what it was, and at last, as the darkness became total, it came to her. There was no noise in the room around her. No murmur of congratulation. No sound of a baby's cry.

Helena's open-topped Morgan bucketed up the rough track towards the house. Mei Lin had sounded panic-stricken on the telephone, and Helena had asked to speak to Elizabeth, in order to ascertain exactly what what was happening. Mei Lin had told her that Elizabeth couldn't come to the telephone. That she was having the baby.

'You mean that her contractions have started?' Helena had asked, puzzled.

'No!' Mei Lin had sobbed. 'Baby come now, Missy Nicholson! This minute!'

She rounded the last corner of the track and saw with relief that the doctor's car was already parked outside the house. In Helena's experience first babies always took their time in coming. She had been in desultory labour for eighteen hours with Jennifer. She stepped out of her car and, as she did, a long agonizing scream froze her to the spot. 'My God!' she breathed, her eyes rounding in horror, and then she broke into a run.

'Something velly wrong, Missy Nicholson!' Mei Lin gasped as she entered the house. 'Baby coming fast and not the right way round!'

The bedroom door was closed against them, but beyond it they could hear the doctor saying urgently: 'That's it! Wonderful! Once again!' And then there was a silence.

The ambulance had rolled to a halt beside Helena's Morgan by the time the doctor walked slowly out of the bedroom. He was a burly man with a thatch of still thick hair and a deeply lined face.

'I'm sorry,' he said to Helena as he stepped into the corridor. 'The baby is dead.'

Helena pressed a fist to her mouth. 'Oh, no!' she whispered, sinking down on to a chair. 'Oh, no!'

'I'm sorry,' he said again bleakly. 'It was breech and it was six weeks premature.' He rolled his shirt-sleeves down, fastening his cuffs. 'I've given Mrs Harland a sedative and I don't think she will regain consciousness until she reaches the hospital. She'll have to stay in for several days.'

'Can I travel with her?' Helena asked.

The doctor nodded and then turned away from her towards the ambulancemen, giving them low terse instructions. Half an hour later, the small doll-like body of the baby, heavily swathed in white linen, was carried out of the house by an ambulanceman, and into the ambulance. Elizabeth was transferred next, her eyes closed, her hair tangled and damp, her skin bloodless.

Helena turned towards Mei Lin. 'Please telephone Mr Harland for me,' she said tonelessly. 'Tell him I'm accompanying Mrs Harland to the hospital. And tell him that the baby is dead, Mei Lin.'

Mei Lin nodded. She had already telephoned Raffles Hotel in Singapore, leaving a message for Mr Elliot to telephone home immediately.

'What shall I tell Mr Elliot when he telephones back, missy?' she asked anxiously.

Helena pushed a dark fall of hair away from her face. Singapore was sixteen hundred miles away. It would be days before he returned. He couldn't be left for all that time thinking that he had become a father. 'Tell him the truth,' she said bleakly. 'Tell him that Mrs Harland is in the maternity hospital in Victoria and that the baby is dead.'

'Yes, missy,' Mei Lin said unhappily, and then, as Helena followed Elizabeth's stretcher to the door, she said: 'Missy Harland will not die, will she, Missy Nicholson?'

'No,' Helena said thankfully. 'Tell Mr Elliot that she will be all right, but that she will have to stay in the hospital for several days.'

Mei Lin nodded, and Helena stepped out into the waning sunshine and crossed the flower-filled terrace to the waiting ambulance. It had been the baby that had prompted Elizabeth to leave Adam and go and live with Raefe. And now the baby was dead. As the ambulancemen closed the doors behind her, she wondered if the baby's death would change anything. If perhaps now Elizabeth would return to Adam.

The ambulance began to jolt over the stony track that led down to the coast road, and in the Moses basket near to her a shock of spiky black hair peeped from the tightly swathed sheeting. Tears stung Helena's eyes. Raefe's child and Elizabeth's child. She didn't even know its sex. She clasped her hands tightly in her lap, hoping fervently that Adam would be at the hospital and waiting for them when they arrived.

# 7

There was an appalling few minutes as they approached the hospital and Elizabeth drowsily recovered consciousness. 'My baby . . .,' she murmured to Helena. 'Where is my baby?'

Helena had squeezed her hand tightly and wished to God that the doctor was with them to answer her, instead of following behind them in his own car.

'The baby died, Elizabeth,' she said gently. 'I'm so sorry, darling. So very sorry.'

She gave a long low cry, memory returning, and then she twisted her head sharply away, the tears falling unrestrainedly.

Once at the hospital she had been transferred to a private room far away from the maternity ward and the healthy lusty cries of the newborn. An ambulanceman had carried the Moses basket into the hospital, but it did not reappear in Elizabeth's room. Helena wondered where it had been taken and if they would ever see its lifeless dark-haired little occupant again.

'I must ask you to leave now,' a nurse said to her. 'Mrs Harland needs medical attention, and the doctor is on his way to her.'

Reluctantly Helena let go of Elizabeth's hand. 'I have to leave the room, Elizabeth, but I'll only be outside, in the corridor.'

Ever since their brief exchange of words in the ambulance, Elizabeth had kept her head averted from Helena. She now turned it slowly, her face deathly pale, her eyes bruised black with grief. 'I want Raefe,' she said simply.

Helena felt her eyes sting with tears. 'I'll get him for you,' she said thickly. God in heaven, what on earth had possessed him to leave for Singapore at a time like this? Mei Lin had said that he could be contacted at Raffles, but that didn't mean that he would be resident there for the duration of his trip. If he was in Singapore on business, then he would most likely be visiting his rubber plantations up-country. Which meant that it could be days before he could be contacted, perhaps even a week or longer.

Trying to get a long-distance telephone connection to Raffles from the telephone in the hospital foyer would be a near-impossible task, and she didn't even attempt it. Instead she telephoned Alastair, telling him briefly what had happened and asking him to do his damnedest to get in touch with Raefe. Then, after only a moment's hesitation, she dialled Adam's number.

He left for the hospital immediately. He had been pruning roses when she had telephoned, and the secateurs were still in his cardigan pocket, stray rose-clippings clinging about his person as he hurried limpingly up the hospital stairs and along the corridor to her room.

'I'm sorry, Mrs Harland is resting. No visitors are allowed for another twenty-four hours,' the staff nurse on duty said primly.

'Rubbish,' Adam said, anxiety overcoming his customary good manners. 'I'm her husband! I want to see her now. Immediately!'

'Oh, of course. I'm sorry, Mr Harland,' the staff nurse said, flustered. The ward sister had given her to understand that Mrs Harland's husband was in Singapore and had still not been contacted. 'I'm sorry,' she repeated. 'I hadn't realized your identity. You may see her for five minutes, but I must ask you not to stay a second longer. Normal visiting hours finished an hour ago. The night staff will be coming on duty in ten minutes' time. Please come this way.'

Adam followed her into a dimly lit room, pity and rage

and hope all striving for supremacy. His pity was deep and genuine. He knew how much Beth had longed for a child. He knew what her pregnancy had meant to her. And now it had all come to nothing.

His rage was directed at Elliot. How could the man have left her when she was so near the end of her pregnancy? Helena had said that he was in Singapore on business. Adam very much doubted it. He had heard rumours that Alute, the Malay girl Elliot had squired so openly and for so long, had left Hong Kong for Singapore. If she had, Adam could well imagine the purpose of Elliot's visit. And if it wasn't Alute, then it would be another woman. Elliot had never been renowned for faithfulness. Not to his wife; not to his girlfriends. And now, quite obviously, he was being unfaithful to Beth.

A nerve jumped convulsively at the corner of his clenched jaws. Now, at last, Beth would know Elliot for what he was. A no-good rogue, incapable of deep feelings for her, or for anyone else. When she was strong enough to leave the hospital he would take her away, so that she could recuperate. They would go to Australia or New Zealand, or maybe even America. Hope intoxicated him. When Beth had needed Elliot, he had not been at her side. He, Adam, had been at her side. As he always would be.

'Oh, my dear, I'm so sorry,' he said huskily as he leaned over her, kissing her tenderly on her forehead, appalled at how white and exhausted she looked. 'I'm so very, very sorry.'

Elizabeth closed her eyes for a moment, summoning up what little strength remained to her. It was typical of Adam that, even though she had lost the child that had driven them so irrevocably apart, there was no underlying note of satisfaction in his voice. His sympathy was sincere and deep. His generous compassionate nature would have been incapable of anything less. Yet she didn't want his commiserations. She wanted Raefe, and Raefe was still hours, perhaps even days, away from her.

'Thank you for coming, Adam,' she said, forcing a small smile. 'It was very sweet of you.'

'Sweet of me, be damned,' he said thickly, sitting down on the chair beside the bed and taking her hand. 'You can't think that I would leave you on your own at a time like this?'

'Helena has been with me,' she said tiredly, touched as she always was by his loving concern for her. There were deep shadows beneath her eyes, and her voice was so weak he could barely hear her.

'You need to rest,' he said gruffly. 'You're in no condition even to talk. I'll come back in the morning and we'll discuss where you can go to recuperate. New Zealand, perhaps, or maybe America.'

'Yes,' she said wearily, 'New Zealand would be nice.' She closed her eyes. New Zealand and Raefe. Perhaps they could make another baby there. Perhaps, with Raefe, the agonizing hurt would heal.

Adam rose heavily to his feet. She was already asleep. He looked down at her long and tenderly, and then he turned and walked slowly from the room. He would be there when she awoke. He had no intention of returning to the Peak, not even for a change of clothes. If there was nowhere he could stay in the hospital, then he would check into one of the nearby hotels. If he was needed, he would be with her within minutes.

Helena was waiting in the hospital corridor. 'How is she?' she asked as she stepped towards him.

'Exhausted,' he said, grateful for her presence. 'I'm going to ask if I can stay at the hospital tonight. If not, then I'll book into one of the nearby hotels. Either way, I'll be here within minutes if she should need me.'

Helena looked at him oddly. 'I don't think they will let you sleep here . . .,' she said doubtfully. 'I don't think they would even let Raefe sleep here.'

'My God! I should hope not!' Adam said explosively. 'If I had my way, the bastard wouldn't even be allowed in to see her!'

Helena took his arm. 'Elizabeth isn't the only one who needs a good night's sleep,' she said firmly. 'You've undergone a long period of stress, Adam. If you won't return home, then at least book into a hotel. Trying to sleep on a couple of chairs in one of the hospital waiting-rooms isn't at all a good idea. And it isn't necessary.'

'I'm going to take her away,' he said as she led him down the corridor towards the stairs. 'New Zealand or America. Somewhere she can forget the last few months and we can start again.'

Helena swung her head sharply towards him. 'Have you told her that?' she asked incredulously. 'Has she agreed?'

He looked at her in surprise. 'Why, yes, of course. She said New Zealand would be nice,' he said, as they began to walk down the brightly lit stairs.

Helena stared at him helplessly. Despite his greying hair and his now pronounced limp, he still had the deep-chested chunky build of a useful-looking middleweight, yet there was a naïvety and a vulnerability about him that aroused all her protective instincts. She didn't for one minute believe that the death of her child had altered Elizabeth's feelings for Raefe. Whatever Elizabeth had said to him about New Zealand he had surely misunderstood.

'Don't make any plans, Adam,' she said gently. 'Not until she has seen Raefe. It would be fatal.'

Her hand had been resting lightly on his arm, and he pulled himself away from her, saying savagely: 'For a sensible woman, you can be very obtuse, Helena! She won't want to see Elliot! Why should she? He's let her down in the most awful way that a man *can* let a woman down! Whatever might once have existed between them, it's over now!' And he swung away from her, hurrying out of the hospital foyer and into the forecourt, the secateurs still bulging incongruously in his cardigan pocket.

Helena sighed and pushed her hair away from her face. It was no use going after him. Whatever she said, he wouldn't listen. She pushed her hands deep into the pockets of her skirt and was halfway to the hospital carpark before she remembered that her Morgan was not there, but miles away, parked beside tubs of geraniums and carnations and sweet-smelling stocks.

Wearily she altered direction, walking towards the street. She would have to get a taxi. And even when she arrived home there would be little comfort awaiting her. Alastair was on duty and wouldn't be able to see her until the end of the week. The children would be in bed. She scanned the street, looking for the familiar light of a taxi-cab. If Adam had been sensible, they could have enjoyed a meal together and a reviving drink. But he hadn't been sensible, and she was tired and on her own.

'Damn!' she said bad-temperedly to the world at large as a taxi finally slid to a halt beside her. 'Why does a man who is so nice have to be so pathetically idiotic?' There was no answer, and she climbed dispiritedly into the cab, unhappily aware that the main cause for her depression was not the death of Elizabeth's baby, or Alastair's unavoidable absence. It was something far more disturbing. Adam's stubborn belief that he and Elizabeth were on the point of reconciliation.

The next morning, when Elizabeth awoke, her room was full of flowers. 'Your husband sent them,' the nurse who took her pulse and checked her blood pressure said. 'Aren't they gorgeous?'

They were, but Elizabeth was still unclear whether the sender had been Adam or Raefe. If it had been Raefe, then it meant that he knew what had happened, and was on his way to her side.

'Is there a card with them?' she asked, pushing herself slowly into a sitting position.

The nurse beamed and passed one across to her. It read simply: 'From Adam, with love.'

She put it down on the counterpane. She should have known that if Helena or Mei Lin had succeeded in contacting Raefe he would not have wasted time in thinking of flowers. He would have slammed the telephone receiver down on the rest and left immediately for the airport. She thought of him hearing the news in a distant impersonal hotel bedroom, and her heart twisted in anguish. 'Oh, my sweet love,' she whispered. 'Hurry back so that I can comfort you. So that we can comfort each other. . . .'

When the doctor came to see her he stayed with her a long time, making sure she understood that there was no reason why she should not, in the future, bear healthy children. She had been grateful for his kindness but she had not wanted to think of other, as yet unborn children. She wanted only to grieve for the child she had lost. When he had gone, she had lain weakly back against the pillows and cried and cried, and the doctor, when a member of the nursing staff told him of her reaction, had nodded with satisfaction. Tears were far healthier than silent numbed grief. 'She's going to be all right,' he said prophetically. 'She's a much tougher little lassie than she looks.'

Adam came in to see her the minute he was allowed to do so. The ward sister had told him of her tears, and that they were not only perfectly natural, but also healthily therapeutic.

'What she really needs is rest,' she had said. 'Please don't overtire her by staying with her for too long.'

Her hair was down around her shoulders, making her look ridiculously young. She had dried her tears, but her face was still pale and there were dark shadows beneath her eyes.

'Did you sleep, sweetheart?' he asked, sitting down beside her, pulling the chair as near to the bed as he possibly could.

'Yes.' She had been given sedatives and painkillers, and her sleep had been deep and unnatural. A faint smile touched her mouth. 'You're still wearing your gardening cardigan, Adam. Where on earth did you spend the night?'

He grinned sheepishly. 'I didn't like to travel back home, in case you needed me. I slept the night round the corner, at the club.'

'Oh, Adam,' she said, a catch in her voice, 'you're the kindest person I know.'

She had said the same thing to him scores of times before. When she was a little girl; when he had comforted her after Jerome's death. When they had been happy together at Four Seasons. Hope for the future surged through him. 'You'll be out of here within ten days to two weeks,' he said, euphoric at once more making plans with her, once more contemplating a future together. 'We can leave straight away for New Zealand. The doctor says you'll be perfectly strong enough.'

She stared at him uncomprehendingly. 'I'm sorry, Adam. I don't understand. . . .'

'I'm taking you to New Zealand to recuperate,' he reminded her tenderly.

Her eyes widened, a new expression coming into them, but before he could understand it there came the sound of an angry altercation in the corridor.

'Mrs Harland's *husband* is with her at present!' the ward sister was protesting indignantly. 'Only husbands are allowed to visit so early in the day!'

There came the sound of a deep dismissive reply, and then the door flew open and Elizabeth cried, 'Raefe!' the sound seeming to come from her very soul. Her arms were outstretched and, even as Adam stumbled, disconcerted, to his feet, Raefe strode to her side, crushing her in his arms.

The ward sister ran into the room, saying: 'Only *husbands* are allowed. . . .' And then stood stock-still, her eyes wide with disbelief at the sight of Adam, standing futilely by, while his wife was kissed with demented passion by the man who had just stormed into the room.

'Oh, my love!' he whispered fiercely against her hair as she clung to him. 'Oh, my sweet, sweet love!'

Adam blundered towards the door. He knew now what expression had been in her eyes in the last few seconds before Elliot had burst in on them. It had been horror at the enormity of his assumption. And pity.

'Mr Harland!' the sister cried. 'What is happening? I don't understand!'

Adam pushed uncaringly past her. He understood. He had seen Beth's face as Elliot strode towards her, and it had been transfigured with an expression of such love that he had hardly been able to breathe. Never, in all the years they had lived together, had he seen her look at him like that. He couldn't even conceive of it. He staggered out into the corridor. Finally, and at long last, he understood. She was never going to come back to him. It was over. Finished.

A Junoesque figure was running down the corridor towards him, dark hair cascading untidily round a beautifully boned, expressive face. 'Adam! Oh my God! Are you all right, Adam?' He allowed her to seize hold of his arm, to take some of his weight. 'What's happened?' she asked urgently. 'Is it Elizabeth? Is she dead?'

He shook his head. 'No,' he said, his voice cracked with defeat and weariness. 'No, she's not dead, Helena.'

Helena glanced swiftly down the corridor. The door to Elizabeth's room was open, and the ward sister's voice rose clearly. 'Only *husbands* are allowed to visit, Mr Elliot!'

'Oh God,' she said beneath her breath, understanding. She turned once more towards him. 'Come along, my dear,' she said compassionately. 'Let's go and have a coffee somewhere.'

He nodded. She was an inch or two taller than him with her wedge-heeled sandals on, but he didn't mind. There was something very comforting about Helena. Something he had begun to depend upon.

Raefe had arranged that the baby be buried in the Elliot family vault. The quiet simple service, attended only by themselves and Helena, brought Elizabeth a measure of peace. Raefe had intended that she have a long period of rest and recuperation when she was discharged from hospital, but she had shaken her head vehemently at the thought. She didn't want rest. It would give her too much time in which to brood. She wanted to ease her pain in work.

For the first few weeks, to avoid her becoming overtired by the journey into Kowloon, Raefe arranged that a chauffeured car bring Li Pi to the house and that her lessons take place in the large sunlit room that looked out towards the sea.

The war being waged by the Japanese on the Chinese had intensified in recent weeks, and Li Pi had begun to smile less and less. 'Fighting is taking place just beyond the border now,' he said to her at the beginning of June. 'Red Cross trucks bring wounded from China into Hong Kong every day. It is growing bad. Very bad.'

'It's horrendous,' Helena said to her on the telephone. 'Several schools in Kowloon have been turned into makeshift hospitals, but I'm sure the wounded that are brought over the border are only the tip of the iceberg. I drove up towards Fanling yesterday, and the smell of dead bodies was unmistakable. I doubt if any proper burials have been carried out in weeks.'

'You are going to have to leave,' Raefe said to her grimly when he returned from a visit to Government House and a meeting with Sir Mark Young.

'Leave?' She looked up at him, startled. 'I don't know what you mean.' She was sitting on the sofa, her legs curled beneath her, a music score in her hands. She put it down as he sat beside her.

'The government is going to demand that all European women and children leave the Colony immediately,' he said wearily. 'It will be official tomorrow.'

She had known that something was very wrong for days. Intelligence meetings now took place in Hong Kong, as well as in Singapore, and they had begun to last until late into the night. 'Are the Japanese going to attack?' she asked quietly.

'The government thinks so. The fighting in China is only miles away now.'

'But that's against the Chinese. It doesn't necessarily mean that the Japanese will turn their attention towards us.'

'No,' Raefe agreed, 'but it's a risk the government can't

take. It's been arranged that two Canadian ships, the *Empress of Asia* and the *President Coolidge*, take evacuees to Australia.'

'How soon?' she asked, her voice fearful.

His hand tightened on hers. 'By the end of the week,' he said bleakly.

She had not argued with him, because she had known it would be pointless. He loved her, and he would miss her as agonizingly as she would miss him, yet rather than have her remain in Hong Kong in danger he would carry her forcibly aboard the *Empress of Asia* himself. If she was to stay behind when other women left, then she would have to do so by subterfuge.

Very early the next morning, before Raefe was awake, she tiptoed downstairs and telephoned Helena.

'Thanks for the information,' Helena said appreciatively. 'It might be sensible to leave now, but I don't think I will. Not yet.'

'Will you have any option if it's a government demand?' Elizabeth asked curiously.

'I'm a State Registered Nurse,' Helena reminded her. 'I haven't practised for years, but that makes very little difference in a situation like this. No one enlisting as an auxiliary nurse or air-raid warden or stenographer or cipher clerk will have to leave. They will be too necessary.'

'Thanks, Helena,' Elizabeth said, now knowing what it was she had to do.

'Darling, I really would be happier if you left for Australia,' Ronnie said miserably. Julienne was sitting at her dressing-table. She was wearing an oyster silk lace-edged camisole and nothing else, and was carefully varnishing her finger-nails a searing scarlet.

'I am not going, *chéri*,' she said for the twentieth time. '*C'est compris*? Understood?'

'No, I don't understand,' Ronnie said irritably. 'All the other wives are going. It isn't just the usual scare. This time it really does seem as if something is going to happen.'

113

Julienne inspected her nails carefully. 'What is going to happen is that I am going to stay here, with you,' she said, waving them gently in the air to encourage them to dry. 'I am *not* going to be packed like a sardine aboard a ship crammed with hundreds of crying fretful children. *Merde alors*! How can you ask it of me?'

He felt ashamed of the relief he felt. The thought of Julienne thousands of miles away was unthinkable. 'Perhaps you're right,' he said, standing behind her and sliding his hands down over her shoulders. 'It's just scaremongering. It won't come to anything.' His hands slid lower, cupping her breasts.

'Be careful of my nails, *chéri*!' she protested laughingly.

'To hell with your nails,' he growled, lifting her up in his arms and carrying her towards the bed. 'Let's celebrate the fact that you're staying here with me, where you belong.'

'But of course,' Julienne said, a delicious shiver rippling down her spine. 'After all, I love you very much, *chéri*. It is something you must never forget!'

Raefe spent the next two days making arrangements for Elizabeth to leave aboard the *Empress of Asia*. He was tightlipped, his face grim. He didn't want her to go, but there was no alternative. And God knew when he would see her again.

Her cases were packed and sent down to the docks to be winched aboard. She had hardly spoken to him since he had told her what it was she must do, and he guessed it was because if she spoke she would also cry.

Adam telephoned her, his voice harsh with anxiety. 'Are you leaving aboard one of the evacuee ships, Beth?'

She looked across to the desk where Raefe was checking her travel documents. 'Yes,' she lied, hating herself for the deception she was playing on both of them.

'Thank God!' he said thankfully. 'Perhaps you would have a word with Helena. She's adamant that she's staying. I can't seem to make her see sense at all!'

'Yes,' Elizabeth promised, wondering what on earth

would happen when the *Empress of Asia* sailed without her.

She went through all the motions of leaving. She said goodbye to Mei Lin and she clung to Raefe in the last few minutes before he led her outside to the car.

'Oh God, but I love you, Lizzie!' he said thickly, his face ravaged by grief at the prospect of parting from her.

She wanted to tell him, her very soul crying out in protest at the deceit she was exercising. But she knew that if she told him she had no intention of leaving he would force her to do so. The only way she could remain was to carry out this charade of pretence.

Both ships were berthed at the Kowloon docks, their funnels spouting black smoke as hundreds of rickshaws and cars descended on to the dockside, spilling out women and children and mountains of luggage.

For one brief second, as he walked her across to the foot of the gangplank, she wondered if, for his sake, she should leave with the others for Australia. She looked up at the high sides of the ship, the rails crammed with waving, departing women, and then back at him and knew that she could not do so. Most of the women who were leaving had children. If the baby had lived, then she knew she would have gone without a second thought. But the baby had not lived, and if war came to the Colony there would be plenty of work for her to do. She wasn't a trained nurse, but she was competent and quick-witted. An overworked hospital would surely be able to put her to use.

'I love you!' he said savagely when the time came for them to part. 'Only you, Lizzie! For ever!'

The tears spilled down her cheeks. She had never lied to him, never been deceitful, and her guilt was crucifying.

'I love you, too,' she whispered, touching his strong-boned face with her hands. 'Oh, my darling, I love you, too!'

There had been hordes of people pushing past and around them. Unable to endure any more, he had kissed her deeply and had then swung on his heel, forcing his way

115

through the crowds back to the Chrysler, knowing that if he stayed a second longer good sense would desert him and he would plead with her to stay.

She had watched him through her tears, wondering what expression she would see in his eyes when next they met. He would be furiously angry. She was prepared for his anger and knew that she could bear it. But what if there was another expression in his eyes? What if he was disappointed in her? What if her childish deceit diminished her in his opinion?

Dark was beginning to fall, and the last clutch of anxious women were boarding. Elizabeth began to make her way back down the gangplank, easing her way past a member of the crew. 'We're sailing in a few minutes' time, ma'am,' he said warningly.

'I've forgotten something. I won't be a minute,' she lied.

The dockside was crowded with husbands waving final farewells. She pushed a way between them, looking for a rickshaw-boy. She would go to Helena's and in an hour's time, when the *Empress of Asia* and the *President Coolidge* were far out at sea, she would telephone Raefe.

'I don't imagine he's going to be very pleased,' Helena said drily as she poured her a large gin and tonic. 'Why couldn't you have told him to his face that you weren't going?'

'Because he would have made me,' Elizabeth said simply.

Helena dropped ice cubes into the glass and did not argue with her. 'If you need somewhere to sleep tonight, or for subsequent nights, there's a room here,' she offered, handing her the gin and tonic and pouring another for herself.

Elizabeth's skin lost a fraction more colour. 'Oh God, Helena, do you think it will come to that?'

'I think he's going to be extremely angry,' she replied. It was an understatement.

'You're *what*?' he shouted down the telephone. 'You're *where*? My God! Of all the idiotic . . . stupid . . . crazy. . . .' The telephone receiver had been slammed down on its rest, the furiously flung words still vibrating in her ears.

'He's angry,' Helena said unnecessarily.

Elizabeth clasped her hands together in her lap to prevent them from trembling. 'Yes,' she said unsteadily, 'he's angry.'

Less than twenty minutes later they heard his car skid to a halt in the street outside. 'I think', Helena said nervously, 'that another gin and tonic is called for.'

They could hear the vibration of his feet as he took the stairs two at a time. He didn't bother to knock. The door rocked back on its hinges and he stormed into the room, his brows pulled together demoniacally, his lips white. 'Do you realize the danger you've put yourself in?' he thundered, seizing her by the arms and pushing her down into a chair. 'Do you realize what you've done? There'll be no other sailings for God's sake! You'll have to stay here now!'

'I want to stay here,' she said quietly, her face white. 'I've enlisted as a volunteer nurse.'

He ran his hand through his blue-black hair, staring down at her in disbelief.

'I *wanted* to tell you, but I knew that if I did you would have me locked aboard the *Empress of Asia* until she sailed.'

'Too damned right I would!'

She bit her bottom lip, steadying her voice, and then said: 'If you don't want me to return home with you, I can stay here with Helena.'

His brows shot high. 'What the devil are you talking about? Of course I want you to return home! Jesus God, Lizzie! Don't you realize that I nearly died when I said goodbye to you on that bloody ship?'

'Then, tell me you're not angry with me,' she said urgently, rising to her feet.

His arms closed around her. 'I'm *furiously* angry with you, but I'm not a certifiable lunatic! I'm not going to banish you from my bed!'

In unspeakable relief her arms slid up around his neck. Raefe lowered his head to hers, a blaze of such fierce love in his eyes that Helena discreetly turned away. She poured herself another gin and tonic. Her spare bed was not going to be needed after all.

All through the remainder of the month, reports of heavy fighting beyond the border continued, but the Japanese made no attempt to cross into the Colony. By the end of the month, when Raefe flew down to Fort Canning, it was generally agreed that the crisis was over.

Elizabeth was pruning back the lush azaleas that crowded down from the hillside towards the house when she heard the throb of an engine. She paused, a slight frown creasing her brow. Raefe wasn't due back for two more days at least, and she wasn't expecting Julienne or Helena to call on her. A jeep lurched into view, a cloud of dust in its wake, and she put down her secateurs, removing her gardening-gloves as she walked curiously to meet it. The sun was strong in her eyes, and for several seconds she couldn't see who was driving; then, as it shuddered to a halt and a huge bearlike figure emerged, a huge grin splitting his face, she dropped her gloves to the ground and began to run joyously towards him. 'Roman! Roman!'

He swung her up in his arms easily, swinging her round and off her feet. '*Witaj*!' he said exuberantly, a deep laugh rumbling up from his chest. 'Are you trying to tame the azaleas and hibiscus into a neat and tidy English garden?'

She giggled. 'No,' she said happily as he set her back down on her feet. 'I'm just trying to prevent them from smothering the house completely.'

His grin deepened, his eyes creasing at the corners, his thick shock of dark-blond hair as thick and curly as a ram's fleece. 'Where is Raefe?' he asked as they began to walk towards the house.

'He's in Singapore. But he's only there for another two days. You'll be able to stay until he returns, won't you?'

He shook his head regretfully. 'I'm afraid not,' he said as they stepped into the sun-filled room where her concert grand held pride of place. 'I'm on my way from a brief trip back to Perth *en route* to London. I'm going to apply for a commission in the Royal Air Force. My ship leaves at nine tomorrow morning.'

'Oh!' She was devastated with disappointment. 'Raefe will be furious when he finds out that he missed you! It might be ages before he sees you again.' She paused, her voice suddenly desolate. 'Years, even.'

The shadow of the war fell across them. Roman dismissed it with firm optimism. 'The fighting may be over by the spring. When it is, I shall want you to play for me. In Palestine perhaps.'

She grinned, dizzy at the thought, knowing that he was going to ask her to play for him now and that her fingers itched to do so.

'What is it to be?' he asked, strolling over to the concert grand, his tall powerful physique filling the room. Musingly he ran his fingers over the keys.

'Would you play for me?' she asked impulsively, no longer overawed by him as she had been in the concert hall in Perth, as at ease with him as if she had known him all her life.

'A farewell performance before the rigours of fighter command?' he asked quizzically, his blue eyes grim despite the lightness of his voice. 'Of course I will. There's nothing I would enjoy more.'

He sat himself at the keyboard, adjusting the piano stool, flexing his strong, large, beautifully sculpted hands. She stood beside him, tense and waiting, forgetting all about the war raging in Europe, forgetting even the disappointment that Raefe was not with them. Roman was a conductor, not a pianist, and she was uncertain of what to expect. His fingers touched the keys, and the opening notes of Beethoven's Appassionata filled the room. She sighed rapturously, knowing immediately that, if he had wished, he could have made the piano, not the rostrum, his life.

The music ebbed and flowed, enveloping and consuming her. She closed her eyes, rocked by a feeling of such unity with him in the passion they shared that it was almost sexual. The ordered calm of the *andante* was followed by the great tidal wave of the *allegro*, the musical menace so relentless and mounting that she opened her eyes, wondering how she could possibly bear the terrifying beauty of it. Li Pi had described the last movement of the Appassionata as mounting until, amid the thunder of sudden *sforzati*, the edifice of the world collapses. Lucifer, once the bearer of light, plunging down from heaven into eternal darkness. He had not exaggerated. For several minutes after the final chord reverberated throughout the room, neither of them spoke. Then Roman said: 'I once had the privilege of playing Beethoven on an old piano, an 1803 Broadwood. The excitement of playing the Appassionata on the kind of piano it was composed for was indescribable. I was convinced that the piano was going to break at any moment under the stress, but that terror became part of the wonder of it.'

A shiver of pleasure ran down her spine. 'I know what you mean,' she said, feeling so emotionally and mentally close to him that the breath was tight in her chest. 'It's as if Beethoven is shaking his fist in the face of heaven.'

He nodded, his eyes holding hers, the rapport between them electric. 'Beethoven thought it his greatest sonata,' he said, appalled at the mood that had sprung up between them and trying to bring it back to normal, 'and I'm in complete agreement with him. What about something entirely different? Something lyrical and joyful. The sonata he wrote immediately following the Appassionata. Sonata number twenty-four in F sharp, opus seventy-eight?'

For some unaccountable reason she was trembling. 'It's a devil to play,' she said, her voice unsteady as he rose from the piano stool and indicated that she was to play it.

'It isn't,' he said gently, a smile hovering at the corners of his mouth. 'Not for you.'

Nervously she took his place at the piano. It was as if all her senses were stretched and heightened. Never before

120

had she been in such close intimate contact with someone whose passion for music was as deep and as integral as her own, and it was a heady experience.

Mei Lin came into the room to ask if Elizabeth wanted refreshments for her guest, but though she said, 'Excuse me, missy,' several times, neither Elizabeth nor the huge golden-haired man at the piano paid her the slightest attention.

The long afternoon tapered to dusk. Rachmaninov followed Beethoven; Grieg followed Rachmaninov; Mozart followed Grieg.

The windows were open to the scent of the flowers and the light breeze blowing across the bay. Two gulls skimmed low over the water, dark shadows identifiable only by their long grieving cry. At last, when it was too dark to see any more without leaving the piano and switching on the lamps, Elizabeth leaned back on the piano stool, saying apologetically: 'I'm exhausted, Roman. Whatever is the time?'

'It's time to eat,' he said, closing the piano lid. 'Are there any Polish restaurants in Hong Kong?'

She flexed her tired fingers. 'If there are, I don't know of them. Would you like to eat here? Mei Lin is a very good cook.'

'I'm sure she is,' Roman said agreeably, 'but I think I would like to take you out on the town. I'm staying at the Peninsula and I thought it would be a good idea if we had dinner there. It's one of Raefe's favourite haunts, isn't it?'

She rose to her feet with a smile. 'It's the haunt of every expatriate on the island. If we're going there, I need to change my dress. I spent all morning gardening in this, and it's full of grass and azalea stains.'

'I'll wait for you outside,' he said, walking across to the open door that led to the terracotta pots awash with flowers. 'I want to look at the sea by moonlight. No wonder the two of you love this house. Its setting is pure theatre.'

'I'll send Mei Lin out with a drink for you,' she said, wondering in amusement who would see them dining

121

together at the Pen and what sort of harebrained rumours would result.

She discarded her cotton dress and slipped on a pale mauve voile dress that swirled softly about her legs. Raefe would want her to be a credit to Roman, and she complemented the dress with ivory stockings and ivory kid pumps, sweeping her hair high into a smooth chignon, clasping a heavy rope of pearls around her neck. It was almost as if she were going out on a date and she sat down suddenly on the edge of the bed, overcome with panic. What on earth was happening to her? She loved Raefe. She loved him utterly and completely, and it was impossible that she could feel any emotional or sexual attraction for anyone else. But she had.

The closeness that had sprung up between Roman and herself while they had played Beethoven and Mozart and Grieg together had not just been the closeness of two friends with a shared talent. It had been stronger than that. So strong that she knew with brutal honesty that if it hadn't been for her commitment to Raefe, and her deep love for him, the closeness between her and Roman would have transcended the mental and become physical.

Shocked at her own vulnerability, she went downstairs to join him. He turned towards her, his thick unruly hair gleaming gold in the moonlight, his eyes crinkling at the corners as he smiled down at her. Her panic ebbed, and a feeling of safety swept over her. Whatever her own vulnerability, Roman had a moral strength that could be trusted absolutely. He was Raefe's friend and he was her friend, and it was a friendship he would never violate.

They drove to Victoria in the jeep, the night air warm and scented. Early stars, king stars, burned bright and steadfast, and the moon was pale and luminous as they sped down Chai Wan Road, Pottinger Peak looming dark and magnificent on their left.

In Wanchai the neon lights flashed on and off with dazzling brilliance, a cacophony of noise emanating from the bars and nightclubs.

122

'Just the place for a quiet night out,' Roman said with a broad grin. The laughter that always seemed such a part of being with him welled up inside her.

'The night is only just beginning here. Things don't really start to hot up until the early hours of the morning!'

The Peninsula's dining-room was full as usual, but they had no trouble obtaining a table. Roman had already made a reservation for three, and as Raefe's place-setting was speedily cleared away a sharp pang of regret knifed through Elizabeth.

'I think someone is trying to attract your attention,' Roman said as a waiter brought them long ice-cold gin and tonics. 'The red-haired lady, over there on the left.'

Elizabeth looked in the direction he indicated and encountered Julienne's raised eyebrows and astonished expression. Ronnie, who was for once at her side, looked merely startled at the sight of Elizabeth with a man he had never seen before, but Julienne was in a fever of curiosity.

'Who is he?' she mouthed, collapsing in a fit of giggles as Elizabeth teasingly raised her shoulders as if to say that she didn't know.

By the time their second drink and the menu had arrived, Julienne could contain her curiosity no longer. Promising Ronnie that she would be no longer than five minutes, she rose from their table, making her way, hips swaying seductively, between the tables to join them.

Elizabeth's amusement deepened as she introduced them and saw the naked approval in Julienne's violet-blue eyes.

'*Enchanté*', Julienne said, her eyes sparkling as she sat herself in the chair that had been reserved for Raefe. 'Will you be staying long in Hong Kong, Roman?'

She rolled the first letter of his name in her provocative accent, and Elizabeth could see Roman's smile deepen.

'Unfortunately not,' he said. 'My ship sails in the morning,' and Elizabeth was sure there was genuine regret in his voice. There was certainly genuine regret in Julienne's as she said, her cheeks dimpling prettily: 'That is a pity,

123

*n'est ce pas?* It would have been nice for us to have made friends.'

Elizabeth suppressed her laughter with difficulty. She knew exactly the kind of friendship Julienne had in mind and wondered, not for the first time, where Julienne found her inexhaustible energy.

As the waiter came to take their orders, Julienne rose reluctantly to her feet. If Roman Rakowski was leaving Hong Kong in twelve hours' time, then it was pointless prolonging their meeting; nothing delightful could come of it. All the same, she envied Elizabeth her dinner date, and her eyes, as they met Elizabeth's, indicated that she did.

'Au revoir,' she said to Roman as he rose to his feet; and then, her laughter-filled eyes meeting Elizabeth's, she said, *sotto voce*: 'Be good, *chéri!*'

Roman, as aware of the quality of the rapport that had sprung up between them earlier as Elizabeth had been, and aware of what had ignited it, steered clear of music as a subject as they ate dinner. Instead, he talked about the war in Europe and his hopes of a commission in the Royal Air Force.

'I first started flying when I was in America. Raefe used to let off steam on the polo field, but I've been in love with flying ever since an uncle took me up in a Curtiss Jenny when I was eight years old. If it hadn't been that I loved music more, I would have made flying a full-time career. Now, for a time at least, I'm going to have to.'

Elizabeth was silent. In previous wars, Britain had had to rely on her navy and her sailors. Now she was relying on men like Roman. Men volunteering to fly Hurricanes and Spitfires against the might of the German Luftwaffe.

After dinner, and after she had introduced him to Mei Kuei, her favourite rose-flavoured Chinese liqueur, they left the Peninsula and she suggested that she take a taxi back home and leave him to get an early night before his departure the next day.

'Nonsense,' he said in a voice that brooked no argument. 'I shall enjoy the drive. The landscape fascinates me. By moonlight, it's pure Grand Guignol.'

They spoke very little on the drive back towards the east coast. The night air was now cold, and Roman slipped his jacket around her shoulders, ignoring her protests that he would freeze without it.

'I'm a hardy animal,' he said, his white teeth flashing in the darkness as he grinned across at her.

Male tweed tickled the nape of her neck and her cheeks as she snuggled warmly down in it. He would need to be hardy to survive the rigours that lay ahead of him. She was filled with sudden terror for his safety, shuddering at the mental image of his plane spinning down in flames over the English Channel.

'What's the matter?' he asked, looking swiftly across at her. 'Still cold?'

'No,' she lied, wishing fervently that Raefe was with them, knowing that if he had been he would have sensed her fears and her reason for them.

The whitewashed walls of the house gleamed silver in the moonlight as they approached, the scent of hibiscus and azaleas still heavy in the air.

He slowed to a halt, turning off the jeep's engine, walking round to help her as she stepped on to the uneven ground in her perilously high heels. 'I won't come in,' he said gently, before she had time to ask him. 'Give my love to Raefe. And keep safe, both of you, till this bloody war is over and we meet again.'

He didn't touch her, didn't kiss her goodbye, or hug her, as he had done when they had parted in Perth, and she was deeply grateful.

'Goodbye, Roman,' she said, her voice breaking slightly, uncomfortably aware that the flame that had sprung up between them earlier had erupted once more into life.

'*Do widzenia*,' he said, his voice suspiciously gruff. 'Goodbye, Elizabeth. God bless.'

She turned quickly, walking into the house and not looking back. As she closed the door behind her she could hear the sound of the jeep's engine revving into life and its ever-receding throb as it sped away.

Next morning, even before she was dressed, the telephone rang imperiously; and she knew, as she hurried to answer it, that the caller would be Julienne.

'I thought you might not be in,' Julienne's voice said mischievously. 'I thought that perhaps you would be waving goodbye to Roman's ship.'

'No,' Elizabeth said serenely, refusing to take the bait. 'And now that you have found me respectably at home have you any other reason for calling?'

Unabashed, Julienne admitted that she hadn't. 'You never told me how *devastatingly* handsome Roman Rakowski was when you met him in Perth,' she chastised. 'I thought all musicians and conductors were slim and slender and effeminate. I had no idea he was such a big *gorgeous* hunk of a man!'

Despite herself, Elizabeth laughed, vastly amused at Julienne's misconceptions as to the physical attributes of the greater majority of the musical profession.

'What I can't get over', Julienne continued, with a note of awe in her voice, 'is how *alike* Roman and Raefe are. I know that Raefe is very dark and Roman is startlingly fair and, though they are both tall and broad-shouldered, they are built differently. Roman is a huge *bear* of a man, whereas there is a lean lithe whippiness about Raefe, but despite those differences there is *still* something uncannily similar about them.' She giggled. 'Perhaps it is because there is something feral and a little primitive about both of them. Raefe doesn't give a damn about accepted standards of social behaviour, and I doubt if Roman does, either. It makes both of them very exciting.' She gave a pleasurable sigh, but whether at the thought of Roman or of Raefe, Elizabeth wasn't sure. 'Are you playing tennis today?' she continued, abandoning a subject Elizabeth knew that she would return to again. 'Helena said she would be at the club at lunch-time, and I think Alastair is going to try to be there as well.'

'I don't know,' Elizabeth said vaguely. 'I'll see,' She said goodbye and put the receiver down, knowing that the last thing she wanted at the moment was an afternoon of social gossip at the club. All she wanted was for Raefe to come home. And to be at home when he did so.

When he did return, late the following afternoon, she rushed out of the house to greet him, hurtling into his outstretched arms. 'Darling! I thought you were *never* going to come home! It seems as if you've been away for *ages!*'

He hugged her tight, kissing her deeply. Rapturously content, she twined her arm around his waist as they walked back together into the house.

'We had a surprise visitor while you were away. One you will have been sorry to have missed.'

'I find that hard to believe,' he said, and as he grinned down at her the quality of his smile was so much like Roman's that she missed her step and stumbled against him. His arms tightened around her, and she said, an odd little note in her voice: 'It was Roman.'

They walked up the outside stone steps, past the terracotta pots ablaze with flowers, and into the long large room that they used as a sitting-room.

'Then, you're right,' he said, looking down at her, sensing that something had disturbed her and wondering what it was. 'I am sorry to have missed him. What the devil is he doing in Hong Kong?'

They sat down on a white-upholstered sofa, and she leaned against him. 'He isn't here any longer. He'd been to Australia again and he was just passing through on his way to London. He's going to apply for a commission in the Royal Air Force.'

'I thought he might,' Raefe said, his voice suddenly grim.

They sat in silence for a moment or two, his arm around her shoulders and her head resting against his chest. After a little while he said curiously: 'And what is it that happened whilst he was here that has so disturbed you?'

Her head flew upwards, her eyes meeting his, wide with amazement. 'How on earth do you know that anything has?'

He chuckled and pulled her closer. 'I know everything about you, my love. I know when you're happy and when you're unhappy, and I know when you're fretting your head over something. Now, what is it? Did he ask you to play for him and did you lose your nerve? Or, even worse, did he not ask you to play for him?'

She said slowly: 'It's nothing like that. I did play for him, and he played for me. He's a marvellous pianist.' She hesitated, wondering how she could tell Raefe of the fierce sexual attraction that had sprung up between them as they had played, and which they had both been so painfully aware of. Surely she couldn't tell him such a thing had happened. It didn't mean that her love for him wasn't one hundred per cent total, and that she would ever, in a million years, be unfaithful to him.

His dark eyes held hers, and she knew with a rush of thankfulness that he *would* understand. Between her and Raefe there had never been any secrets and there would be none now. She said awkwardly, sliding her fingers through his, clasping his hand tightly on her lap: 'We played for hours, all afternoon and until it was quite dark, then he took me for dinner at the Peninsula.' She paused, searching for the right words, and he waited patiently, knowing already what it was she was trying so hard to explain to him.

'It was a wonderful experience, Raefe. The music drew us together, and it was as if . . . as if. . . .'

'As if you were lovers?' he asked gently.

She gasped, as if she had been struck on the chest. 'You know! How can you possibly know?'

He fought down the loving laughter that surged up in his throat. 'Because I know you, my love. And I know Roman. And I know what kindred spirits you are. I also know how powerful and erotic such a shared experience can be.'

'Oh!' Relief overwhelmed her. 'I couldn't understand what was happening to me, or why. . . .'

'For a beautiful, wonderfully talented woman, there are times when you are touchingly naïve, my love. Music *is*

128

sexual. At least, I know it is for Roman, and I'm pretty sure it is for you as well. I'm not surprised the sparks flew when the two of you were together.' His winged eyebrows pulled together slightly. 'It wasn't anything deeper than that, was it? You've not suddenly discovered that he's the great love of your life?'

'No, silly,' she said, reaching her hand up and touching his face tenderly. '*You* are the great love of my life! I love everything about you. The way your hair looks blue in the sunlight, the tiny motes of gold that fleck your eyes.' Her voice became husky. 'The touch of your hands on my flesh. . . .'

As she spoke he had begun kissing her, his mouth moving from her temples to her cheekbone, to the corners of her mouth.

'I love you completely and utterly,' she whispered as he slid her down beneath him on the sofa, 'and I always will. Always and for ever.' And then, for a long time, neither of them spoke again.

The news from Europe continued to be grim. France fell. The Germans marched into Paris. In darkened cinemas in Victoria and Kowloon, the Pathé News left expatriates in no doubt at all as to what was happening half a world away. By the end of the summer, the Battle of Britain was under way, the skies above the English Channel thick with Spitfires and Messerschmitts. The Blitz followed. Night after night London was bombed, the flickering newsreels recording horror and devastation, and the dogged refusal of Londoners to be defeated.

In Hong Kong, signs advertising first-aid classes and air-raid precaution lectures proliferated. Work was renewed on defence positions. Barbed wire sprang up around the golf-course at Fanling. More pillboxes were erected. Ammunition-dumps were sited in the hills, discreetly camouflaged. In Kowloon and Victoria sandbags protected government buildings. Beaches were closed to the public and covered with wire fences and machine-gun posts.

In November, Raefe received a letter from Roman in which he said that he had been successful in joining the Royal Air Force, fighting alongside Polish and American volunteers. The letter was heavily censored, and subsequent letters were rare and so briefly worded that the only information they gave was that he was still alive.

They spent Christmas at the house, putting a fir tree up in the large drawing-room and decorating it with tinsel and baubles. Melissa had moved back into the home she had once shared with Raefe, on the Peak. It had been over two months since her last injection of heroin, and she had emerged from her long ordeal quieter and more reflective.

'I'd thought of inviting her to spend Christmas Day with us,' Raefe said to Elizabeth as he helped her fix coloured streamers across the hall.

'Then, why didn't you?' she asked him. She had still not met Melissa, but they had talked several times on the telephone and a hesitant friendship had sprung up between them.

'She's spending the day with Derry. Apparently his affair with Julienne is not going too smoothly at the moment. She's spending less and less time with him and has told him she can't see him at all over the holidays.'

Elizabeth secured the last paper streamer and stood back to admire it. 'Ronnie will be pleased. I don't think he has a girlfriend at all now.'

Raefe grinned. 'Julienne has quite some way to go before she's in the same position. Even if she puts an end to her affair with Derry, there's still her little liaison with Tom. That's been going on ever since Lamoon disappeared.'

They were silent for a moment. Lamoon's disappearance had affected Tom deeply. He rarely socialized now and, apart from Julienne, there had been no subsequent girlfriends.

'What's he doing for Christmas?' Elizabeth asked, frowning in concern.

'God knows. Helena asked him to spend the day with

her and Alastair and Adam, but he refused. I asked him to come to us, but he said he'd prefer not. As Ronnie and Julienne are coming, I can't say I blame him. I don't suppose Julienne would mind, but Ronnie might.'

'Poor Tom,' Elizabeth said compassionately as Raefe's arm slid around her shoulders. 'I can't bear to think of him being so unhappy. Perhaps if he knew for certain what had happened to Lamoon he would be able to begin to forget her.'

'If he knew what had happened to her,' Raefe said sombrely, 'it might even make it worse.'

There was a glimmer of good news in January when Tobruk fell to the Allies, but there was no other good news. German U-boats continued to sink Allied shipping in the Atlantic. German planes continued to bomb London and major cities such as Bristol and Plymouth and Glasgow.

'I feel so guilty,' Elizabeth said to Julienne as they kneeled on the floor of a church hall at a first-aid meeting, cutting up old sheets for bandages. 'Everything is so horrible. Hitler and Mussolini, and London being ravaged by bombs. . . .'

'Why feel guilty?' Julienne, who had never felt guilty in her life, asked practically. 'You are not responsible for Hitler and Mussolini, are you?'

Elizabeth grinned. 'Don't be an ass, Julienne.'

'Then, why feel guilty?' Julienne persisted.

Elizabeth leaned back on her heels. 'Because it is such a terrible time for so many hundreds of thousands of people, and because I have never been so happy.'

'*Alors*! Is that all?' Julienne asked in disbelief. 'Never feel guilty about happiness, Elizabeth. It is far too precious an experience. Do you think this bandage will ever be of any use? It started off three inches wide, and now it's nearly a foot wide! It will have to be a very curiously shaped soldier who finds need of it!'

# 8

In March, Raefe and Melissa's divorce was made absolute. 'Now there is only your divorce to wait for,' Raefe said to Elizabeth, holding her close. 'Why the devil do these things take so long?'

She hadn't answered him. After her stillborn baby, Adam had begun to waver about the wisdom of a divorce. He had withdrawn proceedings and had only recently, reluctantly instituted them once again. She said instead: 'Will Melissa leave Hong Kong now?'

Raefe frowned slightly. His sense of responsibility for Melissa was still strong, but the future he had envisaged for her, and which she had been looking forward to so much, was now no longer possible. A return to London was out of the question. And Melissa had no friends or family in Australia or America. 'I don't know,' he said, his frown deepening. 'There was a time when she couldn't wait to shake the dust of Hong Kong off her heels. Now she says she would much rather stay here than go to a place she doesn't know.'

'You can't blame her. I wouldn't want to go alone to Australia or America, either.'

They were silent, both of them knowing that the day might come when she would have to go. Last summer's invasion scare had died down, and many of the women who had left aboard the evacuee ships had returned; but, though an increasing number of people now believed it would never happen, invasion by the Japanese was still a possibility.

'It might help if her father could be persuaded to leave for Perth or Los Angeles,' he said, his voice full of exasperation as it always was when he spoke of his former father-in-law. 'She won't live with him here, but she might in a different environment.'

'Have you told him that?'

His mouth tightened. 'I've tried to, but he won't even speak to me on the telephone, let alone meet me!'

Three hours later he drove up to the Peak to speak to Melissa. She was on the telephone when he arrived, but she brought her conversation to a quick conclusion, saying: 'That will be lovely, Julienne. I'll look forward to it.'

'Was that Julienne Ledsham?' Raefe asked as he moved towards the drinks-trolley, pouring himself a Scotch and soda.

'Yes.' Her voice was stilted. She had received the same documentation in the post that morning as he had, and she had known that he would call to see her. She had had a long time in which to adjust to the idea of no longer being his wife, and she had thought she had done so. The sensation of bitter shock she felt at the reality came as an unpleasant surprise.

He dropped a couple of ice cubes into his drink. There had been a time when he had been unable to approve of any of her friends. Now he said with a grin: 'What is Julienne up to these days? Is she still leading Derry a dance?'

Melissa felt her tenseness begin to seep away. 'Yes,' she said, a slight smile touching her mouth. 'The last time I saw him he said he was thinking of asking her to marry him.'

At the thought of a confirmed bachelor like Derry even contemplating marriage, Raefe's grin deepened. 'He stands no chance. Julienne is quite happy as she is.'

The slight smile that had touched Melissa's mouth faded. There was never any dislike in Raefe's voice when he spoke of Julienne, and yet Julienne was quite immoral. When *she* had behaved in a similar fashion, he had not

133

shown an iota of tolerance. He had simply refused ever to sleep with her again. She said, with an edge to her voice: 'The Ledsham marriage survives adultery. Why didn't ours?'

He felt a familiar heaviness weigh on his shoulders. Because you are not Julienne, he wanted to say. Because there was no generosity in your promiscuity. No regard for my pride. No love for anyone but yourself. He said instead: 'Because we are not Julienne and Ronnie. When they married, it was with the understanding that faithfulness was not necessary to them. It was for me. It still is.'

'And is Elizabeth faithful to you?'

'Yes.' There was no doubt in his voice. No equivocation.

She felt a flare of her old vindictiveness, wishing with all her heart that he would, one day, find his precious Elizabeth in bed with another man. Jealousy surged along her veins. If he did, would his reaction be the same as it had been with her? Would he discard her and never have anything more to do with her? Or had he discarded her so totally because he had been *relieved* by her adultery? Because it had given him the excuse he needed to free himself of her? She said passionately, with sudden insight: 'My unfaithfulness didn't end our marriage! Our marriage was over long before I tried to make you jealous by sleeping with someone else! It was over within weeks of the wedding when you realized that you weren't in love with me! That you had never been in love with me!'

He turned away from her, unable to deny it, putting his glass back down on the trolley. 'I came here to talk about the future, not the past,' he said tersely. 'You know that you can have the use of this house for as long as you want, but you need to think of where you're going to go when you leave here.'

'London,' she said with equal curtness. 'When this bloody war is over and life returns to normal.'

He sighed, aware that their new-found friendliness was fast slipping away. 'God knows when that will be,' he said, turning once more to face her. 'Hong Kong isn't the safest place in the world, Mel. I'd rest far easier if you were in America or Australia.'

Her eyes met his unflinchingly. 'Elizabeth isn't in America or Australia. Julienne isn't. Nor is Helena Nicholson or Miriam Gresby or a score of other women I could mention. I don't particularly want to stay here, though things aren't quite so bad now that I seem to be socially acceptable once more. If the Germans weren't intent on bombing London to a pulp, I'd be on the first ship home. As it is, I'll wait. Living alone in a city I don't know holds no appeal for me at all.'

'What if I could persuade your father to leave as well?'

She gave a derisive laugh. 'My God! The thought of my father in Australia hardly makes Australia more palatable! And he certainly wouldn't go if the suggestion came from you. He still thinks you're hell-bent on ruining me. If you suggested he should accompany me to Australia, he'd be convinced it was because you had inside information and knew that the Japs were about to land there at any moment!'

He knew that what she said was true. 'Would you leave if Julienne left?' he asked, his eyebrows arching curiously.

'I might, but I can't imagine Julienne leaving without Elizabeth. And I can't imagine the three of us decorously sitting out the war together, can you? The best you can hope for is that Hitler comes to a sticky end, the Germans say "Sorry, chaps" and beat a hasty retreat to their own borders, and the Japanese don't get ideas above their station. Then no one will have to go anywhere unless they want to, and those that do want to will be able to go where they choose. Which in my case is London.'

Raefe chuckled, knowing that there was no use in pursuing the subject further, at least for the time being. ' 'Bye, Mel,' he said, relieved that they were at least parting amicably. 'Give my regards to Julienne when you see her.'

She felt a catch in her throat, not wanting him to go. Not wanting to be left. ' 'Bye,' she said, digging her nails into her palms. Damn it all, she was a grown woman, not a child! And her new-found pride would not allow her to pine any longer after a man who had never loved her. ' 'Bye,' she said more firmly, walking to the door with him. She was going to Julienne's party in an hour's time. She wondered whether to wear her red chiffon or her sapphire-blue silk, and decided on the red chiffon. It would be her first night out as a newly single woman. And at Julienne's anything could happen.

Julienne wandered through her flower-filled drawing-room, checking that the houseboys had distributed enough ashtrays and enough small dishes of savouries. She enjoyed giving parties and did so with effortless ease. However, this evening's party was going to be one with a difference. It was going to be the last party she would ever give as a happily faithless wife.

The flowers were perfect. She had arranged them herself earlier in the day, great lavish bouquets of jungle flowers that filled the house with heady fragrance. In the dining-room, on the buffet-table, silver gleamed and cut glass shone. It was really quite a momentous occasion. The beginning of a life of monogamy, perhaps even of mother-hood. A small smile played on her wide full mouth. The idea had at first appalled and then intrigued her. But before her plans could be put into practice there were one or two things that had to be dealt with.

The first little difficulty was Derry. She was excessively fond of Derry. He possessed a careless gaiety and a zest for life that matched her own. And he was an extremely satis-fying lover. She sighed a little. She was going to miss her laughter-filled, crazily athletic, passionate afternoons with Derry. She restraightened an already perfectly straight Georgian silver table-knife. It was a pity, but it was a neces-sity. She could no longer bear to see Ronnie looking so downcast. He tried to hide his dejection from her, still resolutely flirting with all her friends, but she knew that he did so without any real enthusiasm. It was as if he had outgrown his days of philandering and was waiting wistfully for her to follow suit.

She stepped back from the laden table, appraising it for a second time. So . . . she had come to her decision, and there would be no more Derry, and no more Tom, and no one to replace them. It would, no doubt, be strange at first, but Ronnie would be happier and that would be compensation enough. All that remained was to inform Tom and Derry of her decision.

She crossed to the cocktail-cabinet, mixing herself a very dry Martini. Derry would think she had taken leave of her senses. He might even miss her quite deeply, but he would recover. She wasn't worried about Derry. It was Tom who was causing her concern. She opened the french windows, stepping from the dining-room on to the terrace that ran the breadth of the house. Fairy-lights had been strung among the trees, and Chinese lanterns glowed in the deepening dusk. Tom was not in love with her, but she had become his one source of comfort. Since Lamoon's disappearance, he had withdrawn into himself, no longer socializing, blaming himself for what had happened and for the suffering he was sure Lamoon was undergoing.

No, she could not leave Tom with the same ease as she could leave Derry. He would not trouble to find a replacement for her and he would need one, very much. As it was a task he would not undertake for himself, she knew that she must do it for him, though without his knowledge. She had pondered long and hard over a suitable candidate and had been surprised at the conclusion she had reached. Melissa Langdon.

She wondered at first if her usually sound judgement was letting her down, but on reflection had decided that it wasn't. Melissa was beautiful, lonely, and emotionally insecure. Tom was a good-looking man who possessed a strong sense of protectiveness. The battle that Melissa had successfully waged against heroin addiction would raise her in his estimation, not diminish her. The more Julienne thought about it, the more sure she became. Tom's old-fashioned gallantry had been appalled at the public disclosure of Melissa's private life at the time of Raefe's trial, but Julienne felt that his dismay had been more for the humiliation that Melissa had endured than it had been for the revelations themselves. From the front of the house there came the distant sound of a doorbell ringing. Her guests were beginning to arrive. She sipped the last of her Martini, put down her glass and stepped back into the house to greet them.

By the time Derry arrived the ground-floor rooms were crammed with people, the crush crowding the stairs and spilling out into the garden.

'How are you, old boy? Nice to see you,' Leigh Stafford said to him expansively as he eased himself into the drawing-room trying to locate Julienne.

'Hello there, Derry. Are you going to be playing in the rugger match against the Middlesex?' someone else shouted to him.

A white-jacketed houseboy squeezed his way towards him, proffering a tray of drinks.

'I hear that horse of Ronnie's is still performing miracles!'

'And so it looks as if poor old Roger will have to marry the girl now!'

The laughter and raised voices were deafening. Derry ignored the back-slapping from old acquaintances, continuing his search for Julienne. It didn't perturb him in the least that the party was in her marital home. What did disturb him was the presence of Tom Nicholson's Packard in the drive outside. His suspicions about Julienne and Tom had increased over the last few months, but he still wasn't sure. Were they having an affair? Or was the idea ridiculous? He pushed his way towards the far side of the room where he thought he could see the tell-tale glint of Titian hair. God damn it! She *couldn't* be having an affair with Nicholson! He was too taciturn. Too strait-laced. Sir Denholm Gresby detained him, wanting to know if it was true that Ronnie's horse was odds-on favourite for

Saturday's race. Derry didn't know and didn't care. A peal of delighted laughter confirmed that it *was* Julienne in the centre of the nearby dinner-jacketed group, and as he approached them he saw that one of the dinner-jackets belonged to Tom Nicholson.

He pushed his way determinedly to her side.

'*Alors, chéri!* How lovely to see you!' Julienne said uninhibitedly, kissing him on the cheek. 'You know Tom, don't you? And Charles Mills, and Graham Storey. . . .'

'I want to talk to you!' he hissed in her ear.

'Later, *chéri.* For the moment I have to be the hostess.' Her voice was regretful. When Derry approached her in a crowded room with that look in his eyes, and that expression in his voice, it meant not that he wanted to talk to her, as he said, but that he wanted a quick reckless coupling in a bathroom or a convenient bedroom.

The last exhilarating escapade had been when they had excused themselves from the table at a mutual friend's dinner-party. The nearest available room had been a spare guest-room, the bed piled high with coats. Julienne had been fascinated to discover, as she rearranged her lingerie, that the topmost coat on which they had just fornicated belonged to Miriam Gresby. Ever since, whenever she had seen it on its owner's back, she had eyed it with affection and a dimpling smile of reminiscence.

'To hell with being a hostess!' Derry whispered savagely. 'I need to talk to you, Ju!'

She shook her head firmly. '*Non!*' she said, turning away from him to greet Melissa who had just entered the room. 'Later, *chéri!*'

There was nothing he could do. Tom Nicholson was regarding him coldly. Mills and Storey were eyeing him curiously, and his sister was approaching them, wearing a dazzling red chiffon dress and something of her old sparkle.

'Nice to see you out and about,' he said to her when Julienne had kissed her and completed the introductions.

'Nice to *be* out and about,' she said drily. Both of them

knew that since her return from the New Territories she had not been inundated with party and dinner invitations. The truth, not believed at the time of the trial, had since gained credence. Melissa Elliot *was* a heroin addict. The fact that she had apparently beaten her addiction cut no ice with the leaders of European Hong Kong Society. They had been extremely reluctant to welcome her back into the fold, and social invitations had been few and far between. It had been Julienne, inviting her to join their party at the racecourse, at the beach, at the tennis club, who had turned the tide.

'I say, you're looking pretty gorgeous,' Ronnie Ledsham said to her, coming up to them and slipping his arm around her shoulders. 'How about coming out on to the terrace for a dance?'

He was wearing a sharkskin suit, a silk shirt, and handmade shoes. His blond hair was glossily slicked back, his moustache was meticulously trimmed. There had been a time when she had referred to him disparagingly as an upper-class spiv. She did so no longer. Beneath his heavy-handed flirtatiousness was an easygoing tolerance, and tolerance was a quality she had begun to appreciate.

They weaved their way through the crush and out towards the terrace, and Derry turned once more towards Julienne. She was deep in conversation with Tom Nicholson, and he ground his teeth frustratedly. God damn it! What on earth did she see in the man? And why didn't Ronnie put a stop to it? Was he blind?

The conversation showed no sign of coming to a conclusion and was obviously one that would not have welcomed interruption. He turned away bad-temperedly in search of another drink. The present state of affairs couldn't continue. He would have to have a serious talk with Julienne and soon.

'It really would be a favour to me, *chéri*,' Julienne was saying, her pansy-dark eyes holding Tom's.

'What? Taking Melissa Elliot to the Government House dinner?'

'I know you've been invited ...,' she continued coaxingly.

'And don't intend to go.'

'It is exactly the sort of function that Melissa needs to be seen at again. She has suffered very much, *chéri*, since that terrible trial. Even Raefe has said how very gallant she has been.'

'I'm sure she has, but I can't see that it's any reason for me—'

Julienne squeezed his arm lovingly. 'It is not nice to be a social outcast, Tom. Nor to be lonely, especially when one is so unaccustomed to it. I think you will find the new Melissa very different from the old Melissa.'

'I should hope so,' Tom said feelingly. 'The old Melissa would have eaten me for breakfast!'

Julienne giggled. 'The new Melissa will not do so. I think you will like her very much. She needs someone strong to help her not to care about the gossip and the wagging tongues.'

'All right,' he said reluctantly. 'I'll take her to the Government House dinner, but after that she's on her own again, Julienne. I'm not going to make a habit of squiring her around.'

'Of course not,' Julienne said demurely. 'And now, *chéri*, I think that it is time that we talked about ourselves. There is something that I have to tell you. ...'

It was not quite so easy explaining to Derry that their affair was over and that she was, in the future, going to be a faithful wife. They were in one of the upstairs bathrooms, the door securely locked against all those needing its facilities.

'Use the bathroom downstairs!' Derry roared in answer to an enquiring knock upon the door. There was the sound of aggrieved indignation and then a defeated retreat. 'I don't believe you!' he repeated, his handsome raw-boned face perplexed. 'Why is it over? Nothing has gone wrong between us, has it?'

'No, *chéri*. Everything has been most wonderful,' Julienne said sincerely.

'Then, why, in God's name . . .?' He ran a hand through his thick shock of sun-bleached hair, struggling for understanding.

'I am twenty-seven,' Julienne said with a slight shrug. 'It is time I began to think about settling down . . . of perhaps becoming a mother.'

'You can become a mother any time you want,' he said with a sudden grin, refusing to take her seriously. 'Right now, this very minute, would be as good a time as any!'

He had her pinned against the washbasin and he lifted her skirt, pressing close against her.

'No, *chéri*,' she murmured regretfully, refusing to capitulate to the delicious tide of sensations he was arousing. 'No more. It is over. Finished.'

His grin vanished. Concern began to replace perplexity. 'You're joking, Julienne. You have to be. This is just another cock-tease, isn't it?'

Julienne shook her head, wishing that it was. 'No, Derry,' she said, her accent rolling his name in a way that made his scalp tingle. 'No, I have made up my mind. It is sad, but it is necessary.'

He looked down at her in horror. 'You can't do this to me, Julienne! I love you! I want to marry you!'

She giggled, touching his face lovingly. 'I do not think it would be a very good marrige, *chéri*. I would be always knocking on the doors of cloakrooms and bathrooms, trying to retrieve you!'

He had the grace to grin slightly. He couldn't quite imagine Julienne in the role of the slighted wife. 'I do love you, Ju,' he said thickly. 'I've never enjoyed anything as much as I have the time we've spent together.'

'It has been very special,' she agreed, knowing that the hardest part was over and that all that remained was to say goodbye.

He hesitated and then said suspiciously: 'You're not having an affair with Tom Nicholson, are you, Ju?'

Julienne's eyes held his undeviatingly. 'No, *chéri*,' she said emphatically. 'How can you think such a thing?'

'Promise?'

'I promise.' It was true. She wasn't. Not any longer.

He frowned. At least he wasn't being jilted in favour of anyone else. And he might not be jilted for very long. Julienne would surely get bored with faithfulness, and then they could continue their affair as before. He decided to take advantage of the present and not worry about the future. 'If we're going to say goodbye, then we'd better make the last time very good indeed,' he growled, his arms tightening around hers.

She pressed her hands against his chest, pushing him away. '*Non*! Truly, I meant it when I said I was not going to be unfaithful to Ronnie again!'

'You *can't* mean it, Ju!' His eyes were agonized.

From the far side of the door could be heard the sounds of people impatiently queuing for the bathroom. Her mouth quirked at the corners. 'I shall keep my word, *chéri*, but I shall say goodbye in a way you will like very, very much.' And she slipped down on to her knees before him, her fingers reaching for the fly of his trousers, her tongue moistening her lips in delicious anticipation.

In June, Raefe said to Elizabeth as he drove her to Li Pi's Kowloon flat: 'I saw Lamoon yesterday.'

She twisted sharply towards him. 'You did? Where? Who was she with? Did you manage to speak to her?'

He shook his head, a lock of dark hair tumbling low across his brow. 'No. She was with a prosperously dressed Chinese. They were crossing Des Voeux Road.'

He didn't tell her that the Chinese had been holding Lamoon's arm in a viciously tight grip, or that Lamoon had looked like death, her face gaunt, her eyes wretched.

'Does this mean that she's living at home again? That, even if she isn't allowed to socialize with Europeans, we can at least write to her?'

Raefe bore left on the road curving around Chai Wan. 'I

143

doubt it,' he said sombrely. 'I made a few discreet enquiries after I saw her. The man she was with is a distant cousin. He's also her husband.'

'Oh!' Elizabeth sank back into her seat, deflated. 'Then, her father *did* force her into marriage.' She was silent as they motored on towards Shau Kei Wan. After a little while she said hopefully: 'Perhaps her marriage isn't too unhappy. If he is also a cousin, then presumably she has known him a long time. She may even be happy.'

Raefe said nothing. He had seen at a glance that Lamoon was not happy, but he didn't want to distress Elizabeth unnecessarily. It wasn't as if they could do a damned thing about it.

After a little while Elizabeth said curiously: 'Will you tell Tom?'

Raefe changed gear and swept down towards the Wanchai. It was a question he had considered long and hard. 'No,' he said as he overtook a taxi-cab. 'What good can it do? He's going out with Melissa now, and if I told him that Lamoon was back in Hong Kong. . . .' He shrugged expressively. 'It might spoil things between them, and I wouldn't want that.'

'But, if Lamoon is back in Hong Kong, surely other people will see her and tell him? He might even see her himself.'

Raefe shook his head. 'I doubt it. For one thing, I don't think this is anything but the briefest of family visits. For another, as a traditional Chinese wife, she isn't going to be seen in public very often.'

'But we must let him know that she's alive,' Elizabeth persisted.

A trolley-bus rattled along beside them, crammed to the doors with strap-hanging Chinese.

'And that she's married?' Raefe asked, looking towards her questioningly.

Elizabeth hesitated and then nodded. 'Yes. It's best that he knows. He has to realize that it's finally over. That she will never be able to return to him.'

*   *   *

In August, Elizabeth gave her first concert performance since leaving London. She had been ready to do so for a long time. At the Imperial concert hall, in front of the largest audience the Imperial had seen for several months, she played a selection of works by Mozart, Rachmaninov and Berlioz. The music critic of the *Hong Kong Times* was ecstatic, writing that it was 'an outstanding performance played with the utmost skill and grace', and that her piano-playing 'glowed with rare vitality'.

Friends who had thought they knew her quite well were stunned by the extent of her talent. They had expected to hear a few party pieces nicely executed. They had not expected to hear a Mozart piano concerto and Rachmaninov's Rhapsody on a Theme of Paganini played with almost terrifying assurance.

Miriam Gresby decided it would no longer be socially wise to continue shunning her. At the party afterwards, in the Hong Kong Hotel, she manoeuvred herself to the front of Elizabeth's admirers, saying gushingly: 'What a *wonderful* performance, my dear! I remember when I first heard you play, within hours of your arrival in the Colony. I said then to Denholm that you were *outstandingly* gifted. I'm having a small dinner-party next week. I'm hoping that the Governor will be in attendance, and perhaps the French attaché. I would so much appreciate it if you could join us.'

'I'm sorry, Miriam,' Elizabeth said with commendable politeness, 'but I have commitments next week. Perhaps another time?'

'Oh, but I could change the date. . . ,' Miriam Gresby began, but Elizabeth was already talking to someone else. She drew in a sharp angry breath, knowing that she had been snubbed. To her dismay, she saw that Major-General Grassett was among those waiting to give Elizabeth his congratulations. There was no way, if she was to maintain her position as a leader of Hong Kong society, that Elizabeth could remain absent from her dinner-table. She would just have to swallow her pride and approach her at a later date. She turned away, smiling stiffly at those around her, murmuring: '*Wonderful* piano-playing, wasn't it? Of course, I've heard her play privately *many* times before.'

Julienne Ledsham was standing with her husband on the fringe of the throng. Miriam's smile remained fixed. She didn't like Julienne Ledsham, but Julienne was a very close friend of Elizabeth's. Perhaps if she invited the Ledshams to dinner as well. . . .

'What a *glorious* evening it has been,' she said to Julienne, wondering how anyone with red hair could possibly get away with a dress of searing pink. 'I've always known that Elizabeth was *very* talented, of course.'

'Oh, but of course,' Julienne said, her lips quirking in a smile. 'That is a very lovely coat, Miriam.' She touched the sealskin lightly with her forefinger. 'I imagine it is a coat that can give great pleasure, *n'est ce pas?*'

Miriam looked at her as if she were mad. Allowances had to be made for the fact that Julienne was a foreigner and that often her English left a great deal to be desired, but really! Sometimes she was incomprehensible.

'It is a very *serviceable* coat,' she said, wondering if Julienne was somehow making fun of it. 'I find sealskin the only possible fur in a climate like this.'

'*Mais oui*, I quite agree,' Julienne said, her eyes sparkling wickedly. 'It is *very* comfortable indeed!'

'What was all that rot about Miriam Gresby's coat?' Ronnie asked as they moved away and towards Elizabeth.

'Nothing for you to worry about, *mon amour*, she said, tucking her arm in his. 'Nothing at all.'

All through the summer the news from Europe was grim. After the surrender of Tobruk to the Allies in January, Rommel had mounted an advance towards it. By April the city and port were isolated, the remainder of the Allied force having retreated to the Egyptian border. It was still under siege. In the skies above Germany, RAF bombers continued to make night-time sorties, their losses heavy. Roman was a member of 249 Squadron flying a Hurricane.

They received a card from him in September and then, after that, there was nothing.

'Do you think he's still alive?' Elizabeth asked Raefe anxiously. 'What are his chances?'

Raefe had just returned from an intelligence meeting at Fort Canning, and his face was tired and drawn. 'Not high,' he said sombrely.

To the best of his knowledge Roman had been on active operations since August, and he knew that the average lifespan of a pilot was only three months. It was a statistic that didn't bear thinking about.

In November the aircraft-carrier *Ark Royal* was sunk by U-boats, and the Germans were at the gates of Leningrad.

'It's not going to be a very jolly Christmas, is it?' Helena said to Elizabeth as Elizabeth drove her back to her Kowloon flat after one of the auxiliary nursing meetings.

'There's the Chinese Charity Ball at the Pen tomorrow night,' Elizabeth said, trying to look on the bright side of things. 'Alastair is coming, isn't he?'

'Yes, if he can. There's been something of a flap on this last day or two. Rumours that the Japanese are building up their forces beyond the border.'

'We've had those rumours before,' Elizabeth said cynically.

'Yes, I know.' The Lagonda's top was down, and Helena pushed her wind-blown hair away from her face. 'The trouble is we've heard the cry "Wolf" so often, we may not take any notice when it's the real thing. And then we may get taken by surprise. It's not a very nice thought, is it?'

'Major-General Maltby isn't the kind of man to be taken by surprise,' Elizabeth said drily. 'His last command was the North-West Frontier!'

Helena chuckled. Major-General Maltby had replaced Major-General Grassett a month ago and had made an immediate good impression among both troops and civilians. 'He's rather nice, isn't he? Very English and very correct.'

With a smile Elizabeth agreed, drawing up outside

Helena's block of flats. As Helena stepped from the car, she said: 'Are you going to Happy Valley tomorrow to watch Ronnie's horse run?'

Elizabeth shook her head. The nursing classes she now attended had wrought havoc with her disciplined hours of piano practice. The time had to be made up, and she was going to make some of it up the following afternoon. 'No, I'll see you at the Peninsula tomorrow night. 'Bye, Helena.'

She drew away from the kerb and into the main stream of traffic, humming beneath her breath. The world situation was ghastly, but her own personal situation was blissful. She wasn't sure yet, but she was almost certain that she was pregnant again. 'There'll always be an England,' she began to sing softly to herself. 'And England will be free. As long as England means to you what England means to me.' It was the song they sang every Sunday lunch-time when they all met for drinks at the Repulse Bay Hotel.

Her hands tightened on the steering-wheel as she thought of Roman and of the men like him, fighting lone battles in the sky, facing enemy flak night after night. 'Please be safe, Roman,' she whispered as she drove towards the Star Ferry Pier. 'Please, *please* be safe!'

# 9

The Chinese charity ball at the Peninsula had been given the name the 'Tin Hat Ball'. Its purpose was to raise £160,000 towards the purchase of bombers which Hong Kong then intended to present to Britain. As she parked the Lagonda and walked into the brightly lit, flower-filled lobby, Elizabeth wondered if it would achieve its objective.

She had spent all morning and afternoon at the piano, and her back and wrists ached. If Raefe had been at home with her, she knew she would have been tempted to stay there and give the ball a miss. As it was, he had been at an intelligence meeting at Government House since early morning and had arranged that, instead of coming home, he would meet up with her at the Pen.

As she walked through into the ballroom she saw her reflection in one of the giant gilt-framed mirrors. She had begun to wear her hair down again, and it fell in a long smooth wave to her shoulders, pushed away from her face on one side with a tortoiseshell comb. Her dress was of cream silk, the mid-calf-length skirt falling sensuously over her hips in a swirl of soft pleats. Three long strands of enormous pearls hung from her neck at precisely the right depth of the softly draped neckline. They had been her first present from Raefe, and she wore them at every possible opportunity. She stepped into the ballroom, the silk of her skirt rustling softly against her legs.

Julienne and Ronnie, Helena and Alastair were seated at a large round table at the far end of the room. Tom

Nicholson's white-dinner-jacketed figure was also at the table, and with an involuntary tightening of her stomach muscles she wondered where Melissa was. Julienne had never, as yet, invited Tom and Melissa to any gathering at which she and Raefe would also be present, and she was sure that Tom was equally careful.

As she approached them, Ronnie rose to his feet, pulling back a chair for her, and Julienne said lightly: '*Chérie*, how lovely to see you! You're looking wonderful!' Her eyes flicked curiously from Elizabeth to the door. 'But where is Raefe? I understood he was coming, too?'

'He's at a business meeting; he's coming straight on here when it finishes.' Raefe's frequent visits to Government House were a closely guarded secret.

'That is a pity,' Julienne said with genuine regret. 'But you will be able to keep Tom company. Melissa has at last decided that she is going to leave Hong Kong for America, and she has gone to the New Territories, to the farm, to collect the things she wishes to take with her and to arrange for her other possessions to be put into storage.'

Elizabeth breathed a faint sigh of relief. She was not at all apprehensive about meeting Melissa, but she hoped that when she finally did so the occasion would not be quite so public.

Julienne was wearing a turquoise satin ankle-length gown lavishly encrusted with crystals and beads. The bodice was very décolleté, revealing the lush ripeness of her breasts, the back plunging to her waist. Her fox-red hair was a short riotous mass of curls, tiny tendrils springing forward and lying seductively against her cheeks.

'We are all morose,' Julienne continued, not looking in the slightest morose. 'Ronnie's horse behaved very badly this afternoon. He was, I think, not very well.' She began to giggle. 'At the tote I saw Sir Denholm at the five-hundred-dollar window. I think perhaps he is very angry with Ronnie.'

'So are a lot of other people,' Tom said drily. 'Old Gresby wasn't the only one putting a packet on his wretched horse.'

Both Ronnie and Julienne looked blithely unconcerned, and Elizabeth was sure that neither of them had staked any of their money on their own horse, or had lost any.

'What was the Middlesex rugger match like?' she asked Alastair, changing the subject. 'You were there this afternoon, weren't you?'

'The Middlesex have a long way to go before they play a game of rugger equal to the game played by the Royal Scots,' Alastair said with a grin. 'Still, it wasn't a bad game, all in all.'

Rivalry between the 1st Middlesex and the 2nd Royal Scots was intense, with the Royal Scots considering themselves vastly superior.

Ronnie hooted with laughter. 'My God, Alastair! The Middlesex can thrash the Royal Scots to pulp on a rugger pitch, and you know it!'

A waiter, depositing a fresh round of drinks on the table, mercifully subdued Alastair's reply.

The band was playing 'It's Only a Paper Moon', and on the crowded dance-floor Elizabeth could see Leigh Stafford dancing very stiffly with Miriam Gresby, and Derry Langdon moving with practised ease, a diminutive blonde in his arms. Seeing where her gaze was directed, Helena leaned across to her and whispered: 'Derry's latest is Anthea Hurley.'

'Mark Hurley's wife?'

Helena nodded. Elizabeth looked at the china-doll prettiness of Anthea Hurley with interest, well aware that she had once been one of Raefe's girlfriends. She was dancing indecently close to Derry, and Derry, far from looking pleased with the arrangement, was looking distinctly discontented, his gaze roving constantly around the room.

His eyes met hers and shot swiftly from her to Julienne. She saw by the change of expression in their vivid blue depths that he had at last found what he was looking for. The discontent had given place to open misery. Elizabeth looked away from him, feeling sorry for him, but glad that she had no longer to feel sorry for Ronnie.

'What are the two Canadian battalions like, that arrived last month?' Ronnie was asking Alastair, one hand cradling his whisky and soda, the other resting lightly and proprietorially on Julienne's satin-clad knee. 'Are they going to be any good to us if the Japs chance their arm?'

'Any reinforcements are better than none,' Alastair said drily. 'And they appeared fit enough when they landed.'

'They are extremely confident and well equipped,' Julienne said, determinedly avoiding Derry's pleading gaze. 'I saw them just after they disembarked. They were being led through the streets to Shamshuipo barracks by a magnificent army band. They looked wonderful!'

'Maltby must be grateful for them,' Tom said as the band swung into 'Blue Moon'. 'Especially with this flap that's on at the moment.'

A cascade of streamers were released, drifting down over the heads of the dancers.

'It still leaves us dangerously under-strength,' Alastair said, removing a streamer from his shoulders. 'And I've a feeling that this latest flap is the most serious one yet.'

Julienne could see Derry making his way determinedly towards their table, Anthea Hurley hurrying in his wake. 'Let's dance, *chéri*,' she said, her hand closing over Ronnie's. 'In a moment there is to be a floor-show and then we will not be able to.'

Ronnie obligingly rose to his feet, and by the time Derry had weaved his way through the couples on the dance-floor his quarry had flown.

'Hello, Derry old boy,' Tom said affably. 'How is the polo?'

Derry was a renowned player with an incredible nine-goal handicap. 'Fine,' he lied, turning away from them and once more trying to locate Julienne. Since Julienne had terminated their affair his playing on the polo-field had suffered. At his last match he had ridden like a barbarian and had been disqualified in the second chukker for 'riding at an opponent in such a manner as to intimidate and cause him to pull out'. He had been uncaring, his only wish that the player he had unseated had been Ronnie Ledsham.

A breathless Anthea caught up with him and was embarrassingly ignored by him. Tom, aware that she had once been one of Raefe's passing fancies, decided that it might be best if she was not still at their table when Raefe joined them. He rose gallantly to his feet. 'Would you care to dance, Anthea? I'm wretchedly partnerless at the moment.'

Anthea looked at Derry, obviously hoping that he would object, but as no such objection was forthcoming she had no alternative but unwillingly to acquiesce.

'Why the hell won't Julienne let me speak to her?' Derry said savagely to Elizabeth. 'I haven't seen her alone since the night of her party!'

Alastair, who disapproved of all extra-marital affairs, was listening to him frozen-faced, and Elizabeth knew that at any moment angry words would be exchanged. 'Let's dance,' she said to Derry, rising to her feet.

He nodded obligingly, moving out with her on to the dance-floor. 'I don't understand it,' he said gloomily for the thousandth time. 'We were happy together. I've never in my life enjoyed myself as much as I did when I was with Ju. Why has she spoiled everything? Has she suddenly got religion, or fallen sick? What is it?'

As he led her into a smooth quickstep a smile touched the corners of Elizabeth's mouth. 'She certainly hasn't got religion and she isn't sick,' she said soothingly. 'In fact, I don't think Julienne has changed at all. It is Ronnie who has changed. He still flirts, but he hasn't been seen with another woman for nearly a year now.'

'But what has that got to do with Ju?' Derry demanded, mystified.

'Julienne loves him,' Elizabeth said gently as they skimmed past Tom and Anthea Hurley. 'She may have fallen in love lightly and often elsewhere, but her love for Ronnie has always been the mainspring of her life. Once she knew that her affairs were beginning to cause him anguish, she ceased having them. It's as simple as that.'

'It isn't simple to me,' Derry said grimly. 'I can't eat, I can't sleep, I can't think. I can't even play a decent game of polo any longer!'

The dance was at an end, and it was announced that Miss Hilda Yen was now going to sing for them.

'Let her go, Derry,' Elizabeth said to him pleadingly as the couples around them began to return to their tables.

He looked across to where Ronnie was escorting Julienne from the crowded floor. 'I can't!' he said fiercely, a nerve jumping at the corner of his clenched jaw. 'God in heaven! I love her, Elizabeth. I *can't* leave her alone!'

The floor was emptying, and people were beginning to look in their direction. 'You will make her very unhappy if you don't,' Elizabeth said soberly, and then reluctantly she stepped away from him, leaving him where he stood as she walked back to her table.

Hilda Yen, a beautiful Chinese girl with raven-dark hair streaming silkily to her waist, sang a romantic song in Chinese and, while she did so, Elizabeth wondered if her own friends had felt the same despair when she and Raefe had first fallen in love. She empathized totally with Derry. His love for Julienne was dominated by sexual passion, and she knew from her own experience that once in the grip of such joyous madness there was no room for restraint or common sense.

Hilda Yen's song came to an end and was enthusiastically applauded. The dancing continued, and she waltzed with Alastair and foxtrotted with Ronnie, waiting hungrily all the while for Raefe to enter the ballroom and stride towards her.

Raefe's face was grim as he drove through the darkened streets towards the Peninsula Hotel. He had trusted his informers, not his own judgement, and it was a mistake for which he would never forgive himself.

For weeks, all the information he had received from Shanghai and Canton had been adamant that the concentration of Japanese military activity that had begun to take place in and around Canton was a Japanese preparation for an attack on the Chinese city of Kunming to the north-west. Canton was a mere hundred miles north of Hong Kong, and he had not been convinced. He had voiced his doubts to the British at Fort Canning, but the consensus of opinion was that any visible Japanese preparations around Canton were more likely to be defensive than aggressive. They were taken note of. Reports were written and reports were filed.

His jaw tightened as he swerved to a halt outside the Peninsula's glitteringly lit Palladian entrance. Defensive be damned. There was now at least a full division of Japs mustering on the border, and they were facing south, not north.

He strode into the hotel, cursing himself for not having acted earlier. For not having put Elizabeth on a ship or a plane. For allowing her to remain with him.

'Good evening, Mr Elliot,' a junior manager said respect-fully as he crossed the lobby.

'Good evening, sir,' a bellboy said with genuine warmth as he continued on his way towards the ballroom. Mr Elliot was a generous tipper. The bellboy wished there were more like him.

Raefe acknowledged their greetings curtly. He had only minutes in which to speak to Elizabeth before returning to the tense meeting still in progress at Government House. He had excused himself peremptorily, knowing that he had to tell her himself that an invasion was imminent. That he had to see her. That it might be days, even weeks, before he would be able to do so again.

As he entered the crowded ballroom the orchestra was playing 'The Best Things in Life Are Free'. Ignoring the greetings he received from all sides, he made his way quickly to the far end of the room and the large circular table around which Helena and Alastair, Julienne and Ronnie, Tom and Elizabeth were sitting.

Elizabeth turned her head at his approach, her face

lighting up joyously at the sight of him. 'Darling! I thought you were never going to get here!' It was nearly midnight and, though she had disguised it beneath smiles and laughter, her anxiety had been growing.

He took her hand, drawing her to her feet, saying low and urgently: 'I can't stay, Lizzie. The invasion is imminent. Leave now and return to Victoria. You'll be far safer on the island than you will be this side of the water. Whatever happens, don't be tempted to cross back here. Do you understand me?'

'Yes, but—'

'No "buts".' His dark eyes burned hers. 'Be safe for me, Lizzie! That's all I ask!'

His arms closed tightly around her, his kiss hard and savage, almost brutal. 'I love you!' he said harshly as he drew his head away from hers and then, before she had the chance to ask where he was going, what he was going to do, he was gone, pushing his way through the laughing couples that thronged the floor.

'Well!' Julienne said, her eyes wide. 'What was all *that* about, *chérie*?'

Elizabeth did not answer her. She was still staring after Raefe, fear roaring along her veins. What if anything happened to him? What if he were killed? What if . . .?

The music came to an abrupt end. The president of the American Steamships Line appeared on the balcony above the dance-floor, waving a megaphone for silence. 'Your attention, please, ladies and gentlemen! Your attention, please!' he shouted.

Helena and Alastair, Ronnie and Julienne and Tom, who had all been mesmerized by Raefe's sudden appearance and his abrupt passionate leavetaking of Elizabeth, transferred their attention to him, their smiles and laughter fading.

'Any man connected with any ships in the harbour,' the president of the American Steamships Line continued to shout, 'report aboard for duty. At once!'

There was a second's unbelieving silence, and then

scores of chairs were scraped backwards as men rose hurriedly to their feet, the dance forgotten.

'My God! Is this it?' Ronnie asked, stunned.

'Looks like it,' Alastair said grimly. 'I'd better be getting back to barracks.' He rose to his feet. 'Goodbye, my dear,' he said soberly to Helena. 'I'll be in touch with you at the earliest opportunity.'

She stared at him aghast. All around them men were saying goodbye to wives and sweethearts and making for the doors. As Alastair turned to join them, she pushed her chair away from the table, rising hastily to her feet.

'No! Wait a moment, Alastair!'

He turned and hesitated, and she threw her arms around him, hugging him tight. 'I love you!' she said fiercely. 'I know I haven't said it very often lately, but I do, Alastair! Truly I do!'

He didn't speak. He couldn't. He would have wept with relief, for he had begun to believe that she had never loved him and never would. He held her close for a brief precious moment, and then, his eyes suspiciously bright, he swung on his heel, breaking into a run as he made for the doors.

Julienne and Ronnie, Tom and Elizabeth and Helena stared at each other. The orchestra had begun to play again, but only a few couples had taken to the floor.

'What do we do?' Ronnie asked awkwardly. Both he and Tom were members of the Volunteer Force. 'Do we report for duty, too?'

'I shouldn't think so,' Tom said doubtfully. 'Not until there's been a more official announcement.'

'Raefe said that an invasion was imminent,' Elizabeth said in a low voice. 'He also said that when it came the island would be far safer than Kowloon.' She looked across at Helena. 'You'd better move in with me, Helena. We can go and collect the children now.'

Helena shook her head. She was dressed starkly and sophisticatedly in a black cocktail-dress, and it did not suit her full-blown beauty. 'No,' she said stubbornly. 'I have to stay in Kowloon. The hospital I have been assigned to is there.'

157

'Whatever happens, the Japs will never fight their way as far south as Kowloon,' Tom said, defusing the tension. 'All the fighting will be around the border.'

Ronnie grinned, his natural buoyancy reasserting itself. 'We'll soon shove the little men off,' he said confidently. 'To tell the truth, if this *is* the real thing, I shall be relieved. The sooner it starts, the sooner it will be over.'

Elizabeth rose to her feet. 'I'm going home now,' she said quietly. 'Are you sure you won't come with me, Helena?'

Helena shook her head again. 'Positive. By tomorrow everything will have probably blown over. If it has, I'll see you for drinks as usual at the Repulse Bay.'

'I hope it blows over,' Tom said with a wry smile. 'The uniform I've been handed out as a member of the Volunteer Force isn't exactly Sandhurst standard. The jacket was made for a man half my size, and I'm not sure whether the trousers are long shorts or short trousers; whichever they are, I look ridiculous in them!'

Even Elizabeth found herself laughing as she said her goodbyes, but her laughter faded once she was on her journey home. As the vehicular ferry made its way across to Victoria she stood in the bow, looking out over the silk-black sea. The Peak was in darkness. She didn't know where Raefe was, or when she would see him again. For the first time since they had moved into it, she did not drive home to their house near Mount Collinson. Instead she drove to the apartment in Victoria. It was more central. Wherever Raefe was, she would be nearer to him there than she would be out near the coast, on the east of the island.

The next morning Victoria seemed, on the surface, much as usual. She had a light breakfast and then she telephoned Adam. He hadn't been at the ball the previous evening, and there was still a chance that he knew nothing of the latest rumours.

'Mr Harland not here,' Chan said civilly to her. 'Mr Harland a Volunteer. He been called up.'

She put down the telephone receiver, her earlier optimism diminishing. If the Volunteers had indeed been called up and deployed, then it meant that things had gone further than they had ever done before.

She made herself a cup of coffee, drank it and then telephoned Helena. 'It looks as if there'll be no pre-lunch drinks at the Repulse Bay today,' Helena said wryly. 'The whole garrison has been ordered to battle positions, the Volunteers included. The Royal Scots are on the mainland, up near the border. The Volunteers are somewhere on the island. It's all beginning to look extremely grim.'

'Don't you think you should come over here and stay with me?' Elizabeth said again. 'I'm at the apartment in Victoria, not the house. You can travel by ferry to the hospital each day quite easily. . . .'

'Not yet,' Helena said again obstinately.

'But why . . .?'

'It looks so cowardly,' Helena said briefly. 'Can you imagine the panic among the Chinese community of Kowloon if all the Europeans did a quick flit across to the island? There would be pandemonium.'

Elizabeth didn't argue with her. She had met that note of obstinacy in Helena's voice before and knew that arguing was useless. And, at the moment, there was no imminent danger. Whatever fighting took place, it would take place, as Ronnie had said, far to the north of the New Territories, in and around Fanling.

She went cold suddenly, remembering Melissa. 'Oh my God,' she whispered. 'Melissa. . . .'

'What about Melissa?' Helena had not overheard Julienne and Elizabeth's conversation the previous evening.

'She's out at the farm.' She had no need to say any more. Everyone knew that Melissa had spent much of the last two years living in the isolated Elliot farm in the New Territories.

'Does Raefe know she's there?' Helena asked sharply.

'I don't know. . . . He might do. . . . I have to go, Helena. I have to try to get in touch with him!'

159

She put down the receiver with a crash. Where could she start? Government House? Flagstaff House? Fortress Head-quarters? Where was he likely to be? Hastily she dialled the number for Government House, and a harassed male switchboard operator answered the call.

'Could you tell me if Mr Elliot is at Government House, please?'

'I'm sorry, madam, there's an emergency on. No private calls are being taken.'

'This is very urgent! I have to know if he is there or not. If he is, then I can leave a message.'

'I'm sorry, madam, but—'

'Then, please could I speak to Sir Mark Young?' Elizabeth said in her best cut-glass accent. 'It is Elizabeth Harland speaking.'

The switchboard operator hesitated. He had heard of Elizabeth Harland and remembered seeing a photograph of her in the *Hong Kong Times*. She had been at a dinner, and the gentleman sitting next to her had been the Governor.

'I'll see what I can do, Mrs Harland,' he said doubtfully. 'Please hold the line.'

It was nearly ten minutes before the switchboard opera-tor came back to her. 'Mr Elliot is here, Mrs Harland, but he is in conference and is no way he can be disturbed.'

Elizabeth felt her anxiety begin to ease. 'Please give him a message for me. Tell him that Mrs Elliot is at the farm in the New Territories. Have you got that?'

'Yes, Mrs Harland.' The switchboard operator was begin-ning to understand her concern. If the rumours flying around Government House were true, the last place on earth any woman should be was a farm out in the New Terri-tories. 'I'll most certainly see to it that he gets the message,' he said reassuringly.

'Perhaps if you telephoned me back. . . .'

'Yes, Mrs Harland. I'll do that.' The switchboard operator had also remembered that Elizabeth Harland was the stun-ning ice-cool blonde who had caused such a sensation at the Imperial a few weeks ago.

It was half an hour before he telephoned her back. The message had been passed on to Mr Elliot. Elizabeth thanked him and put down the receiver. There was nothing further she could do. She made two more telephone calls. One to Mei Lin, telling her that she would be staying in the flat in Victoria for the next few days and asking her to join her there. The other to her nursing station. There was no need for her to report for duty as yet, but they would appreciate it if she would stand by in readiness.

It was the strangest Sunday in Hong Kong she had ever experienced. There were no pre-lunch drinks at the Repulse Bay Hotel, no parties, no gossip, no water-picnics. All the men, including the Volunteers, were at battle stations. She wondered where Adam was. Alastair had told Helena that the Volunteers were being deployed on the island and not on the mainland. Presumably he would be stationed somewhere on the coast.

When she went for a walk in the afternoon she could see Royal Navy motor torpedo-boats out at sea, guarding the approaches to the Colony. The sight sent a shiver of apprehension down her spine. After so many years of speculation, it seemed that those who had always said the Japanese would eventually attack had been proved right. Certainly the Chinese thought so. They stood in huddled anxious groups, saying to her as she passed by them: 'Is it true the Japanese come soon, missy?' 'Who look after us when the Japanese come?'

'The Japanese will never reach Hong Kong Island,' she said reassuringly, but the Chinese continued to look anxious. For years the Japanese had ravaged China. They knew very well what to expect if the Japanese also overran Hong Kong. The pictures of Japanese soldiers in Manchuria gleefully bayoneting Chinese prisoners had been widely circulated amongst the Chinese community.

Mei Lin arrived at tea-time, not asking where Raefe was or why Elizabeth had decided to spend the next few days in Victoria. She immediately began to prepare a light meal

161

for Elizabeth, grateful that she hadn't been left in isolation on the east coast.

In the evening Elizabeth read through a Moszkowski score and then, unable to concentrate properly, she wandered over to the windows, throwing them open and stepping out on to the veranda, looking down over the rooftops of Victoria to the silk-black bay. The evening was warm and scented, with hardly a breath of air, the setting sun a riot of crimson and vermilion and vivid streaks of yellow, the stillness unpleasantly reminiscent of the threatening calm before a typhoon. She returned to the music score, trying not to wonder where Raefe was, where Adam was. In a few days, if the experts were to be believed, the Japanese would have attacked and been repulsed and life would return to normal. She could only pray that, when it did so, Raefe and Adam, and Alastair and Tom and Ronnie would all be safe.

She slept restlessly, disturbed by the heat and the atmosphere of waiting and watching. At seven o'clock, after lying awake for two hours, she gave up all hope of further sleep and, wrapping a cotton dressing-gown over her nightdress, she wandered into the sitting-room, drawing back the curtains and looking once more out across the bay.

'Would you like coffee and scrambled egg, missy?' Mei Lin asked, hurrying from her own room to be of service.

'No eggs, Mei Lin. Just coffee and toast, please.'

At seven-thirty Mei Lin hurried down into the street to buy the morning paper. This task was usually that of the houseboy, but as he was still in the main house, and as Mrs Elliot had not asked that he remove himself to Victoria, it was a task she happily imposed on herself. When she arrived back at the flat, she was breathless and terrified.

'We are at war, missy! We are at war with Japan!'

Elizabeth snatched the newspaper, but the only reference to Japan was a small paragraph on the front page reporting that Japanese transport ships had been sighted off Thailand.

'Not the paper, missy!' Mei Lin gasped, trembling violently. 'A policeman told me. He say we've been at war with Japan since quarter to five this morning!'

Elizabeth dropped the paper. If it were true, then she had to report immediately to her nursing station. 'Make some more coffee, Mei Lin,' she said, hurrying into the bedroom and quickly scrambling out of her dressing-gown and nightdress. 'I'm going straight to the Jockey Club. I want you to stay here, do you understand?'

It had been arranged months ago that the Jockey Club would serve as a relief hospital. At least it wasn't far to drive.

'Yes, missy, anything you say, missy,' Mei Lin said, bringing the coffee into the bedroom. 'Do you think—?'

A thunderous noise ripped through the still morning air. The coffee-cup crashed to the floor, steaming-hot liquid seeping into the carpet.

'They're coming, missy!' Mei Lin screamed, pressing her hands over her ears. 'Oh, what have we to do? We will all be killed!'

'Don't be silly!' Elizabeth said sharply, bending down and picking up the broken pieces of china. 'It's only the air-raid warning. You've heard practice alerts before!'

Mei Lin began to cry. Not like this, she hadn't. Not at eight o'clock in the morning. 'No, missy!' she protested vehemently. 'The Japanese are coming! Look!'

She was pointing to the window, and as Elizabeth turned swiftly she was just in time to see fighter planes hurtling down on Kai Tak Airport. Her first desperate hope was that they were Royal Air Force planes on manoeuvres, but then the bombs began to rain down, sheets of flame shooting skywards.

'Oh my God!' she gasped, dragging on her skirt and her blouse. 'Put your tin hat on, Mei Lin, and stay indoors!'

'Don't leave me, missy! Please don't leave me!' Mei Lin sobbed as Elizabeth grabbed her own tin hat and began to run towards the door.

'You'll be perfectly all right here,' Elizabeth shouted

back over her shoulder. 'They're bombing the airport, not the residential areas! Just stay indoors till it quietens down!'

She slammed the door after her, running out into the street. She had left the Lagonda parked by the kerb the previous evening, having been too tired to garage it. Now she yanked open the driver's door, pressing her foot down on the clutch, slamming the gears into first. She had been wrong when she had told Mei Lin that the Japanese were only bombing the airport. They were raining down on Kowloon now, columns of smoke billowing skywards. She thought of the hundreds of Chinese refugees cramming the narrow streets and fought back a sob of rage. The casualties would be appalling, and this was only the beginning. God only knew what was to come in its wake.

# 10

For eight hours there was nothing Raefe could do about the message he had received. When at last the strategy meeting he was attending drew to a close, it was ten o'clock at night. He requisitioned a jeep and, ignoring the request that he remain at Government House throughout the night, he drove at high speed through the darkened streets towards the ferry.

He knew that the Royal Scots were at battle stations in the north of the New Territories, and he knew that a platoon of Punjabis and the Volunteer Field engineers had been given instructions to blow all bridges that would give the Japanese access southwards. If the bridges were blown before he could return with Melissa, then the two of them would be helplessly trapped in the path of the advancing Japanese.

The eight-minute crossing seemed interminable. The minute the ferry docked he revved the jeep's engine, pressing his foot down hard on the accelerator, careering through Kowloon's narrow streets and making for the Tai Po road leading north. He was stopped over half a dozen times by army patrols, but his identity-card and rank as an intelligence officer ensured he was detained for only seconds.

Inky darkness pressed in all around him as he hurtled north. God, what a fool he'd been not to have warned Melissa not to leave the Peak. He knew she had finally made up her mind to leave for America but it had never occurred to him that she would return to the farm to collect any of her possessions. Mountain peaks pierced the skyline in black silhouette. At Pineapple Pass, just north of Tai Po, he was stopped by a large contingent of Royal Scots who warned him that the nearby railway line was soon to be blown and the road impassably blocked.

By the time he reached the farm it was nearly two o'clock. There were no lights on, no signs of life, but the minute his jeep approached the houseboys tumbled out into the darkness, their hands high in the air, certain they were being overrun by Japanese.

'Is Mrs Elliot here?' he demanded, vaulting from the jeep and running towards them.

'Oh, yes *tuan*! Missy Elliot asleep. Take us back with you, *tuan*! Japanese come, but Missy Elliot no believe us!'

He ignored them, slamming his way into the house, taking the wide stairs two at a time, shouting 'Melissa! Melissa!'

She stumbled from the bedroom as he ran down the broad corridor towards her. 'What on earth . . .?' she began, her hair tousled, her eyes still glazed by sleep.

'We're at war with the Japs!' he said tersely, seizing her arm and propelling her back into the room. 'Get dressed! The Tai Po road is about to be blocked and the bridges blown!' As he was speaking to her he was rifling through her wardrobe, tossing a skirt and a sweater towards her.

'But my things!' she protested dazedly. 'I haven't finished packing yet!'

'There's no time now, not unless you want to ask the Japs to help you!'

She stared at him, realization of their danger dawning, and then she hurriedly began to slip her arms out of her négligée.

'I'll be waiting for you in the jeep,' he said curtly, turning away from her. 'Be quick, Mel! Every second is vital.'

The minute he was out of the room she slipped her nightdress over her head, pulling on her underclothes, trembling in her haste.

Raefe hurried down the stairs, calling for the houseboys.

'Is anyone else on the premises?' he asked them as they stood shivering in the doorway.

'No, *tuan*, only us. Please, *tuan*, can we . . .?'

'Get in the jeep,' Raefe said tersely.

They obeyed with alacrity. Raefe followed them, revving the engine into life. Where the devil was Melissa? It was at least five minutes since he had left her. Just as he was about to go furiously in search of her, she came running out of the house, her hair still dishevelled, the buttons of her blouse undone, her jacket in her arms.

Even before she had slammed the jeep's door behind her, Raefe was driving off, bucketing over the dusty track that led to the road, fearful that at any moment he would hear the dull blast of the Tai Po road being demolished.

'When did you hear the news?' Melissa gasped, pulling her jacket around her shoulders.

'We haven't yet, officially, but it's no false alarm. There are at least two battalions of Japs only a couple of miles to the north. They'll be fighting their way southwards within hours.'

'Oh God.' She held on tight to the door as the jeep rocked and careered around pot-holes and gullies carved by heavy rain. 'Where is Tom? Do you know?'

He shook his head. 'No. The Volunteers are all on the island, except for the Field Engineers. They're out here with the Royal Scots and the Punjabis, demolishing bridges and making movement difficult for the Japs.'

The jeep thudded on to a smoother road surface, and Raefe pressed his foot down hard on the accelerator. No one knew he had left Government House. With luck, if the Japs held off till daylight, he could be back without anyone being any the wiser about his absence. Without luck, he would be court-martialled before the war had even officially begun.

'How did you know I was out here?' She asked as they thundered down towards Tai Po.

'Lizzie phoned me. I was in a strategy meeting. There wasn't a damn thing I could do about it for hours. Why the hell did you come up here alone? You must have heard the rumours.'

'I've been hearing rumours for over two years,' she said defensively. 'How did Elizabeth know where I was?'

He swerved to avoid a pothole. 'She was at the Chinese Charity Ball at the Pen on Saturday night. Everyone was there, Julienne included.'

There came the sound of a dull explosion in the distance, and she sensed his knuckles tightening on the wheel. She bit her lower lip. He had known the risks he was taking when he drove out for her, and yet he had done so unhesitatingly. When Elizabeth Harland had informed him of where she was, she must have known what he would do. She hugged her arms, knowing that if she had been in Elizabeth's place she would never have told him.

'We've about another half-mile to go before we reach the pass,' he said, and as he did so his headlights picked out great heavy rolls of barbed wire coiling across the road. He swore vehemently, slamming on his brakes, skidding to a halt. Melissa was thrown violently against the dashboard and one of the Chinese toppled from the rear jump-seat and into the road. The vicious wire was all around them and Raefe shouted at the Chinese to stay where he was and not to move.

'Can we get free of it?' Melissa asked fearfully.

Raefe yanked open the glove compartment. There was a spanner and a pair of pliers. A very small pair of pliers. 'God knows,' he said grimly. 'Can you yank the sleeves out of your jacket so that I can wrap them around my hands?'

She did so, her heart in her mouth as he began to work, inch by inch, severing the wire that was jammed up against his driver's door, edging his way out of the jeep, slowly and bloodily cutting and clipping.

It was an hour before he furiously kicked the last remaining section of wire away. As he did so there came the sound of another explosion, this time behind them, to the north. Neither of them spoke. If it was the bridge over the Sham Chun that had been blown, it would make no difference to their journey to Kowloon. But if the blowing of the Sham Chun was a signal for the other objectives to be demolished, then they would find themselves on the wrong side of a mass of impassable rubble.

It seemed an eternity before Raefe said with relief: 'Whatever the hell it was they just detonated, it wasn't the railway or the road.' In the light of his headlights the entrance to the pass loomed eerily, the troops still standing by like wraiths. They waved him down, and he skidded to a halt, flashing his pass.

'You've only just made it, sir,' one of the soldiers said respectfully. 'We're all set to blow the line the minute the word comes through.

'Is the rest of the way clear into Kowloon?'

'Yes, sir.'

Raefe pressed his foot once more on the accelerator. They were going to make it. Half a mile further on there was an ear-splitting crack, and the jeep veered violently out of control as a front tyre burst.

He fought down his rising frustration, bringing the jeep under control and bumping to a halt. 'Will it take long to change the tyre?' Melissa asked nervously as he sprang to the ground.

There was a moment's silence and then he said savagely: 'It wouldn't have done, if we had a spare tyre, but it looks as if we're the victims of a bloody fifth columnist.'

'But we're not in danger now, are we? I mean, the road is clear behind us and the Japs certainly won't be bowling down behind us. Not with the Royal Scots out in strength.'

He had grunted agreement, his immediate problem being not the Japanese but his superiors who would soon be wanting to know where the hell he was.

The remainder of the journey was conducted at a snail's pace, and it was nearly eight o'clock by the time they crawled into Kowloon's crowded outskirts.

'I'm going to dump this and put you in the first taxi I see,' he began to say, and then was deafened by the screaming approach of planes, wave after wave of them, hurtling down from the north towards Kai Tak.

There was no time for them to take shelter. Split seconds later bombs rained down on the airfield, and then a plane wheeled away from the others, swooping low over Kowloon. Raefe jammed on the brakes, shouting to the Chinese to run for cover. As he grabbed Melissa's hand, dragging her from the jeep, there was a terrific whistling sound and then the crash of an exploding bomb blasted their eardrums. There were other planes screaming over-head now, and a stick of bombs falling directly in their path. There was a culvert at the side of the road, and Raefe threw Melissa down beside it, rolling on top of her as the bombs cracked the street wide open. He was deafened by the crash of impact, by screams; blinded by dust and thick black acrid smoke.

An eternity later he raised his head, looking back across the road. The jeep was a flaming mass of twisted metal. Chinese were running in all directions, some with their clothes on fire, some with blood running down their faces.

Melissa was sobbing hysterically beneath him, her hands pressed desperately over her ears. Another plane dive-bombed, and he ducked his head, tightening his hold of her; and then, as the explosion thundered in his ears, he was wrenched away from her, lifted bodily into the air and slammed down twenty yards away in the middle of the blazing road.

He choked for breath, heat searing the back of his throat, dust filling his mouth. As he stumbled to his knees amid billowing smoke, he half-fell against a soft moist object. He looked down at it, swaying dizzily. It was an arm, bloodily severed from the shoulder. He clapped his right arm to his left, reassuring himself that they were both still intact, and then he saw the bleeding body to his right. It was a Chinese, still alive, screaming frenziedly, his arm and shoulder socket a hideous black hole.

He staggered to his feet, running back between burning cars to the culvert and to Melissa. She was lying face down,

170

part of her skirt and her blouse ripped from her body, blood pouring from a gash in her head. He felt her pulse and then ripped another length of material from her torn skirt, making a pad with his handkerchief and bandaging it clumsily in place. He had to get her to a hospital, and the hospitals would be crammed with the Chinese victims of the attack. Scooping her up in his arms, he ran with her across the road and into a maze of side-streets. The Kowloon hospital would be the nearest. It was crazy to wait for an ambulance, even though he could hear their sirens screeching towards him. Glass littered the streets, doors hung crazily askew, sobbing terrified Chinese ran in all directions. He could taste blood in his mouth and wondered where it was coming from, and then he weaved round the last corner and into the forecourt of the hospital, and a white-coated figure was running towards him.

'What the hell happened?'

'Bombs! A whole stick of them! There must be thirty dead!'

Melissa was swiftly taken from him and placed on a trolley. 'Who is she?' the doctor asked as a nursing attendant began to propel the trolley at high speed towards an examination room.

'My wife. My ex-wife.'

The sound of sirens pierced the air as the first of the ambulances returned with their bloody cargo.

'It doesn't look good,' the doctor said a few seconds later as he examined Melissa. 'Nurse, have this patient prepared for theatre at once.'

It was only then that Raefe realized that the nurse at the doctor's side was Helena.

'Yes, doctor.' Helena was already doing as he instructed.

As Helena started to peel away what was left of her clothes, Melissa groaned, her eyes flickering open. 'Raefe?' she whispered with difficulty. 'Raefe?'

He took her hand, bending over her, saying gently: 'I'm here, Mel. I'm with you.'

For one brief moment her fingers pressed feebly against

171

his and a smile touched the corners of her mouth. 'Good
. . .,' she exhaled. 'Good, I'm so glad. . . .' And then her
eyes closed and she was still.

'Doctor Meredith!' Helena called urgently. The doctor
was instantly back at her side. He felt for Melissa's pulse,
lifted the eyelid of one eye and then did all he could to
resuscitate her. His efforts were in vain. 'It's no good,' he
said at last. 'She's dead.'

He couldn't waste time in further commiserations; his
casualty ward resembled a battlefield. The curtain
whisked behind him, and it was left to Helena to say: 'I'm
sorry, Raefe.'

He stood looking down at the face of the girl he had
married only brief years before. There had been a time,
when he had been standing trial for Jacko Latimer's murder, when he had thought her death would be a matter of
supreme indifference to him. It was no longer. Over the
last two years they had slowly and painfully forged a new
relationship. A relationship based on acceptance of the
past and one far finer than anything that had gone
previously.

'Thank you, Helena,' he said thickly. He couldn't stay.
His duty was at Fortress headquarters. 'Make sure her
body is treated with respect.' he said, and before she could
suggest that she tended the deep gash over his left eye he
had spun on his heel, striding between the wounded and
the dying that were being brought in off the streets, breaking into a run as he reached the door.

Julienne had reported early to her nursing station and had
been told that she was not needed as yet. Volunteers were,
however, needed at the Peninsula Hotel, and she was
asked if she would report for duty there and help the Red
Cross nurses turn it into a temporary hospital. She had
happily agreed and driven to the Peninsula in her little
Morris, enjoying the novelty of being up and about so early
in the day. It was still not eight o'clock. She giggled to
herself, wondering what Ronnie would say when she told

him. It was a standing joke between them that in all the years they had been married she had never been up and dressed before ten o'clock.

The Peninsula Hotel was a hive of activity when she arrived. Bellboys were busily rolling up the luxurious carpets, guests were cheerfully helping to stack chairs and tables at the far end of the ballroom, and blackout material was being hastily cut to fit the windows.

'Morning, Mrs Ledsham,' a bellboy said, pausing in his work to give her an admiring grin as she walked exuberantly into the lobby, her shoe heels high, her skirt tight and with provocative side-splits similar to those the Wanchai bar-girls wore in their cheong-sams.

'Bonjour,' Julienne returned, her smile wide. 'Where can I find the Red Cross sister in charge?'

The sister in charge regarded her with despair. 'We are no longer playing at war, Mrs Ledsham,' she said coldly. 'We *are* at war. Kindly remove your make-up and nail varnish and then assist the other nurses in preparing cots for the wounded.'

Julienne was about to make a most unsuitable reply when her future nursing career was saved by a tall good-looking Dutchman who was standing at one of the far windows.

'My God,' he called out to them, 'come over here and look at this!'

They did so and stared in disbelief at the planes bearing down towards Kai Tak Airport.

'They must be ours,' Julienne uttered, aghast. 'They can't possibly be Japanese.' And then, a moment later, the bombs began to fall.

Within a few hours of leaving the lush splendour of the Peninsula's ballroom, Alastair found himself in the far north of the New Territories. His orders were straightforward. He and his men were to maintain observation on the frontier and report any Japanese troop movements. They were also to ensure that all bridges were successfully demolished and then they were to withdraw in an orderly manner to the Gin Drinkers' Line, further to the south, where a stand would be taken. All through Sunday, the Japanese were well within their sights, massing on the far side of the border, but making no move to attack.

'They will, though,' Alastair said grimly to his captain. 'Just give them enough time and they will.'

At ten minutes to five on Monday morning he received a terse message over the field-telephone, telling him that Britain and Japan were officially at war. By seven-thirty the Japanese were pouring over the border and Alastair was leading his men into the first bloody engagement of the war.

Elizabeth drove straight to the Jockey Club. The streets that had been so quiet the previous day were now choked with cars and trucks as people hurried to their posts. She drove with one hand nearly permanently on the car horn, refusing to be intimidated by daredevil rickshaw-boys or the crowded one-decker buses that kept hurtling past her.

'It looks as if this is really it,' Miriam Gresby said nervously to her when she arrived.

Elizabeth looked at her in surprise. She had never known Miriam to be anything but aggressively bombastic. To her horror she realized that the older woman was frightened. 'Come on, Miriam, it will soon be over' she said with an optimism she was far from feeling. 'Let's get to work.'

A lorry was already discharging equipment, and they set to, ferrying camp beds into the Jockey Club, putting them into position, helping with the setting-up of the operating-theatre on the first floor. Within an hour their patients had begun to arrive. Most of them were very old and sick, refugees who had been sleeping rough on the streets of Kowloon for weeks, some of them for months.

'Oh God, who would have thought one bombing raid could cause so many injuries?' a tired-looking blonde said to Elizabeth at lunch-time as they snatched a sandwich and

174

a cup of coffee. 'If this is only the beginning, how are we going to cope with what comes later?'

The morning raid was followed by others. A military post, established in the nearby members' enclosure, let off deafening rounds of anti-aircraft fire as the planes swooped low overhead and, though no bombs were dropped in their vicinity, the noise and the sight of the smoke still billowing over Kowloon rendered most of their patients half-senseless with terror.

It was ten o'clock at night before she was told to go home and get some rest. She walked wearily out to her car, her legs and her back aching, her head splitting. For the moment the skies were silent. Perhaps, she thought as she turned the key in the ignition, the rumours about the Japanese not being able to see in the dark were true. She fervently hoped so. She needed a decent night's sleep if she was to face another equally arduous day in a few hour's time.

Mei Lin ran to greet her, sobbing with relief. 'Oh, missy, I think something terrible happen to you! All day I've been here alone and there has been such noise and such smoke!'

'It's over for the moment, Mei Lin,' Elizabeth said wearily. 'Pour me a gin and tonic, will you?' She eyed the chairs and the sofa longingly but did not sit down. She had an urgent telephone call to make before she allowed herself such luxury.

She dialled Helena's Kowloon number, praying that the line was still in working order and that Helena was back from the Kowloon Hospital.

When Helena's calm deep-toned voice answered the insistent ringing, she leaned against the wall in relief. 'Helena? It's Elizabeth. You can't continue to stay over in Kowloon with the children; it's far too dangerous. Drive over here and stay with me, please.'

'No' Helena's voice was as tired as her own. 'It's impossible, Elizabeth. The situation in the hospital is beyond belief.' She paused for a moment and then said: 'There's something I have to tell you. . . .'

'Then, you must send the children over here! I'm going to telephone Li Pi in a minute. I want him to come here, too. He could bring the children with him. . . .'

'Melissa is dead. Raefe brought her into the hospital at ten past eight this morning.'

Elizabeth slid slowly down the wall until she was sitting on her heels. 'Oh, no,' she whispered. 'Oh, no.'

'They were caught in the raid this morning. She was alive when he brought her in, but she died within minutes.'

Elizabeth was silent. It was a strange experience, feeling grief for a woman she had never met; a woman who had once been the centre of Raefe's life. Whatever she said would sound trite, and so – as there were no words to describe her feelings – she said nothing.

'I'm grateful for your offer to take the children,' Helena said tactfully, when they had both been respectfully silent for a moment, 'but they are just as safe here as they would be in Victoria. The bombing is going to be pretty indiscriminate.'

'I wasn't thinking only of the bombs,' Elizabeth said soberly, wrenching her thoughts away from Melissa. 'I was thinking of the Japanese advance.'

'They won't advance very far. The Royal Scots will be sending them back across the border with their tails between their legs. They're certainly not going to advance south as far as Kowloon.'

'All right,' Elizabeth said reluctantly. 'But, if things change for the worse, promise me you'll send the children to me.'

'I promise,' Helena said affectionately. 'Goodnight, Elizabeth. I must get some sleep. I'm back on duty in five hours and I've never been so tired in all my life.'

Elizabeth grinned. 'Me, too,' she said wearily. 'Goodnight, Helena. God bless.'

Mei Lin brought her an ice-cold gin and tonic, and she sipped it gratefully as she dialled Li Pi's number. He was as adamant as Helena that Kowloon was in no worse danger than Victoria. 'I will come to you if necessary,' he promised at last, 'but not before.'

She had been forced to put the telephone receiver down with both her objectives unrealized.

'Will you be out all day again tomorrow, missy?' Mei Lin asked her, her slant eyes wide and frightened.

Elizabeth sank down into one of her chairs. 'Yes,' she said, wondering how she would find the strength to get undressed and go to bed. 'If there are air raids tomorrow, Mei Lin, you must go down to the shelters. You will be safe there.'

Mei Lin gave a little sob. The thought of the dark, crowded shelters terrified her almost as much as the thought of the Japanese did. 'Yes, missy,' she said obediently, but she had no intention of doing as Elizabeth suggested. She would hide in the apartment, under the table, as she had done all day. The apartment was in an elegant European area. The Japanese would surely not bomb European houses. Such an outrage was inconceivable. If she was going to be safe anywhere, she would be safe beneath Missy Harland's table.

'I run you a bath, missy,' she said, eager to please, feeling suddenly braver. 'Japanese soon run away from British soldiers. Everything soon all right again.'

# 11

Everything was not soon all right again. For the next two days the bombing and shelling of Kowloon and Victoria continued. The casualties at the Jockey Club increased from a steady flow to a barely containable torrent. The supplies that had seemed so adequate when they were being offloaded from the lorries now proved to be barely sufficient. Old sheets were torn into strips for bandages. Chlorine and rock salt were used to eke out the diminishing supplies of disinfectant. The fierce enthusiasm which most volunteers had exhibited on the first day began to be replaced by ever-increasing anxiety.

'I don't understand it,' Miriam Gresby said petulantly. 'What are our troops doing? Why aren't the planes being shot down?'

'Because land-based anti-aircraft guns aren't very effective,' Elizabeth said with as much patience as she could muster, 'and we haven't planes of our own in which to do battle with them. What planes we had were all destroyed in the first raid on Kai Tak.'

'Nevertheless, *something* should be done,' Miriam said querulously. 'It's been three days now, and my nerves are in shreds.'

Very little outside news filtered through to Adam and his fellow-Volunteers manning a pillbox on the south side of the island, overlooking Aberdeen harbour. On Wednesday morning a motorcycle messenger gave them the news that there had been fierce fighting in the New Territories since first light on Monday, and that the Japanese had broken through the Gin Drinkers' Line and were now fighting their way towards Kowloon.

'Jesus,' one of Adam's companions said, stunned, 'I thought the Gin Drinkers' Line was supposed to be as far south as the Japs would get.'

Adam had thought so, too, and now he watched the sea-approaches to Aberdeen harbour with even greater vigilance. If any Japanese sailed into the sights of his gun, they would have a very nasty surprise indeed.

'Do you think they'll try to make a surprise landing?' a former clerk in the Hong Kong and Shanghai Bank asked him nervously.

'I wish they would,' Adam said grimly. impatient for action. 'I just wish to God that they would!'

Up on the heights of Sai Wan Hill, looking out towards Kowloon and the mainland, Ronnie had been under intermittent air attack for two days.

'The bastards really mean business, don't they?' he said to Leigh Stafford, who was his platoon commander.

'They do, and the military made a gross error in underestimating them,' Leigh Stafford said bitterly. 'All that cock about the Japanese air force being of a low standard and their bombing poor! Their bombing was accurate enough at Kai Tak. Every bloody plane we had was destroyed before it could take off! They've got us by the short and curlies, old boy. These next few days are going to be critical. If they once chase us off the mainland, we'll be under siege and they'll be able to lobby us with mortar fire from Kowloon all day and all night.'

By dusk on Tuesday, Alastair and his men had made a bloody but planned retreat to the Gin Drinkers' Line. Here, in the underground tunnels and pillboxes and observation posts of the Shingmun Redoubt, they were to make their stand against the Japanese and prevent any further advance to Kowloon.

'It isn't exactly the Ritz, is it?' he heard one of his men say as they hurled themselves down into the dank claustrophobic depths of tunnels that had been dug and cemented years before, as a precaution against an attack that no one had believed would come.

It wasn't the Maginot Line, either. Alastair had long been dubious as to the benefits of fighting from such a fixed position, and his doubts grew by the moment. Some embrasures in the pillboxes were so constructed that it was impossible to depress the machine-guns sufficiently to cover the steep slopes below them. The scrub-filled ravines that surrounded them offered treacherously covered approaches to any attacker, and the rugged jagged terrain made mutual support between positions a near-impossibility.

'When an attack comes, we'll use the redoubt mainly for cover,' he told his men crisply. 'Our main fighting positions will be on the outside.'

There was a general murmur of relief, but when darkness fell, and when the attack came, it came with such suddenness and such ferocity that it was in the dimly lit passageways and foul-smelling pillboxes that most of them died.

Alastair had time only to press one hand against the breast pocket containing Helena's photograph and then the screaming hordes swarmed down on them, heedless of the Royal Scots' machine-gun fire, heedless of the casualties they were suffering.

Grenades were lobbed through pillbox embrasures and hurled down ventilation shafts; steel doors were blown in, exits were sealed off.

'The bastards are coming in!' Alastair yelled, leaping away from the guns and towards the tunnel from which he heard the pounding of running feet and frenzied cries of *'Banzai! Banzai!'* *'Kill! Kill!'*

In the smoke-filled acrid-smelling darkness, Alastair let off every round in his pistol and then, as ever more Japanese surged forward over the bodies of their dead

180

comrades, he resorted to a bayonet, knowing that he would never now marry Helena. Never even see her again. Blood was pouring from a bullet wound in his shoulder and from a shrapnel wound in his head.

'They're falling back, sir!' a young corporal, fighting hand-to-hand alongside him, cried out triumphantly.

There was a second's respite as the Japanese no longer tried to storm the passageway, and then a grenade came whistling towards them, landing and rolling on the floor between Alastair and the corporal. There was no room to back away from it, nowhere to sweep it to. Alastair saw the youngster's terrified face and then, with a savage cry of '*Helena!*' he hurled himself on to it, taking the full force of the blast, his flesh and blood spattering the cordite-fumed tunnel and raining down on the unconscious but barely injured boy.

The first intimation Helena had that the Gin Drinkers' Line had given way and that the troops were in retreat was when Miss Gean, her hospital matron, took her to one side and informed her that the news was grave and that, as she knew Helena had children still in Kowloon, she was giving her permission to leave her post and remove them to the greater safety of Hong Kong Island.

'But what of everyone else?' Helena had asked, aghast. 'Are the other nurses to leave, too?'

Miss Gean shook her head. 'No,' she said briefly. 'Even if the troops withdraw to the Island, we shall not. We are needed here and we shall stay here.'

Helena ran from the hospital still in uniform. She drove through the bomb-blasted streets in her open-topped Morgan, cursing herself for her blind belief in the Royal Scots' ability to thrash the Japanese. She had foolishly put her children's lives at risk, ignoring Elizabeth's pleas that she take them to Victoria while it was still relatively easy to do so. Once the news Miss Gean had imparted to her became general news it would be impossible to get a place on one of the ferries. And God only knew what would happen to Jeremy and Jennifer if they fell into the hands of the Japanese.

She screamed to a halt outside her block of flats, running up the stairs. There was still time. She could have the children and their amah at the ferry within fifteen minutes, and then Jung-lu would take them direct to Elizabeth's. She mustn't think of Alastair. Alastair would be safe. Alastair would come back to her. She would be able to tell him that she was sorry she had been so hesitant about marriage. That she had changed her mind. That she wanted to marry him more than anything in the world.

'Missy Nicholson! What happen? What wrong?' Jung-lu gasped as she raced into the flat.

'The Japanese are approaching Kowloon! Pack one bag and then I'm taking you and the children down to the ferry. You are to go and stay with Mrs Harland in Victoria. This is the address. Her household staff will be expecting you.'

'No, missy,' Jung-lu said, shaking her head vehemently. 'Me not leave Kowloon. My family here. My mother, my father, my cousins.'

Helena was already throwing the children's toilet things and a change of clothes into a large canvas holdall.

'Where are we going, Mummy?' Jeremy was asking curiously. 'Can I take my toy soldiers?'

'Want to take teddy,' Jennifer said, toddling round the room after Helena. 'Please can I take teddy?'

'Of course, darling,' Helena said, adding toy soldiers and a teddy bear to her mental list of absolute essentials that had to be taken with them.

'You *must* take the children to Victoria,' she said fiercely to Jung-lu. 'I have to return to the hospital. I'm desperately needed there!'

Jung-lu shook her head. 'No, missy, I not leave my family. Not now, not even for you.'

The canvas bag was nearly full. Helena scooped up her silver-framed photograph of Alan and laid it on top of the clothes, and zipped it up. Please, God, she was thinking, don't let Alastair be killed, too. Don't let the grieving begin all over again.

'You can return immediately you have left the children with Mei Lin,' Helena said, casting a last, hasty look round the room to make sure that she had not forgotten anything of vital importance.

'No.' Jung-lu's mouth had set defiantly. 'Sorry, missy, me no go.'

Helena felt sobs of frustration rising in her throat. She had brought all this on herself with her damnable optimism that such a move would be unnecessary. If she took the children herself, Miss Gean would understand. After all, she had given her permission to leave the hospital and not to return. But, in Helena's eyes, leaving now would be deserting her duty. The little hospital had been originally built to accommodate a hundred bed patients, and now there were close on a thousand Chinese crammed in the wards and corridors, all of them hideously wounded as a result of the savage air raids and all of them desperately in need of help. No, she could not remain in Victoria with the children herself, not if there was an alternative way in which she could be sure of their safety. The alternative way occurred to her as she lifted Jennifer high in her arms and picked up the bulging holdall. Li Pi. Li Pi was still in Kowloon, and she knew that he had been as adamant as she had been in refusing Elizabeth's request to take shelter with her in Victoria.

' 'Bye,' she shouted to Jung-lu in the last few seconds before she closed the door of the flat behind her. Any anger she had felt had now dissipated. She only prayed that wherever Jung-lu went she would be safe. The Japanese were reputed to be utterly merciless where the Chinese were concerned.

She bundled the children into the car, driving through the rubble-filled streets towards Li Pi's luxury apartment.

'. . . and so you see, I really would be most grateful if you could take the children to Elizabeth's for me,' she said, trying to sound less desperate than she felt.

183

'Is this the man who teaches Aunty Lizbeth to play the piano?' Jeremy asked curiously, looking round at the unusually bare room and the concert grand piano dominating it.

Li Pi smiled down at him. 'Would you like to be able to play the piano?' he asked.

Jeremy nodded, his eyes bright. Helena took a deep steadying breath. Perhaps she had been wrong in keeping panic from her voice. Perhaps Li Pi had not appreciated the seriousness of the situation. 'Our troops are no longer holding the Japanese,' she said carefully. 'They are in retreat. It is only a matter of days before they reach Kowloon.'

Li Pi had been bending down, talking to Jeremy. Now he stood upright, holding Jeremy's hand, and said: 'And so you wish me to take the little ones to Victoria?'

Helena nodded. 'Please, Li Pi. They will be much safer there. Even if the Japanese do reach Kowloon, they'll never be able to cross to the Island.'

'No,' Li Pi said smilingly. 'Of course not.'

Helena stared at him, suddenly certain that it was not what he really thought. Oh God, she thought despairingly, am I being an optimistic idiot again? *Could* the Japanese invade the Island? '*Prince of Wales* and *Repulse* are on their way to us,' she said confidentially. 'Once they arrive, the Japanese will give us no more trouble.'

Li Pi had nodded and smiled and said: 'I will be more than happy to take the little ones to Victoria for you. But I would not put my faith in battleships that have still not arrived, Mrs Nicholson. The Japanese have probably already taken them into account.'

Tom had found himself with the Volunteer Field Engineers, helping the Royal Scots blow up the bridges over the Sham Chun. When the Japanese had poured over the border at seven-thirty in the morning, he had been on his way to give a message to a nearby platoon and from then on remained with them, cut off from the Engineers, fighting with the Royal Scots as they withdrew to battle positions on the Gin Drinkers' Line, a few miles to the left of the Shingmun Redoubt. By early Wednesday morning, they were falling back even further, this time to Golden Hill, where he had often walked with Lamoon.

There was no pleasant walk in store for him on the night of 10 December. Exhausted by the retreat from the Gin Drinkers' Line, weighed down with equipment and ammunition, he followed his orders, climbing and crawling up the steep slopes in almost total darkness.

'At least we'll be able to see the bastards coming from here,' one of his companions said as they finally hauled themselves to the bare summit.

Tom wasn't so sure. At the Gin Drinkers' Line the Japanese had attacked in rubber-soled shoes, approaching so silently that no one had been aware of their presence until they were nearly on top of them, their uniforms heavily camouflaged by twigs and grass inserted in the cross-stitching.

He slapped his arms around himself, trying to keep warm, trying to forget the fact that he was tired to the point of exhaustion and desperately hungry.

'Have a tot of rum,' his companion said dourly. 'It's the only breakfast you'll get today.'

The attack came as dawn was breaking. Mortar shells rained down on them, the impact area igniting in sheets of flame, a thick pall of smoke enveloping them as they fired relentlessly back, only to be savagely mortared yet again. Tom hurled himself forward, firing his Bren gun, hurling hand-grenades, shouting barrack-room obscenities at the Japs that he didn't even know he knew. All around him men were falling, screaming out in pain, the ground beneath their feet slippery with blood. He heard a voice to his left yelling for him to get under cover but he ignored it. 'Bastard!' he yelled as he ran forward like a Dervish, his Bren gun firing. 'Mother-fucking *bastards!*'

He heard a voice at his side saying, 'I've bought it, mate,' and he turned his head fleetingly just in time to see his breakfast companion, a look of disbelief on his face, slide to the ground. Tom ploughed on, in a man-made fog of smoke and dust and cordite fumes. The earth seemed to be blowing up all around him. The noise was deafening. And then, inch by inch, he knew he was being pushed back. They were losing the fight for Golden Hill, just as they had lost the fight for the Gin Drinkers' Line.

When the order finally came for them to pull back to less exposed ground closer to Kowloon, Tom sobbed in bitter rage and frustration. They were being defeated. Defeated by bloody mother-fucking *Japanese*.

They had scarcely reached their new positions when a further order came. The mainland was to be evacuated, anything of any use to the enemy was to be denied them. Cement works, power stations, dockyards, all were to be destroyed. From now on, all further fighting would take place on Hong Kong Island.

Helena had safely deposited Li Pi and the children aboard the ferry the previous day and was sincerely glad that she had done so. Gunfire could be heard in the Kowloon streets, the air raids had increased and the Chinese dead lay in the streets, their bodies rotting alongside the living. The medical staff of the Kowloon Hospital, doctors and nurses, were gathered together and sombrely told that despite the evacuation of the troops it was the Governor's wish that they all remain at their posts.

Even in the hospital, the sound of the disorder in the streets could be heard. Windows were being smashed in Nathan Road; riots had broken out, and looting was rife. Helena returned to her terrified patients, wondering where Julienne was, where Elizabeth was, and if Alastair and her children were safe.

Tom fumed and swore all the time he was being driven down towards Kowloon Point. After all they had gone through, he and his companions were being ferried down to the embarkation point in a bus! To Tom it was the final indignity.

'Looks a bit nasty round 'ere, don't it?' one of the men who was with him said as they saw evidence of looting and a rotting pile of Chinese dead.

Tom was just about to turn his head away from the chaotic street scene when he went rigid, the blood draining from his face. 'Lamoon!' he uttered with a strangled cry. 'Lamoon!'

She was pushing and battling her way in the midst of the crowds streaming towards the docks.

He couldn't believe his eyes. For a long near-fatal moment, he couldn't even move. 'Lamoon!' he shouted again as the bus continued to speed away from her. 'My good Christ! Lamoon!'

He leaped to his feet, ignoring the shouts and cries around him. 'Let me off this bloody bus!' he yelled, and then, not waiting to see if it would stop, not caring if he was court-martialled and shot, he launched himself from the bus platform and into the road.

He fell heavily, rolling over and over, scrambling to his feet and running back up the street shouting 'Lamoon! Lamoon!' like a man demented.

She stood still as the crowds milled around her, turning her head to see where the shouts were coming from, her almond eyes wide and fearful.

'Lamoon!' he shouted at the top of his lungs, barrelling his way through the hurrying Chinese. 'Oh, good God! Lamoon!'

When she saw him she swayed on her feet, kept upright only by the pressure of people jostling and pushing her.

He cleaved his way through the throng, his eyes blazing with joy. 'Lamoon!' he uttered as he swept the last human barrier easily aside. 'Oh, my love! My darling! Lamoon!'

She fell into his arms, her head against the broad safety of his chest, tears streaming down her face. He crushed her against him, sobs of thankfulness and joy rising in his throat. 'Oh, my little love,' he uttered chokingly. 'Where have you been? What did they do to you?'

Air-raid sirens screamed into life.

'I thought I would never see you again!' she said rapturously, raising her face to his.

All around them Chinese and Europeans were running for cover.

'My love, my life,' he whispered thickly, lowering his head to hers, kissing her with all the pent-up passion of months of longing.

There was a sudden blinding roar as the planes swooped down on the narrow streets. 'Quick!' he yelled, seizing her wrist. 'I'm sure as hell not going to be killed now!' He sprinted with her across the road, thrusting her into a doorway, shielding her with his body. The sky darkened as the planes roared overhead, and then there came the terrible whistling sound of falling bombs.

'Don't let me die! Dear God, don't let me die!' he prayed silently for the first and only time since the war had begun. He couldn't die, not now he once more had Lamoon. He had to be alive to protect her; to love her; to keep her safe.

The bombs tore into streets some distance away. The ground rocked beneath their feet, a shower of white concrete dust falling over their heads and shoulders.

'Is it over?' Lamoon shouted above the roar of falling buildings and the continuing scream of sirens.

'I think so.' Cautiously Tom lifted his head, peering upwards. The sky was as blue and as clear as it had been minutes earlier before the attack. 'Come on, I've got to get out of here. Where were you going when I saw you?'

They were back out in the street; to the left of them, about half a mile away, tongues of flame were shooting skywards, great billowing clouds of smoke beginning to choke the air.

'The ferry,' she gasped as they weaved and dodged through the crowds erupting from the street-shelters. 'I thought it would be safer on the Island.'

'Damned right it would!' Tom said grimly. My God! The mere thought of what might happen to her if she fell into Japanese hands made him go cold with terror.

'The trouble is I haven't got a permit!' she gasped as he

188

lunged across the street towards a taxi-cab abandoned by its driver.

'To hell with bloody permits!' Tom expostulated, half-throwing her into the front seat of the taxi and running round to the driver's seat. 'Let's hope this old jalopy has some petrol in it!'

It had, and seconds later they were speeding through the congested streets towards the docks.

'You haven't told me what happened to you yet,' he said, swerving to avoid the fire engines and ambulances screaming their way towards the fires and the injured.

'I was married,' she said simply.

He jerked his head towards her, the taxi-cab veering dangerously. She gave a small smile. 'It is over now.' Her smile faded. 'He was killed in a raid. We were visiting my father.' She looked away from him, out to the ravaged streets. 'They were all killed. My father. My brothers. There is no one left.'

'Yes, there is,' he said gently, removing one hand from the wheel and placing it over hers.

Her eyes were bright with tears as she turned her head once more towards him. 'I love you,' she said softly. 'For all of my life, I love only you, Tom.'

Kowloon City Pier was in a shambles. European women, amahs and small children in their wake, were thronging the area streets deep. Extra launches were waiting to ferry them across to Victoria, taking on board so many passengers that by the time they put out into the channel it seemed a miracle they didn't sink beneath the weight.

Tom shouldered his way through the crush towards a Royal Naval Volunteer seemingly directing operations. 'This lady has lost her permit,' he said urgently. 'She needs to be able to cross immediately. . . .'

'Sorry, mate,' the harassed naval officer said. 'No one crosses without a permit.'

All around them children were crying, frightened by the noise and the crush and the unmistakable smell of fear.

'To hell with that!' Tom said furiously. 'This lady is

Lamoon Sheng and my fiancée! I want her aboard one of these boats, Lieutenant!'

'I don't care if she's the Queen of Siam,' the Lieutenant said, rapidly checking permits and waving thankful women through towards the launches. 'She's a Chink and she hasn't a permit and she'll have to wait, is that understood?'

Tom's eyes blazed and his fist clenched. Lamoon pulled desperately on his arm, begging him to come away, and then a deep voice shouted out: 'Over here, sir! The Chinese are storming the boats!'

Just as Tom was about to hit him, the lieutenant turned, forcing his way towards his junior officer, and Lamoon almost sobbed with relief. 'Please let's go away, Tom. I'll cross later, when there is no longer a panic.' Very faintly, above the noise and shouts around them, both of them could hear the distant sound of gunfire.

'There isn't going to be a later,' Tom said harshly. 'The Japs can't be more than a couple of miles away.'

'There's room in this boat,' the nervous underling who had been left in charge said to Tom. 'And would you go as well and try to keep order? These women will have the boat six feet under the way they're carrying on.'

Tom didn't need to be asked twice. He hurled Lamoon forward on to the pier, running with her towards the launch. He would take her to the Hong Kong Hotel. He was known there, and the name Sheng was known there. At the Hong Kong Hotel even in war, she wouldn't be just another 'Chink'. And then he would rejoin his unit, though how the hell he would ever find it again he couldn't imagine.

In the Kowloon Hospital the stench drifting in from the streets was almost insufferable. Bodies were beginning to decompose where they had fallen, sewage was seeping from bombed and broken mains, hundreds of tons of fruit and vegetables were rotting as the refrigeration system in the godowns broke down.

190

Helena's patients lay squeezed into any inch of space they could find. The lucky few lay in beds; others lay under the beds, on the floor, in the corridors. Operations in the two small operating-theatres were continuous. By Friday evening, Helena couldn't remember when she had last slept, or eaten, or even taken a drink. Her uniform was stiff with blood, her finger nails caked with it. There was no more disinfectant, no linen for bandages, and their precious water-supply was dwindling fast.

All through Friday night she tended the maimed and the dying and the dead, not thinking of Adam or Alastair, not even thinking of her children, knowing that if she did so she would not be able to continue. Instead she staunched hideous wounds, stitched gaping holes in arms and thighs, and tried to give comfort to young men who had lost legs and would never walk again.

At 9 o'clock the following morning, the pitch of the noise drifting in from the surrounding streets altered ominously. There was no sound of bombs falling or air-raid sirens screaming into life. Seconds later there came the heavy tramp of marching feet and the doors were kicked open by Japanese soldiers, rifles at the ready, bayonets fixed.

The Chinese began to scream, struggling to leave their blood-stained beds, to drag their injured bodies to a place of safety.

The leading Japanese officer ignored them. He was grinning at Helena, his eyes behind his gold-rimmed spectacles lustful as they feasted on her Junoesque proportions and her magnificent bosom.

'You come . . .,' he said leeringly, jabbing his bayonet only inches away from her face. 'You come with Japanese Officer. You find out what defeat for European women means.'

# 12

Raefe had spent the last week at Fortress Headquarters, helping the British interrogate Japanese informers, trying to elicit enough information out of them to enable General Maltby to assess where his preciously few troops could best be deployed.

The main decision was whether to keep troops back in a central position, moving them forward in strength to meet an attack when an attack came, or to spread them out, trying to cover as much of the coastline as possible.

The information that Raefe was able to pass on was not decisively helpful. He was told that the Japanese would land by parachute, at night, in the central area around Wong Nei Chung Gap. This information was disregarded as the Japanese had not yet, at any time, operated a bombing raid at night and the feasibility of landing an army of men by air over the treacherous ground of the gap was practically nil.

A second informant said that the Japanese would cross to the island from the Devil's Peak Peninsula, west of Kowloon, landing at Sau Ki Wan. The Devil's Peak crossing was the shortest of all possible crossings; and, foreseeing that it was one the Japanese would want to use, withdrawing forces had been ordered to scupper ships in it, making the channel impassable.

'They won't be able to cross at that point,' a senior officer said confidently. 'They're going to land on the south coast where we least expect it.'

General Maltby did the best he could in an impossible

situation. Keeping the vast majority of troops in a central position until an attack came was not a feasible option. He did not have enough trucks to facilitate the speedy movement of large numbers of troops to any one spot. Instead, he deployed the Canadian troops to the south of the island, the Indian regiments to the north coast, the Punjabis to the west of Victoria, the Rajputs to the east, overlooking the Lei Yue Mun Strait. The Royal Scots and the Middlesex remained centrally, as many units as possible being supported by the Volunteers.

By the Friday evening Raefe knew that there was little left for him to achieve at Fortress Headquarters and he was thirsting for action. His orders were clear. As an undercover agent for the British, if and when Hong Kong fell, he was on no account to allow himself to be captured. He was to escape, making his way to the Japanese-held mainland and then travelling through enemy territory to Chungking in free China, where he would help the Chinese form British-led guerrilla units. They would be an Asian counterpart of the French Maquis, doing everything possible to undermine and dislocate the authority of the enemy.

Meanwhile, with the Japanese still making no move to land, Raefe's sense of impotence was acute. 'At least let me join a Volunteer Unit,' he begged Landor. 'I can't remain buried away here any longer. It will only create suspicion about what I am really doing. And if word gets to the Japanese, I'll have even less chance of making a successful getaway should the need arise.'

Permission wasn't given until Thursday the 18th. By then the Japanese were swarming all over the island, and Raefe found himself holding the honorary rank of captain and commanding a unit whose officer had been killed. And fighting by his side was Adam Harland.

Elizabeth remained on duty at the Jockey Club. On Friday evening it had been announced on the radio that *Prince of Wales* and *Repulse* had been sunk off Singapore. She had heard the news with stunned disbelief, knowing that there was now no real hope for Hong Kong's survival. The next morning she was greeted with the news of the mass evacuation from the mainland. By midday the Japanese could be clearly seen on the Kowloon waterfront, sandbagging buildings and setting up gun emplacements.

When her long hours of duty came to an end, she did not grab what sleep she could. Instead, ignoring an air raid and almost constant mortar-fire, she drove through the wrecked streets to the flat and Mei Lin.

'No, Missy Harland,' Mei Lin said tearfully, 'Missy Nicholson not come. Children not come. Oh, when will it end, Missy Harland? When will it be safe again?'

There was nothing that Elizabeth could do. There had been no telephone link to Kowloon for days. If Helena was trapped there, she could only pray that she and the children were alive and well. If she wasn't trapped there, if she had managed to join the other civilians in the previous day's mass evacuation, then she could only pray that they would eventually turn up at the flat. That when she was next able to drive home she would find Helena waiting for her.

As the week progressed the streets of Victoria became a nightmare. The bombing and mortar fire were incessant, the thousands of Chinese refugees pathetically easy targets. The hospital was hit and hit again, even though a large red cross had been painted on the roof. One of the operating-theatres was wrecked, and one shell went right through the top floor, causing many casualties. On Wednesday, 17 December, fourteen bombers attacked the crowded streets of the Central District and the Wanchai.

'They're softening us up,' one of the medical orderlies said darkly. 'You mark my words, this will be the last day they content themselves with bombs and shells. This time tomorrow the bastards will have landed!'

Elizabeth wiped the back of her hand wearily across her forehead. Once the Japanese landed she would probably never see Mei Lin again. An hour later, when there was a lull in the terrible bombing, she made a dash for her car, determined to make one last trip to the apartment. She would collect as much tinned food and bed-linen as she could transport to eke out the rapidly dwindling hospital supplies, and give anything remaining to Mei Lin.

The roads were so cratered and bomb-blasted, so littered with fallen tram-wires and lamp-standards, that they were nearly impossible to negotiate. It took her nearly an hour to make the five-minute journey. As she neared the apartment apprehension began to cramp her stomach muscles. The area had received several direct hits. Fires were still raging out of control, doors and window-frames hanging lopsidedly from buildings whose frontage had been ripped away. An ambulance clanged vociferously in her wake. Air-raid wardens were climbing cautiously over a mound of rubble that had once been a human habitation.

Her hands slid sweatily on the wheel; she felt sick and disorientated. It couldn't be her apartment block. It couldn't. She stumbled from the car, running across to the men still searching the smoking wreckage.

'This your 'ouse, lady?' one of them asked solicitously in a cockney accent.

'Yes,' she gasped, hardly able to breathe. 'My apartment was here. . . .'

'Ain't here no longer,' the cockney said unnecessarily. 'Anyone in here when it caught it?'

She shook her head, weak with relief. 'No, I told my amah always to go down to the shelter.'

'We've found one!' another male voice shouted from a few yards away. 'A Chinese! A girl! Poor kid must have been hiding under the table. Didn't even have her tin hat on.'

Elizabeth began to struggle towards him, slipping and sliding over the blasted concrete and shattered wood and the incongruous remains of her kitchen.

The air-raid warden heaved a table-top away and bent down, beginning to lift Mei Lin from the rubble. 'You take 'er 'ead, I'll take 'er feet,' the cockney said, hurrying to his assistance. 'Cor blimey, what a nasty mess and no mistake.'

Mei Lin's golden skin was covered with a white film of concrete ash. Dark red blood oozed through the bodice of her blouse, her head lolling back at a grotesque angle as they lifted her free.

'She your amah, luv?' one of the men asked Elizabeth.

She nodded, the tears streaming down her face.

'She was a silly girl,' the air-raid warden said as they transferred Mei Lin's body to a stretcher. 'Table-tops are no protection against Jap bombs. When will they ever learn?'

The two men lifted the stretcher and began to carry it with difficulty back down over the constantly shifting wreckage.

'Pretty though,' the cockney said, looking down at Mei Lin's still, white face. 'Very pretty little thing she was.'

Elizabeth slipped and slid in their wake. She had been pretty. She had been pretty and sweet-natured and touchingly loyal. And she had died alone, hiding in terror from the thundering volley of falling bombs.

'You all right, miss?' the air-raid warden asked as they lifted the stretcher and pushed it into the rear of an ambulance.

Elizabeth nodded, her tears falling unrestrainedly. She had been tending the dying and laying out the bodies of the dead for over a week, but Mei Lin's death was the first death to touch her personally.

She watched as the ambulance doors slammed shut, crippled by fear. Where were Helena and the children? Where was Li Pi? Where were Julienne and Alastair and Ronnie? Where were Adam and Raefe? Were they safe? Were they alive and well, or were they, too, lying dead and maimed, the victims of a Japanese bomb or a mortar-shell?

She walked slowly back towards her car. She had no way of knowing what was happening to any of them. She could only continue her work at the Jockey Club and pray fervently that the war would soon end. There had been rumours that the Chinese were sending troops to their aid. If it were true, and if they arrived within the next few days, then it was just possible that the Japanese would capitulate and that there would be peace by Christmas.

The drive back to the Jockey Club was grim. Now that the raid was over, the Chinese had swarmed from the shelters and re-formed in long, disorderly queues for food. Nearly all of them looked as if they were in need of medical treatment. With sores openly exposed, their clothes often little more than tattered rags, they waited with rusty tins and battered bowls for the daily distribution of rice and beans.

'We have been requested to send someone to help with the sick at the Repulse Bay Hotel,' her nursing officer said to her when she returned. 'Will you go? I'm afraid the military are unable to provide an escort, but it shouldn't be too bad a drive if you go at dusk. There's not much chance of a raid then.'

The Repulse Bay. Elizabeth thought of the laughter-filled, happy afternoons she had spent there. 'Yes,' she said wearily. 'I'll go.'

The nursing officer managed a small smile. 'At least Repulse Bay won't be under intensive air attack like Victoria is. It should be quite a picnic out there. I almost wish I were going with you!'

Thursday had been an unusually cold and damp day, and Ronnie's discomfort was acute. He hadn't had a hot meal for twenty-four hours and he couldn't remember the last time he had slept. Ever since ten in the morning, bombers had been flying over Victoria and even now, late at night, black smoke from the Anglo-Persian Company's petrol and oil-storage tanks at North Point billowed into the air. The Japanese batteries in Kowloon had his position under almost constant mortar-fire. Of the seven men in his platoon, one was seriously wounded by shrapnel and another was out of commission with violent stomach pains and diarrhoea.

'Nerves,' Leigh Stafford had muttered disparagingly. 'There's nothing physically wrong with the fellow. He's just shit-scared.'

Ronnie didn't blame him. He was pretty shit-scared himself. At tea-time they had seen about two hundred Japs approaching the Devil's Peak Pier. They were obviously unconcerned about the scuppered ships in the channel. The landing was imminent, and it was going to take place exactly opposite his gun position.

'I'm ready for the little yellow bastards,' Leigh Stafford said fiercely, conscious of the need to give a good impression to the younger man. 'I've waited for this moment a long time.'

The night was so dark they could barely see a yard in front of them. Heavy cloud obscured the moon, and thick black smoke from the still burning oil-tanks hung chokingly low. The rubber boats and rowing boats and sampans sliding out into the channel did so unobserved, shielded from sight by the high sides of the grounded merchant ships.

'There's something out there,' Ronnie muttered edgily, his eyes straining into the darkness. 'I can feel it in my bones.'

'Blast those scuppered ships,' Leigh Stafford said viciously. 'I can't see a bloody thing for them.'

A huge flare of burning oil shot suddenly skywards, fleetingly illuminating the channel, the scuppered ships and the scores of small craft edging their way round them.

'I can see them!' Ronnie rasped, adrenalin shooting along his veins. 'There's a battalion out there! And it's coming this way!'

'Position, men!' Leigh Stafford commanded, forgetting his weariness, forgetting his hunger. 'Get ready to fire!'

Out of the darkness the black shapes of boats and men began to take on substance.

'Targets!' Leigh Stafford commanded, his voice throbbing; and then, as shadowy figures began to leap for the shoreline: 'Fire!'

'My God, there's an entire Jap army down there!' the corporal *hors de combat* howled. 'There's bloody hundreds of them!'

'Keep firing!' Leigh Stafford bellowed. 'We mustn't let them gain a foothold! For Christ's sake, keep firing!'

They kept firing, and for a few miraculous minutes held the disembarking Japs at the water's edge. In the distance, at either side of them, they could hear the guns of the anti-aircraft batteries roaring into action.

'We'll soon send them on their way!' Leigh Stafford crowed but, even as he spoke, more boats were sliding ashore, more men sprinting and leaping over the bodies of the dead and wounded.

'They're going to overrun us!' Ronnie shouted as, despite the withering fire, heedless of their casualties, the Japanese swarmed on towards them. 'There's no way we can hold them!'

A hand-grenade was lobbed through a loophole and just as speedily lobbed back again.

'We *have* to hold them!' Leigh Stafford shouted back, and then another grenade entered the pillbox, exploding and blasting them off their feet. Cement and plaster rained down on them. Ronnie could hear someone screaming and prayed to God that it wasn't himself.

'Out!' he heard Leigh Stafford shout chokingly through the dust and fumes and blinding smoke. 'We have to get out!'

Ronnie was in full agreement with him. He staggered to his knees, his uniform ripped, blood trickling down into his eyes, half-falling over the corporal who had been suffering so violently with stomach ache. He was suffering no longer. He had taken the full force of the blast and had been almost cut in two, sliced open from the neck to the navel, his entrails spilling bloodily to the floor. Ronnie gagged, falling over two more prone bodies as he struggled in the older man's wake.

The Japanese were all over the pillbox now, exhorting them to give themselves up. To surrender.

'It's no good, old boy. We have to do as they say,' Leigh panted, throwing down his revolver and stepping out of the pillbox towards the Japs, his hands raised.

'No!' Ronnie screamed at the top of his voice, but it was too late. The gentlemen's war that Leigh Stafford imagined he was fighting was no gentlemen's war at all. The Japanese jeered at him in derision as he did as they demanded, falling on him, bayonets raised, plunging them time and again into his defenceless body.

Ronnie raised his revolver and fired and kept on firing. A piercing pain in his shoulder sent him stumbling to his knees and then, as they closed round him, a blow to the back of neck sent him sprawling to the ground. He couldn't see, couldn't hear, couldn't breathe. There was blood in his nose and his eyes and his mouth. Julienne! he thought desperately. Julienne! And then he was dimly aware of the Japanese surging away from him, away from the pillbox. He lay motionless, fighting back cries of pain as scores of rubber-soled feet pounded past him on their way inland.

'Bastards,' he whispered as the last reverberation died away and he crawled in crucifying agony on his hands and knees. 'Bastards! Bastards! *Bastards!*'

Adam heard the news of the landings in the early hours of Friday morning. 'The Japs have landed on the south-east coast,' he was told tersely.

'Get yourself and your men over to Brigade Headquarters. That's where they are heading.'

Adam had slammed down the telephone receiver and immediately given the order to abandon their position. Brigade Headquarters was at the Wong Nei Chung Gap, and the gap stood on high ground in the virtual centre of the island. If it fell into the hands of the Japanese, then they would have achieved a terrible tactical advantage.

'Who are we linking up with, sir?' one of his men asked as they rocketed across country in an army truck.

'I don't know,' Adam had retorted grimly. 'And I don't

care. Just as long as we throw the bloody Japs back into the sea!'

Julienne had been posted, much to her disgust, with Miriam Gresby. She would have preferred a more congenial companion, especially in a dressing station as isolated as the one they had been detailed to. They were to the east of Wong Nei Chung Gap, their patients mainly men from the Rajputs who had come under intense shelling from the Japanese batteries in Kowloon. It was a small station with only three medical officers, a British nursing sister, four other British Voluntary Aid Detachment nurses, three Chinese Voluntary Aid Detachment nurses and three medical orderlies. By the time the Japanese swarmed inland early Friday morning, they had over a hundred patients in their care.

'The Japanese have landed,' the senior medical officer said to them grimly. 'I've just been warned that they are coming this way.'

Julienne did not pause in her ministrations to a young Canadian boy whose leg had been blown off by a shell. If the Japanese came, they came. There was nothing that she could do to stop them. But she was damned if she was going to cringe with fear at the mere mention of their name.

'My God! You know what they'll do to us if they capture us, don't you?' Miriam Gresby hissed to her, twisting her hands convulsively and ignoring the boy whose wounds she had been in the process of dressing.

'No.' Julienne was applying sulphur to a pus-ridden stump. 'But, whatever it is, talking about it will make no difference.' She looked across to the young boy Miriam was neglecting. His face was shiny with sweat, his knuckles clenched against the pain. 'Your patient needs you to finish changing his dressing, Miriam.'

Miriam's lips tightened, querulously thin without their usual careful application of lipstick. 'Don't take it upon yourself to tell *me* what to do, Julienne Ledsham! I'm not surprised you're unconcerned at the prospect of rape! It's exactly the kind of activity you enjoy, isn't it?'

Julienne was surprised at how little anger she felt. Miriam had always been a fool and now she was a frightened fool. 'No,' she said, readjusting a draining-tube. 'I have never had any experience of rape, Miriam, and I doubt if I would enjoy it at all. Would you like me to help you with that bandage?'

They worked together in silence, Miriam's hands trembling as she lifted her patient's leg and Julienne deftly bound the cumbersome dressing-pad into place.

At the slightest sound all eyes swivelled towards the doors, the patients lying still, tense and apprehensive.

'We are a hospital,' one of the Chinese nurses said nervously to Julienne. 'The Japanese will not harm sick men, surely?'

'No,' Julienne said reassuringly. 'Of course not.' But she remembered the stories she had heard of Japanese behaviour in China and she was not at all sure.

'They're coming,' one of the medical orderlies said suddenly. 'I can hear them.'

Julienne wiped away a trickle of blood from the corner of the mouth of a Rajput whose right lung had been pierced with shrapnel. He was dying, but he was still lucid. 'What is happening, Nurse?' he whispered. 'Why has it gone so silent? What is wrong?'

She took his hand, giving it a comforting squeeze, saying gently and praying that she was speaking the truth: 'There's no need to worry about it, Sergeant.'

The outer doors of the dressing station were slammed open and a barrage of running feet thundered towards them. Julienne's hand tightened on the hand of the dying Rajput, and then the doors to the ward were flung open and a squad of Japanese with rifles at the ready and bayonets fixed burst in on them.

'Out of beds!' they screamed. 'Out of beds!'

'This is a hospital,' the senior medical officer said forcefully, stepping forward and addressing himself to the officer

202

in charge. 'These men are all seriously injured. They cannot leave their beds. I must ask you to withdraw—'.

The officer raised his rifle butt, hitting him full across the side of the head, sending him sprawling across the floor. 'When Japanese officer gives order, English pigs obey! Now, out of beds! Everyone out of beds!'

Those who could began to try to do as they were ordered; those who couldn't remained helplessly where they were.

'Out! Out!' a Japanese screamed, jabbing his bayonet towards the young Canadian boy Julienne had been so recently tending.

Julienne withdrew her hand from the dying Rajput's and flew across to the injured Canadian, throwing herself in front of him.

'*Non!*' she spat, knocking the bayonet aside as contemptuously as if it were a toy. '*Ça n'est pas possible!*' Her riot of Titian-red curls tumbled from beneath her crisp white headdress, her grey cotton nursing dress was creased and spattered with blood, her violet-dark eyes blazed. 'This patient has only one leg! He cannot stand! Do you understand? He cannot stand!' She spread her arms wide so that the Japanese could approach no further.

The Japanese goggled at her and stepped backwards, and as he did so his commanding officer barked an order. It was the signal for a bloodbath.

The retreating Jap retreated no further; he lunged forward, and with a cry of horror Julienne flung herself protectively over the body of the helpless Canadian. The bayonet went through the flesh of her arm and into the Canadian's stomach, skewering them bloodily together. Through her screams of pain, Julienne was aware of the other soldiers, pausing for a moment half-crouched over their bayonets, and then storming forward, dragging patients from their beds and bayoneting them with murderous glee.

A booted foot was stamped down on her pinioned arm as the Jap sought leverage to wrench his bayonet free. As she slithered bloodily to the floor she caught a glimpse of Miriam Gresby cowering in a corner and of one of the Chinese nurses being hurled away from the patient she was trying to protect. A bayonet went into the senseless body of the senior medical officer, another through the throat of the dying Rajput.

Julienne crawled to her hands and knees, slipping and sliding on the blood-soaked floor, trying to reach a scalpel, a surgical knife, anything that would end the life of one of the beasts rampaging around her. There were no instrument-trays within her reach, and she staggered to her feet, sobbing in frustration, deafened by the screams of the dying men and the shrill gleeful laughter of the Japanese.

'Murderers!' she howled as she lunged forward towards the nearest Jap. 'Murderers!' and she hurled herself at him, clawing at his face with the hand of her uninjured arm, her nails raking his flesh.

The rifle butt came down hard on the side of her head, sending her sprawling in blinding agony to the floor. All around her, as she lay unable to move, barely conscious, she could hear the screams of the dying Rajputs. Then there were no more screams, only gasping agonized groans, and then silence.

'What are you going to do with us?' Miriam Gresby's voice quavered. 'Dear Lord, what are you going to do with us?'

Julienne tried to move. Her vision was dislocated, objects dancing and merging together, but she was sure that she could see the glint of metal just inches away from her.

'You soon see,' a Japanese said to Miriam as the nurses were dragged from wherever they had tried to hide and were hauled, stumbling and falling, over the bodies of the dead medical staff and the few patients who had managed to die on their feet.

Julienne's hand stretched an extra fraction of an inch further. It was a knife. A surgical knife. Her fingers closed around the haft.

'How old are you, Englishwoman?' the Jap snapped at Miriam.

Julienne lifted her head, the knife safe in her grasp, dizzily trying to focus. Miriam looked as if she were about to faint. Her steel-grey hair, usually so elegantly styled, now hung damply against her cheeks. Her hands, naked without their lavish decoration of rings, looked pathetically old.

'Forty-seven,' she said waveringly.

The Japanese hooted with laughter. 'Too old,' he said derisively. 'Too old, old woman. No good.' And as the four British girls and the three Chinese girls were herded forward she was pushed contemptuously aside.

One of the Chinese girls was whimpering in fear; another was praying rapidly and urgently, a rosary sliding with desperate haste through her fingers. The men pressed round them, bloody and sweaty, jostling for position, and then the screams began.

Julienne held the knife concealed in the palm of her hand. She would only be able to kill once, but she would kill with merciless relish. Brutal hands seized her, throwing her on to her back, and she could see nothing but lustful yellow faces closing in on her, and rampant cocks held in blood-soaked hands.

She had only one hand in which to hold the knife, but she held it firm and as the first of her ravagers fell on top of her the knife slid unerringly in and up beneath his ribs. She saw an expression of dumb amazement on his face, heard his choking intake of breath and knew it would be the last he would ever take. As his companions realized what she had done, they fell on her with howls of rage, but Julienne was triumphant.

The Jap whose dead body was being dragged away from her to make way for the others had been the Jap who had so brutally bayoneted the young Canadian.

'*Vous avez été vengé, chéri,*' she whispered as her victim's comrades fell on her like ravening wolves. You have been avenged.

# 13

The night sky lightened imperceptibly, presaging dawn, as Adam and his companions hurtled in their army truck towards Wong Nei Chung Gap.

'How the hell did the bastards manage to get so far inland so quickly?' their driver asked as he took a perilous corner at the foot of Shouson Hill with a screech of tyres.

'God knows,' Adam said tautly. 'They must have overrun the Rajputs on the north coast *and* the Volunteer batteries at Sai Wan Hill and Jardine's lookout.'

'Ronnie Ledsham was at Sai Wan Hill,' one of the men behind him said as the truck bumped and rocked over the uneven ground. 'I wonder if he copped it or not?'

'That bloody horse of his ought to cop it,' another voice said darkly. 'I lost a bloody packet on it last Saturday.'

There was a burst of nervous laughter, and then the driver said brusquely: 'Pack it in, chaps. I can hear gunfire.'

Adam leaned forward tensely, straining his eyes into the darkness. To the left was the dense black mass of Mount Nicholson, and with a stab of memory he recalled Beth leaning against the rails of the *Orient Princess* as they steamed into harbour, and Tom Nicholson pointing out to her Victoria Peak and Mount Butler and Mount Nicholson, and laughingly saying that he liked to think Mount Nicholson had been named after an ancestor of his. He wondered where Tom was now. He had always liked Tom and had stayed friends with him, as he had stayed friends with Alastair and, to a lesser extent, with Ronnie.

There was a rattle of gunfire, and the flank of the

mountain was suddenly thrown into lurid relief as flames from exploding mortar shells soared skywards.

'Jesus, but they're bloody close!' the man who had lost a packet on Ronnie's horse said apprehensively.

'The Japs aren't heading towards the Gap, they're *on* the Gap!' the driver gasped, as volley after volley of machine-gun fire ripped out over the sound of the rifles and the crump of exploding shells.

Adam's hand tightened on his rifle. They had only the ammunition in their belts and a small supply of hand grenades. His driver flashed him a quick glance. 'It looks as if we're not going to be meeting up with anyone, sir,' he said grimly. 'It looks as if we're going to be on our own.'

'Keep your eyes on the road,' Adam ordered, and as he did so a machine-gun opened fire on them. Bullets raked the windscreen, spattering across the chest of the driver, burrowing into the door. From behind him Adam heard screams as men were hit and his own voice yelling at them to get down. The truck was veering wildly out of control, and he seized the wheel, trying to hold it on the road, to drive through the crucifying hail of fire.

'I'm hit, sir! I'm hit!' the youngest member of his platoon shrieked, stumbling towards the front of the truck, blood pouring down his face and over his hands.

'Get down!' Adam shouted at him as he fought to hold on to the wheel, to keep the truck on the road.

There was another withering blast of fire, and the young corporal screamed in agony, lifted off his feet by the momentum of the shots plummeting into him. When he fell, it was bloodily forward, over the rear of Adam's seat. Vainly Adam tried to free himself of the boy's weight, but it was too late. He had lost control of the wheel, and before he could regain it the truck toppled off the edge of the road, crashing and rolling and splintering down the side of a ravine.

Adam was sandwiched between the driver and the dead corporal, and when the disintegrating truck finally rocked and slithered to a halt on the scrub-filled dark hillside he knew he owed them his life. Without the protection their bodies had afforded, he would have been smashed to a bloody pulp.

Pain screamed through his shoulders and legs as he tried to move, tried to free himself from them. He had to get out of the truck before the petrol-tank exploded or a hand-grenade went off, and he had to get his men out with him.

'I've got you, sir,' a voice panted, and Adam recognized the voice of Freddie Hollis, the middle-aged punter who had lost money on Ronnie's horse. 'Just hang on tight, sir, and I'll have you free in a jiffy.'

'Get back!' Adam shouted to him. 'The petrol-tank is about to go!'

'Not yet, it isn't,' Freddie gasped, with the confidence of a man accustomed to long shots. 'Not till I've got you free, it isn't.'

With a massive heave, he pulled Adam from beneath the weight of the dead driver and out of the truck's shattered cab.

Adam crawled painfully on his hands and knees, looking about him with horror. 'What about the others?' he asked, stumbling to his feet, sick and stunned. There was no movement from the wreckage. No sound.

'I didn't see what happened to the two who were behind me,' Freddie said, fighting for breath. 'But the three in front of me are all goners.'

With a choked cry, Adam staggered forward towards the wreckage.

'There's nothing you can do for them!' Freddie protested urgently. 'We need to get the hell away from here!'

Adam was in complete agreement with him, but before he left he had to satisfy himself that he wasn't leaving wounded men behind him. His hands, moving feverishly and bloodily over the darkened shapes of the mangled bodies still trapped in the rear of the truck, assured him that he was not.

'Come *on*, sir!' Freddie hissed. 'That tank is going to go any minute.'

Adam sucked his breath between his teeth. Apart from

one man, his entire platoon had been wiped out without even having had the chance to fire on the enemy.

'Let's go,' he said harshly, hardly able to speak for grief, and they began to run and stumble over shale and between stunted Chinese pines. As they did so, there was another long chattering burst of machine-gun fire and the petrol-tank was hit, exploding with hideous force, flames leaping into the air, the heat blasting their retreating backs.

'That was a near one,' Freddie gasped, throwing himself face down on the scree.

They lay still for a few moments, trying not to think of the bodies being incinerated only yards away from them.

'Come on,' Adam said, when the machine-gunner had been given time to direct his attention elsewhere. 'We have to try to skirt this ambush and regain the road. Somehow or other, we still have to make it to the Gap.'

'I can't see a bloody hand in front of my face,' Hollis whispered back to him. 'Can't we just sit it out until it gets light?'

'And find a score of Japs having breakfast fifty yards above our heads?' Adam asked savagely. 'No, we can't. Our orders were to make it to the Gap and give what assistance we could. And that is what I intend doing.'

Hollis sighed. Adam had always been a stickler for discipline. He knew he could always refuse and say his legs wouldn't carry him, but he didn't fancy the idea of spending hours alone on a treacherous hillside with the Japs breathing down his neck. 'I'm with you, sir,' he said resignedly. 'Lead the way.'

Adam led the way. Slowly and carefully they traversed the scree, the pre-dawn darkness intensified by a thick fog rolling in from the sea. Finally, bruised and bleeding, they crawled back on to the road a good hundred yards further on from the point where they had been ambushed.

'We can't just stroll along it as though it's Pall Mall on a Sunday morning,' Hollis whispered apprehensively. 'What is it you intend doing?'

'What I don't intend is getting shot,' Adam retorted crisply. 'We'll cross to the higher ground, taking what cover we can, but keeping the road in view to give us our bearings.'

Crouching low, rifles in their hands, they ran across the narrow road and into the scrub beyond.

'I can hear an engine,' Hollis said suddenly. 'Coming towards us from the Gap. Is it one of ours, or one of theirs, do you think?'

Adam listened tensely. 'It's one of ours,' he said with sudden certainty. 'It's a Bedford, I'm sure of it.'

As the truck lumbered into view and he saw the familiar-shaped bonnet, he sprang forward, waving it down.

The truck skidded to a halt and the driver leaned out, yelling: 'Don't go any further that way! The Gap's alive with Japs!'

'There's a party of them this way as well,' Adam warned. 'They've got a machine-gun positioned above the road.'

'Jesus Christ! Which way am I to go, then?' the driver asked desperately.

'Back the way you came,' Adam snapped, disgusted at the man's determination to retreat. 'And you can take my corporal and myself with you.'

The driver rammed his truck once more into gear. 'No bloody fear,' he said forcefully. 'I'm not driving back into that hell-hole! Everyone is falling back. There's only one other platoon still trying to fight their way through to HQ and that's led by a madman. He's about five hundred yards ahead of you.' And with that, he pressed his foot down hard on the accelerator and sped away.

'Did you tell him about the Jap ambush?' Hollis asked curiously as Adam sprinted back across the road.

'Yes. He seems to prefer it to whatever is happening at the gap.'

'And what *is* happening at the Gap?' Hollis asked, knowing damn well that he would soon be finding out. If Adam had been going to retreat, he would have hitched a lift with the departing truck-driver.

'Hand-to-hand fighting by the sound of it,' Adam said, dropping down into the scrub and beginning to run at a steady pace. 'There's one platoon still trying to fight their way through, though.'

'And we're going to join it?' Hollis asked, falling into a run at his side.

'Yes,' Adam panted, wondering how long he could keep up his speed over rough ground. 'We damn well are!'

The sound of fighting was all around them. Dawn was beginning to break, and as the pale gold light seeped over the horizon it was easier for them to locate the sources of fierce enemy rifle-fire.

'Jesus, Mary and Joseph!' Hollis said as they threw themselves to the ground for the twentieth time. 'The bastards are forming a ring round the Gap. No one is going to get out of there!'

There was the sound of a truck accelerating wildly, speeding in their direction down the nearby road. They raised their heads cautiously, and as the British army truck veered into view a barrage of shell shots were let loose on it. There was a scream of brakes and it keeled over, the cab a mass of flames. Spurts of fire flicked along the ground, and splashes of dust pitted the road. No running figures fled from the truck's rear. It lay where it had fallen, burning brightly and the shell-fire died.

'Poor devils,' Hollis said thickly. 'They were making a run for it. There's no sense in trying to go any further. The Japs have the Gap. The best thing we can do is to try to retreat.'

Adam's mouth tightened obstinately. He hadn't waited years for a military confrontation in order to make a retreat before he had even engaged the enemy. 'No,' he said stubbornly, 'we're not retreating while there's still a platoon fighting ahead of us. We're going to join up with them and fight with them.'

A shell exploded in a dip of ground to their left, showering them with debris.

'But there's no point!' Hollis protested when he had satisfied himself that he was still all in one piece. 'Even if we manage to fight our way through to Brigade HQ, we'd never be able to fight our way out! It's surrounded!'

211

The pale gold of early dawn was deepening to rosy red. Adam crouched on his haunches, looking around him. They were above the Gap, and the gullies and ravines running down to it from the surrounding mountains were full of Japs. Brigade Headquarters was a hundred yards or so on the west side of the Wong Nei Chung Gap Road, and he could see the bunkered roofs and the nearby company shelters half-buried in the hillside, and the ammunition-dumps. The Japs had closed in a tight ring around them, but they had still not broken through. From all around the Headquarters there were pockets of fierce fighting, and the one nearest to them was now clearly visible.

Adam's fingers tightened purposefully around his rifle. There were six men, probably seven – all, apart from the officer leading them, in volunteer uniform and all running low through the dense undergrowth towards a Jap machine-gun post. He didn't wait to see what would happen when they came within firing distance of it.

'Come on!' he snapped to Hollis. 'There's a party going on, and we've been invited! Get moving!'

Braving sniper-fire and falling shells, they raced over the pot-holed ground. 'Christ! I don't know who those chaps are in front of us, but they've been busy!' Hollis gasped as they swerved to avoid the bodies of butchered Japs. 'What are they fighting with – carving-knives?'

Adam didn't answer. His heart was pounding against his chest, the blood drumming in his ears. 'Please don't let my leg let me down,' he was praying as he ran and leaped and surged down the hill towards the Volunteers in front of him and then, as the Volunteers opened fire on the machine-gun post, and he hurled himself into battle alongside them, he found himself uttering the prayer of a man who had entered into battle over three hundred years earlier. 'O Lord! Thou knowest how busy I must be this day,' Sir Jacob Astley had prayed before the battle of Edgehill. 'If I forget Thee, do not Thou forget me.'

Bullets, heavy and hissing, flew past his head like swarms of angry bees. Mortar-shells began to plop down into the ground around him, exploding in sharp blasts and sending shrapnel flying. One of the men in front of him caught a piece in his throat and fell to his knees, choking on blood.

'We have to put the gunner out of action!' the officer leading the Volunteers yelled.

Adam was aware that Hollis had fallen, but whether through injury or to take shelter from the withering blast of machine-gun fire he didn't know.

'I've got a grenade!' he shouted, aware that the men he was fighting with had long since exhausted such supplies.

'Then, give it to me, man!' the officer exhorted, whipping round to face him. His steel helmet was gone, his dark hair falling sweat-damp across his forehead; his bayonet dripped blood from his earlier hand-to-hand engagement; he had an ugly gash in his left forearm; and his eyes blazed with fanatical determination.

Adam felt himself falter and half-fall as he thrust the grenade into the officer's blood-soaked hand. 'Thanks!' Raefe said with an exultant grin. 'This will put the bastard out of action! Give me all the cover that you can!'

There was no place to hide, no place to take cover. If Elliot was going to lob the grenade with any hope of accuracy, then he was going to have to expose himself suicidally to enemy fire.

As Raefe sprang forward, heedless of the gunfire ricocheting round him, Adam opened fire at the machine-gunner with his rifle. Bullets beat down on him like hail, and other pellets bounced off the ground, casting gigantic firefly sparks into the air. Through the smoke and fumes he saw Raefe raise his right arm and lob the grenade with deadly accuracy. Crazily, as the machine-gun post erupted in screams and smoke and flames, all he could think was what a magnificent spin-bowler Elliot would have made.

'Thank God,' Hollis croaked, crawling up beside him. 'That bloody gun has been silenced.'

'Not for long!' Adam whooped gleefully. 'Now we can turn it on the bastards and give them a taste of their own medicine!'

There was still heavy sniper-fire as he crouched low, sprinting forward to Elliot's side. 'That was bloody marvellous!' he enthused, seizing Elliot's uninjured arm and slapping him on the back. 'I've never seen anything like it! Why the hell you're not gutted with bullets I'll never know!'

'I've got my fair share,' Raefe said wryly as the blood continued to run down his left arm. 'Now let's put this machine-gun to good use.'

Adam didn't move. He suddenly realized what it was he had done. This man he was congratulating on his foolhardy bravery was the man he hated most in the world. The man who had taken Beth away from him. The man he yearned to put a bullet through.

Raefe grinned, and for the first time Adam was aware of the force of the man's personality. Of the reckless zest for life that had so attracted Beth. 'I know what you're thinking, Harland,' he said as a shell whistled close over their heads, 'But forget it for the moment. All that matters now is that we get through to Lawson.'

'Brigadier Lawson?' Adam asked, wondering what the hell Elliot was doing holding the rank of a British army captain.

Raefe nodded grimly. 'He's in there with only a handful of men. The Winnipeg Grenadiers who were with him were detailed to Jardine's lookout shortly after midnight. His only reserve company left two hours ago to try to capture Mount Butler.'

'Then, who has he got in there with him?' Hollis asked, reaching them in time to hear the tail end of the conversation.

'Clerks, cooks, signallers, storemen,' Raefe said tersely. 'They're putting up a hell of a fight, but you can see for yourself what the odds are.'

Another shell plummeted heart-stoppingly near them.

'Yes,' Hollis said fervently. 'I can, but I don't see what we can do about it. We can't take on the entire Jap army single-handed. There must be two divisions at least swarming over these hills.'

Adam and Raefe ignored him. The other Volunteers who had been pinned down by fire were now running low towards them. Of the six, there were only four left.

'We leave two men here to man this gun,' Raefe said decisively. 'The rest of us keep going forward, is that understood?'

Hollis squirmed slightly. He wasn't a coward and he didn't like being made to feel like one. If the madman giving the orders had an ounce of sense, he would realize that continuing to go forward was nothing short of suicide. As it was, he didn't have sense, and of the two options open to him he much preferred the thought of remaining with Adam, whom he had begun to regard as a lucky mascot.

'If Captain Harland is staying with the gun, I'll stay with him.'

'I'm not,' Adam said unhesitatingly. 'I'm going forward with Captain Elliot.'

Hollis wondered what the odds were on them ever coming back. 'All right,' he said fatalistically, 'I'll go forward, too.'

They had gone only fifty yards when a party of Japanese surged over the lip of the hill, bearing down on them with frenzied shouts of 'Banzai! Banzai!'

In the long hideous days afterwards, when Adam had plenty of time to remember and reflect, it was Raefe's sheer physical strength that remained his clearest memory. As hand-grenades fell among them like fine rain, Raefe shouted blasphemous encouragement to the men he was leading, and hurled unspeakable oaths at the enemy. When his rifle would no longer fire, he clubbed the Japanese to death with the butt. When his bayonet remained pinioned in the body of a Jap who had been bearing down on Hollis, he wrested a sword from an officer and decapitated him with it; he picked up grenades and threw them back at the attacking hordes; he fought with his boots and with his bare fists. He wasn't one man, he was ten men, and by the time the Japanese lay dead around them Adam knew that he would never again be able to speak of him with contempt.

They lay on the ground, among the fallen Japs, gasping for breath. Hollis was badly wounded, blood pouring from a shrapnel wound in his leg. One of the original Volunteers had died at the end of a Japanese bayonet thrust, his last anguished cry being for his mother. Adam had been wounded in the shoulder and the thigh but he could still lift his arm, still limp at a creditable rate on his good leg.

The gunfire in and around the Headquarters was fiercer than ever.

'They're still holding out,' Adam panted, 'Surely to God there should be reinforcements breaking through soon?'

Raefe was just about to answer him when he saw a score of Japs emerge from the scree of the east side of the Wong Nei Chung Gap Road and take up sniper positions perilously close to the beleaguered Headquarters. Dragging himself to his feet, he waved Hollis and Adam on behind him. Before they had gone a dozen yards, they could see more Japs, this time on the roof of the Medical Aid shelter, only thirty feet or so from Brigadier Lawson's command post.

'We can't get there in time to be of any use,' Hollis gasped, and then he heard Raefe Elliot's savage intake of breath and Adam's choked cry. Down below them, where the gap road wound through the converging hills, towards Repulse Bay and the sea, the Brigade Headquarters was completely surrounded and under a barrage of gunfire. Half a dozen men, one of them in the distinctive uniform of a brigadier, burst out of the shelter, firing from the hip. They were almost instantly cut down.

'Oh God,' Hollis said, sinking to his knees. 'Oh God! Oh shit! Oh hell!'

Adam and Raefe looked down on the now silent Headquarters, the skin stretched tight across their cheekbones, their mouths grim. There was no more gunfire, only exulting Japanese swarming down into the bunkered recesses of what had been Brigadier Lawson's command headquarters.

'What now?' Adam asked bleakly, turning away, unable to bear seeing any more.

Raefe was silent for a minute. The Japanese had closed in a tight ring all around them, and he knew they would have to fight just as fiercely to break out of the ring as they had had to do to break into it.

'We head towards Repulse Bay,' he said at last. 'The Japanese will have their work cut out consolidating their positions on the ground they've taken. Any counter-attack will have to come from East Brigade, and they're down around the bay and the peninsula.'

Hollis groaned. 'But that's nearly two miles over rough ground. There's no way that I shall be able to make it.'

'There's an advanced dressing station between here and the bay,' Raefe said, helping Adam haul Hollis to his feet. 'We'll leave you there. They'll soon patch you up.'

They were so exhausted by the time the dressing station came into view that none of them noticed how suspiciously quiet it was.

'I'll get them to put a pad on this wound in my thigh,' Adam said as they limped up to the door. 'It isn't deep, but it's bleeding like the devil. . . .'

The door swung open, and he didn't speak again. Not for a long time. It was a charnel house. The senior medical officer lay directly across their path, hideously bayoneted. Men with only stumps for legs lay half-dragged from their beds, bayoneted to death despite their obvious wounds.

Hollis choked, vomiting over the floor as Adam and Raefe stepped disbelieving forward. The nurses had been herded together, and lay in a pathetic discarded heap, their broken bodies bearing dreadful witness to the way they had been used before death.

'Christ Almighty!' Adam whispered, turning his head away. 'It's beyond belief. . . .' It was then that he saw her. She was lying apart from the other nurses, a dead Jap only a few feet away from her, a surgical knife protruding from his chest.

Adam sobbed, kneeling down at her side. 'The bastards,' he wept, taking her hand. 'The unspeakable, unbelievable, goddamned *bastards*!'

Every muscle and tendon in Raefe's body was rigid. Lizzie! he was screaming inside his head. Lizzie! Lizzie! If the Japs had raped and murdered once, they would rape and murder again.

Adam turned his chalk-white face towards him. 'What about Beth?' he whispered hoarsely. 'What if the Japs over-run the Jockey Club?'

Raefe was taking off his jacket, bending down towards Julienne. 'There's a huge concentration of troops around the Wanchai and the Jockey Club,' he said tersely, praying to God that they were still there. 'Lizzie will be safe.'

His voice was odd, so tight that it was almost strangled. With unutterable tenderness he wrapped the jacket around Julienne, closing her pansy-dark eyes.

'At least she took one of the bastards with her,' he said, and as he spoke Adam realized that it wasn't rage or horror that was transforming his voice, but tears.

'We can't just leave her here,' Adam said helplessly. 'We can't just leave any of them here. It's indecent. It's—'

A noise from a large cupboard only a yard or two away from them made them both spring to their feet.

'Bastard!' Adam sobbed, leaping forward and yanking open the door, his bayonet ready in his hand.

Miriam Gresby toppled out on top of him, no longer elegant and aggressive and well groomed, but a barely recognizable incoherent wreck.

'They killed them all! Killed them! Take me away. Oh, take me away!' she sobbed, sinking to the floor at Adam's feet, grasping his hands and then, as he tried to help her to her feet, his legs. 'Oh God, help me! They killed them! Raped them!' Her words were lost in a fit of hysterical sobbing.

Raefe looked down at Julienne. She was still beautiful, despite the obscene way she had died. Her spicy red hair clung in damp, curling tendrils around her kittenish face, her full, soft lips were tranquil. He pressed the first two fingers of his hand against his lips and then bent down, pressing them against hers. ' 'Bye, Julienne,' he said huskily. '*Au revoir, ma petite.*'

'What are we going to do with Miriam?' Adam asked, as she sobbed and clung to him.

Raefe stood up, took one last look round the ward and the dead men bayoneted in their beds, and said: 'We'll take her with us to the Repulse Bay.'

The scene he had just imprinted on his memory would stay with him for life. Whatever the outcome of the fighting now taking place, he made a deep, bitter resolve that the world would know of the infamy of the Japanese who had overrun the dressing station. 'If I die,' he said harshly to Adam, 'make sure that what has happened here becomes public knowledge.'

Adam nodded, determining to make sure no harm came to Miriam. She was a witness to what had taken place, and one day, maybe years hence, she would be able to tell her story and the perpetrators would find themselves on the gallows.

It was a long miserable retreat to the bay. Hollis's leg wound was severe and, though Adam bound it as best he could with pads he found at the dressing station, the blood was still oozing through, dark and thick, as they limped their way across the hills towards the hotel.

'I don't feel too good, old boy,' Hollis said with difficulty to Adam as the long low gleaming-white hotel finally came into view. 'I don't think I'm going to make it.'

'Of course you're going to make it,' Adam retorted grimly, grateful for the fact that his thigh had stopped bleeding and that the wound in his shoulder had proved to be not seriously incapacitating.

'Help Corporal Hollis,' Raefe said brusquely to Miriam Gresby, wondering how soon it would be before he was able to commandeer a car or a truck and storm a way through the Japanese-held centre of the island to the Jockey Club.

'Sorry about this, Lady Gresby,' Hollis said with a weak grin. 'I never thought we'd get to know each other quite so intimately.'

Miriam sobbed and allowed him to rest his arm round her shoulders and they traversed the last few yards of uneven ground and dropped down on to the road. It was blessedly clear.

'Thank God,' Adam said with heartfelt relief. 'At least the Japs haven't reached the bay.'

As they limped towards the sumptuous splendour of the hotel gardens they were seen, and over half a dozen guests ran out towards them.

'Jesus Christ! What's happened?'

'Lady Gresby! It *is* Lady Gresby, isn't it?'

'Give that man to me, I can support him.'

The voices clamoured around them, and Raefe said tersely: 'The Japs have overrun Brigade Headquarters at the gap. Are there any troops at the hotel? Any telephone communication?'

'We have a platoon of C Company of the Middlesex,' a middle-aged man incongruously dressed in a white dinner-jacket and evening trousers said, 'and some naval ratings and a small party of Royal Navy Volunteer Reserves. About fifty men in all.'

'Who's in command?' Raefe asked as he led his depleted party between the luxuriant flowerbeds that lay at the hotel's rear.

'Second Lieutenant Peter Grounds,' another of the guests, who was helping to carry Hollis, said. 'He's very competent. He has everything under control.'

'And the telephone?' Raefe asked, desperate to communicate to Fortress Headquarters the atrocity that had taken place at the dressing station, and to reassure himself that the Jockey Club had not suffered similarly.

'There's a civil telephone link. Second Lieutenant Grounds is keeping in touch with Fortress HQ on it.'

Raefe breathed a sigh of relief and stepped bloodily and dirtily inside the familiar opulent confines of the Repulse Bay Hotel.

# 14

'We've had reports of other atrocities,' he was told when he had made his own report. 'The fifth anti-aircraft battery of the Volunteers was bayoneted to death *after* they had made an honourable surrender. The Silesian Mission at Shaukiwan has been overrun and the medical staff butchered.' The second lieutenant eyed the ugly gash on Raefe's· forearm. 'You'd better get that seen to. We have a resident nurse here, a formidable Scotswoman, and also a couple of auxiliary nurses. They'll soon sort you out.'

Raefe walked slowly out of the luxurious lounge that was serving as a temporary military headquarters, and towards the room being used as a sickbay. For the first time since the fighting had begun, he felt unbelievably tired. There was no immediate danger now to send the adrenalin surging along his veins, no outlet for the bitter, burning hate that had consumed him ever since he had stood amid the carnage of the advanced dressing station. His orders from Fortress Headquarters had been precise. He was to stay at Repulse Bay, giving whatever assistance he could, and helping in the formation of sorties against the encroaching Japanese. If the island was overrun and there was no further hope of driving the Japanese back across the straits, then he was to avoid capture and make his escape to Chungking, where he would continue the war, giving help to British intelligence. He ran his hand through his hair. The word 'surrender' had not been used, but it had been implicit. And he had categorically been refused permission to try to cross the island and reach Happy Valley and the Jockey Club.

'Lizzie,' he groaned to himself as he stepped inside the crowded sickbay. Ever since he had gazed down at Julienne's mutilated broken body, he had been consumed by an emotion totally alien to him. He had been consumed by fear. 'Lizzie, Lizzie,' he prayed again to himself, his knuckles clenching white. '*Please* be safe! *Please* survive!'

And there she was. Her grey cotton nursing dress was creased and blood-spattered, her lovely face was tired and drawn, but she was there, only yards away from him, her blonde hair coiled low at the nape of her neck, her smile reassuring as she sponged the dried blood from Hollis's leg.

'It's going to need several stitches, Lance-Corporal Hollis,' she was saying in her low warm voice. 'And we don't have a doctor. . . .'

'Lizzie!' He didn't give a damn about Hollis's leg. He didn't give a damn about anything any more. '*Lizzie!*'

She spun round, dropping the bowl she had been holding, the blood draining from her face.

'Just a minute . . .,' Hollis protested plaintively. 'I don't mind there being no doctor, but at least let me have a nurse!'

She left his side, she left the upturned bowl on the floor, she took three paces across the room and, like an arrow entering the gold, hurled herself into Raefe's outstretched arms.

'Oh my love, my darling, my sweet, sweet love!' he murmured hungrily against her hair, her skin, as he crushed her against him like a man demented.

'If he gets that sort of treatment for a flea bite to his arm, why didn't I get it for my leg?' Freddie Hollis complained to the rest of the fascinated bedridden onlookers.

'It's because he's a captain,' someone said cheekily. 'Captains always get special privileges?'

'Wish I was a bloody captain, then,' another voice chimed in. 'I wouldn't mind that sort of privilege.'

'I can't believe it!' she said joyously, her face upturned to his. 'I've been so worried about you! There have been such dreadful reports. Every time I heard of a Japanese advance or the massacre of a volunteer unit, I kept thinking that perhaps you were there. That you were lying out on the hillside dreadfully injured or even dead!'

'Not me, Lizzie,' he said, and the old grin was back on his mouth. 'I'm like a bad penny. I always turn up.'

'Kiss me!' she said urgently. 'Oh God, make me believe it's true and that I'm not dreaming! Kiss me!'

He lowered his head to hers and, as the wounded Canadians and Hollis clapped and cheered, he kissed her long and deeply, overwhelmed by the love he felt for her, knowing that she was his for life.

'Very nice!' Freddie called out to them weakly. 'But what about my leg? If it doesn't get stitched up soon, it won't be worth wasting the catgut on it!'

'Oh goodness!' Elizabeth gasped, horrified. 'Lance-Corporal Hollis's leg!' And she fled from Raefe's arms, making effusive apologies to a vastly entertained Freddie and running fresh water and filling a clean bowl.

'When you've finished with that reprobate, I have a slight scratch on my arm that needs loving attention,' Raefe said, grinning down at Freddie who was gallantly winking up at him. 'And you have another patient, too. Adam.'

'Adam!'

She spun her head round to him, and Freddie groaned in despair. 'Never mind Adam Harland,' he said with feeling. 'If it wasn't for him, I wouldn't be in this pickle. Adam, "First-to-the-Front" Harland will just have to wait his turn.'

Elizabeth returned her attention to his injured leg. 'Is he badly hurt?' she asked tremulously.

'No, a bullet grazed his shoulder, and there's a peppering of light shrapnel in one leg.' He paused and then said: 'He's quite a fighter. If he hadn't come to our assistance, I doubt if I would still be alive.'

She put the bowl and the sponge unsteadily down. 'Do you mean that you and Adam have been fighting together?'

223

Raefe nodded, amused at seeing how competent she was in a task so alien to her. 'Yes – and, if I say so myself, we made rather a good team.'

'I'm going to give you an injection before I start suturing,' she said to Freddie. 'It will help numb some of the pain, but it's not going to be very nice.'

'Oh God,' Freddie said, raising his eyes to heaven. 'I knew my luck would run out eventually.'

Raefe watched as she began to put in the sutures. He couldn't tell her about Julienne now. He didn't want to have to tell her at all. He said quietly: 'I'll see you later, Lizzie. After you've had a chance to say hello to Adam.'

She nodded, grateful for his sensitivity, wondering how Adam must feel at having had to fight alongside a man he felt so much contempt for.

It was eighteen hours before she and Raefe had an opportunity to be alone together. She had been on duty all day and she remained on duty all night. It was only at six the next morning that she was able to leave the sickbay and the wounded Canadians who had been brought in from the gap. As she stepped out into the wide, lushly carpeted corridor, Raefe was waiting for her, his arm in a sling.

'Your senior companion dealt with me herself,' he said, sliding his free arm around her waist. 'And a very efficient job she did, too. How was Adam's leg? Is he going to have any problems with it?'

She leaned wearily against him, rejoicing in the physical and emotional strength he afforded her. 'No.' She had cleaned and bandaged Adam's leg and shoulder herself. It had been a strange experience, knowing that Raefe was only rooms away from them, that they were all now together in an intimacy from which there was no escape. 'He won't be able to fight any more. He can't move quickly and he should never have had to walk so far over such rough ground. What he needs is rest, but it isn't something easily obtained at the moment, is it?'

'No,' Raefe said, his arm tightening around her. 'Which

is why we must take our opportunities while we can.'

In an hour he was to leave with a hastily assembled party of the Middlesex, their destination the Japanese-infested Gap. He did not tell her of his imminent departure. He wanted their lovemaking to be as joyous, as uninhibited, as it had been in the sun-filled bedroom of the home he doubted either of them would ever see again.

'Come with me,' he said, his voice thick with rising passion. 'I have a surprise for you.'

If anyone had told Elizabeth that an unoccupied bedroom could be found in the hotel, she would have laughed in disbelief. Ever since the Japanese had overrun the New Territories, nervous residents from all parts of the island had made their way towards Repulse Bay, regarding it as a possible haven of safety. There were now a hundred and eighty of them, cheek by jowl, with two hundred soldiers and with more stragglers arriving every hour. De-luxe suites were being shared by elderly American men and Chinese babies; by aristocratic Englishwomen and by the young wives of French and Portuguese businessmen. At night, every bed, every sofa, every chair was occupied. The idea of finding privacy was ludicrous. Until Raefe opened the door of the huge walk-in linen-cupboard and turned the key in the lock behind him.

'Now,' he said huskily, pulling a blanket from a shelf and tossing it to the floor. 'Let me show you how very much I've missed you, Lizzie!'

Afterwards, whenever she remembered their love-making in the small lavender-scented linen-room, it seemed to her as if it had taken place in slow motion. She had kneeled facing him on the rough blanket, and he had tenderly touched her face with his hands, his forefinger caressingly tracing the pure line of her cheekbone and jaw. Then, as her excitement mounted unbearably, he removed her white nursing cap and the slides holding her hair so primly at the nape of her neck, and her hair had slid, heavily and silkily, over his hands, spilling down on to her shoulders.

225

'You are so beautiful, Lizzie,' he had breathed reverently. 'So incredibly, amazingly beautiful.'

He had kissed her forehead, her temples, his mouth tantalizingly skimming the corner of her mouth and bending to the nape of her neck. Then, with slow deliberation, he had begun to undo the buttons of her dress.

'I love you, Lizzie. Love you,' he whispered hoarsely as he slipped it down over her shoulders, exposing her shoulders and her brassièred breasts, and she had risen in a smooth fluid movement, letting the dress fall to her ankles, stepping free of it, kneeling down once more before him for his adoration.

Gently he had removed her white lace brassière, cupping her breasts in his strong olive-toned hands, his thumb-tips brushing the rosy-red nipples, his eyes darkening in pleasure as he saw them harden proudly. He lowered his head to them, his thick shock of blue-black hair soft against her skin as he pulled gently with his mouth on first one nipple and then the other, his tongue lapping and circling, his teeth softly pulling. She heard herself groan in submission, felt the hot dampening between her thighs as exquisite chords of longing vibrated deep within her vagina.

'Oh, Raefe, I've missed you so,' she whispered as his hands ran caressingly down over her breasts to her waist, and then down over the full gentle curve of her hips and her thighs. Not until she was brought to near-insensibility with need of him, did he swiftly rid himself of his shirt and pants, easing her down on the floor beneath him. Restraining his own passion with iron self-control, he lowered his head to the mound of golden curls between her thighs, his hands caressing her flesh as his tongue found the small pearl of her clitoris.

She lay in an ecstasy of passivity, her arms stretched languorously out above her head, moaning with pleasure as his tongue moved slowly, hot and sweet. At last, when he could bear no more, he covered her body with his own, parting the lips of her damp vagina with strong sure fingers. 'Oh God, Lizzie!' he groaned as he entered her. 'I love you! Only you! For ever!'

They moved slowly at first, two lovers with an intimate knowledge of the other's need, savouring every step of their climb towards a long-drawn-out magnificent climax. Her hands slid over his shoulders, up towards the nape of his neck, her fingers burrowing in his coarse black curls; their bodies would no longer allow them to halt upon the way. Her hips ground relentlessly against his, her breasts crushed against his chest as he drove deeper and faster into her. She heard his name on her lips, felt her back arch, her nails score his flesh as they reached a mutual peak of earth-shattering cataclysmic relief, no longer two separate identities, but one.

Afterwards she lay in his arms, tears wet upon her cheeks, and before he gently drew away from her she said softly: I'm having another baby, Raefe. I've thought I was for a week or two. Two days ago I was sure.'

He looked down at her, his hair falling low across his brow, his near-black eyes brilliant with love. 'This time it will be all right, Lizzie,' he said huskily, his hard-boned face certain.

Her arms tightened around him. The Japanese were advancing indefatigably; the world they had known was falling apart. And yet at that moment, lying in Raefe's arms and sharing with him the joy of her pregnancy, she had never been happier.

It wasn't until they were dressed and the door of the linen-room was closed behind them that he gently told her of Julienne's death.

She had been too shocked, too grief-stricken for tears. 'Oh, no,' she had whispered, time and time again, 'Oh, no! I can't believe it! I won't believe it! Not Julienne. It isn't possible!'

'I'm sorry, my love,' he had said, holding her close, hardly able to believe himself that Julienne's dauntless buoyancy was stilled for ever. 'But it's true. Miriam Gresby was a witness. And one day the Japanese who overran that

227

dressing station will pay for what they did. On the gallows.'

He had kissed her and left her, knowing that she would have to come to terms with her grief herself. That he could not help her. She had gone white-faced to the room she was sharing with ten other women, and knowing that she would have to be back on duty in the sickbay by lunchtime she had desperately tried to sleep. But despite her physical exhaustion sleep was a long time in coming. She thought of Julienne, laughing and merry and dazzling. It seemed inconceivable that she would never see her again. Never hear her infectious giggle. Never again be dazed by her outrageous, good-humoured behaviour. And when she thought of Ronnie, living a life unsustained by Julienne's irrepressible zest, she turned her face to the wall and wept.

Six hours later she went back down to the sickbay and reported for duty to the Repulse Bay's resident nursing sister. The sister's face was harrowed as she told Elizabeth that Second Lieutenant Peter Grounds had been killed while leading an attack on the hotel's garage.

'On the garage?' Elizabeth had asked, stunned. 'You mean the Japanese are in the grounds?'

'I'm afraid so,' the nursing sister said grimly. 'And they had prisoners with them. Second Lieutenant Grounds led a very brave attack on the garage to free the men the Japanese were blatantly ill-treating and, though the attack succeeded and the Japanese have been flushed out, Second Lieutenant Grounds died in the confrontation.'

From then on the hotel was in an atmosphere of siege. Adam helped the staff and guests to sandbag the windows, and when one of the guests, a Dutch engineer, suggested that they use a large drain as an air-raid shelter Adam was in keen agreement with him. The drain was more than big enough, at least eight feet in diameter, and it ran from the rear of the hotel, beneath the road, emptying out on to the beach. All through Saturday, and Saturday night, everyone who was able worked under the Dutchman's direction, inserting an entrance and ventilation shafts. By the time Raefe and the men from the Middlesex returned from their bloody and abortive attempt to rid the gap of Japanese, women and children from the hotel were sheltering snugly in the drain, equipped with sandwiches and coffee, and temporarily safe from the shells which were now landing with terrifying frequency.

'This isn't like a usual Sunday at the Repulse Bay, is it?' Adam said drily to Elizabeth the next day as he helped the Dutchman tap a central-heating pipe for water. The hot-water system had been turned off owing to lack of fuel, but as the hotel's water-supplies were dwindling fast the water in the boilers and the pipes could not be allowed to go to waste.

Elizabeth smiled wearily. It certainly wasn't. She remembered the Sunday pre-lunch drinks they had enjoyed with Ronnie and Julienne, and Helena and Alastair, and Tom, with Ronnie gustily leading them into a rip-roaring rendering of 'There'll Always Be an England.' Now there was no singing. The stink of unflushed lavatories permeated every room; the cocktail bar and the card room and the dining-room were full of weary soldiers, exhausted after their hopeless expedition to the gap.

Raefe ran towards them. 'We're coming under sniper-fire from the rear of the hotel,' he shouted urgently to Adam. 'We need your ability as a marksman to try to pick them off.'

Adam's face tightened, not because of Raefe's presence, but with resolution. 'Just let me have the chance!' he said fiercely, grabbing the rifle that Raefe thrust at him. 'Where are the bastards?'

'About fifty yards away, on the west side.' Raefe gave Elizabeth's shoulder a quick squeeze and then spun on his heel, breaking into a run after Adam.

That night, Major Robert Templar of the Royal Artillery was sent by Fortress Headquarters from the Stanley Peninsula to take command of the various units milling beneath the hotel's roof. The situation was blatantly desperate. A party of Volunteers had fallen back on to the hotel earlier in the day, telling of bitter fighting taking place not only in the centre of the island, but all along the southern coast as well. They had been part of East Brigade's last desperate attempt to recapture the Gap, and they were all that was left of their party.

'You'll be pleased to see one of them,' Raefe had said to Elizabeth as he directed the line of fire from a sandbagged window. 'It's Derry.'

'Derry!' She had run down the candlelit corridors to the main lounge where the newcomers were drinking preciously rationed coffee and taking what rest they could. He looked for all the world as if it were any normal Sunday evening. His tin helmet was crammed on his sun-bleached hair at a rakish angle, giving him the look of a medieval pikeman. His raw-boned handsome face was smeared with dust and smoke, but his grin was wide, his eyes undefeated.

'Derry!' she cried, squeezing past half a dozen soldiers and a squalling Chinese toddler. 'Derry! How wonderful!'

He swung her up in his arms, whirling her around, smacking a large kiss on her cheek. 'You look as beautiful as ever,' he said appreciatively, 'but do you think that grey is really your colour?'

She had giggled and felt for one brief delirious moment that the world had returned to sanity. And then she remembered Julienne. He saw the expression on her face change, and with dreadful premonition his own smile faded.

'What is it?' he demanded, the hair on the back of his neck rising. 'What's happened?'

'It's Julienne,' she said, stepping away from him, her voice thick with pain. 'She's been murdered by the Japanese.'

He had stared at her disbelievingly for a moment, and then with an anguished cry he had turned, forcing his way back through the crowded lounge and out into the darkness.

'I don't understand it,' Adam said later to her. 'Where did

he go? We need every able-bodied man we have to defend the rear of the hotel.'

Elizabeth thought of the dark hills outside the hotel, infested with Japanese. 'I think', she said slowly, 'that he's gone to kill all the Japs that he can.'

For the next twenty-four hours she hardly saw Adam and Raefe, and Derry did not return. A three-man committee had been formed to try to bring some order to the chaos, but there were some problems that were insurmountable. Food and water were fast running out. By dusk on the 22nd, there were only enough rations left for a further two days. Many of the sick and injured desperately needed the services of a doctor, but despite many agonized requests over the telephone to Fortress Headquarters there was no doctor that could be spared. The sanitation was abominable, and if it hadn't been for the Dutchman organizing parties of volunteers with pails Elizabeth was sure that an epidemic would have broken out.

When the order came through from Fortress Headquarters on the Monday night that all troops were to evacuate the hotel and leave the civilians to the mercy of the Japanese, she was horrified. 'But it's an invitation to murder,' she said to Raefe, aghast. 'How can Headquarters even suggest it?'

'Because it's the only hope there is of saving lives,' he said, hoping to God that he was speaking the truth. 'Our position here is untenable. There is no way that we can fight our way out. The Japs are in the grounds and all around us. When they close in for the kill, it will mean the annihilation of everyone within the hotel's walls.'

'And if the troops leave?'

'Then, as civilians, the guests and staff will have a slight chance of survival,' he said tautly, knowing the gamble that was being taken. If the Japs about to storm them were the same troops who had stormed the dressing station, then the chance of anyone surviving was slim.

She was silent for a moment and then said, her voice so

231

low he could hardly hear her: 'Will you be going with the troops? Is this goodbye for us again?'

He took her hands, holding them tightly in his. 'I'm leaving with the troops and I'm taking you with me.'

She gasped, staring up at him bewilderedly.

'Not only is the hotel untenable,' he said grimly, 'the whole island is untenable. There can be no alternative to an eventual surrender. When that happens, my orders are clear. To evade capture and escape, and I'm certainly not leaving you behind to face the Japanese. Not after what happened to Julienne. From now on, where I go you come as well.'

The exodus of troops took place at 1 a.m. the following day. All alcohol in the hotel was carefully destroyed so that the Japanese would not be tempted into a drunken orgy of raping and looting. The last telephone message was received from Fortress Headquarters and then the telephone lines were ripped from the walls. The evacuation was to be made via the drain tunnel leading to the beach, and then south across country to Stanley, where the Japanese had not yet penetrated. As the troops assembled, all in stockinged feet so that they would make less noise, Adam took Raefe to one side. 'Beth's told me what you plan to do if there's a surrender. I'm coming with you. I want to continue the fight against these murdering bastards, and I won't be able to do that if I'm stuck in a prison camp somewhere. I will be able to do it from Chungking.'

Raefe's hesitation was fractional. Adam's leg injury was a nuisance, but not gravely incapacitating. And he was a fearless fighter. Two of them would be able to give far greater protection to Elizabeth than one of them could. 'All right,' he rasped. 'If it comes to it, we go together.'

Slowly and apprehensively, the troops began to file out towards the drain.

'Been nice knowing you, Nurse,' one of the cockney Middlesex said to Elizabeth, never imagining for a moment that she was going to go with them.

'See you in good old London town,' another said, giving her an appreciative wink.

One of the Volunteers, leaving with the rest of the troops, hesitated at the last moment and then changed into a suit of civilian clothes and disappeared upstairs. 'Put his trousers and jacket on,' Raefe said tersely to Elizabeth. 'You'll be far less conspicuous.'

They waited until the end of the line and then, wishing the white-faced apprehensive civilians luck, they slipped into the drain, aware that the Japanese were only feet above their heads.

Emerging in the darkness of the beach, they ran, taking whatever cover they could, to the Lower Beach Road and on past the Lido until they reached the main Island Road. No shots were fired at them. No Japanese were laying in wait.

'We've done it!' Adam whispered exultantly to Raefe. 'We've slipped past them!'

In the still darkness a familiar voice could be faintly heard. It was the redoubtable Dutchman, and he was shouting out into the darkness from the hotel: 'Come in . . . come in . . . No soldiers here! No soldiers here!'

They paused for a moment, overcome with fear for those they had left behind, and then the long line of figures once more broke out into a steady run, off the road, into the hills, and over the rough treacherous ground to Stanley.

# 13

They reached Stanley Village at six in the morning, and by the time they did so every one of those who had fled the hotel knew that the battle they were waging was hopeless. The Japanese had control of all the high ground, and they had come under heavy sniper-fire several times. At one point, as they had skirted South Bay, they had stumbled over the bodies of dead Canadians, their hands tied behind their backs, their bayonet wounds hideous witness to the way they had died.

The brigadier in charge of the troops assembling in Stanley for a last-ditch stand was adamant that he would keep on fighting, even if it meant doing so with his hands and fists.

'And it looks as if he'll have to,' Raefe said sombrely to Adam. 'There are hardly any mortars and no mortar-bombs. All the heavy machine-guns have been knocked out, there are some spare rifles, a small quantity of hand-grenades and bayonets, and that's all.'

'Then, it will have to do us,' Adam said, his jaw set hard. 'I just wish to God we could catch some sleep before we go into action again.'

'You've no chance,' Raefe said with his old grin. 'The Japs are on Stanley Mound, and that's where we're going now, with the Royal Rifles.'

Adam wiped his hand across his forehead. He was exhausted to the point of collapse. His shoulder hurt and his leg throbbed, but he would have died rather than let the younger man know how beaten he felt. The minute they arrived in Stanley, Beth had offered her services to the overworked dressing station, and seeing her hurry off, uncomplaining about her long days and nights without sleep, and the arduous walk they had just endured, he had wondered if he would ever see her again.

A barrage of shells exploded uncomfortably near to them. 'Come on,' Raefe said, his grin dying. 'Let's show the bastards the battle isn't over yet.'

Elizabeth swayed with fatigue. There was nowhere for the wounded to be evacuated to. Apart from small isolated pockets of resistance, the Japanese had control of the entire island. Bombing had cut the water-mains, and the water-tanks had been hit by shell-fire. Nearly the only thing that could be done for the hideously maimed men was to pour sulphur into their gaping wounds.

All through the long bomb-blasted day, she remained at her post, not knowing where Adam and Raefe were, praying that they were still alive.

'My arm!' a young boy was screaming. 'Aaaahhh, my arm! Please, please, somebody help me. Oh, my arm!'

Running across to him, Elizabeth could see that the trooper's arm had been riddled by shrapnel from an exploding shell and was hanging in shreds, blood pouring out of the terrible wounds.

'Staunch the bleeding, Nurse,' the medical officer said to her tersely. 'Let's see if we can save it or not.'

By nightfall her hands were slippery with blood. The shell-fire was almost ceaseless, and the Japanese on Stanley Mound had not been forced into a retreat. Instead, they were steadily gaining ground.

'There's only one way we can go now,' one of the wounded men said to her bitterly as she dressed his leg, 'and that's into the bloody sea!'

Up on the smoke-blackened slopes of Stanley Mound, Raefe and Adam fought side by side, exhorting each other forward, firing their rifles until their rifles were too hot to hold.

'Watch your fronts, men!' Raefe yelled suddenly. 'There's another wave of them coming!'

He saw Adam drop to one knee, firing at the chest of the Jap who was leading the charge. The shot went wild, and as Raefe pulled the pin from a grenade, holding it for as long as he dared and then hurling it underarm into their midst, he was aware that the Japanese officer was nearly on top of Adam.

Adam staggered to his feet, the Jap too near for him to take aim and fire. Desperately he grasped his rifle by the barrel, wielding it club-fashion. The Jap knocked it contemptuously aside, and as Adam fell there was the gleam of a sword raised high above his head. With a blood-curdling cry that put the Japanese shrieks of 'Banzai! Banzai!' to shame, Raefe hurled himself at Adam's attacker, circling his neck with his good arm, wrenching it back until it broke and the Jap fell against him like a rag-doll. He had his back to the enemy for a second too long. The bullet hit him in his right shoulder, spinning him round, and then Adam was giving him covering fire as they ran and leaped to the nearest dip of ground they could find.

'It's Christmas Day in the morning, Nurse,' an injured cockney who had trekked with them from the hotel said, incredulity in his voice. 'It don't seem possible, do it?'

Elizabeth stared down at him. The days and nights had long since merged into one. Christmas. She thought of Christmas two years ago; of walking the sun-drenched streets of Perth with Raefe; of Roman Rakowski giving them the painting of the boy David.

'No,' she said, hardly able to speak for weariness. 'It doesn't seem possible at all.'

Towards dawn she was able to snatch a couple of hours of desperately needed sleep, and when she awoke it was to the news that Stanley Mound had fallen to the Japanese and that a retreat was going to be made to Stanley Fort at the very tip of the Peninsula.

'Did Captain Elliot and Captain Harland return?' she asked fearfully.

Her informant gave a hopeless shake of his head. 'God only knows,' he said despairingly. 'It's a shambles.' And then, as an afterthought: 'Merry Christmas. I've spent better, haven't you?'

It was lunch-time before she knew for certain that they were both still alive.

'I've just dug a bullet out of Captain Elliot's shoulder,' one of the medical orderlies said. 'He's lost a lot of blood but he insisted on returning to the front.'

'He wouldn't have been hit at all,' one of the Volunteers who had been fighting with them said, 'not if he hadn't broken the neck of the Jap about to decapitate Captain Harland.'

Elizabeth put out a hand to steady herself. 'Is Captain Harland safe? Is he hurt?'

'No,' the Volunteer said cheerfully. 'He was going like the bloody clappers the last time I saw him. The British bulldog at its best, that's Captain Harland. He can certainly show some of the youngsters a thing or two!'

Just after lunch she heard the rumours that there had been a general surrender, but the fighting around them continued. 'The Brigadier won't believe it,' one of the medical orderlies said crisply. 'Says he's fighting on until he receives orders in writing that he's to stop.'

Two hours later a staff car carrying a British staff officer and flying a white flag crossed the enemy line to Brigadier Wallis's headquarters. Minutes later the men were listening, stunned, as they were bitterly told that Hong Kong Island had surrendered to the Japanese.

'By order of His Excellency the Governor and General Officer Commanding, His Majesty's forces in Hong Kong have surrendered,' a young captain read from the order Wallis had issued to all the units under his command. 'On no account will firing or destruction of equipment take place as otherwise the lives of British hostages will be endangered. Units will organize themselves centrally forthwith.'

237

Elizabeth stood, the tears streaming down her cheeks. It was over. All the fighting and all the suffering had been in vain. Hong Kong had fallen. The Japanese were triumphant.

When the advancing Japanese had disappeared into the darkness, Ronnie had begun to drag himself forward, inch by inch, aware that blood was coursing freely from the wound at the back of his neck and that, try as he might, he could not raise himself to his knees, let alone to his feet. As dawn broke, he heaved and hauled himself on to the dust-blown road and then, his last reserves of energy expended, lay semi-conscious, face down, praying that the vehicle to discover him would be British.

'We thought you were a goner, mate,' a voice was saying jovially, and he was aware of excruciating pain in his neck and his head as he was bounced and shaken. 'Then I recognized that blond thatch of yours and I said: "Cor blimey, if it ain't Ronnie Ledsham." We'd still have left you where you were, but Lance-Corporal Davis said he badly wanted a word with you. Something about a horse that he put a week's money on and that limped home last.'

Ronnie tried to smile, but his facial muscles wouldn't respond. He was in the back of a truck and, if God was good to him, there would be a hospital bed and morphine at the end of his journey.

'From the way those Japs tried to decapitate him, they must have had money on his horse as well,' another voice said, and there was a ripple of laughter.

A shell exploded in the road ahead of them, and the truck-driver swerved sharply. Pain streamed through Ronnie, robbing him of all coherent thought. When they reached the nearest hospital, he was unconscious again.

The next thing he heard was an incredulous voice saying: 'You're a lucky bastard, Ledsham. There can't be many men who survive a sword-blow to the back of the neck.'

Ronnie struggled to open his eyes. The hideous shaking and bumping had stopped. He was prone and blessedly immobile, and there was a large dressing supporting the back of his neck. He focused hazily on a weary-looking doctor and managed a mockery of a grin. 'It would take more than a Japanese sword to put me out of the running,' he croaked gamely. 'Where am I?'

'Hospital,' the doctor said, satisfied that his patient would live.

'Thank God,' Ronnie whispered thankfully, and once more closed his eyes.

Six days later, when a sombre-faced chief medical officer informed the men in the crowded ward that Britain had surrendered, Ronnie was one of the few who were elated by the news. As far as Ronnie was concerned, it meant that he had survived the fighting, and it meant that he would soon be reunited with Julienne again.

'What do you think the Japs will do with us?' a soldier asked him.

Ronnie, now one of the walking wounded, was helping a hard-pressed nurse to change a dressing on the boy's leg. He shrugged his shoulders slightly, wincing with pain as he did so. He still felt as if he were recovering from the world's worst hangover. 'Intern us, I suppose,' he said optimistically. 'Life will be uncomfortable for a time, but it won't last for ever. Nothing does.'

The little nurse at his side remained silent. She had heard hideous rumours of the brutal treatment meted out to patients and staff in some of the more isolated dressing stations, but they were rumours her own patients were still blessedly ignorant of. Only minutes ago a jeep had screamed up to the hospital and a high-ranking officer had hurried inside for urgent talks with senior members of the staff. Seconds later, orders had been given for all stocks of alcohol on the premises to be destroyed, even though such stocks were proving enormously valuable as substitute antiseptics and painkillers.

'It's being done in the hope it will prevent the Japs indulging in a drunken orgy of rape,' one of her colleagues had said, white-faced with fear. 'But there will be plenty of alcohol to be looted from the shops in the Wanchai and, if they find out what we've done, it may make them madder than ever.'

The staff officer who had been despatched from Fortress Headquarters to warn the hospital of the treatment they might expect was striding past the end of the ward on his way back to his car when he caught a glimpse of Ronnie, supporting a patient's leg as a nurse deftly bandaged it. He knew Ronnie well, having often shared a drink with him at the Jockey Club, and he stood stock-still, the blood leaving his face.

'What is it, sir?' the medical officer escorting him back to his car asked curiously.

'That man, Ledsham. His wife was one of the nurses raped and murdered in the attack Major Elliot reported.'

'Christ!' The young medical officer looked in Ronnie's direction, horrified.

The staff officer tightened his lips and turned in the direction of the ward. 'I have to tell him,' he said resolutely. 'The man can't be left in ignorance.

'But what if the report is incorrect?' the medical officer asked, hurrying at his side. 'So many nurses have been transferred from post to post. She may not even have been there when the attack took place.'

'She was there all right,' the staff officer said grimly. 'Captain Elliot identified her himself.'

Ronnie turned round at the officer's approach. As an American, and an American once more in civilian clothes, he knew better than to reveal to a British officer just what good news he personally thought the surrender was. From the hospital window he could see white flags fluttering in the streets, and for the first time in what seemed an eternity there was no sound of exploding shells or detonating bombs. 'Good morning, sir,' he said, mindful of his drinking companion's rank and feeling very chipper. His Volunteer's uniform had been so saturated in blood that it had had to be destroyed and no replacement could be found.

Ronnie had been grateful. He felt much more comfortable in the tussore trousers and white linen shirt and slip-on shoes that had been given to him.

The staff officer felt sickly disorientated. It was impossible to talk to Ronnie and not remember the other occasions they had talked. The crowded laughter-filled bar at the Jockey Club. The parties at the Ledsham home on the Peak. The palm-filled Long Bar at the Peninsula.

'I need to talk to you, Ronnie,' he said, wondering how the man would take the news. There had always been gossip that the Ledsham marriage was on the rocks, gossip fed by Ronnie's blatant army of girlfriends. But the staff officer remembered that there hadn't been quite so many girlfriends of late and, even when there had been, he had always had the uncomfortable feeling that Julienne Ledsham had known all about them and had not thought them worth her notice.

'What is it going to be for us all?' Ronnie said chattily. 'Internment at Shamshuipo Barracks?'

The staff officer didn't know. It probably would be. The Japs would have to put them somewhere. He said, wishing that he had never looked into the ward on his hurried dash towards his car: 'I'm awfully sorry, Ronnie, but Julienne is dead.'

Ronnie's smile remained fixed on his face. 'What was that you said? I don't think I heard you correctly.'

'Julienne is dead,' the staff officer repeated gently. 'I'm sorry, old chap, I—'

'I don't believe you!' Ronnie backed away from him, laughing nervously. 'I don't believe you. There's been a mistake.'

The staff officer shook his head. This was far worse than he had thought it would be. 'No, Ronnie, it was Raefe Elliot who telephoned the report into Fortress HQ. The dressing station to which Julienne was posted was overrun in the early hours of the nineteenth. There was only one survivor, and that was Lady Gresby. The rest of the nursing staff were raped and murdered. Elliot identified Julienne himself.'

241

Ronnie was swaying slightly, taking in great gulps of breath, trying to speak and failing.

'As soon as it's possible to do so, we'll make sure her body and the bodies of those who died with her are brought back to Victoria and decently buried. . . .'

Ronnie stared at him.

The staff officer clapped him comfortingly on the arm and then turned, marching swiftly out of the ward.

Ronnie continued to stare after him and then looked towards the windows. The white flags were still fluttering.

'Thank God the fighting is over,' a man in a nearby bed said to him, seeing the direction of his gaze. 'We're just going to have to tolerate the bastards now, aren't we?'

Dead. Raped. Murdered. Julienne. It wasn't possible. They were going to start a family. They were going to have years of happiness together. Years and years of it. He began to walk slowly towards the door, in the staff officer's wake. The ward behind him was so crammed with injured men, the nursing staff so overworked and exhausted, that no one noticed him leave. Julienne dead. He stood in the street in the Wanchai, looking dazedly around him. Scores of British and Canadian soldiers were squatting quietly on the pavements, smoking as they dispiritedly awaited the arrival of the Japanese. The streets were riddled with potholes, littered with damaged cars and abandoned trucks. Steel helmets and gas-masks and armbands lay discarded in the gutters.

'We're just going to have to tolerate the bastards now, aren't we?' The words rang in his ears, and he shook his head fiercely. No, by God! Never. Julienne was dead, and the world had gone dark around him. The bulky dressing at the back of his neck made his movements difficult, and he raised his hand, feeling for the Elastoplast that secured it, ripping it free.

At the corner of the street a group of soldiers sat beside an empty jeep, tommy-guns on the ground beside them. 'Have you finished with those?' he asked them tersely.

They looked up at him, hungry and weary unto death.

'Everyone is finished with them,' one of them said bitterly. 'We've surrendered, didn't you know?'

'I haven't,' Ronnie said and bent down, lifting two of the tommy-guns and throwing them into the back of the jeep.

'And where do you think you're going with that lot?' their sergeant-major asked, making no move to apprehend him.

'I don't know,' Ronnie said, frozen-faced, as he opened the jeep's door and slipped behind the steering-wheel. 'Anywhere, just as long as there are Japs.'

'Then, you've got an easy task!' the sergeant-major said with a savage laugh. 'Because there's nowhere on this bloody island that there *aren't* any Japs!'

Ronnie turned the key hanging in the ignition. At the third try the jeep hiccuped into life.

'Maniac,' the sergeant-major said as Ronnie pulled away from the kerb and drove away down the bomb-blasted street. 'My God, what wouldn't I give for a decent meal and a drink of beer!'

Ronnie drove slowly. He wanted to think of Julienne. He wanted to remember her. He knew where there would be Japs. The hills around the gap would be thick with them. He drove away from the built-up streets and the shell-pocked buildings and the piles of Chinese dead. There hadn't been a day when he had been unhappy with her. There had never been a day when he had arrived home and she had not been pleased to see him. The streets petered out behind him. He could see the Japs now, hundreds and hundreds of them, squatting down on their haunches at the side of the road, awaiting the final order for the victory march into Victoria. None was disturbed at his approach. The surrender was hours old. White flags flew. The fighting was over.

Ronnie creaked to a halt at a curve where Stubbs Road merged into Wong Nei Chung Gap Road. The stench of rotting bodies fouled the air. He wondered how many men still lay out on the hillsides. He wondered how many of them were not yet dead, just dying horribly, with no access to food or water, terribly maimed.

He walked round to the rear of the truck and lifted the

tommy-guns out, tucking one under each arm. She had never knowingly hurt him. Not ever. She had loved him more than she had ever loved anyone else. He had been her life as she had been his. The Japs had seen him now and were looking across at him curiously. Some of them were beginning to rise to their feet.

'Bastards!' Ronnie howled, flinging himself down on his belly and opening fire on them with the first of the guns. 'Bastards! Bastards! Bastards!'

Tom stood, heartsick, at the gates of Murray Barracks. He and the other men he had been fighting alongside had been ordered to retreat there hours earlier when the surrender had been declared. The fighting was over. The Japanese, with an army Hong Kong society had always regarded as a ludicrous joke, had beaten them to their knees. Tom's shame was so intense that he wanted no one else to see it, and so, instead of remaining dispiritedly with the rest of the men, he stood alone, wondering if Lamoon was still at the Hong Kong Hotel. Wondering if she was still safe.

The next morning, Boxing Day, the Japanese came into the barracks and lined them all up and searched them. The weather was beautiful, the sun blazing down from a brilliant blue sky as they stood before the Japanese on the parade-ground. A Japanese private, attracted by the silver badge on the fore-and-aft cap of an adjutant to the Middlesex, pulled the hat from the adjutant's head. Tom felt his stomach muscles tighten. There had already been gross scenes of unnecessary violence, and now they waited tensely as the adjutant said in a calm voice to the Japanese warrant officer in charge: 'Tell that man to give me my hat back.'

Immediately the warrant officer strode towards him, screaming abuse, giving him a series of hard insulting slaps across his face. Tom looked uneasily at his neighbour. If this was how things were going to be, life as a prisoner of war beneath the Japs was going to be no picnic.

Two days later they were herded together and told they were crossing to Kowloon to be interned at Shamshuipo, the barracks that had once been home to the Middlesex. Degradingly they were marched through the streets, hemmed in by grinning Japanese sentries in ill-fitting shabby uniforms. The Chinese watched them, cowed and dejected. There was no one to arrange food distribution for them now. No one to protect them from the bullying victors. White flags hung desultorily from windows, interspersed with the Japanese flag of the rising sun. The streets were filthy, littered with the bodies of dead Chinese, the bombed and shattered sewers giving off a dreadful stench. Tom's eyes narrowed as they passed close to piles of the dead. Some of the bodies did not look as if they had been out beneath the sun for long, certainly not since Christmas Day. Which meant that they had died since the surrender. He thought of Lamoon and was nearly crippled by the fear he felt. The European women at the Hong Kong Hotel would be taken away to internment camps. But what would happen to Lamoon? Would she be taken with them, or would she be left to fend for herself, just one more to add to the many thousands of Chinese now openly starving?

'Think there'll be a chance to cut and run for it?' the man marching next to him asked, low-voiced.

'I don't know,' Tom replied. It had been exactly what he had been thinking himself. Breaking free from the column as they were marched past the Hong Kong Hotel, seeking out Lamoon and fleeing with her. But where to? Chungking, the wartime Chinese capital, was over a thousand miles away. There would be a British embassy there, and safety, but between Hong Kong and Chungking lay hundreds of miles of Japanese-occupied territory.

As they neared the shell-pitted walls of the Hong Kong Hotel, he looked hungrily towards the windows. If only he could see her! If only he could reassure himself that she was still safe! He scoured every window for a glimpse of her, but she wasn't there. Sick at heart, he trudged on towards the ferry, wondering when he would see her again. Wondering if he would ever see her again.

Lamoon wearily wiped her forehead with the back of her hand. Ever since her arrival at the Hong Kong Hotel she had taken on the role of nurse, and for the last six days and nights had hardly slept. She did not know that British and Canadian troops were being marched past the hotel on their way to internment until long after they had been herded down to the pier and the boats waiting to take them across to Kowloon.

Even though there might have been the faint chance of seeing Tom among their numbers, a part of her was glad that she had not witnessed their humiliation. She could not bear to think of it. It seemed beyond belief that the soldiers of the greatest empire the world had ever known were being jeered at and laughed at by Japanese troops.

The Europeans around her were stunned with shock, dazed by the finality of the capitulation, pathetically incredulous.

'But where were the Chinese? I thought the Chinese were sending an army to help us?' an elderly British woman asked, time and time again.

'Perhaps they will come now,' another said hopefully. 'Perhaps we will be relieved.'

Lamoon remained silent. She knew that if the Chinese army had been able to reach them it would have done so, but it was three years since the Japanese had driven the Chinese army back across country in order to capture Canton, and there had been no sign since of the Chinese being strong enough to regain the territory lost, territory that would have to be crossed before they could reach Hong Kong.

It had been on her second day in the hotel that she had overheard one of the auxiliary nurses saying worriedly to a colleague: 'But we can't just leave two European children in the care of an elderly Chinese. It isn't right.'

'They won't be parted from him,' her colleague replied

wearily. 'The little boy is adamant that his mummy said they had to remain with the old man. Though he's only five or six, he objected like the very devil when it was suggested he and his sister should be cared for by one of the women with children his own age.'

'If it comes to internment, then they'll *have* to be separated,' the first nurse said darkly. 'The Japs have no respect for the Chinese. They certainly won't waste food on them by feeding them in camps.'

Lamoon had tried not to think of what might happen to her if the Europeans in the hotel were interned. She had looked across to the old man and the two children that the nurses had been discussing, and had stared at them incredulously. She had never met Tom's nephew and niece, but she had seen photographs of them and had been struck by the little boy's likeness to Tom.

'Why is that lady looking at me like that?' Jeremy said, turning to Li Pi; and, as he did so, Lamoon's suspicions deepened into certainty. There was something in his movements that bore a definite Nicholson stamp. She hurried across to them, saying shyly to Li Pi; 'My name is Lamoon Sheng. I am a friend of Mr Tom Nicholson and Mrs Helena Nicholson. . . .'

Li Pi's anxious face creased into a smile. 'I, too,' he said with gentle dignity, 'am a friend of Mrs Nicholson.'

'And these are her children?' Lamoon asked as Jeremy and Jennifer stared gravely up at her.

Li Pi nodded. 'I was entrusted by her to take them to Mrs Harland's.' His smile faded, and he looked again very old and very anxious. 'But Mrs Harland's apartment has been destroyed by bombing and so we came here. The management know me. My name is Li Pi.'

His name meant nothing to Lamoon. She thought, as the Europeans thought, that he was an old family retainer. She stared at him, saying horrified: 'And Mrs Harland? Is she safe?'

For the first time Li Pi's suffering showed in his eyes. The thought of Elizabeth's brilliant talent being snuffed out by

247

the blast of a Japanese bomb was almost more than he could bear. 'I do not know,' he said fearfully. 'The local ARP men told me that one body was found. A girl's body. But they said that she was Chinese.'

They looked at each other, both knowing the mistakes that were so easily made when bodies were hastily removed from blasted buildings. 'We must pray,' Li Pi said, sensing how deep her concern for Elizabeth was. 'It is all that we can do now.'

For the next four days Lamoon had prayed. She had prayed for Tom, and for Helena and for Elizabeth. And she had prayed for herself and Li Pi and the children. On the day after Boxing Day, when the Japanese had stormed into the hotel, the children had clung to her fearfully.

'We're not going to be taken away from you, are we?' Jeremy had whispered, and Jennifer had begun to whimper, holding on to Lamoon's skirt, her eyes big and wide as bandy-legged Japanese had swarmed through the rooms with fervent shouts of 'Long live the Emperor!'

'No,' Lamoon had said to him reassuringly, her heart hammering painfully as she wondered what she would do if such an attempt was made.

'All American, all British, all Dutch together,' the Japanese officer in charge ordered.

'What is to happen to us?' a young American woman asked bravely. 'Where are our husbands?'

The Jap found her last question beneath contempt and did not deign to reply to it. 'You are going to Japanese internment camp,' he said magnanimously. 'All things there will be good. Food will be plentiful and conditions will be pleasant. I hope that you appreciate this kindness from the Imperial Japanese Army. As you know, the soldiers of Nippon are always kind to women.'

No one listening to him believed him. As the Europeans were pushed and jostled together, the Chinese refugees who had taken shelter with them were driven at bayonet point out into the street.

'I must go,' Li Pi said to Lamoon unsteadily, releasing his

248

hold of the children's hands. 'They may allow you to stay with them, but they will never allow me. I cannot cause an incident. Not in front of the little ones. Joi Gin.' Goodbye.

'No!' She tried to catch hold of his arm, but he had gone, and as she took a step after him a Jap bore down on her, a bayonet in his hand.

'All Chinese out!' he shouted, seizing her shoulder.

Jennifer tightened her hold on Lamoon's skirts, beginning to cry. Jeremy stood white-faced. 'Let go of her!' he said bravely to the savage-looking Jap. 'Don't you dare to hurt her!'

Lamoon, terrified that he would be hurt, began tearfully to try to disentangle Jennifer from her skirt, and the young American, who had asked what was to happen to them, stepped forward. 'That young woman is not Chinese,' she said authoritatively, not knowing if Lamoon was or not. 'She is Eurasian, and those children are hers. She must be allowed to remain with them.'

The Jap paused, uncertain.

'That is correct,' the nurse who had been anxious at Li Pi's guardianship of them said with equal certainty. 'If we go into internment, she must be allowed to come with us. And the children also.'

The Jap hesitated for a moment and then nodded. 'You go with others,' he said to Lamoon. 'But you bow to Japanese officer. Everyone must bow to Japanese officer!'

Lamoon bowed, tears stinging her eyes as the children huddled at either side of her. For the moment she and the children would remain together, but what would happen to Li Pi? How would he survive the harsh brutality that the Japanese were meting out to the Chinese?

The American woman crossed the room towards her, defying the Japanese order that she remain subserviently stationary. 'Come along,' she said forcefully. 'Stay with me. We don't want you being separated from the rest of us again, do we?'

Lamoon smiled gallantly through her tears. She had found a friend. She was determined that she would also find

Helena. And one day, if God was willing, she would also find Tom and Li Pi again. 'Thank you,' she said, with a hint of her habitual shyness. 'I would like that very much.' And with the children's hands clasped tightly in her own she crossed the room to where the European women were waiting for instructions as to where they were to go.

Only the thought of the children, the absolute necessity of surviving in order that she might be reunited with them, enabled Helena to endure the days and nights after the Japanese ransacked the hospital. At one point she had been forced to lie on the bodies of the dead while the Japanese had abused her again and again and again. When news had come that she was being taken across to Hong Kong Island to be interned in a civilian camp at Stanley, she had sobbed with relief.

The ferries had been crowded with numbed dazed civilians, the women's eyes black-shadowed at the experiences they had undergone. Helena barely recognized the harbour. The water was green and dirty, full of the wreckage of junks and sampans, and thick with floating distended corpses. She averted her eyes, lifting them upwards towards the towering grandeur of the Peak, taking comfort in its enduring beauty.

Trucks ferried them down towards Stanley, the scenes of devastation so dreadful that many of the women began to weep. Bodies still lay unrecovered on the hillside, burned-out remains of jeeps and trucks bearing silent witness to the ferocity of the fighting that had taken place.

At the gates of what had once been a large rambling gaol, they halted. There was a great mass of civilians already there, suitcases by their sides, pathetic bundles of personal belongings tucked beneath their arms.

'Where are they from?' Helena asked urgently, feverishly searching the bewildered defeated faces for a glimpse of Elizabeth. For a glimpse of Jeremy and Jennifer.

'Heaven only knows,' the elderly lady crammed next to her said. 'Victoria probably or Repulse Bay. I heard there were a lot of civilians trapped at Repulse Bay.'

She couldn't see the distinctive gleam of Elizabeth's pale gold hair, but suddenly she saw a lone Oriental face. A very beautiful face. 'Lamoon!' she shouted, leaning over the side of the truck and waving furiously. 'Lamoon!'

Lamoon's head turned swiftly in Helena's direction, and then as Helena continued to call her name and wave furiously, and as Lamoon saw who it was calling out to her, her face lit up with unalloyed joy and she began pushing and shoving through the milling crowd, towards the stationary truck.

'Lamoon!' Helena shouted again, and then she saw the tiny figure in Lamoon's arms and the slightly bigger one running at her side, and tears of joy began to flood down her cheeks. 'Oh God!' she gasped, leaning out over the side of the truck, her arms outstretched. 'Oh God! Thank you! Thank you!'

A guard was racing towards them, but by the time he roughly pushed Lamoon and Jeremy away from the truck Lamoon had thrust Jennifer up into her arms. She could see that Jeremy was undisturbed at the Jap's action, too overcome by relief at seeing her again to care that he would have to wait a little longer before he could throw himself into her arms.

'Let's go in there defiantly,' she shouted down to him as the gates opened and the trucks began to move forward. 'Let's go in there singing!' And, pressing Jennifer's cheek closely against hers, she began to sing in a clear lovely contralto: 'There'll always be an England.'

The motley assortment of civilians in the accompanying trucks and the civilians on foot took up the strain. 'And England will be free!' they sang out, their heads high, their hearts filled with determination to survive as they entered Stanley Gaol. 'As long as England means to you what England means to me!'

# 16

In the hours immediately following the surrender the men on the Stanley Peninsula were dazed and bewildered, exhausted beyond belief. Elizabeth continued to care for the wounded, crippled by guilt at the knowledge that she would soon be leaving them. Raefe made a final report to Brigadier Wallis, informing him of the instructions he had been given. Adam hurriedly collected provisions for their long march.

'The Brigadier wants us to take two men with us,' Raefe said as they met together at dusk. 'Captains Henry Bassett and Lawrence Fisher. Bassett speaks fluent Cantonese and Fisher is a doctor. Bassett, especially, will be useful if we should become split into two groups or if anything should happen to me.' Elizabeth took a sharp intake of breath, but he ignored it, saying to Adam: 'Are you sure you want to come? It's going to be quite a trek.'

Adam knew that Raefe was obliquely referring to his lame leg. 'I'm coming,' he said staunchly. 'I've lived with my lameness for years, and it's never hindered me. It isn't going to do so now just because it's been peppered with shrapnel.'

Raefe didn't argue. If Adam had been anyone else, he would have adamantly refused to have him as a member of the party. As it was, a strange bonding had been forged between them as they had fought and risked their lives for each other. And he couldn't order Adam to stay behind. Not when he was going to take Elizabeth with him. 'All right,' he said tersely, knowing at least that Adam would give his life for Elizabeth if it became necessary. 'What provisions have we got?'

They had tins of bully beef and sardines and condensed milk and, strangely, Quaker Oats. 'It was all I could scrounge,' Adam said apologetically.

Knowing how long it was since any of the hundreds of dispirited troops around them had eaten, no one argued with him.

'When do we leave?' Elizabeth asked quietly.

'In an hour. When it's dark. Bassett and Fisher are to meet up with us down on the beach.'

'And where do we go first?' Adam asked as Raefe spread a Crown Lands and Surveys Office map out on the ground before them.

'We're requisitioning the motor-boat that the Chinese have been trying to ferry provisions across the bay in. It's old and it's leaky, and it's too great a risk to try to make for the mainland in it, but if we can reach Lamma Island there will be a motor torpedo-boat waiting for us off the west coast.'

Adam had long ago realized that Raefe had connections with military intelligence. If Raefe said there would be a motor torpedo-boat waiting for them, then he believed him.

'With luck, the motor torpedo-boat will be able to land us at Mirs Bay, to the north-east of the New Territories. There are Chinese guerrilla forces in action there, and we should be able to rely on them for help.'

'And then we walk?' Adam asked, tracking the coastline on the map with his forefinger and halting when he reached the broad expanse of Mirs Bay.

Raefe nodded. 'Sixty miles to Waichow. That will be the most difficult part of the journey. The ground is mountainous and it will be infested with Japs. From Waichow things should become easier. We'll then be within the territory of the Chinese Regular Forces, and we'll also be able to travel by boat. The East River runs from Waichow to Leung Chuen, about two hundred miles further north. From there we will be on foot again until we reach Kukong, and from Kukong we should be able to travel to Chungking by rail.'

'What will you do then?' Adam asked him, squatting on his haunches and looking across at Raefe curiously.

'My orders are to stay there and help the Chinese form British-led guerrilla units. There's also going to have to be an organization established to arrange the escape of prisoners of war and internees from Hong Kong. If there is, I'd like to be a part of it.'

Adam remained silent. There was a British embassy in Chungking, and no doubt he would also find himself under orders, but he had no intimate knowledge of China and could not speak Cantonese. His orders certainly wouldn't be the same as Raefe's. He would probably be sent to India or Burma, somewhere where he would have to take a back seat until the war was over. It occurred to him that he would, in all likelihood, have Elizabeth with him. They were still husband and wife. He wondered if the same thought had also occurred to Raefe, but if it had he gave no sign of it.

His sleek black hair fell low across his brow, and his high-cheekboned face was weary. 'Let's go,' he said, and Adam noticed that as he rose to his feet he did so without his usual pantherlike speed. The sling he had discarded so contemptuously shortly after leaving the Repulse Bay Hotel was still discarded but his bandaged arm and shoulder were obviously giving him pain. Adam felt a wave of apprehension flood through him. It was twelve hundred miles to Chungking, and without Raefe their chances of ever reaching it were virtually nonexistent. As they hoisted their haversacks on to their shoulders and began to walk down towards the beach, he took comfort from the fact that Raefe would not be attempting it if he wasn't confident of success. He would put his own life at risk without so much as a second thought but he wouldn't put Beth's life at risk also.

From the darkened beach they could see fires raging intermittently all along the coastline. 'The Japs are probably putting private houses to the torch,' Captain Bassett said to them, and Elizabeth shivered, thinking of the home she and Raefe had shared and which she was now sure she would never see again.

Captain Bassett was a short, chunkily built young man with fair straight hair and a ready smile. If he had been stunned at Elizabeth's presence on the beach and the realization that she was to accompany them across China, he had hidden it magnificently. As they walked across the pebbled beach and into the shallows to the waiting motor-boat, he told her that he spoke not only Cantonese but French, Italian, Urdu and Pushtu as well. He asked her if she was Scandinavian, with an eye to learning another language as they trekked, and was disappointed when she disillusioned him.

Captain Fisher was far more taciturn and reserved. He had taken Raefe to one side, objecting strongly to the presence of a woman on such an arduous undertaking, and his objections had been curtly overridden. Mrs Harland, he was told, was coming with them. As they scrambled across the beach he looked across at Adam Harland curiously. He didn't look a very influential figure. Fisher wondered what pull he had that ensured a man like Elliot giving way to him over the question of his wife.

The Chinese, who had been ferrying provisions to the troops cut off on the peninsula, risking heavy enemy fire each time that they did so, had remained with their boat.

'We go now,' they said anxiously as Raefe helped Elizabeth aboard. 'The Japanese coastal batteries quiet now. We go now, while it's safe.'

As they squatted down in the damp smelly boat, Elizabeth saw the dark shape of a child huddled in the bow. She smiled reassuringly, but the pale little face, barely visible in the darkness, did not smile back.

'Is this your little boy?' she whispered to one of the boatmen as the boat's engine throbbed into life and they began to chug steadily out from shore.

The Chinese shook his head, answering her question in Cantonese.

'It's a girl, not a boy, and he says he doesn't know who she is,' Raefe interpreted for her, his eyes scanning the shoreline behind them for signs of activity from any of the Japanese coastal batteries. 'He says their village was bombed and that after the bombing he found her crouched in the bottom of his boat. She's been here ever since, living on whatever scraps they can give her. Her parents are dead.'

The child continued to stare at Elizabeth, her eyes wide and dark. 'But she looks as if she's starving!' Elizabeth protested, horrified.

Raefe glanced across at the child. The bewilderment in her eyes and the dumb acceptance of her fate he had seen all too often before.

When Elizabeth began fumbling in her rucksack he didn't deter her, even though Fisher said coldly: 'We haven't enough rations to hand out willy-nilly.'

Elizabeth ignored him, pressing a tin of sardines into the child's hand. She was huddled up and so thin and scrawny that it was impossible to judge how old she might be. She was possibly seven or eight, though her eyes were ages old.

The tin was seized eagerly and pressed close against her chest, as though defying anyone to remove if from her.

'It's all right,' Adam said reassuringly to her. 'It's yours.' And then a brilliant arc light blazed out from the shore and shells slammed into the water around them.

Elizabeth threw herself down on the waterlogged floor of the boat, pulling the child with her. Adam heard Raefe give a low harsh cry as machine-gun and rifle fire opened up on them; and then, just when Adam thought all hope was lost, the blazing light swung sharply away from them to the east as another target, more worthwhile than a village motor-boat, came into their sights.

Adam began to ease his way towards Raefe, saying urgently: 'What is it? Have you been hit?'

'No!' Raefe snapped harshly, hunched in the stern, peering out in the darkness as he tried to see what vessel had attracted the Japs' attention.

Adam sat back, knowing better than to persist with his

questioning. He stretched out a hand to Elizabeth, pulling her back into a sitting position, and the child crawled upright with her, huddling against her for comfort as every minute took them further and further away from the coastal guns.

Eventually all sound of gunfire faded. The night wind was bitterly cold, and Elizabeth hugged the thinly clad child, trying to warm her as best she could.

'It seems ironic that when we pick up the motor torpedo-boat we're going to have to backtrack on ourselves, rounding the Stanley Peninsula in order to reach Mirs Bay,' Captain Fisher said as Lamma Island appeared in the darkness, a low black hump.

'It can't be helped,' Raefe said brusquely. 'No motor torpedo-boat could have come ashore to take us off. This one is lying out of sight of the Jap guns on the west side of the island. Once we're aboard her, she can keep well away from land as she rounds the peninsula and travels up the New Territories coastline.'

'If she's there,' Fisher said drily. 'What happens if she's not?'

'The motor-boat will stay anchored for four hours on the east side of the island. If we don't pick up the motor torpedo-boat, then we return to it and tomorrow night we try to cross to the west side of Kowloon and strike out for the Chinese border from there.'

'That sounds a dodgy proposition,' Captain Bassett said with a shiver. 'I shouldn't fancy our chances anywhere within a twenty-mile radius of Kowloon. Mirs Bay sounds much more attractive.'

The Chinese at the helm turned off the engine, and the boat rode ashore on stones and sand.

'How far to the east coast?' Fisher asked as they waded ashore.

'A mile, perhaps less. It's a very narrow neck of land here,' Raefe said abruptly, his jacket pulled close about him.

Elizabeth crossed the sand towards him, slipping her

257

hand into his, needing brief physical contact with him to express her relief that so far none of them had been hurt. Raefe gave her hand a tight squeeze and then released it as he strode across to the boatmen, confirming with them that they would wait for four hours in case they should return.

Captain Bassett looked after him, and then back to Elizabeth, bewilderedly. He had been given to understand that she was Harland's wife. If she was, and if she was also Elliot's mistress, then the trek ahead was going to be fraught with more than one kind of danger.

Raefe took the lead, and they set out on a wide earth-covered path winding through the sweet-smelling fir trees. They had only gone twenty yards or so when Fisher halted abruptly. 'We're being followed!' he hissed. 'Listen.'

Everyone froze, listening intently. There was nothing to be heard but the soughing of the wind in the trees.

'You're mistaken, old chap,' Captain Bassett said, heaving his rucksack into a more comfortable position on his back. 'Come on, that motor torpedo-boat won't wait for us for ever.'

Once more they began to move forward, walking in single file, Elizabeth immediately behind Raefe, and Adam behind her, Captain Fisher and Captain Bassett taking it in turns to bring up the rear.

The track climbed steeply at one point and then began to run down towards the sea. 'I can see it!' Adam whispered to Raefe, pointing out a single boat low in the sea. 'How do we manage to attract its attention without making any noise and alerting any Japs that might be lurking around?'

'We can't,' Raefe said with unusual sharpness. 'We have to take a risk.'

Hurriedly they scrambled down to the shore, and then Captain Bassett stripped off his shirt and began to wave it furiously as they all shouted across the sea at the top of their lungs. Minutes later they could see a skiff being lowered, and Elizabeth leaned against Raefe, weak with relief.

258

'It's going to be all right,' she said as his good arm closed around her waist. 'Once we're aboard the boat, we'll be relatively safe.'

There was a small sound from behind them, and this time they all heard it. 'What the devil . . .' Captain Bassett expostulated, whipping round, his gun in his hand.

A small weary figure began to walk towards them across the narrow strip of sand.

'It's the child!' Adam said incredulously. 'She's followed us.'

'Then, she'll have to go back,' Fisher said brusquely. 'It's bad enough that we have to take the responsibility for a woman without having a child tagging on as well.'

The child, sensing how unwelcome she was, hung back. Elizabeth looked pleadingly across at Raefe. 'We can't leave her here! She'll starve! At least let us take her with us as far as Mirs Bay. There'll be a village there. People. We'll be able to find someone to leave her with.'

'My God, I've never heard of anything so ridiculous!' Fisher began contemptuously.

'*Please*, darling!' Elizabeth said urgently. 'It will only be another few hours and then she will be safe as well!'

Raefe looked across at the pathetic figure of the child. Her dress was ragged, offering her no protection at all against the cold night wind, and her feet were bare. 'All right,' he said curtly. 'But she's your responsibility, Lizzie. No one else's.'

The skiff had grounded ashore, and a dark-uniformed figure was herding Bassett and Fisher aboard. Elizabeth ran across to the little girl. 'Come on,' she said, taking her hand. 'Stay close to me.'

Adam looked at Raefe curiously as they were ferried from the skiff to the boat. The bones of his face seemed to have taken on sharper lines than usual, and beneath his heavy jacket his injured arm hung far more awkwardly than it had previously done.

The captain of the boat immediately commandeered Raefe, and Adam was unable to ask him again if he was all right.

259

Crouching low in cramped but far drier conditions than they had experienced on the motor-boat, they slipped out into the China Sea at a brisk twenty knots. They sailed steadily east through the darkness, giving the gaunt outline of the Stanley Peninsula a wide berth and then continuing northwards along the indented coast of the New Territories, towards Mirs Bay.

'Where do you want us to put you ashore, sir?' the captain asked Raefe as the first rays of dawn began to streak the sky.

'There's a small bay, just north of Nam-O,' Raefe said, glad of the disguising darkness as he stood at the captain's side. 'Put us ashore there.'

The captain sailed in as near to the coast as he dared and then the skiff was lowered into the water and they climbed down into it, shivering with cold as they were paddled ashore.

'What now?' Adam asked as they wearily waded ashore just as the sun was rising. 'It's pretty lonely here. How far do you think the village is?'

Raefe looked grey with exhaustion. 'Not far,' he said tersely. 'About half a mile.'

'Can't we lay up here?' Henry Bassett asked him and then, seeing the look of veiled contempt that Fisher gave him, added hurriedly: 'I was thinking of Mrs Harland. She must be extremely tired.'

Elizabeth was, but she shook her head in denial, sensing that Raefe desperately wanted them to push on. 'No,' she said, still holding the hand of the little Chinese girl. 'Please don't worry about me, Captain Bassett. I'm fine.' She smiled at him, and Captain Bassett felt a rush of heat to his groin. Even in the darkness of the previous evening he had realized that she was a remarkably beautiful woman. Now, in the pale golden light of the rising sun, he saw for the first time just how beautiful. Her silvery-blonde hair was pulled away from her face, secured at the nape of her neck with coral pins. Her green-gold eyes were thickly lashed, full of staunch endurance. He noted the creased and blood-spattered uniform beneath the army jacket that she was wearing for warmth, and wondered what her civilian profession was. Probably she didn't have one. Her husband, Adam Harland, was obviously crazily in love with her if the concern in his eyes whenever he looked across at her was anything to go by. As Captain Elliot was.

Henry Bassett wondered if Adam Harland knew of the liaison between his wife and the Captain. There was such a close sense of unity between them all that he thought he couldn't possibly know. Still pondering on the relationship of his companions, he brought up the rear as they walked away from the beach and inland, between carefully tended paddy-fields to the village.

'It's a Hakka village,' Raefe said briefly to Adam as they began to enter it. 'The people should be friendly, but I doubt if there will be any Chinese guerrillas there to give us help. If there aren't, we shall just have to press on by ourselves.'

Although it was still very early, half a dozen small children ran to meet them, waving their arms in greeting and shouting for others to come and see the funny foreigners. The children led them into the heart of the village, past primitive dwellings with pigs nosing for food, and into a small paved courtyard with a fung-shui tree growing in the centre.

'This is obviously the village square,' Adam murmured to Elizabeth as an elderly headman in a blue cotton jacket and long trousers invited them all to sit down with him around a large stone table. The village women, wrinkled and bent from hard work in the fields, and dressed in traditional black trousers and tunics, grinned toothlessly at them and offered them tea.

They drank it gratefully, and Adam remembered the first time he had drunk Chinese tea, sitting with Beth in the little teahouse near the waterfront on their first morning in Victoria. It seemed so long ago, so much a part of another age, that he couldn't believe it was barely two years.

Raefe had been speaking to the headman in Cantonese,

261

with Captain Fisher watching him closely. At last he turned round to them, saying briefly: 'The headman is going to give us one of his young men as a guide to the nearest guerrilla camp. He has also invited us to eat with them.'

'Jolly good show,' Captain Bassett said cheerily, beaming good-naturedly at the women as they brought rice-bowls and chopsticks and set them on the table in front of them.

'I need to talk to you,' Raefe said quietly to Adam, and while Elizabeth was busily filling the little Chinese girl's bowl with rice and vegetables and fish from a large central dish he quietly slipped away from the table.

Adam followed him towards the fung-shui tree, full of his old apprehension. He had known something was wrong ever since the coastal battery had opened fire on them when they were crossing to Lamma Island.

'You're going to have to go on without me,' Raefe said to him harshly when they were out of earshot of the others.

Adam stared at him, stupefied. Whatever he had expected, it had not been a calamity of these proportions. 'But you *have* to come with us,' he gasped. 'It's over a thousand miles to Chungking! We don't stand a chance without you!'

'You don't stand a chance with me,' Raefe said grimly, and slowly and with difficulty he opened his heavy army jacket.

The makeshift pad was dark with blood. Near-black deoxidized blood.

'Oh my God,' Adam whispered. 'I knew it! I knew you'd been hit!'

'And I knew there wasn't any point in letting anyone know,' Raefe said drily and Adam was horrified at how difficult he was finding it even to speak. 'I just wanted . . . to be sure that you had a guide.'

He swayed on his feet, and Adam seized his arm, supporting him. 'What do you want me to do?' he asked urgently, knowing with sickening horror that Raefe could not possibly survive his wound.

'The maps and compass and medical supplies are . . . in

my rucksack,' he said, beads of sweat trickling down from his forehead. 'The Hakka guide will take you to the guerrillas.' He paused, drawing in a deep ragged breath, and then said: 'Keep on the right side of Fisher. He's an irascible devil, but you need him.'

'Elizabeth won't leave you behind,' Adam protested. 'We'll stay here, in the village. . . .'

Raefe shook his head. 'No,' he said adamantly. 'This is Japanese-controlled territory. It isn't safe. If the motor torpedo-boat was sighted as we came ashore . . . then there'll be Japs here within the hour. You have to leave now. Immediately.'

'Beth will never agree to that! There's no way on God's earth that I could persuade her to leave you behind.'

Raefe managed a slight grin. 'I know,' he said, 'and I'm glad.' He drew in a deep steadying breath, and when he could speak again he said: 'Leave Lizzie to me. I'll tell her that I'm bringing up the rear and will meet up with you at nightfall. But, for God's sake, don't allow her to talk to me for more than a few seconds or she'll guess the truth.'

'Oh Jesus,' Adam said brokenly. 'Oh God!'

Raefe licked his lips. 'I want you to do one thing for me, Adam.'

'Anything!' Adam was near to tears. This was the man he had hated with every fibre of his being, and it was the man whose death was nearly going to destroy him with grief.

'Lizzie is pregnant.' He saw the incredulity in Adam's eyes, and the old grin touched the corners of his mouth again. 'Look after her for me, Adam. And look after the child.'

Their hands were tightly clasped. Adam could feel the tears streaming down his face. Elizabeth was walking towards them, revived by the hot tea and the plentiful food.

'Are you having a private conversation, or can anyone join in?' she called out good-humouredly.

'Don't let her stay with me!' Raefe hissed fiercely

to Adam. 'Not for a second longer than necessary!'

Adam gave Raefe's hands a last tight squeeze and then turned away, unable to speak. Elizabeth did not notice his distress; she had eyes only for Raefe and was shocked at how exhausted and gaunt he looked. 'You haven't eaten,' she said gently. 'You'll feel better if you do.'

He gathered up the last reserves of his strength and flashed her a brilliant down-slanting smile. Her hair was like spun gold, and he longed to reach out and touch it, but he knew that if he did so his shaking hand would betray him. He leaned against the tree, feigning his old nonchalance. 'I want you to leave with Adam and Bassett and Fisher,' he said, making a superhuman effort to keep the pain from his voice. 'I'm going to bring up the rear, keeping well behind.'

She nodded. She didn't like the idea of marching all day without him at her side, but he was in command and she had no intention of making his task any harder than it already was.

'Jung-shui doesn't want to remain behind in the village. She wants to come with us. Can she? I'll share my rations with her and make sure that she is no trouble.'

'Jung-shui, is that her name?' He was playing for time, trying to think. It might be best if the child went with her. Having such a responsibility might help her through her grief when she discovered that he would not be rejoining her. 'Yes,' he said, knowing that Fisher wouldn't like it but that Adam would be able to deal with the situation. 'Take her with you if you want, but you'll have to be parted from her eventually.'

Elizabeth was not so sure. The child had no family. The idea of keeping her with her permanently had already begun to take root.

Adam was looking across at them anxiously. Raefe knew that in a second he was going to do as he had asked and ensure that Lizzie remained with him no longer. 'You must go,' he said harshly. 'The others are waiting.'

'And I'll see you tonight?' She was smiling up at

him, all the love she felt for him glowing in her eyes.

'Yes,' he said, feeling his heart break within him. 'I'll see you tonight, Lizzie.'

She stood on tiptoe, uncaring of what Captain Bassett or Captain Fisher thought, and kissed him tenderly on the mouth. 'I love you,' she said, thinking joyously of all the years that lay ahead of them, and then she turned swiftly on her heel, picking up her rucksack and following Adam as he began to stride quickly out of the village in the Hakka boy's wake.

The village children scurried along at their side, and at the edge of the village Adam paused, thanking the village headman for his hospitality and his help. As Bassett and Fisher shook hands with other village elders who had come to wave them on their way, Elizabeth turned for a last glimpse of Raefe. He was leaning against the fung-shui tree, looking as relaxed and as insolently nonchalant as he had been the first time she had set eyes on him, in the Hong Kong Club's bar. The sun gleamed on his tumbled dark hair, sheening it to blue-black, and an odd ironic smile touched the corners of his mouth as he lifted his hand in farewell. She pressed her fingers to her mouth, blowing him a kiss, and then she turned, plunging after Adam as he strode out on to the narrow path leading between the paddy-fields and towards the hills.

Despite their lack of sleep, they trekked all day. At one point, as they reached a high ridge, they could see the shimmer of the sea and then it was lost to view as they clambered down into a ravine thick with fir and bamboo. Jung-shui kept up a valiant pace at Elizabeth's side, not asking where they were going, not caring, grateful merely to have Elizabeth's protection.

Shortly after midday their young Hakka guide became increasingly nervous, constantly stopping and cupping his ear, as if listening to sounds that the rest of them couldn't hear.

'What is it?' Adam asked nervously. 'Are we being followed?'

'Not sure,' the Hakka boy said succinctly and then, moving with ever-increasing caution, he cut away from the track, leading them up a steep slope through shaded groves of bamboo. At the summit he lay flat, signalling for them to follow suit. They did so only just in time. A Japanese patrol was marching down the track, in the direction of the village.

'It would seem a good moment to take a rest,' Lawrence Fisher said drily, heaving his rucksack wearily from his shoulder.

The Hakka boy nodded in agreement, speaking rapidly in Cantonese to Henry Bassett.

'He says we should stay here until dusk, in case there are more patrols following,' Henry translated. There were no protests; everyone was desperate for rest.

'What about Raefe?' Elizabeth whispered urgently to Adam. 'Will he be safe?'

Adam thought of Raefe, his life-blood seeping away beneath the heavy army jacket. 'Yes,' he said abruptly, not able to look her in the eyes. 'He'll be safe.'

At dusk they began to walk again, bypassing many villages that had been bombed and were now charred ruins. It was shortly after midnight when they reached the guerrilla headquarters at Wang Nih Hui.

'Thank God,' Henry Bassett had said thankfully, sinking down on to a pile of straw. 'I couldn't walk another step.'

'You'll have to tomorrow,' Fisher said tartly.

Henry didn't care about tomorrow. Fully clothed, he closed his eyes and in seconds was asleep, snoring loudly.

'I don't understand,' Elizabeth said worriedly to Adam. 'Where is Raefe? Why hasn't he caught up with us?'

'He will do,' Adam said, wondering how the hell he was going to break the news to her. 'Try to sleep, Beth. We're going to have just as long a trek to face in the morning.'

She slept restlessly, waking often, aware that Raefe had still not joined them. At dawn the guerrilla camp bustled into life. Sausages were provided for them and also the unexpected luxury of hot cocoa.

'Today we have to cross the Tah Shui-Shao road which is heavily used by Japanese patrols and convoys,' the guerrilla leader told Henry Fisher, squatting down at his side. 'A party of our men are going ahead now to plan the best way of crossing it.'

Bassett relayed the information to the others. Adam and Lawrence Fisher received the news in silence, knowing very well what fate would be in store for them if their attempt failed and they were captured by the Japanese.

'We can't leave!' Elizabeth protested urgently to Adam. 'Not until Raefe catches up with us.'

Bassett and Fisher were hoisting their rucksacks on to their backs. The young Hakka boy was showing no signs of returning to his village but was standing with the guerrillas, obviously intending to stay with them.

'We have to go,' Adam said as the guerrillas and Bassett and Fisher began to file out of the camp.

'We can't go! I won't go!' Her distress tore at his heart.

'You have to, Beth,' he said, knowing that the terrible moment could be postponed no longer. 'Raefe isn't going to join us. He was injured when we came under fire from the coastal battery. He's staying behind at Mirs Bay so that he won't slow us up.'

'I don't believe you!' She took a step backwards. 'I don't believe you! It isn't true! Oh, please tell me that it isn't true!' Her eyes were frantic, her face bloodless.

'My dear, I'm so sorry,' he said compassionately, reaching out to take her in his arms. 'Raefe knew that if you were told you wouldn't leave him, and he *wanted* you to leave him. He *wants* you to be safe.'

'No!' she said, pressing the back of her hand against her mouth. 'Oh, no!' And then she turned, beginning to run away from the guerrillas and Fisher and Bassett, running in the direction they had come from. Running towards Raefe.

He sprang after her, seizing her wrist, swinging her violently towards him. 'It's no good!' he protested desperately. 'You can't go back! There are Japs on the road!'

'I don't care!' She was fighting him, struggling to get free. 'I'm not leaving him to face capture alone! I'm going to him! There's nothing you can do to stop me!'

'He won't *be* there when you return!' he shouted at her; and then, hating himself for his brutality, he said as gently as he could: 'He was dying, Beth!'

She sucked in her breath, staring at him unbelievingly, and then she began to scream.

He had never struck a woman in his life and he would have thought himself physically incapable of striking Beth. His hand caught her savagely at the side of her face, stunning her into silence. 'He's dying and there's not a goddamned thing anyone can do about it!' he roared savagely. 'Now, for God's sake, don't make his dying alone worthless! Don't bring the Japs hurtling down on men who are risking their lives to help us!'

She was sobbing hysterically, the tears streaming down her face. He tightened his hold of her, dragging her in his wake. 'Come along,' he said brokenly, his rage dying, tears scalding his own eyes. 'We have to catch them up, Beth. We mustn't be left behind.'

# 17

She remembered very little of the long arduous journey to Chungking. They crossed the Tah Shui Shao road, narrowly escaping being sighted by a convoy of Japanese trucks. From there on the way became very steep, and Henry Bassett began to suffer acutely from the heat. Adam relieved him of his rucksack, carrying it along with his own as they trudged over rough ground, each day and every day. A week later they reached Waichow and then, for a blissful few days, they were able to travel by barge up the East River to Leung Chuen.

Only the conviction that Raefe was still alive sustained her. The people in the village where they had left him had been friendly. They would have taken care of him and they would have hidden him from the Japanese. One day they would be reunited. So sure was she of it that it gave her the strength she needed to cope with the lack of food and the lice-ridden blankets that served as bedding and the constant never-ending weariness.

At Leung Chuen they were given a lift to Kukong in a truck driven by a captain in the Chinese Nationalist Forces, and from Kukong they travelled by rail to Chungking, with money loaned to them by the staff of Kukong's Methodist mission.

'I never thought we'd make it,' Henry Bassett kept saying. 'Truly, I never thought we'd make it.'

Adam smiled at him wearily. There had been times when he, too, had doubted that they would ever reach Chungking. The two-month trek had broken his health, and he knew it. He would never be robust again. He scarcely recognized himself when he entered the luxury of a bath-room at the British embassy and looked at himself in the mirror. He had become an old man. His still thick hair was no longer grizzled, but pure white, and his luxuriant beard made him look like a grotesque and semi-starved Father Christmas. He began to clip it and then to soap the stubble, razoring it off, marvelling at Beth's constitution. She looked so delicate and fragile, and she had proved to be so tough. She was still carrying the baby, her thickening waistline visible witness of its continuing existence.

They had been greeted by embassy officials as husband and wife, and treated as such, both of them too weary to face the inevitable confusion that would follow if they stated that they were separated.

'This is much easier,' Adam had said to her, 'especially in view of your condition.'

Elizabeth had been uncaring as to whether it was easier or not. Her one concern was how soon she would be able to receive confirmation that Raefe was alive.

'There'll be official lists of all prisoners of war captured, won't there?' she had said to him, her eyes harrowed, her face ivory pale.

'Yes,' he had answered, wondering if the Japanese would be mindful of the Geneva Convention, 'but it will be months, possibly longer, before the Red Cross will have access to such information.'

'Then, I'll wait,' she had said quietly, her hand passing lightly over her rounding stomach. 'But Raefe is alive, Adam. I know he is.'

Within hours of his arrival he had been asked to make an official report to the military authorities. He did so, giving all the information he could about the situation in Hong Kong. He also told them of the atrocities that had taken place at the dressing station, giving an estimated number of the dead and of the way they had died. He also told them of how Raefe had been gravely injured and of how he had stayed behind rather than hamper the others' escape chances.

Colonel Lindsay Ride, who had been commander of the Hong Kong Volunteers' field-ambulance and who had escaped from Shamshiupo, reaching Chungking only days before them, said quietly: 'In your opinion, could Captain Elliot still be alive?'

Adam hesitated for a moment, thinking of Beth and of her fierce insistence that Raefe had survived, and then said quietly: 'No, sir. Captain Elliot knew that his wounds were fatal. He knew that he was dying.'

There was a small silence, and then Lindsay Ride said: 'Thank you, Captain Harland. That will be all.'

Adam had known there would be no further posting for him. He was physically unfit for active service of any kind.

'We can't get you back to England, old boy,' a colonial officer had said to him regretfully. 'The best we can do is fly you and Mrs Harland to Rangoon. Rangoon is still safe. From there, with luck, you might be able to get a flight out to India.'

Elizabeth had refused to leave until official permission was given for her to take Jung-shui with her.

'If you want to adopt her, the Methodist mission will help,' Adam said, appalled at the prospect of leaving the little girl behind. 'Have I to go and see them for you?'

'Please,' she had said, squeezing his hand gratefully. He was looking after her as he had always done, with infinite tenderness. But, even though they were living outwardly together as man and wife, it was inconceivable to either of them that sexual relations should be resumed between them.

In April they left for Rangoon, taking Jung-shui with them. The international situation had worsened. Singapore had fallen to the Japanese, and even Rangoon was no longer secure. A week after their arrival they were hurriedly ferried on an army flight to Calcutta.

'Which is where we'll be staying for the rest of the war, I expect,' Adam had said resignedly.

Elizabeth had watched the earth falling away beneath them and had wondered where Helena was, and Li Pi, and

271

Alastair and Tom and Ronnie. She was sure that she knew where Raefe was. He would have recuperated from his wounds now and would be leading Chinese guerrilla units into the New Territories in the fight to oust the Japanese. And if he wasn't, if he had been captured, then he would be in an internment camp, and she had only to wait for the war to end and for him to be released.

British officials in Calcutta made them as comfortable as possible, putting a bungalow at their disposal. Adam found something reminiscent of Hong Kong in the colonial way of life still being clung to by their European neighbours. Elizabeth was vaguely surprised when he mentioned it to her. She noticed very little any more. She had withdrawn into herself. Waiting for the baby to be born. Waiting for the war to end. Waiting for Raefe to return to her.

He had moved heaven and earth to find a piano for her, and on the day it was moved into their large drawing-room he knew that his fears about her mental health were groundless. The old discipline soon claimed her. She practised for seven or eight hours a day, remembering all that Li Pi had taught her, striving for perfection in order to be worthy of him.

In July the baby was born, and the hospital staff, taking it for granted that her attentive husband was the father, were astounded when she asked that the name of Raefe Elliot be entered on the birth certificate as the father.

'What are you going to call him?' Adam asked her, standing at the foot of the bed as she held the dark-haired shawl-wrapped baby close against her breast.

She smiled up at him, her hair falling loosely around her shoulders so that she didn't look a day older than the eighteen-year-old girl he had married. 'Nicholas Raefe,' she said, her cheeks flushed with happiness, her eyes so full of love that his heart twisted within him. He felt no jealousy, no bitterness, that the child she was holding was Raefe's. Those emotions had all died within him when his respect for Raefe had been born. But he did feel almost unbearable regret. If only the child she was nursing was *his* child. If only he and Beth and Jung-shui and the baby could be a family together.

'Why Nicholas?' he asked, knowing that it was a dream that would never come to fruition. She was living with him now, quite contentedly, as a sister might live with him. But she would not stay with him. Not when the war was over.

'Because I like the sound of it,' she said, and her joy was so deep that it had reached out and touched him and he found himself smiling, saying tenderly, his heart full of love for her: 'So do I, Beth. So do I.'

In September, Colonel Ride forwarded them the information that Tom Nicholson was a prisoner of war in Shamshuipo Camp, in Kowloon, and that Mrs Helena Nicholson was a civilian prisoner in Stanley internment camp and that her two children were with her.

'Thank God,' Adam said, time and time again. 'Oh, thank God that they are safe!'

In October they received the news that Alastair Munroe had died in the fighting at the Shingmun Redoubt. There was still no news about Ronnie or about Raefe.

'And we're damned lucky to know about Helena and Tom and Alastair, and to have Ride as a source of information,' Adam said sombrely. 'There must be thousands of families not knowing if husbands and fathers and sons are alive or dead.'

'Raefe is alive,' she had said with quiet confidence. 'I know he is. I can feel it in my blood and in my bones. He's alive and he's going to come back to me.'

He hadn't argued with her. He was sure that she was wrong, but to tell her so would be to rob her of the hope that was sustaining her.

In January of the following year came the news that Ronnie Ledsham was dead. The information from Chungking was far more explicit than normal official information would have been. 'He died at the Gap.' Adam said bleakly. 'God alone knows what he was doing there. He was supposed to be at Sai Wan Hill.' He put down the telegram, his hand trembling slightly. 'He was by himself and there were over a dozen dead Japs scattered around him.'

Tears slid down Elizabeth's face. 'He must have known about Julienne,' she whispered, all the old grief surging through her. 'He did what Derry did. He went out and fought the bastards by himself.'

In early 1944 they returned to England via Portugal, and Elizabeth travelled down to Four Seasons with Jung-shui and Nicholas Raefe. Adam remained in London. He had known that she had not wanted him to accompany her. Four Seasons had once been their marital home. Returning to it together would have meant that she wanted their lives to continue together. And she didn't. Now that they were back in England she wanted him once more to begin divorce proceedings. She wanted to be free in order that she could marry Raefe.

Jung-shui stared out of the train window at the neat fields and the woods and the rolling splendour of the Downs. 'It's very pretty, isn't it?' she said with gentle gravity.

Elizabeth had hugged her tight. 'Yes, darling, it is *very* pretty, and it's your home now. I do hope that you will like it.'

Jung-shui had given her an accepting smile. 'Nicholas has never seen it before, either, has he? Do you think Nicholas will like it, too?'

'Yes,' Elizabeth had said, tears glittering on her eyelashes. She looked out over the familiar countryside, wondering if Raefe had ever seen Sussex. He had been educated in England, but that had been at Harrow. Probably he had never had any reason to travel south to the Downs and to the sea. It was difficult to imagine him in the Sussex countryside, tall and lean-hipped and olive-skinned. She wondered what the villagers in Midhurst would make of him, and she wondered how much longer she would have to wait before she could share a drink with him in the village pub and walk with him on the Downs and by the sea.

Princess Luisa Isabel was waiting on the station platform

to greet them, as Elizabeth had known she would be. She had written to her from Calcutta and from Portugal, and that morning, when she had telephoned her from London and told her that she was travelling down to Midhurst on the two o'clock train, Luisa had been almost incoherent with delight.

Now she ran along the platform towards them, a slightly plumper Princess Luisa than Elizabeth remembered, but still with a ridiculous little hat dipping coquettishly over one eye, and still with fox furs swinging.

'Luisa!' she cried, running towards her, Nicholas Raefe held in one arm, Jung-shui clinging to the hand of her free arm. 'Luisa!'

Fox furs and an exotic fragrance enveloped Jung-shui and Nicholas Raefe, the tiny pillbox hat and its veil tilting more precipitately than ever.

'What *beautiful* children!' Princess Luisa Isabel crowed, cupping Jung-shui's golden face in her gloved hand, winning the little girl's heart at once. 'And is this your brother? My, isn't he a big boy? I thought he would still be a baby!'

'Not a baby,' Nicholas Raefe said as Elizabeth set him down on fat little legs. 'Can walk. Babies can't walk.'

Laughing and crying, Elizabeth threw her arms around the older woman. 'Oh, I'm so glad to see you again. Luisa. I'm so glad to be home!'

Luisa had driven them through the high-hedged winding Sussex lanes in a splendid Rolls-Royce that attracted the attention of everyone they passed.

'However do you manage to get the petrol for it, Luisa?' Elizabeth had asked incredulously. 'I thought everything was rationed to the hilt?'

'It is,' Luisa had said mischievously, 'but I have my contacts. The worst thing about the war has been that I have been without a chauffeur. Every time I obtained one, the Army commandeered him for what they termed "essential war work".'

Elizabeth hugged her arm, laughing at her silliness. 'Oh, Luisa, if only that *was* the worst thing about this horrid, horrid war!'

Luisa stayed with her for two weeks. An advertisement for a housekeeper was inserted in *The Times*, and a pleasant, middle-aged Scotswoman applied for the job. Her husband had died in the fighting as British troops had fallen back on Dunkirk, and Elizabeth immediately engaged her, impressed by the woman's quiet courage as she set about building a new life for herself, alone.

When Luisa had reluctantly departed, the house had seemed oddly empty. She had wandered through the rooms, looking out of the windows at Jung-shui and Nicholas Raefe romping together on the terrace. They, at least, were safe. She thought about Helena's children, wondering if they had suffered during the long years of internment, and she thought, as she always did, about Raefe. Whether he had been free or a prisoner, he, too, would have suffered. Four Seasons would be a haven for him when he returned to her. A place where he could rest and recuperate and where their lives together could begin anew.

She busied herself in transforming a sunny ground-floor sitting-room into a study for him, decorating and furnishing it herself. She planted roses along the south wall of the house, Zephirine Drouhin and Ophelia and Madame Alfred Carrière, so that the house would be clothed in blossom. She worked hard at her music, knowing how eager he would be that her dreams of the concert platform should be speedily fulfilled.

It was a rain-washed April day when her first visitor, apart from Adam and Luisa Isabel, arrived. She was on the terrace dressed in an old violet-shaded tweed skirt and a lavender jumper, with her hair pulled away from her face and tied at the nape of her neck with a hair ribbon borrowed from Jung-shui. She was lifting and dividing the clumps of Michaelmas daisies that grew along the edge of the terrace by the house wall when she heard the sound of a car approaching.

She put down her trowel, taking off her gardening-gloves and walking along the terrace to the shallow stone steps that led down to the drive. Adam hadn't telephoned to say that he would be visiting her but, then, their relationship was so close that there was no reason why he should have done so. The car swung round the curve in the drive and she stood still, rocked by surprise. The car wasn't Adam's carefully polished Daimler, but a battered old Morris that reminded her, with a sudden pang, of the little battered old Morris that Julienne had driven in Hong Kong. It surged to a halt twenty yards or so away from her, and a big bear of a man in RAF uniform removed himself with difficulty from its cramped interior.

The April sun shone on his thick shock of dark-gold hair. There was the word POLAND on his shoulder-flash. For a moment she was overcome by an overpowering sense of *déjà vu*, remembering Hong Kong and the perfume of azaleas, and then she was running down the steps, shouting incredulously: 'Roman. Roman!'

White teeth flashed in a dazzling grin, and then, moving with an athletic grace and agility rare in a man of his size, he strode towards her. She took the last few steps two at a time, hurtling into his arms, hugging him tight. 'Oh, Roman! How wonderful! I can't believe it's really you!' she gasped, looking up at him with shining eyes.

'*Prosze! Prosze!* Whenever I come upon you unexpectedly, you are always knee-deep in flowers,' he said, his grin deepening; and then, as she continued to hug him: 'If I'd known I was going to get this sort of welcome, I'd have visited earlier.'

Laughter bubbled up inside her as she feasted her eyes on him. Even in RAF uniform there was a hubris about him that was totally mid-European.

'You don't mean to say that you're *stationed* near here?' she asked disbelievingly as he reluctantly released his hold of her and she tucked her arm through his, leading him towards the house.

'I'm afraid so. I'm about ten miles away at Westhampnett.'

She began to giggle, joyously light-hearted. Roman was

home, and soon Raefe would be home. 'Oh, but, Roman, that's *wonderful*!'

She led him across the terrace and through the open french windows into a large drawing-room dominated by her Steinway grand.

'I'm glad to see that you are still working,' he said affectionately, moving immediately across to see what it was she had been playing.

She nodded. All of a sudden the world was once again a sane place. She had someone to talk to about music again, and she had someone at her side who was a bridge into the past, a living proof that the most unexpected reunions took place every day.

'Chopin,' she said a trifle defensively. 'I find him so soothing.'

He gave a deep chuckle. 'You forget that I am a Pole, Elizabeth. There is no need to apologize for playing Chopin to me!'

She laughed, as at ease with him again as she had been in Perth. On the podium he was Roman Rakowski, maestro. But here, in her drawing-room, he was Roman, her friend. The man she had drunk Brudershaft with. With easy confidence she sat at the piano, and he stood by her side, filling the room with his presence.

'Chopin is far more than a rose-coloured salonist surrounded by violets,' he said, the old bond of their mutual passion enclosing them in a world of their own. 'He must be played with verve and daring.'

For the first time since her last lesson with Li Pi, she sat down at the piano and played to a critical audience. It was bliss. A totally freeing experience that made her feel as if she were alive again after long months of hibernation.

'*Dziekuje*! That's good' he had said, his deep rich voice full of encouraging enthusiasm. 'Now play a waltz. The waltzes are marvellous, a little hackneyed perhaps, but who cares? They are unsurpassably beautiful.'

The war faded from her consciousness. She played waltzes and then nocturnes. The great Fantasy in F minor, and the Barcarolle, the Polonaise-Fantaisie.

'Oh, wonderful!' Roman had said exuberantly, running his hands through his hair in a gesture she remembered from Perth. 'These nocturnes show Chopin's enormous talent for condensation. He is a *much* greater composer than he is often made out to be. You must always play him like that, Elizabeth, dynamically and with inner drama.'

When she had played the last note of the Polonaise-Fantaisie, he was quiet for a few moments, the question he had not asked hanging in the air between them. As she closed the lid he said quietly: 'Tell me about Raefe.'

She told him, sitting in front of a log fire, serving Earl Grey tea from a Crown Derby teapot into wafer-thin cups. He listened in silence, not interrupting her, making no comments, until she said finally: 'And so there is nothing for me to do now but to wait for him.'

The log fire spat and crackled.

'And his name has not been listed by the Red Cross as a prisoner of war?' he asked, his Slavic high-cheekboned face sombre.

She shook her head, and something moved within him, an emotion both shocking and disturbing. 'No,' she said, not seeing his quick frown, or the way his brilliant onyx eyes had suddenly darkened. 'But, then, there must be hundreds and hundreds of men who are still alive but whose names aren't on any list. I don't imagine the Japanese are being very co-operative with the Red Cross, do you?'

He had shaken his head, rising reluctantly to his feet, knowing that it was time for him to go.

'Oh, must you go so soon?' she asked, disappointment flaring through her eyes. 'I want you to meet the children. Jung-shui is down in the paddock, riding the pony I bought her for her birthday. Nicholas Raefe is with his nanny. She's a local girl from the village and she takes care of him while I practise. She's taken him to feed the ducks at the local pond, but they'll be back at any moment. Please stay.'

He had been sorely tempted, but he also knew that he

had to have time to himself to think before he stayed with her any longer, or before he agreed to see her again. She was desperately in love with Raefe, and one day, God willing, Raefe would be returning for her. To fall in love with a woman so unobtainable would be crass foolishness, and he wasn't a man who suffered foolishness easily.

'*Nie.*' he said, rising to his feet, his great height and massive shoulders seeming to fill the room. 'I'm sorry, Elizabeth, but I must go.'

She had walked with him out to his car, urging him to visit her again, her loneliness, when he had driven away, so acute that it almost robbed her of breath.

It was a week before he telephoned her and said that he had leave the following weekend. He had never been down to Brighton. Would she care to drive there with him and have lunch?

She had accepted unhesitatingly. This was what she would one day do with Raefe; that she was doing it now with Roman seemed to her to be the best-possible omen.

They went to Brighton and a few days later they took Jung-shui and Nicholas Raefe to Bodiam Castle and picnicked, chilly but happy, beneath the great Norman battlements. From then on, he had visited her regularly, swinging Nicholas Raefe up on to his shoulders as they walked the Downs or the seashore, Jung-shui hurrying eagerly along at his side, chattering about her pony and her English school while Roman listened to her with genuine interest, displaying a patience rare in a man of his mercurial talent.

The war in Europe was rapidly coming to a close, and she knew that he couldn't wait for the day when he would be demobbed and able to return once more to the concert platform.

'Where will you go first?' she had asked as they had walked a steeply shelving pebble beach where once, a thousand years earlier, Julius Caesar's Romans had first struggled ashore.

'Palestine,' he had said unhesitatingly. 'Nowhere in the

world is there a people so hungry for music. I want to give every ounce of support I can to an orchestra that will one day be the greatest orchestra in the world.'

She thought of the men who composed that orchestra, the great musicians of eastern Europe who had fled Hitler's pogroms.

'Perhaps I shall play with them one day,' she said with a little smile.

'You will,' he had said with fierce confidence. 'And when you do I shall conduct you.'

Roman's regular visits, interspersed with visits from Adam and from Princess Luisa, relieved her relative isolation, but her sexual loneliness remained acute. There were times when she lay in bed at night, damp with longing, when she almost wished that she had never been awakened to sexual passion. She hungered for sexual relief so fiercely that it shocked and appalled her. 'Not sexual relief!' she would say furiously to herself as she swung her legs from the bed and walked over to the window, pulling back the curtains and looking out over the moonlit terrace and the garden to the Downs beyond. 'Raefe. It's Raefe that I'm hungry for. Raefe that I miss.'

But on 8 May, when Winston Churchill announced over the wireless that German armed forces had surrendered unconditionally, it was sexual need that brought her world tumbling down around her ears.

Roman had been on leave that day, and the minute the announcement was made he ran towards his car, leaping into it and surging away from camp in the direction of Four Seasons.

Elizabeth's housekeeper had already run to her with the news, and they had stood in the large slate-floored kitchen, celebrating the event with cooking sherry.

'Find a flag!' Elizabeth said joyously to Nicholas Raefe's nanny. 'We must fly a flag from the windows!'

'But no one will see it, ma'am. We're over a mile from the road,' the young nanny had protested, dazed by the momentous announcement and the generous amounts of cooking sherry that Elizabeth was pouring for her.

'It doesn't matter!' Elizabeth had said determinedly. 'We must fly a flag!'

They had found a flag in one of the garages and hung it from the window above the main door, and then Jung-shui and Nicholas Raefe had begged to be allowed to go into the village, where bells were ringing and people could be distantly heard singing.

'I'll take them, ma'am,' the nanny had said, eager to take a part in the festivities, and Elizabeth had waved them off, and her housekeeper had begun to bake a special cake for the children's tea, listening to the wireless and the commentator's description of the crowds gathering outside Buckingham Palace and 10 Downing Street.

Elizabeth walked back towards the drawing-room, sensing her housekeeper's need to be on her own. After all, her husband would not be one of the men thankfully returning home. Her joy at the announcement of peace would also be mixed with a fresh surge of personal grief.

She had stood in the large sun-filled room wondering when and if Raefe would receive the news, and then Roman's battered Morris had surged to a halt in the drive, and she had run towards the french windows to greet him.

He had taken the shallow stone steps in two giant bounds and was halfway across the terrace towards her when she catapulted into his arms. 'Isn't it the most wonderful news!' she exulted, flinging her arms around his neck. 'It *must* mean that war in the East will be over soon as well!'

When he had driven through Midhurst, perfect strangers had been flinging their arms around each other and kissing each other, and it seemed the most natural thing in the world that he should crush her against him and kiss her exuberantly.

The exuberant sexless kiss that he had intended died almost before it was born. Like a spark setting a tinderbox alight, the instant their lips touched, reason and sanity left them. Her mouth parted, her tongue sliding past his, her

282

fingers tightening in the thick mat of his hair. His response was immediate; he swung her up in his arms, striding with her into the drawing-room, lowering her to the rug as he tore off his jacket, his tie, his shirt. She didn't even remove her clothes, with her skirt pushed hastily up to her hips, her brief panties pushed to one side to allow him to enter her, she pulled him down on top of her, half-senseless with need. He gasped her name, unzipping his trousers, plunging into her hot and hard, and as he felt his sperm shoot from him like hot gold he knew with dreadful certainty not only that he loved her, but also that Raefe was dead. He couldn't have made love to her, his body would not have allowed him to, if Raefe had still been alive.

She was sobbing beneath him, her cries no longer the savage cries of satisfied love, but of horror and grief and deep burning shame. 'Oh, no!' she sobbed, twisting and turning in an effort to be free of him. 'Oh, no! Oh, Raefe! Raefe! What have I done? Oh God, what have I done?'

He eased his weight off her, saying awkwardly: 'Elizabeth, please . . .'

'No!' She pushed her fists against his chest, fighting to be free of him, the tears streaming down her face.

'Elizabeth, please . . .,' he began again as he rose unsteadily to his feet, but she wouldn't listen to him.

'No! Oh God, please go away! Please go away and never come back!'

He stood for a moment, his magnificent shoulder and arm muscles glistening with sweat, and then he slowly reached out for his shirt and began to put it back on. He picked up his tie, crushing it into his pocket, hooking his jacket with his finger and swinging it defeatedly over his shoulder. Because of a moment's uncontrolled passion, everything that had been forged between them now lay in irreparable ashes. His pain was so intense that he didn't know how he was surviving it.

'You have to listen to me, Elizabeth,' he said again, his voice raw with urgency.

'No!' She was trembling convulsively, hugging her arms

around her as though holding herself together against an inner disintegration. 'No, please go! Oh, please go!'

'I love you,' he said with fierce simplicity. 'I wouldn't have done such a thing if I didn't love you.'

'No!' she whispered again, shaking her head, the tears still falling. 'I don't want to listen! Please leave me! Please go away!'

There was nothing further that he could do. From outside, he could hear the distant sound of the village bells ringing joyously, and knew he would never be able to listen to them again without reliving the pain he now felt.

'Goodbye,' he said thickly. 'I'm sorry, Elizabeth, more sorry than you'll ever know.' And with his heart breaking within him he turned away and walked out of the room.

She covered her face in her hands, sobbing convulsively. Oh God, how could she have done such a thing? How could she have pulled another man down on top of her in such hungry urgent need?

'Oh, Raefe, I'm so sorry,' she gasped. 'So very sorry. Oh, please come back to me, my love! Please come home!'

# 18

He telephoned her early the next morning, but she refused to speak to him. He wrote to her, and she destroyed his letters unread. The shame she felt so mortifying, so total, that she couldn't even imagine ever facing him again.

In June, Adam drove down to see her, and as soon as she saw his face she knew that he brought bad news with him. 'What is it?' she said fearfully, rising from the piano stool and walking swiftly across to him. 'What has happened?'

'I'm sorry,' he said, taking her hands. 'Truly I am.' Ever since they had returned to England he had been ceaseless in his efforts to try to trace Raefe as a prisoner of war. Now, at last, he had official notification, but it was not the kind of notification that Beth had been so steadfastly awaiting. She knew immediately.

'No,' she said, taking her hands away from his. 'I don't believe it! He's alive, I know he is!'

Slowly Adam took the piece of paper from his inside jacket pocket. 'He's missing, presumed dead, Beth.'

She wouldn't look at the paper he held out to her. She turned on her heel, walking away from him, staring out through the french windows to where the roses were in early bloom. 'No,' she said, and her voice was quiet and sure. 'He's alive, Adam. And he's going to come back to me.'

On 16 August the Japanese surrendered and war in the East was finally over.

'Soon Daddy will be home,' she said joyously to Nicholas Raefe, cuddling him on her knee. 'Soon he will be able to come for walks with us and he'll teach you how to play cricket and football, and we'll have such lovely times together, just you wait and see.'

Nicholas Raefe had looked at her lovingly. He had been waiting so long to see the daddy who was only a name to him that he didn't really mind waiting a little longer. He couldn't imagine what this strange daddy would be like and he didn't really need him to teach him how to play football and cricket, because his Uncle Adam already did that. He kissed her on her cheek, wriggling from her knee, running on sturdy little legs to where Jung-shui was waiting for him down in the paddock.

Now, every day, she waited for news. A Hong Kong Fellowship had been formed in London for the wives and widows and relations of prisoners of war and those interned, and she had attended the London-based meetings regularly, hoping to glean some information about Raefe from the newsletters that the Fellowship published at regular intervals and that were a great comfort to many. Extracts were published from POWs' letters, though they contained only reassuring news, for otherwise the Japanese censors would not have let them through. At the end of September the Fellowship was informed that over a thousand men, former prisoners of war in Hong Kong, had sailed aboard the *Empress of Australia*, her destination Vancouver, via Manila.

'They are beginning to come home,' Elizabeth had whispered to herself. 'It can't be long now. Oh, please, Raefe, please write. Please let me know where you are!'

But he didn't write, and she knew that it was because he could have no idea where she was. She would have to wait for the Army to redirect his letters to her. Helena wrote to her, her letter forwarded by the Red Cross. She was alive and well, though after the years of imprisonment much slimmer than before. She would be returning to England at the earliest opportunity.

'And Lamoon is with her,' she had said joyously to Adam. 'Isn't that incredible? Lamoon is with her, and she and Tom are going to be married at the earliest opportunity.'

The first ship to arrive in England, bearing Hong Kong prisoners of war was the *Ile de France*, sailing from Canada. Members of the Hong Kong Fellowship were advised by the authorities that it was not advisable for them to travel to Southampton to meet the returning men. The men were going to be whisked straight away to resettlement camps for at least three days and there would be no opportunities for reunions until then. Elizabeth had taken not the slightest bit of notice. She would be there when the *Ile de France* docked, even though there was still no confirmation that Raefe would be aboard, and even though the authorities still adamantly held to the view that he was missing and presumed dead.

Adam drove her down to Southampton, terrified at what her reaction might be if Raefe was not among those disembarking. It was a chill autumn day, and they had to wait with a small huddle of other eager relations for the men to begin to file down the gangplanks and once again touch English soil. She stood, her coat-collar up against the cold breeze, her eyes fiercely bright. He would be one of those disembarking. He *had* to be.

Gaunt face after gaunt face hurried down the gangplank. A woman standing next to her gave a joyous cry and ran forward, calling out to one of the hunched emaciated figures with his kit on his shoulder. Elizabeth saw the look of disbelief on the man's face: saw his disbelief turn to wonder and then to joy as he slung his kit to the ground and opened his arms wide.

In single file the men continued to disembark, but there was no tall broad-shouldered figure with a pelt of blue-black hair. Only tired men, thankful to be home again, slightly bewildered that there were so few people at the docks to greet them.

When the last men had disembarked, she still stood there, her coat-collar turned up against the wind, her eyes overly bright.

Adam touched her gently on the arm, and she said fiercely: 'There will be other ships, Adam. Lots of other ships.' And then she didn't speak to him again, and he drove her back through the winding country lanes to Four Seasons in silence.

That night he asked her if she would remarry him. She stared at him, her green eyes brilliant, knowing why it was that he was asking her.

'No,' she said, her throat dry. 'Raefe is still alive, Adam.'

'Oh, my dear,' Adam said tenderly, taking her hands and holding them tightly in his. 'And if he isn't? Will you marry me then, Beth? Will you let us be happy as we used to be?'

Tears sparkled on the thick sweep of her lashes. 'No, Adam,' she whispered, loving him with all her heart, but loving him as a friend. 'No. Those days are over. They will never come again.'

There were other ships bringing back POWs and internees as she had said there would be. Helena and Jeremy and Jennifer arrived home on 28 October, having sailed via Manila and Singapore and Colombo and Aden. She drove up with Adam to Liverpool to meet them, and as Helena walked towards them, her square-jawed, high-cheekboned face still beautiful despite the gross amount of weight she had lost, Elizabeth gave a low sob.

'Helena. Oh, Helena!' she cried, running towards her and hugging her tight. 'Oh, Helena, I'm so glad to see you!'

'The feeling is mutual,' Helena had said unsteadily, and there were lines around her eyes and mouth that had never been there before.

Adam had held her close, shocked at the suffering etched on her face, knowing that she, too, was probably shocked at the change in him. He was still only fifty-four, but the fighting and the trek to Chungking had taken their toll of him and he knew that he had prematurely aged, his limp now severely pronounced, his hair snow white.

'Oh, Adam,' she said, kissing him on the cheek, her deep blue eyes bright with tears. 'It's so wonderful to see you again!' And suddenly, as he tucked her arm in his and began to lead her towards their waiting car, he no longer felt so old and so decrepit.

'It's wonderful to see you, too, Helena,' he had said, his voice thick with emotion. 'Beth has a room ready for you and the children at Four Seasons. You will stay there, won't you? For as long as you want.'

'Yes,' she had said, and then, as the children clambered into the rear of Adam's Daimler, she said bleakly: 'You know that Alastair is dead, don't you?'

Adam had nodded. They all knew the way that Alastair had died, and he had been posthumously awarded the Victoria Cross.

'I loved him and was a fool and never really realized it,' she said, her voice unsteady with regret and grief. 'I shan't ever make the same mistake again.'

'No, my dear,' he said, knowing now what the future held for him and full of the kind of happiness that he had thought he would never feel again. 'I know that you won't.' And he walked round to the front of the car, sitting behind the wheel, knowing that, although Beth's long years of waiting were still not over, his own years of waiting had finally come to an end.

'And neither of us ever saw Li Pi again,' Helena said quietly.

They were sitting at the dining-table at Four Seasons. Jung-shui and Nicholas Raefe had welcomed Jeremy and Jennifer. Jung-shui with shy gravity, Nicholas Raefe with boisterous exuberance. They had gone immediately down to the paddock to view the pony, and after a specially indulgent high tea they had retreated to Nicholas Raefe's bedroom where they had played a spirited game of Monopoly until it was time for bed. Now the house was quiet, and Elizabeth and Helena and Adam sat around the candlelit dining-table and Elizabeth clasped her hands lightly in her lap and stared down at them.

'He may still be alive,' Helena said tentatively, but all of them knew that there was very little hope. He had been old and he had been Chinese. His chances of survival in Japanese-occupied Hong Kong would have been tragically slim.

'Tell us about Tom and Lamoon,' Adam said gently, knowing how deep Beth's grief was at the thought of Li Pi's death and wanting good news to leaven the bad.

Helena smiled, and her mane of dark hair, now heavily streaked with grey, swung forward against her cheeks. 'They were married in Shamshuipo camp three days after liberation. The troops were still confined there because there wasn't anywhere else for them to go, and Lamoon and myself hitched a lift from Stanley to Shamshuipo and Tom said he'd waited so long to marry her that he wasn't going to wait any longer, and he insisted that the padre marry them immediately.'

'Let's give them a toast,' Adam said, rising to his feet and crossing to the cocktail-cabinet where he knew a bottle of Sauterne lay hidden, saved by Beth for just such an event. He uncorked the wine, pouring it into their glasses.

'To Tom and Lamoon,' he said, raising his glass high. 'May they know only peace and happiness from this day forward.'

'To Tom and Lamoon,' Elizabeth and Helena echoed, and for both of them tears were not very far away.

Christmas came and went, and still there was no news of Raefe. 'There were other camps apart from the ones in Hong Kong,' Elizabeth said obstinately when Adam gently asked her if she shouldn't now accept the official report of his death. 'There were camps in Singapore and Formosa and Manchuria. Quite a lot of officers from Hong Kong were sent to Shirakawa Camp in Formosa. He may have been there. He may have been sent anywhere.'

'But the men in those camps are all accounted for. The authorities have lists of their names and nearly all of them have been returned home.' Adam said, his heart hurting at her steadfast refusal to face reality.

'Not all of them,' she said, her face pale, deep shadows bruising her eyes. 'Not Raefe.'

In the New Year he told her that he had asked Helena to marry him and that Helena had accepted.

'I'm so pleased,' she said, hugging him tight. 'It's the most sensible thing that you've ever done, Adam. She'll make you a marvellous wife.'

'We're going to be married in April, on Helena's birthday. You will be there, my dear, won't you?'

'Of course I'll be there,' she said lovingly. 'Wild horses wouldn't keep me away.'

In February, Tom and Lamoon drove down to Four Seasons. They were on a visit to England so that Lamoon could meet Tom's parents and be formally welcomed into the family.

'This is quite like old times, isn't it?' Tom said as they sat round the dinner-table with Adam and Helena, happily unaware of the shadow that passed across Elizabeth's face.

Lamoon looked as impossibly lovely as ever, her almond eyes shining with happiness, her cheong-sam glitteringly exotic. The years in captivity had sat lightly on her, but there were flecks of grey in Tom's dark hair and his lean face still bore traces of the emaciation he had been suffering from when he had been released.

'If only Alastair were here,' Helena said quietly, 'and Julienne and Ronnie, then it really would be like old times.'

They were silent, all of them thinking of the past; and suddenly, as clearly as if it were a vision, Elizabeth could see Alastair, laughing and talking in the Jockey Club Bar, and Ronnie, his blond moustache as trim and sleek as that of a matinée idol, and Julienne, her mop of spicy red curls tumbling around her heart-shaped face, her eyes dancing with mischief. Somewhere in the background, she was sure that she could hear the faint rousing strains of 'There'll Always Be an England', and then Alastair and Ronnie and Julienne faded into the background and she could see only Raefe.

He was standing nonchalantly at ease, his hair falling low across his brow, his dark eyes looking at her with love and tenderness. And again she saw the smile on his mouth, the same ironic smile with which he had bade her goodbye at the village on the shores of Mirs Bay. She sat absolutely still, waiting for him to come nearer to her, but the sound of singing faded and Tom was saying: 'We shall be returning to Hong Kong on the twentieth. I still have my job with the government and, even if I hadn't, I couldn't imagine living anywhere else. It's my home.'

Small drops of ice were dripping down her spine. The ghosts were all receding and Raefe was receding, too.

'There'll be a lot of changes there now,' Adam was saying. 'I'm surprised the Chinese didn't hold out to have it handed back to them.'

Suddenly, and with absolute certainty, she knew that he was dead. She rose abruptly to her feet, trembling violently, her face chalk white.

'The day will come,' Tom said, pouring more wine into his glass. 'The British government will have to surrender Hong Kong to the Chinese eventually. . . .'

'Excuse me!' she said in a strangled voice, spinning on her heel and walking swiftly from the table.

'And then what will become of it?' Helena was asking Tom curiously.

Tom was holding Lamoon's hand, and Adam was watching Helena's face, thinking how beautiful she was. None of them realized that Elizabeth had left the table for anything more than to bring in the dessert. None of them realized how deeply distressed she was.

She stood in the hall for a brief second, and the sound of their laughter drifted out to her. Tom had been reunited with Lamoon. Adam was reunited with Helena. But she knew now that she would never be reunited with Raefe. The belief had sustained her and given her strength for over three years, but now that belief was gone. Raefe himself had personally come to her and gently removed it.

The kitchen door was open, the desserts standing on a

tea-tray, waiting to be transferred to the dining-room. She ignored them. Without pausing for a coat or a jacket, she ran from the house and across the gravel of the drive towards the garages. Her car was parked alongside Adam's Daimler and Tom's hired Ford. She opened the door, slipping behind the wheel and turning the key in the ignition. She didn't know where she was going and she didn't care. With a screech of tyres she reversed out of the garage, swinging the wheel round and shooting down the drive and out into the dark high-hedged lanes beyond.

He was dead. The realization beat at her in waves. He was dead and he was never, ever going to return to her. She drove south, across the South Downs and down towards the sea. He had said goodbye to her in the dusty Chinese village, and he had meant goodbye, but she had not meant goodbye. Not goodbye for ever.

'I can't live with it,' she whispered as she raced seawards, out to the loneliness of Selsey Bill. 'I can't live with such pain! It isn't possible!'

The sea gleamed, slickly and blackly, and she brought the car to a halt, opening the door and slamming it behind her, running down to the beach, slipping and sliding over the loose pebbles until she reached the shingle and the gentle creaming waves.

He was dead and he was never coming back to her. 'Oh, Raefe!' she cried in agony, raising her face to the night sky. 'Oh, Raefe! Why did you leave me? Why did you go?' And then she sank to her knees on the sea-deep sand, and covered her face and wept.

# Epilogue

The sun heat hotly on her back, and the azure blue South China Sea glittered. She had survived that night on the English coast, as she had survived the hundreds of agonizing nights that had succeeded it. There had been her music, and Jung-shui and Nicholas Raefe, and somehow because of them she had found the will to live and the courage to endure.

She rose slowly to her feet. This was the last of her pilgrimages. Yesterday she had visited Julienne's grave and had laid a posy of exotic blossoms on it, and then she had driven to the military cemetery at Stanley. She had laid flowers on Alastair's grave and on Ronnie's and Derry's and had walked slowly up to one of the graves on which the inscription on the headstone read only 'Known but to God'. She had ordered the small bouquet of flowers especially. It was an English bouquet of all the flowers that grew at Four Seasons and that he had never seen there. Creamy white roses and yellow-eyed daisies and pale lilac anemones with indigo hearts. She had stood for a long time, thinking about the past, knowing that finally she had come to terms with it.

The intervening years had brought their own happiness. She had achieved her dreams of concert-platform stardom and she remembered the words she had whispered to herself on the first night that she played to a large audience. 'For you, Li Pi,' she had whispered, 'and for you, Raefe, my love.' And she had not let either of them down.

Slowly she walked back down the hill to her car. People

were beginning to emerge from the long, white, peaceful serenity of the hotel for early-morning swims. Lamma Island was beginning to take on shape and form as the early-morning heat-haze lifted and disappeared. She opened her car door and slid behind the wheel. She had no more doubts, no more uncertainties. The man who had loved her for seven years was waiting for her in their hotel suite, and in two hours' time she would become his wife.

She drove away from the bay and up Repulse Bay Road towards Wong Nei Chung Gap. New buildings were springing up on the hillsides, luxury homes standing where the Rajputs and the men of the Middlesex had so bravely died. The road topped the gap and began to wind down towards Happy Valley and the outskirts of Victoria.

She had served a long and lonely seven years. There had been no other men in her life, not until three months ago when she had found herself staring in stupefied horror into Roman Rakowski's fierce grey eyes.

They were on the concert platform of the Hollywood Bowl. The Los Angeles Symphony Orchestra was to play Tchaikovsky's Piano Concerto No. 1 and Mahler's Symphony No. 9 in D, under the German conductor Otto Klemperer. She was guest pianist. Rehearsals had gone satisfactorily and, though it was the first time she had played in the immense natural amphitheatre of the Bowl, she had her nerves well under control.

The orchestra had taken its place on the concert platform to enthusiastic applause. She herself had walked out to a warm reassuring welcome from the stunningly large audience. But still Klemperer had not taken his place on the podium. There were impatient coughs and mutterings from the open-air auditorium and a sense of growing unease from the members of the orchestra. There had been rumours that the sixty-seven year old conductor was not in good health; in rehearsal he had looked tired and strained.

The minutes spun out, and she half-expected the musical director to walk out and apologize for the

295

conductor's absence owing to sudden indisposition. Just as it seemed they could wait no longer for him, there was a cheer from the audience and an outburst of applause. Elizabeth breathed a sigh of relief, closing her eyes as Klemperer strode towards the podium. In these last few seconds before she commenced to play, she needed to steady herself, to harness the adrenalin surging along her veins, to be in complete and utter control. Klemperer reached the podium amidst continuing applause. She flexed her fingers, drew in a deep calming breath, and opened her eyes, fixing them on Otto Klemperer.

Only it wasn't Klemperer. It was Roman. The world shelved away beneath her feet, leaving her sick and giddy. Roman saw the shock she had sustained, saw the blood drain from her face, the black satin evening gown she wore emphasizing her pallor. The applause at his entrance finally died down, and he lifted his baton, his eyes riveting hers.

'Don't go to pieces!' he silently pleaded with her. 'Remember who you are and what you are! Play for me as you played for Klemperer!'

The breath was so tight in her chest that she was in physical pain. She could read the messages his eyes were sending and she tried vainly to comply with them. Just when she thought she couldn't possibly move, when she thought she was frozen for ever, she remembered the tiny candlelit restaurant in Perth where they had drunk Brudershaft together. Slowly the pain in her chest eased.

He gave her a sudden grin, and she felt the world right itself on its axis. She was going to play for Roman as she had played for Klemperer. A sudden blaze lit the backs of her eyes. No, she was going to play far, far better than she had played for Klemperer. She was going to play better than she had ever played in her life before.

He sensed her returning confidence, and his thick eyebrows, so many shades darker than his deep-gold hair, rose queryingly. She gave an imperceptible nod of her head, and relief flooded through him. He brought his baton down in a characteristic firm downbeat, and from the moment that her fingers touched the keys he knew that the rapport between them was total.

The excitement in the audience was palpable. Elizabeth felt as if she were riding a magic carpet as she and the orchestra entered into another world. Their collaboration was brilliant, flawless, as the dialogue between them flowed and ebbed and climaxed in a surge of spirit and sound at the end of the long first movement.

There was hardly a breath from the audience in the pause before the second movement. Elizabeth knew that her sleekly coiled chignon was damp with perspiration, that she was playing on a level she had never reached before. Roman leaned forward on the podium, his eyes blazing into hers as softly, almost imperceptibly, he summoned in the strings. The flute entered, delicate as the pipes of Pan, and then Elizabeth, and then Roman merged them all into a Ukrainian dance of rhythmic pungency.

In the rondo finale the battle for ascendancy between piano and orchestra reached a climax so passionate, so earth-shaking, that when Roman's arms whipped them all into the final desperate chords Elizabeth thought she was going to die. She physically sagged over the piano as the last notes died away and the audience exploded into frenzied applause. Dazedly she raised her head high, trying to orientate herself. Roman's face was sheened with perspiration as he stepped weakly down from the podium and walked towards her. The audience was on its feet as he did so, shouting, stamping, clapping. . . .

'Amazing!' Roman shouted over the din of the applause. 'You were wonderful! Incredible!'

His hand gripped hers, his eyes blazing triumphantly with love and pride as he raised her to her feet. Unsteadily, her knees so weak she couldn't imagine how they were supporting her, Elizabeth walked off-stage with him.

'It's a good job the Bowl has no roof!' Roman was shouting. 'Otherwise it would have been lifted off!'

They paused for a second off-stage, the applause drumming against their eardrums; and then, their hands tightly gripped together, sweating and trembling, they walked back on again. The orchestra was stamping its feet, the audience shouting hoarsely 'Bravo!' and 'Encore! Encore!'

They took bow after bow, and at last Roman shouted across to her, laughing: 'It's no good! We'll have to play the last movement again!'

It had been the triumph of her career, and it had been the moment when she had known that her destiny and Roman's destiny were irrevocably linked, as her destiny with Raefe had been.

The streets of Victoria were beginning to hum with life. As she drove towards their hotel she could see a giant placard advertising their forthcoming concert, and on a newspaper-stand she saw the giant headline, 'RAKOWSKI AND HARLAND TO MARRY! Concert platform greats to tie the knot!'

She smiled to herself, wondering what the next day's headline would have been if her pilgrimage had had a different outcome. It had been Roman who had suggested they return to Hong Kong. Roman who had realized that there could be no future for them until the past lay at peace. She parked the car outside the hotel, and Lee Yiu Piu hurried to open the heavy glass doors for her. She smiled at him, walking into the opulent foyer, conscious of the buzz of newsmen hurrying towards the flower-filled room where, in a little while, she would marry.

She pressed the button for the lift, unnoticed by them, wondering why it had taken her so long to realize that this was what Raefe would have wanted for her. He would not have wanted her to live alone and he would not have wanted her to grieve for ever. His great gift to her had been in showing her how deeply and passionately she could love. And in loving Roman the love she had felt for Raefe was not diminished; that love, and the richness it had bequeathed to her, would be hers for ever.

She walked down the deeply carpeted corridor to her hotel suite and quietly opened the door. Princess Luisa Isabel was removing her wedding bouquet from its cellophane cover and laying it carefully on the bed. Jung-shui was surveying herself in the full-length mirror, her sleek black hair decorated with a single white rose, her bridesmaid's dress emphasizing her willowy slenderness and burgeoning fifteen-year-old breasts. Nicholas Raefe was busily trying to pin a carnation to the lapel of his morning suit, his dark hair tumbling untidily in the way it always did, and in a way which never ceased to make her catch her breath. He was ten years old now, and already had the lean whippy look to him that had been so characteristic of Raefe.

It was Roman who saw her enter the room first; Roman who swiftly strode across to her, taking her in his arms. She leaned against him, hugging him tight, and then he gently tilted her face up to his and said, his handsome strong-boned face revealing none of the anxiety he was feeling: 'Are all your ghosts laid to rest, my darling?'

'Yes,' she whispered softly, loving him with all her heart, grateful for his patience and his understanding and his acceptance of the place Raefe held in her life, and always would.

'Then, let's get married,' he said huskily, and as Princess Luisa Isabel handed her her wedding bouquet, and as Jung-shui and Nicholas Raefe announced that they were both ready for the wedding and had been waiting for her for ages, a deep smile of happiness curved her lips and she turned, her arm in the arm of her husband-to-be, walking with him out of the room and along the corridor and down the stairs, to where the newspapermen and photographers were waiting.

THE END